THE FIRST BLADE OF OSTIA

Also by Duncan M. Hamilton

THE SOCIETY OF THE SWORD TRILOGY

The Tattered Banner

The Huntsman's Amulet

The Telastrian Song

SHORT TALES OF THE MIDDLE SEA

The Swordsman of Tanosa

THE FIRST BLADE OF OSTIA

DUNCAN M. HAMILTON

ISBN-13: 978-1505245387
ISBN-10: 1505245389

'Our swords shall play the orators for us.'

Act I, Scene II

Tamburlaine the Great, Part I

Christopher Marlowe

PROLOGUE

BRYN HELD HIS breath. Around him, over fifty thousand people did the same. This was the moment they had all been waiting for. In the weeks since the announcement was made, this was all the city had talked about. In the months before that, most conversations speculated as to whether it would ever happen. Nobody could quite believe that it would. Now Baldario and Rosetto were finally facing one another and Bryn was lucky enough to be there.

Bryn felt his father squeeze his hand. Like Bryn, his gaze was fixed on the two men standing in the centre of the Amphitheatre. Both were tall and slender, in peak condition. Nothing in their appearance allowed a choice between them.

Neither swordsman, both Bannerets of the Blue, had been defeated in a duel for nearly a year, and for weeks they had vied with one another for the title of First Blade of Ostia. Baldario would move into the lead, only to be caught and then passed by Rosetto—then the situation would reverse. Several weeks before, the tally of their victories had become equal, and everyone knew the only way for one to be declared the best was for them to face each other.

The duel began, but with so much at stake neither man seemed willing to make the first strike. They circled one another for what seemed like an age, as the massive crowd watched in complete silence. The only sound came from the combatants' boots on the sand.

The tension grew so great Bryn thought it would snap him in two. He had to remind himself to breathe. Baldario pounced and fifty thousand voices sighed as one. Rosetto parried and danced back, his feet a blur, his reputation for perfect footwork well deserved. Baldario went after him, his style more aggressive. Their blades flashed in the noon-day sun, clashing back and forth. The crowd had fallen silent again; Bryn could hear each strike of blade, each stamp of boot.

The swords moved so quickly Bryn could barely follow them. How could they keep up such a pace? He imagined himself there, facing one of them, so vividly that he found himself short of breath. What must it be like to stand there in front of so many? Adored by their fans, hated by those of their opponent. Bryn couldn't decide which of them he preferred, having supported both at various duels over the year. He pushed the thoughts from his head; they were only distracting him from the greatest duel in decades.

Baldario drove Rosetto back across the arena floor, almost to the barrier, each step accompanied by half a dozen strikes and parries. Rosetto riposted. Bryn jumped to his feet and cried out.

'Oi! Si'down, ya little oik!'

Bryn's father pulled him back down onto the wooden bench and nodded an apology to the man behind. Bryn grinned sheepishly before returning his attention to the duel. There had not been a scoring touch, which Bryn had expected. Baldario had dodged Rosetto's riposte, but Rosetto had the initiative now. He searched for a weakness in Baldario's defence with probing attacks, building the tempo and intensity with each one. The furious exchange continued in a blur of steel and limbs. It was said Rosetto owned a Telastrian blade, but had declined to use it today as Baldario had nothing to match it. He said the victor would be decided by man, not metal. Such honour.

Even at his age, Bryn realised that he was witnessing two masters in action. He might never again see swordsmanship of such quality. He wanted more than anything to be like them, to be a Banneret—perhaps one day even a Banneret of the Blue, the highest achievement of skill—to dedicate himself to perfecting the art of swordsmanship at the Academy up on the hill, and to finally take his place on the Amphitheatre floor as all the greats had done. He looked back at his father and wondered at the possibility, all thoughts of the duel momentarily gone.

CHAPTER ONE

S TEEL SHRIEKED AGAINST steel as the two blades slid along one another. Bryn stumbled back as Dornish shoved forward once the hilts clunked together. He tried to correct his balance but had little time as his opponent came forward again, fast and aggressive.

Bryn parried once, twice and tried to riposte, but he was blocked and forced back with another assault before he had time to think. Their blades flashed in the beams of sunlight that came in through the windows lining one side of the salon. Bryn continued to retreat, defending with each step, knowing that there was not much farther he could go.

He swept Dornish's blade to the side and reversed the movement of his arm, then lunged forward with a quick thrust and a hard stamp of his foot on the wooden floor. The sound echoed around the salon and was joined by the rasp of metal on metal as Dornish swatted his blade away. He followed quickly with another thrust as the sweat that had been pooling at his eyebrows finally broke through and dripped into his eyes.

He squinted the stinging liquid away with repeated blinks as Dornish seized the initiative that had so briefly been Bryn's. He parried, left, right. It was the defence that Bryn was most comfortable with, one that he had used many times before.

Despite still being on the receiving end, it allowed him to settle into something of a rhythm and it set his opponent up for an attack above the waist. He was being obvious about it though, he wanted Dornish to think that was where his next attack would be going.

Bryn parried again and quickly feinted toward Dornish's heart, the move he hoped would be expected. Dornish committed himself to defending against it and mid-thrust Bryn changed direction, angling his wrist and driving the button-tip point down into Dornish's thigh.

The strike made, he backed away and took his guard once more. Had the blades been sharp his opponent would now be wounded and unable to fight effectively. It was as good as a killing blow. Any competent swordsman would be able to exploit the wound and bring the duel to a favourable conclusion.

Dornish saluted in acknowledgement of the skilled hit, took his guard but then lowered his sword after only a moment.

'That will be sufficient,' Master Dornish said.

Finishing his final exams at the Collegium was a major life event for Bryn. He had spent the past six years at the Academy, and the seventeen prior dreaming of reaching that moment. It was the same for his classmates and the celebrations were unsurprisingly wild. Wild enough that he found himself sitting in the Master of the Academy's office the following morning, his chief drinking partner, Amero, sitting beside him looking as though he had reached the transition point between drunk and hung-over.

'Might I remind you, gentlemen, that members of the Collegium are held to a higher standard than the rest of the Academy? You're supposed to be setting an example for those coming up behind you,' Master dal Damaso said.

Bryn struggled to hold down the contents of his stomach,

and Amero seemed unable to focus on anything in particular, looking dazed and confused.

'Sixty-two shattered ale mugs. A broken table. Three broken chairs and a tavern keeper who feels "gravely insulted",' dal Damaso said. He raised an eyebrow at the last grievance.

Despite his best efforts, Bryn could not recall any altercation involving a tavern keeper. His recollection being as it was—and the few fragments of the previous night that he could remember being what they were—he could see no point in denying it. However, Bryn thought he saw a hint of a smile on dal Damaso's face. Maybe the punishment might not be as severe as he feared.

'I hope for your own sakes that you weren't responsible for emptying all of those mugs alone,' dal Damaso continued. 'I trust you will be making good the repair bill in short order?'

'Yes, Master, we will,' Bryn said. Amero still didn't seem to know where they were and did not utter a sound. Admittedly, Bryn wasn't entirely clear on how they ended up in the Master of the Academy's office, and there were significant gaps in his memory of the events of the previous few hours. His brain wasn't working well enough to try to put the pieces together, so he didn't bother trying.

'There is also a captain of the City Watch who will require a written apology. I assume I can trust you to see to that also.'

'Of course, Master,' Bryn said. 'I'll take care of it before the end of the day.'

'Perhaps you might want to dry out a little more before you put pen to paper. Contrary to what the students here seem to believe, I'm not overly fond of having to deal with irate Officers of the Watch. You are both dismissed.'

It had gone better than Bryn expected, and the thought of being able to crawl back into bed was as much of a relief as getting away with only a chastisement.

Bryn sat uneasily on the chair by the office door. He had his fingers laced tightly on his lap and his knuckles were white with tension. For every year of the past six he had gone through the same experience, waiting to be called in for his examination results and annual debrief—but this was the final time. Although each felt as though it was the most important, a potentially catastrophic life event, this was the one he would carry forward for the rest of his life. He had already earned the right to be called Banneret on graduation of the Academy proper two years previously, but to graduate with colours from the Collegium would set him apart from his fellows, acknowledging him as among the best of the very best. He had long thought it nothing more than an impossible dream, but now? Could he have finally achieved it?

After his last interview with the Master, he knew he had exhausted whatever goodwill he'd generated in previous years, but he had behaved himself since the evening after their final examination and fulfilled all the requirements made of him to put to rights the trail of destruction caused by their night of revelry.

The door opened, which startled Bryn and pulled him out of his self-destructive thought process. So much hung on the news he would get in the next few moments. It felt as though there was a maelstrom in his stomach.

'Major dal Damaso will see you now, Banneret,' the adjutant said.

Bryn jumped to his feet and straightened his uniform. The palms of his hands were sweaty and attracted little balls of lint that then refused to come off, adding to his agitation. He realised that the adjutant was still watching him so he allowed his hands to drop to his sides and walked into the office.

Major Abrixio dal Damaso, Banneret of the Blue, had been Master of the Academy for over a decade. He was always referred to as a major rather than a banneret, which was something that

Bryn had wondered about. Bryn had spent the greater part of his life struggling to become a banneret and now that he was one, he took great joy in using the title. He would take even greater joy in being able to add 'of the Blue' to it if the news he received in the next few moments was positive.

'Please sit down, Banneret,' the Major said.

Bryn did as he was bid, and felt light headed as his anxiety reached near breaking point. He took a deep breath and tried to distract himself by examining the carvings on the wood panelling lining the walls.

'Congratulations are in order, Banneret of the Blue Bryn Pendollo.' Dal Damaso stood and offered a large hand across the table.

Bryn revelled in the sense of relief, achievement and satisfaction. He stood and shook dal Damaso's hand. 'Thank you, sir,' he said. He had finally achieved what he had worked for all of his life. It was almost too much to take in. 'I was beginning to convince myself that I hadn't passed.' He said it absently, his jumble of thoughts refusing to fall into order.

'Nonsense, but understandable all the same. It doesn't seem all that long ago that I was having this same conversation from your side of the desk—even if it was. Now please sit. The first thing you have to remember is that I am only "sir" on the battlefield. In this office we are now brothers and my name is Abrixio. I know from personal experience that will feel odd at first, but the sooner you get comfortable with it the better. You're now a member of a group of elite swordsmen. Only the very best accomplish what you have achieved and both you and your family can be very proud.'

'Thank you again, Abrixio,' Bryn said. Using his former master's first name was indeed an odd feeling.

'Excellent. Top of your class all the way through the Academy, and now top graduate of the Collegium. Quite an achievement indeed.'

Bryn tried to contain the elation coursing through his body.

'Now,' dal Damaso said, 'have you given any thought to what you're going to do next?'

'A little. In truth I've spent so long thinking about just getting to this point, I haven't given any serious consideration to what would come after,' Bryn said. It was a lie; he knew exactly what he wanted to do. It was just that voicing it aloud felt foolish. For so long it had been nothing more than a childish dream. To admit it to a man like Major dal Damaso made him feel like a child with outlandish fantasies. No matter how many things there had been to occupy his mind over the years, this notion had remained ever present in his head since the first time he had seen men fight with swords. It was the reason that brought him to the Academy; he wanted to duel in the arenas.

Abrixio leaned back in his chair. 'That's not unusual. There are really only three viable options for one such as yourself. Without independent means you'll be making your living with your sword, which means soldiering, bodyguarding, or the arena.'

Bryn's heart leaped when dal Damaso mentioned the arena.

'My suggestion to you would be the army. You've displayed excellent leadership quality and, your somewhat irreverent traits aside, I think without the influence of some of your more privileged classmates, you will carve out a good career for yourself in a regiment. As a Banneret of the Blue you'll be able to get a decent commission without having to buy one. I don't mean to sound partisan, but my own former regiment would be delighted to have you. At this time of year I always contact them to see how they're situated and there's an opening for lieutenant should you choose to go in that direction…'

'I'm not going to dismiss it out of hand,' Bryn said, 'but to be honest, I've always quite fancied the idea of going to the arena.'

'It's a fine choice and you certainly have the individual

combat skills to thrive there. I'd urge you to consider it carefully though. There's far more to the arena than just being an excellent swordsman. There's a large pool of swordsmen struggling to make a living in the arena; far more than are successful. Talent is only a small part of it, and I've seen a number of very skilled bannerets fail to make a life for themselves there.'

Bryn knew it would not be easy, but he had wanted it for so long, and he was certain that ability and hard work would be enough to see him good. It might take time, but he could persevere.

'Then there are the problems caused by success to think about. At first the life will seem mundane enough, not much different to sparring here every day, but with a little luck you'll find yourself duelling in front of crowds of thousands, even tens of thousands. The Amphitheatre can accommodate over fifty thousand spectators. Quite a terrifying concept, I've always thought, being watched by that many people. Dealing with the celebrity is something that also needs to be given careful consideration. It takes a certain type of person. I know that it might be difficult for a young man to see the drawbacks to that, but believe me, they exist and they are many. I'm not entirely convinced you have the type of personality that will thrive under that scrutiny.'

Bryn disagreed, but he said nothing. He would deal with anything that might come when necessary.

'I'm the first to admit that I may be wrong and I don't want you to feel that I'm trying to steer you in the direction of military service. All I would ask is that you take the time to consider your options; don't rush into anything. It's also worth considering staying here to continue your studies as a Fellow of the Academy, or travelling to one of the other academies to study there for a while. It's not as glamorous or well-paid a pursuit, but it is worthwhile and can be immensely satisfying on a personal level.'

'I'll think on it,' Bryn said, his mind already set.

'Well, that's everything I think. My door is always open to you, if I can be of help. Good luck with whichever path you choose. And congratulations once again.'

As Bryn left the office, he mulled over what he had been told. The advice dal Damaso had given him was good and it would be foolish to dismiss it out of hand, no matter how focussed he was on the arena. The arena was what he had always dreamed of, though, and it was finally within reach.

Bryn was of modest means; he had no titles or lands and would not inherit any, so he had to make money with his blade. The arena represented the best opportunity for this, and even if a military career was more respectable in the long term and would give greater chance for social advancement, the money he could earn from a few years of duelling in the arena was very tempting. Not only was it a boyhood dream, it offered the opportunity to amass great wealth in a short time. A little luck and success was all it took.

As pressing as the decision was, his first priority was to clear his things out of his room in the Academy and find somewhere to live in the city. He would be able to return to his family home until he had scraped together enough coin to pay for somewhere himself, but that wasn't a solution in the longer term—or even the short term, when he thought about it.

'Did you pass?' Amero's familiar voice came from behind Bryn.

'Yes, of course I did,' Bryn said.

'Me too,' Amero said. He wore a smile so wide it almost split his face. He walked down the corridor that their rooms were off with his usual casual swagger. 'Only second place though. I assume I have you to thank for that?'

'I'm afraid you do,' Bryn said.

'Whatever will you do with all those swords of honour?'

Bryn smiled. 'I'm sure I'll think of something.'

'Hard to believe we're done here. I've spent more of my life in this place than anywhere else. I'll be glad to see the back of it, though. Now I can get on with my life.'

His words struck a note with Bryn, and it was the first time that he had given any thought to how he felt about finishing there. He was not glad at all to be leaving; he was keenly aware of how much he was going to miss the place. Bryn had been incredibly happy at the Academy. What lay ahead felt so uncertain, frightening even.

'So where to next?' Amero said. 'Back home?'

'I expect so. For the time being anyway, until I can afford something of my own. I don't really fancy moving from here into a rat pit just to be independent, though.'

'Well, I might have just the thing,' Amero said. 'I've a place in Oldtown, it's big enough for two and you'd have your own room. It's yours if you want it. After getting used to there being so many people around the whole time, I'm not keen on rattling about the place on my own.'

'Thanks, but I doubt I could afford the rent in Oldtown. Not for a while anyway.' It would be a very long time before he might be able to afford the rent in such a desirable part of the city. Possibly never.

'I'm not too worried about the rent; I just want a friendly face around. How about rent free for the first month and then we can agree to a nominal amount?'

An offer that good wasn't likely to come along again. He and Amero had been friends all the way through the Academy and had spent a lot of time training together since moving to the Collegium. It would feel odd him not seeing him regularly anyway.

Bryn shrugged. 'Sounds good. Why not.'

Amero looked back and took one final look across the Academy's front quad. His things were already packed and on the way to Oldtown. He felt an odd and unwelcome sense of nostalgia as he surveyed the grounds, from the campanile in the centre to the imposing training halls behind. He had spent six years there, and they had been happy for the most part. It was never his choice to go to the Academy however, and that fact would always sour his memory of the place. Few things in his life had been of his choosing, and none of them important. The thought made him angry. Resentful.

He had done what he was told, worked hard and made the best of the years, but he was a man now and would make his own choices. A visit home was the first thing on his agenda. It would be the test. It would prove he had the resolve to step out from his father's shadow.

CHAPTER TWO

T HERE WAS NO getting away from his pursuers. He was on foot; they were on horseback. The young man was exhausted and had no more running left in him. He stopped and dropped the deer to the ground. He should have left it where he killed it, but it was a fine beast; plenty of good eating. He wouldn't be getting it home now. He turned to face the men as they drew to a halt next to him.

'Now tell me, m'lad,' the lead rider said. 'Where did you get that hart? A fine beast like that must cost quite a bit.'

The young man shrugged.

'A fine answer,' the horseman said.

He looked tall, but everyone did when in the saddle. The young man had seen him on his feet though, so knew it to be true. A hard looking man. The years hadn't softened a single one of his edges. Not one to be caught by with a poached deer, the Lord of Moreno.

'Even someone as thick as pig shit knows that poaching is illegal,' Lord Moreno said. 'Are you as thick as pig shit?'

'No, sir. I… I don't know.' The young man hadn't realised that noblemen cussed just like regular folk.

'You don't know?' Lord Moreno leaned back in his saddle. 'Do you know who I am, at least?'

The young man nodded. 'The Hammer, sir. Lord of Moreno.'

'Right first time. Well done.'

The young man forced a smile.

'Do you know why I'm called the Hammer?'

The young man shook his head.

'When I wasn't much older than you are now, I was leading my first army. In truth it was so small it could hardly be called an army, but there I was in the south at the head of a force of armed men doing what I'd always dreamed of. Not long after, a far larger Auracian force moved into the area, and I was ordered to retreat. Do you know what I felt when I heard that?'

The young man shook his head.

'I felt exactly the same as you did when you saw that magnificent hart.' Lord Moreno leaned forward in his saddle, closer to the young man. 'I felt hungry—and like you, I ignored the rules. I disobeyed that order.'

The young man's mouth opened slightly. For the first time since sighting the horsemen riding toward him, he felt hopeful the dungeon might no longer be in his future. Perhaps the Count wasn't so harsh a man after all.

'We were down in the southern mountain passes; I can't recall the name of the mountain now, but for a time the locals took to calling it the Anvil. I manoeuvred my troops all morning until I had the Auracians exactly where I wanted them, with their backs to the Anvil. Then I smashed them. Every last man. What most people don't know however, is that nearly half that Auracian army surrendered once they realised they were beaten. Not one of them lived though. I had every last one of them killed. Do you know why I did that?'

The young man shook his head.

'I did it because if you allow a man to put down his arms and return home, he'll be back to fight you again the next year. It's the same way as if I allow you home now, you'll be out poaching another deer next week.' Moreno turned to his men. 'String him up!'

⟡

'Did you enjoy that?' Amero asked.

'Of course not,' Renald, Lord Moreno said. 'But it was necessary. He stole. Others will think twice before doing the same. Letting him go would have been an invitation.'

Amero thought of the young man swinging from the tree by his village. He had pleaded as the rope was secured around his neck, invoking a wife and two young children. He was no older than Amero. He couldn't imagine being responsible for a family. For children.

'Call at my study when we get back to the house,' Renald said. 'There's something I want to discuss with you.'

'Of course, Father.'

⟡

While studying in the Collegium, Bryn had been a front-runner in the Competition—a duelling contest that attracted the very best swordsmen from all of the academies dotted around the Middle Sea. Although he had been knocked out before the final, getting as far as he did earned him the right to a duelling licence.

The licence was there to prevent just anyone who chose to from entering himself into the arena. It had been introduced after it briefly became fashionable for out-of-shape bannerets well past middle-age to try to prove their continuing virility by duelling in public. After several had been maimed or mortally wounded, and one portly gentleman far beyond the age of sixty keeled over and died from a heart attack before the duel had even started, a stand was taken. Despite the joy of the crowd at the spectacle of aristocrats making fools of themselves, the licensing system was introduced.

Duelling was not exclusively the remit of bannerets. A number of men who had not graduated from an academy—former soldiers usually and occasionally street toughs with lofty dreams—entered themselves onto the duelling lists, so the tests introduced to obtain the licence also ensured they were of the required standard.

For Bryn, exempted from the requirement to be tested for his licence, the process was simple, and more importantly, fast. He went to the Bannerets' Hall in the centre of the city of Ostenheim and registered on the list of active duellists. His name was added to the pool of combatants and duels would be arranged for him, starting with modest venues in the city with no more than a few hundred spectators. When he became more successful, he would be in a position to arrange his own matches—but until then he would have to be satisfied with whatever he was offered. After he had entered his name on the list, it was time to move his things from the Academy down to Amero's apartment in Oldtown.

Amero was angry with himself when he felt a flutter of nerves as he knocked on the door to his father's study.

'Come in.'

Amero felt a chill at the sound of his father's voice. He did as he was bid.

'Good morning, Father,' Amero said.

Renald dal Moreno did not even look up from his papers when Amero entered. There was a moment of uncomfortable silence before he spoke.

'So, Banneret of the Blue. You must be very pleased with yourself,' Renald said.

'It's something few enough achieve,' Amero said.

'I'm not convinced it wasn't a waste of a couple of years,' Renald said.

Amero bit his lip in frustration. It had been his father's command that he stay on and attend the Collegium.

'Still,' Renald said, 'as you say, not many can get it, so the fact that you have is a credit to yourself and our house. It will also carry weight with the men you will command.'

'Men I will command?' Amero said. He realised they were reaching the crux of the matter, and an argument was not far off.

'Yes. I've arranged a commission with Breganzo's Medium Horse. They're a good regiment led by officers from the best families. They've a reputation as good fighters, not just a social club for idlers and wastrels.'

'It didn't occur to you to discuss it with me first?' Amero said.

'Why would it? You have a different regiment in mind? If it's suitable, I'm willing to consider it.'

'I have no regiment in mind. I have no desire to be a soldier,' Amero said.

Renald stood suddenly, and Amero flinched. He cursed himself silently. His father paced back and forth with his arms akimbo. Closer to seventy than sixty years, he still had a trim, athletic figure and broad shoulders. Only his receding hairline and the grey on his stubbled chin gave away his age.

He had earned the name 'Hammer of the South' in his youth. The massacre he had so delighted in recounting to the young poacher was credited with securing Ostia's southern border for two decades. If he chose to wear all his military awards and decorations, Amero doubted he would have the strength to stand under the weight.

'You realise,' Renald said, 'that every Count of Moreno has held a military command before inheriting the county.'

'Of course I do, Father,' Amero said. 'I'm hardly likely to forg—'

'Shut your impertinent mouth!' his father said.

Amero flinched again. He was prepared for this, but it didn't make it any easier. 'Since I was born, I have done everything you have told me. Without question, without complaint.

How am I going to take your place if I've never made a decision for myself?'

'That's what your time in the regiment will be for,' Renald said, his brow furrowed as he studied Amero.

'Taking orders from others?' Amero asked. 'What's there to be learned from that?'

Renald sat. 'What did you have in mind?' he said, his voice quiet again.

It was unnerving how quickly he could go from rage to calm. Amero had nothing in mind. He hadn't given a thought to it, never truly believing he would end up doing anything other than what his father decided on. 'The arena,' he found himself saying, only because he had listened to Bryn going on about it for so long.

Renald frowned, then leaned back in his chair. 'The arena. You plan to make a fool of yourself. A mockery of our family name?'

'I plan to make my own decisions,' Amero said. 'For my own reasons.'

Renald gave Amero a hard look. 'There's more of your mother than me in you. Every time I look at you, I see that deceitful whore's face.'

'Perhaps I'm not yours,' Amero said, spite dripping from his voice. As the only heir, it was the most injurious thing he could think of.

Renald barked a laugh. 'No chance of that. There are those who can tell such things. I had three of them confirm who sired you. I wasn't going to take your mother's word for it.'

'If you hadn't spent most of your life gallivanting along the borders killing anyone who even looked at Ostia, she might not have felt the need to find comfort elsewhere,' Amero said.

'An aristocrat's life is bound to the state. I did my duty, keeping the borders secure. She should have done hers and kept her legs closed while I was away.'

Although Amero knew his father was hurt by what she had done—the conversation would not have been happening if the wound was not still sore—the calm, cold way he could speak of it was unnerving, and in a strange way admirable. Every time Renald spoke of Amero's mother, he could feel his own temper flare. To be able to control it so masterfully would be a fine talent. Opening his mouth would only have revealed his feelings, so he kept it shut.

'Still,' Renald said. 'We know how all of that ended.'

'We do,' Amero said. He cursed himself for the waver in his voice.

'Don't look at me like that, boy. I didn't put the knife in her hand.'

'You might as well have, when you killed Serlo.'

'She was my wife,' Renald said, anger flaring in his voice. 'He should have known better. There could have been no other resolution.'

Amero took some grim satisfaction in finally having provoked a reaction, but the exchange did nothing other than leave a bitter taste in his mouth.

'The regiment expects you by the end of the week. Get out of my office.'

Amero had spoken modestly, a trait not usually attributable to him, when describing the apartment as 'big enough for two'. It was at least as big as the apartment that Bryn had grown up in as part of a family of five. It was in the most expensive part of Oldtown, the original site of the city before it expanded to its present size, and living there was the height of fashion for young aristocrats. Were it not for Amero's generosity, Bryn would have been limited to a one-room affair in the top of a building tucked away behind Crossways, or perhaps something in a less salubrious part of the city. Once all of his possessions had been moved down, he had barely filled the closets in his room.

There had always been something to do at the Academy, always something to keep your mind busy. Once he had unpacked, he realised that there was no routine for him to follow anymore. Amero was out of the city, visiting his family at their country estate for a few days, so Bryn had the apartment to himself and he was noticing the quiet and loneliness. Having grown up in a large family he had never encountered it before. From there he had gone straight to the Academy where there were always people around, always noise and activity.

The quietness and the lack of purpose felt strange. He could remember many occasions in the Academy when he'd wished he had a moment to himself, but now that he had the entire day he couldn't think of a single thing to do. The thought was troubling, but he tried to occupy himself with plans for his future. He had decided upon a career in the arena, so he needed to put in place a regime that would allow him to perform at his highest possible level. He took a pen and bottle of ink from his room and scavenged around the apartment for some paper.

Having found some he sat down on one of the plush armchairs in the living room and began to plan out a training schedule. He based it heavily on the one that had been made out for him by his tutor, Willard Dornish, in the Collegium in preparation for the Competition. The training had put him in the best form of his life. If he could reach that level again without access to the facilities of the Academy he would be very pleased, and in a strong position to begin his career on the duelling circuit. He was under no illusions that he could reach the top of the duelling ranks, but that wasn't necessary to make a good living and who knew how his swordsmanship might develop in coming years? He was far from being in his prime yet, and the thought of being First Blade of Ostia was very appealing indeed.

As he began to plan, drawing up a list of all the areas he

would need to address, it became clear to him that he would need some form of training facility. The thought had been in the back of his mind for some time, but only now did it need to be addressed directly. He considered going back to the Academy and asking Major dal Damaso to allow him to train there when the halls were not being used, but that was not his preferred solution. He wanted to move forward, not back.

In order to do well in the arena he would also need regular access to skilled training partners. A private salon was the usual route for duellists, but Bryn couldn't afford the fees. If there was no other option, he would have to see if his family could help him, but that was a course he'd rather not take. He wanted money to flow from him to them now that he was no longer a student. He would explore all the other options before he started looking into private salons.

As he considered the reality of what had seemed like a very attractive career choice, the problems kept mounting up. The best option he could come up with was to go to the Bannerets' Hall and look around to see what was on offer there. As a banneret he was a member—but the only time he had been there was to get his licence and the place had struck him as being little more than a club for bored aristocratic bannerets to while away their days reminiscing about old feats of swordsmanship that grew greater with each passing year. It was not an activity that Bryn had any time for, but it had decent training facilities, and he was running short on alternatives.

Bryn sighed and looked down at the blank piece of paper. Staring at it wasn't getting him anywhere. He needed to get out to clear his mind. He grabbed his cloak from the finely crafted brass hook by the door and headed out into the city.

CHAPTER THREE

I N A CITY where duelling was an obsession, a match could be found at almost any hour of any day of the week. The arenas ranged from dank, dark cellars where down-on-their-luck bannerets and thrill seekers would fight to the death on a stretch of floor painted black to hide the blood stains in illegal duels, to the Amphitheatre, where the very finest exponents of the sport plied their trade.

In between, there were numerous arenas of varying size in the city, encompassing those that could accommodate a few dozen spectators to the boutique arenas on the fringes of Highgarden, where the exclusive audiences sat on silken cushions.

Bryn stopped at the first small arena he encountered, paid the admission fee and went in to watch. He wasn't expecting much on a weekday afternoon. It would be jobbing swordsmen trying to make some extra money for the most part, men who made up the lower end of the Ladder, the city's fencing ranking system.

He bought a packet of candied nuts and sat on the wooden plank that served as a seat and tore open his folded paper parcel. A duel was already underway and he absently chewed on the nuts as he watched the duellists in an equally distracted fashion, his thoughts still dominated by his own nascent career.

The combatants weren't up to much. There were a couple of exchanges that made Bryn cringe. It didn't look like either man had any formal training. They were probably soldiers, as they didn't have that thuggish look that the toughs from the city's streets and criminal gangs tended to acquire through broken noses, cauliflower ears and knife fight scars. Their swordplay might have sufficed when mingled with kicks, punches, elbows and knees, but as physical contact was forbidden in the formal duels of the arena they left a great many openings in their defences, none of which were exploited by the other.

There were no more than a dozen spectators in the arena, and Bryn could see why if this match was illustrative of the standard. The duel ended on the expiry of the time limit, the result inconclusive. Both men—Bryn had a hard time calling them duellists—had worked up a good lather of sweat in the afternoon sun, but no excitement or appreciation in the audience. They saluted and made their way from the sandy arena floor to their payment of a few florins for their exertions.

The next pairing came out onto the floor, and Bryn could see that this match would be different. The first man looked little different to the previous pairing. He was a scrapper rather than a dancer, as Dornish would have put it. The second man was the complete opposite.

He was tall, slender, and broad in the shoulders. Completely bald and with a jet-black, pointed beard, it looked as though he shaved his head by choice rather than necessity. He had perfect posture and moved lightly on the balls of his feet, as though his well-built frame weighed nothing at all. Bryn shifted onto the edge of his seat, his attention grabbed by his expectation of what was to come.

The Master of Arms walked onto the arena floor and gestured to both duellists to take their places on either side of the black mark at its centre. The small audience chatted critically and in lacklustre tones about the previous match.

'Banneret Panceri Mistria of Maestro Valdrio's Salon, and Corporal Selvo Septra of Count Bragadin's Second Regiment of Light Foot,' the Master of Arms said. That done, he retreated to the edge of the arena floor to watch for breaches of the rules.

'Duel!' he shouted.

The audience ceased talking and returned their attention to the duel. Mistria danced back three steps, anticipating Septra's flamboyant slashing attack. Mistria was gone before Septra had even swung his sword, confirming Bryn's expectation that he would move well. Septra's was the type of weapon handling that got soldiers on the battlefield killed, but it was something that Bryn had noticed a number of times with professional soldiers. When they got to the arena, they left all the common sense beaten into them in battle at the door, and tried to conform to some ostentatious notion of what was expected of professional duellists.

As Septra came to the end of his attack, now within the reach of the taller Mistria, the banneret's arm shot out—no other part of his body moving even a fraction—the rounded tip of his sword moving smoothly with precise direction, connecting with Septra's chest over his heart. Septra nodded in concession of the touch and returned to the black mark without needing to be told by the Master of Arms.

So the duel continued. It was a master class in swordsmanship and Bryn was surprised that he had not encountered Mistria before, or at least heard his name. Mistria was clearly five or so years older than Bryn, which could have put them at the Academy at different times. However, for a man of that skill to have gone unfêted in the arena for any length of time was surprising. It was possible that he was new to it, in which case Bryn felt certain there were great things in store for him.

Bryn left after that match, returning to the ominously blank piece of paper. He still had no idea what to put on it. After seeing Mistria duel, he did however have a greater sense of urgency. That was what he wanted from his career, that unharried sense of mastery and control, and he wasn't going to get there sitting around procrastinating.

When Amero returned that evening, he found Bryn sitting in an armchair, fingers covered in ink and several crumpled balls of paper lying around on the floor.

'What in the gods' names are you doing?' He breezed into the room, followed by two servants carrying baggage and didn't wait for an answer. 'The bad news is, I can't cook,' Amero said. 'I've known you long enough to be quite confident that you can't either, and the idea of eating the mystery meat special in taverns every night doesn't fill me with much enthusiasm. The good news is, I managed to pinch one of the cooks from home. He's installing himself in the servants' quarters above and will come down to cook us up something as soon as he's finished.'

Cooks? Servants quarters? What next? Even being exposed to members of the more privileged classes while in the Academy had not given Bryn any idea that life in Amero's apartment would be like this. While in the Academy, everyone had much the same living conditions irrespective of position in society, the only real differences being down to seniority. Being in the Collegium had put Bryn at the top of that pile.

'I wasn't expecting you back so soon,' he said.

'No, I hadn't planned on it, but I decided to come back this morning,' Amero said. 'Countryside's too quiet at this time of year. Got bored. So, what have you been doing when not dipping your fingers in the inkwell and crumpling up paper?'

'I'm trying to work out how to best train for the arena. I can use the facilities in the Bannerets' Hall, can't I?'

Amero scrunched his face in distaste. 'Yes, if you want to

choke yourself on dust and poison yourself on rusty old blades. I doubt if anyone has been in the hall there in a century. All the old farts in there spend half the day asleep in armchairs in the lounge, the other half talking up what great swordsmen they were in their youth. Never heard of anyone going there to train.'

It confirmed Bryn's opinion that it was little more than a social club for bannerets. 'Any ideas then? I really need to find somewhere. Not to mention a training partner, or at least access to some sparring partners.'

'Well, I think I can help you on the training partner and sparring front. I had a think about it when I was at home, and I quite fancy the idea of duelling myself. Father wants me in the army.' Amero's face darkened for a moment, but he quickly regained his composure. 'A nice uniform's all well and good, but to be honest the idea of getting hacked to bits by some bloody barbarians gods-only-know-where doesn't sound as nice as the adulation of all the young women of the city. You're too much of a prude to take advantage of it, and it would be a shame to let it all go to waste. Point is, I'm going to go to the arena too. I can't see any reason not to continue training and sparring together as we did in the Collegium; that worked out quite well for both of us.'

'What are you going to do for a licence? It takes ages to get one—months at least, often longer,' Bryn said. 'I was lucky to get one from the Competition.'

'Taken care of,' Amero said. 'I got in touch with an old pal from the Academy who owes me a favour. His father has some pull with the Bannerets' Commission, so I asked him to speed my licence along. I expect to have it by the end of the week.'

It was nice to have contacts, Bryn thought. Were it not for the fact that he had gotten his licence by default, he would have been waiting half a year at least. However, there was something odd about the way Amero was behaving. He seemed awkward, ill at ease. Bryn would have suspected him to be lying, were there any reason for him to do so. Perhaps he was tired after the journey back to the city.

'What does your father think of that?'

'Not much, but it's not up to him anymore,' Amero said. 'So, training?'

'Yes, that sounds good,' Bryn said. 'Any ideas of where we might train?'

'No. Not really,' Amero said. 'I think the best plan is to spend a couple of days taking a look at the private salons around the city. There are a few better known ones that might be worth a look, but anywhere with the space that isn't too busy and has enough equipment to keep us going should be fine. We can think about a coach or a trainer at a later point, once we're up and running.'

Bryn cringed at the mention of the private salons, but they did seem to be the only realistic option. Hopefully they could find one that wouldn't be too expensive. It also struck him that although going to the arena had been his idea, Amero seemed to have grabbed it enthusiastically and taken charge of its direction. The thought made him uncomfortable. He wanted to be independent, not reliant on his friend or anyone else.

CHAPTER FOUR

THE NEXT MORNING Bryn and Amero began their search. As Amero seemed to have a better idea of what was available, Bryn allowed him to lead the way. He was worried though. For Amero, cost was not something that mattered, or even existed. His wealth was as good as limitless. Bryn, no longer the beneficiary of a generous scholarship at the Academy, had no source of income and only very meagre funds to tide him over until he started getting matches.

His concerns grew after their first stop, not just at the potential expense of the salon Amero had taken them to but also at the attitude to training there. After their second, he knew unless he retook control of matters he might actually find himself agreeing to one of the places out of sheer frustration with the prospect of having to look at any more.

The salons that Amero had taken him to could at best be described as vanity salons. They were all very well appointed with the best equipment and facilities that one could desire. There were plush changing facilities, with both cold and hot running water, something of an extravagant novelty in the city. There were lounges, fully equipped with servants, bars and catering. In effect, they were miniature versions of what he had imagined the Bannerets' Hall to be like, but far more exclusive.

The salons struck Bryn as being more like brothels than places for jobbing swordsmen to go when they needed hard training, harsh criticism and a place that was devoid of any distraction. Amero seemed keen on both of the ones they visited that morning, and had spent some time chatting with people that he knew, all aristocrats with nothing better to do with their time than play with swords and spend money.

The cost of joining one of these places would be enormous, and while he had little doubt that Amero would offer to cover his fees at the first sign of the issue being raised he had absolutely no desire to join one of them, nor to sink farther into his friend's debt.

At their final stop of the morning, there were several bannerets from the same house as Amero at the Academy. Always more social than Bryn, he chatted with them while Bryn took a closer look at the facilities. Once Amero had finished catching up with his aristocratic friends, he returned to Bryn where he stood watching the various activities with barely veiled contempt.

'Which of them do you fancy then?' Amero said. 'I've no real preference; any of them are fine by me. Cavzanigo's Salon of Arms is slightly more prestigious, but as you can see the crowd here is younger, so it probably suits us a little better. Like I said though, the choice is all yours.'

Amero was a superb swordsman—his taking second place in the Collegium ranking being proof of point—and if he applied himself more seriously could be a threat to any other, Bryn included. The problem was that this was just a lark for Amero, something to keep him from idleness and the trouble that brought. He would never need to earn a living with his sword. He had enough money to throw a bag of gold crowns into the harbour every day for the rest of his life and still have more than he knew what to do with. For Bryn, this was too important to approach flippantly. He would have loved the comfort of being relaxed and casual about it, but he could not. His prosperity would be largely dependent on how hard he trained. In a place such as the salons they'd visited there would be no chance to get serious work done.

Amero knew how to work hard when he had to. At the Academy there were times where no amount of natural talent or luck would be enough, but as was the case here the Academy had just been a diversion for Amero. Talent had carried him on into the Collegium, but again, once he had earned the honour of being a banneret his reasons for continuing his studies were more to have something to do other than drink, gamble and wench than the professional opportunity that being a Banneret of the Blue brought.

Despite their many years of friendship, Bryn had never been able to work Amero out. His decision to join Bryn on the duelling circuit was just another example of his confusing behaviour. There were many other ways for young gentleman bannerets to keep themselves out of trouble, which were far more in keeping with the position of a high aristocrat.

Nevertheless he had achieved as much as Bryn, entirely on merit. He was a Banneret of the Blue, the highest accolade and testament to skill that a swordsman could earn, and had decided to follow a road that not many aristocrats chose. Perhaps that was why he had taken it.

The two salons they had been to represented exactly the type of places Bryn expected Amero to end up. Neither was close to suitable for what Bryn wanted. The question that remained was how he could put his opinion to Amero without causing offence.

'I'd have to say that neither of them are really what I had in mind,' Bryn said. He paused to try and gauge Amero's reaction, but it was impossible to tell what he was thinking. It always was.

Amero looked around for a moment, as if thinking things over. 'What *did* you have in mind?'

'Something a little less fancy for starters,' Bryn said. 'It's nice and all, but I just want somewhere to train hard with no distractions, no socialising.'

'That's reasonable I suppose. Anywhere specific?'

'No, that's the problem. We're going to have to keep looking until we find it,' Bryn said.

'Not "we" I'm afraid. I only have the morning free, so it'll have to be you doing the rest of the legwork. Have a look around. If you find something you like, I'll take a look and if all else fails we can always come back here.'

They parted company and Bryn went to the Bannerets' Hall to take a look at the register of fencing salons kept there. Every salon in the city had to register in order to conduct business. He would make a note of a dozen or so and spend the rest of the day and the next also looking. He was not willing to choose the first that seemed suitable only to find later that he preferred another.

He went into the records office at the Hall where two large tomes were brought out for him. The practice seemed to be to keep a running record, with the new salons being added to the end of the list. Unfortunately there did not seem to be any indication of which ones were still in operation. Bryn reckoned that every building in the city would have to contain a salon if each of those listed was still running. Even the Ostians weren't that devoted to swordsmanship.

He made a note of the names and addresses of the dozen most recent entries on a scrap of paper and pushed it into his pocket. They were scattered across the city, but he had immediately discounted those situated in Lowgarden and Oldtown. They were likely to be similar to the salons he had already visited that day.

A group of them were clustered in the streets around Crossways, the large market square that dominated the centre of the city, so he decided to try there first.

It was still early in the summer, but it was already growing uncomfortably warm in the middle of the day. Over the next few weeks the wealthy parts of the city would become quieter as the aristocrats who had country estates left for them to escape the heat and stink of the city at the height of summer. That wasn't an option for someone like Bryn, but he had spent his entire life in the city and was used to the experience, uncomfortable as it was.

The central part of Ostenheim—that which lay between the two rivers flowing through the city—was always busy. The city was home to over two hundred thousand people and that was its beating heart.

Other than a few wide main streets that ran through the city from its gates, converging on Crossways, Ostenheim was a warren of twisting streets, alleys and lanes that snaked between her tall, pale brick buildings. The salons Bryn was looking for were all situated on these small streets, away from the main thoroughfares.

The first was not difficult to find. He knew the street, as it was only a short distance from the apartment he had grown up in. Bryn had yet to call home since moving out of the Academy or inform his mother about his new living arrangements, and he felt guilty about it. He could not put it off much longer, but there always seemed to be something more pressing.

The salon was listed as being on the top floor of its building. When he got there the name had been crudely scratched off the list of occupants on the door. Bryn swore, hoping he was not going to waste his day with similar experiences.

He was relieved to find that the next salon was still in operation. Like the previous one, this salon was on the top floor of the building, four stories up. The immediate issue that came to mind was how far it was from Amero's apartment in Oldtown. Trekking home after hours of training through busy streets didn't fill him with much enthusiasm, but he thought it would be foolish to come all the way here and not take a look.

Bryn went up the stairs and into the salon, and was pleasantly surprised by what he saw. It was far closer to what he was looking for. The entire loft of the building had been opened up into one large room. It was well lit with windows set in the dormer roof and it was tidy, but there were no traces of luxury. The advantage of being on the top floor was that it was high enough for a gentle, cooling breeze to pass through the open windows. Gone were the comfortable rest areas and the swarm of servants buzzing around ensuring that all of their clients' needs were attended to. Gone too were the bored looking gentlemen lounging around, trying to decide if they would actually pick up a sword rather than just chat about doing so. This was a place where serious training was carried out and there was plenty of it in evidence.

It was busy, which was a problem. There were at least twenty men sparring, doing exercises or waiting their turn to do so. The room was full of the sounds of sword play; boots stamping on the wooden floor, the chink of steel against steel, the gasps of exertion. It smelt exactly how Bryn thought a salon of arms should: of leather, sweat, and oily steel.

He wanted somewhere that would allow him to focus but also where he would be able to get the attention from the fencing masters that he wanted. If he was going to pay out the subscription fees required, he wanted to get full value for money and this place struck him as being too hectic. He was disappointed—it was otherwise exactly what he was looking for.

It didn't take long before the arrival of a new face was spotted, and a man of middle age with greying hair pulled back into a tight ponytail walked over.

'Can I help you, sir?' he said.

'I'm looking for somewhere to train,' Bryn said. 'I came to have a look at your salon.'

'Very good. I am Banneret of the Blue Gendo, assistant to Maestro Valdrio. There isn't much more to see than what's before you; we offer no frills and no luxuries. Most of the men here are either in the arena or work in private service. We also have the occasional army officer preparing for a posting.'

'Is it always this busy?' Bryn said. There wasn't much room

for anyone else to train there; if it was that busy every day he would need to look at other options.

'I'm afraid it is, and has been for a while. One of Maestro Valdrio's duellists has won several notable duels recently, which has attracted quite a few new duellists to the salon. Might I ask what your own circumstances are?'

'I've just left the Collegium,' Bryn said. 'I'm intending to try for a career in the arena. I need somewhere to train, for myself and another Collegium graduate. I'd like regular access to a trainer also.'

'I think we should have room for another couple of regular attendants, Bannerets of the Blue are always especially welcome, but I'm afraid Maestro Valdrio's schedule is entirely taken up. I or one of the other assistants are usually available; we are all Bannerets of the Blue. If you wish I can talk you through our fees and what we can offer in terms of training.'

The crowd gave Bryn pause for thought. He could not help but get the feeling they were taking every advantage of their new-found status to bring in as many new clients as possible. If the salon's fencing master was completely preoccupied with their new star, then it seemed unlikely that Bryn would be able to get the type of attention he was hoping for.

'Thank you,' Bryn said. 'I don't think that will be necessary right now.'

'Very good, please don't hesitate to call back if you have any further questions.' He nodded his head in a Banneret's salute and walked away.

Bryn returned the gesture and turned to leave. As he was making his way down the stairs he passed by a bald man, exquisitely dressed in purple clothes with silver-thread embroidery that were cut to resemble fencer's kit, but were slightly more relaxed for day-to-day wear. He had a neat moustache and pointed beard and carried himself with a level of confidence that was bordering on arrogance. Despite this, he shrugged his black cloak over his shoulder and stepped to the side politely to let Bryn pass.

Bryn gave him an appreciative banneret's salute, assuming this man to be a banneret also. There was something familiar about him, but it wasn't until he was out in the street that he realised it was the impressive man he had seen duelling in the small arena. He racked his brain, and eventually remembered the duellist's name. Panceri Mistria. He had an air of success about him, something that Bryn very much wanted for himself.

Bryn spent the remainder of the afternoon calling at the other salons on his list, becoming more disconsolate as each one fell short of what he wanted. There were two that came close, but neither was ideal. After nearly a full day trudging around the city, he was beginning to think his expectations were unrealistic and was ready to give up on the idea of finding exactly what he was looking for, frustrating though it was.

They all offered some of the things that he had liked about Valdrio's but were quieter and would allow for him to get both the space and attention he felt he would need to progress on the duelling circuit. However, none of them had it all. Perhaps he was being picky, having been thoroughly spoiled by access to the best facilities and the very finest fencing masters when he was in the Collegium. He hoped that the couple he had earmarked would be acceptable to Amero, but he was hot, tired and grimy from his day's wanderings and had no interest in looking at any more.

He decided to leave his search at that, cheered by the prospect of having a cook waiting back at the apartment.

CHAPTER FIVE

A S BRYN WALKED it occurred to him that he would be passing by one of the other salons on his list and it would be lazy not to stop there on his way home.

The quickest route back to the apartment from Crossways was straight toward the harbour, around its edge and over the Westway until he reached the old city walls, which marked the boundary of Oldtown. The salon was in Docks, the part of the city that was filled with warehouses, trading companies, mixed with apartments, inns and taverns that were frequented by a tough crowd; dock workers, sailors, thugs, and mercenaries. It could be a rough part of the city, hosting some of its least salubrious streets, and rents were appropriately low. It did not bode well for the salon Bryn was investigating, but he would give it the benefit of the doubt. At least it would be cheap.

The address brought him to a small building tucked between two larger warehouses. It was rundown and looked as though it hadn't been in use for some time. The windows were grimy and the woodwork was bleached and rotting. It had obviously been many years since anyone had thought of painting it. His first thought was that the building was derelict and that any salon had long since closed.

Out of curiosity, he pushed on the door. It creaked open to

reveal a large open plan interior, punctuated by the wooden pillars that held up the roof of the single storey building. It was bright and airy, with a number of open skylights in the roof letting in both light and fresh air.

There was no sign of damp or water damage on the floor, so they couldn't have been open for long. His footsteps echoed on the wooden floor, which was swept clean, but any traces of varnish had long since vanished. He looked around and realised what an ideal space it was for training in. Perhaps he should try to see if the lease was available and set up there himself. Amero would be more than able to provide the meagre funds that would be needed. His planning was brought to a halt by the sound of footsteps that were not an echo of his own.

'Can I help you?' a voice said.

Foreign. Estranzan perhaps?

'Yes,' Bryn said, as he turned to face the direction of the voice. It belonged to a man of average build and cropped salt-and-pepper hair. He had a thick moustache that had been left much to its own devices, contrasting strongly with Bryn's own finely sculpted effort. He was standing at the doorway to another small room at the back. 'I was told that there's a fencing salon here.'

'You have been informed correctly,' the man said.

Bryn didn't speak for a moment, expecting something more in the way of information but it didn't appear to be forthcoming. 'I was wondering if you could tell me where I might find the salon's master.'

The man's clothes had seen better days; they weren't rags, but they were shabby which gave Bryn to presume that he was merely a caretaker.

'I am the master,' he said. 'This is my salon. Banneret of the Starry Field Baltasar Bautisto at your service.'

An Estranzan then. Bryn's initial guess had been correct.

'I'm Banneret of the Blue Bryn Pendollo. I'm looking for somewhere to train. I thought I'd come to have a look at your salon.'

Bautista eyed him suspiciously. 'What is the nature of your training?'

'I'm planning on competing in the arena. I'm looking for a basic salon where there will be few distractions. Coaching also.'

'This isn't the most well-appointed salon that you will find.' Bautisto walked forward from the doorway and gestured to the open space of the room with both hands. 'I dare say it might be the worst. But it is clean and dry, and there are no distractions to be had other than the whores who ply their trade on the street outside after dark.'

It was hardly the most compelling sales pitch. 'Thank you for your time, Maestro Bautista. I'll give it consideration. I've viewed several salons today and will need time to make my decision,' Bryn said. He felt uncomfortable being the only other person there, and a sense of something akin to pity for a Maestro with no students. Despite the emptiness of his salon, Bautisto didn't seem particularly motivated to entice one.

'You would consider a salon without testing it?' Bautisto said, cocking his head inquiringly.

'Well, I suppose not.' It struck Bryn that he had been slipshod in his approach thus far. He knew what he was looking for in terms of facilities by sight, but the only way to truly gauge a salon's worth was to train in it.

Bautisto ducked into the back room without another word and re-emerged a moment later carrying a rapier and matching parrying dagger. Neither were particularly ornate, 'tools rather than jewels' as Dornish would have called them.

'The arena is generally fought with both sword and dagger, I suggest that is what we use now. I have practice blades if you would prefer...'

An unusual approach, but Bryn was willing to play along. 'Live steel will be fine,' he said.

He undid the fastening of his cloak and allowed it to drop

from his shoulders to the ground. He unsheathed his rapier and dagger and dropped his sword belt on the cloak.

'Shall we begin?' Bautisto said.

Bryn nodded and dropped into a low, wide stance, flexed at his knees with his body leaning forward. He held his dagger out in front of him at waist level, his rapier farther forward and a little higher. It was a neutral posture, that of a man not sure what to expect.

'Fine form,' Bautisto said, before launching into an attack of a precision and speed that surprised Bryn. It was a little more enthusiastic than he would have expected of a friendly spar with sharp blades, but nothing he couldn't cope with.

Bryn parried with both sword and dagger, stepping back with each attack to invite Bautisto to overreach himself. He was not to be easily drawn however, moving forward lightly on the balls of his feet, never over-committing his weight and always remaining balanced.

He paused to invite attack and Bryn was only too eager to oblige. He thrust forward from his low guard, stepping forward with his rear foot to follow in with a secondary attack with his dagger. Bautisto danced backward, swatting both out of the way but instantly reversed and launched into a perfectly executed counter with his rapier that almost caught Bryn off guard. He parried it out of the way but took two fast steps back to give himself a chance to reform his guard, both surprised and impressed by the Estranzan's ability to change tempo. Bryn found himself enjoying the bout.

They continued back and forth for several more exchanges before Bautisto stopped, stood straight and lowered his blades.

'Excellent form all-round,' he said. 'I can see some areas that might need work, but I think you have a very solid technical foundation. Should you choose my salon I would be very pleased to work with you.'

Bautisto was agile and fast. His technique was exceptional, albeit distinct from what was the norm in Ostenheim. Before they sparred Bryn had been trying to get out of the salon as quickly but as politely as possible, now he found it hard to imagine training anywhere else.

Bautisto had easily been a match for any of the tutors in the Collegium and it was only with strenuous effort that Bryn had been able to keep up with him. There was no doubt that he would learn from Bautisto and he felt that the man's skill was enough to make up for the grotty location. Hopefully Amero would feel the same way and agree to train there. The consideration of cost never even entered his mind. This was the right place.

Bryn felt his anxiety build as he and Amero turned the corner onto the street where Bautisto kept his salon. He had been deliberately cagey in his description of the place, knowing that the only thing to speak in its favour was the man himself. The salon could be improved upon without much difficulty, but as it was, there was little to recommend it on first glance.

He stopped outside and it took Amero another two steps before he realised that they had arrived. He looked at the shabby exterior and then to Bryn, a bemused expression on his face.

'This is it?' he said.

'This is it,' Bryn said. He stepped forward and opened the door. His memory had done little to alter the first impression given by the interior, neither embellishing nor degrading it. Clean, but grotty and run down. He cleared his throat loudly, but there was no response.

'Maestro Bautisto?' he said.

The Estranzan master swordsman appeared from the back room and walked toward them.

'Banneret Pendollo, I had not thought to see you again,' he said. From the sound of his voice he was genuinely surprised. 'This is the friend you spoke of? I am Banneret of the Starry Field

Baltasar Bautisto.' He gave a curt bow of his head, not offering his hand.

'Banneret of the Blue Amero dal Moreno, pleased to make your acquaintance.' He returned the saluting nod, but there was no mistaking his disdainful countenance. 'I wonder if you might excuse us for a moment, I'd like to have a word with my friend.'

'Of course, gentlemen, take all the time you need,' Bautisto said. He wandered off toward the back room leaving Bryn and Amero alone.

Bryn could feel his body tense.

'Are you serious?' Amero said. He clearly wasn't looking for an answer. 'A short-arse Estranzan with a head like a pot scrub and a salon that looks more like a convalescent home for rats? What are you thinking?'

'Just give it a chance,' Bryn said. 'The salon is clean, bright and large. Everywhere else I went was crowded, expensive and full of distractions. As new members, we wouldn't have been able to get access to the maestro in those salons for months at best, if ever. Bautisto is good. I sparred with him yesterday and he's as good as any I've come across. I promise you that we'll both learn from him. Give it a month, and if you don't agree, we can go somewhere else.'

Amero looked around for a moment, very obviously not happy. His plans of a little training intermixed with relaxed socialising would not be realised here—but he had not dismissed it out of hand, which Bryn took as a good sign.

Amero let out a deep sigh. 'One month, and if this little ponce doesn't have me winning duels with both hands tied behind my back I'm going to be signing up at Cavzanigo's faster than you can say "greasy Estranzan shyster".'

'Fine. I really don't think you'll be disappointed,' Bryn said.

CHAPTER SIX

'AGAIN!'

Bautisto's Estranzan accent was beginning to occupy a regular place in Bryn's nightmares. Bautisto ran both he and Amero harder than Bryn thought was possible. Nothing he had done before, either in the Collegium or in preparation for the Competition, had come close.

Sweat pooled at his eyebrows and his arms burned. Holding his sword out in front of him took supreme effort. From the expression on Amero's face, it appeared that he felt much the same way.

After two weeks of training Amero had yet to make another complaint about the salon or their trainer, other than the occasional offhand remark about him having missed his true calling as a slave driver. It could have been down to the fact that he was simply too tired to moan and trek across the city to find himself a nice spot on a couch in Cavzanigo's, but he had not complained and that made Bryn feel satisfied.

Bryn pulled his tired and meandering thoughts back to the present and responded to Bautisto's command. He dropped back into what Bautisto referred to as the 'first guard', the position he favoured for both initiating and receiving attack. Bryn's feet felt as though they were attached to blocks of lead and he just couldn't move them quickly enough to satisfy Bautisto.

'Faster!' Bautisto yelled. When he became particularly animated, which was something in itself considering how energetic he was ordinarily, his face went bright red and the veins in his forehead bulged. It could be distracting and at times Bryn felt genuine concern for his health, but to give any indication that he was not concentrating fully would result in a tongue-lashing or another routine of exhausting exercise.

He tried to move his feet faster, but they burned and felt so heavy nothing made them move the way he wanted. His sword felt like it had doubled or tripled in weight, and the ache in his shoulder provided an unwelcome distraction from the pain in his feet. A child with a wooden sword could have bested him with little difficulty.

'That is enough for today. Eat, and sleep at least ten hours. I will see you in the morning.' Bautisto turned and went back to his small room, leaving Amero and Bryn wavering with exhaustion. Amero slumped to the ground and sat cross-legged and hunched over, drawing in deep breaths of air. Bryn spiked the ground with the tip of his training sword and leaned on it, trying to shift some of his weight from his legs onto the makeshift support.

They hobbled home, as they did each afternoon once Bautisto was done with them. They must have seemed like two drunks as they swayed on exhausted legs and bumped into one another. Amero's cook had been told to have food ready for them when they arrived back. They would eat in silence, then Bryn would fall asleep mid-afternoon, either on one of the couches in the living room or if he had the energy left, he would crawl to bed.

Bryn had spotted Mistria's name on a billboard for a duel in one of the city's larger arenas, one of those in the tier directly below the Amphitheatre, and was determined to go and watch no matter how tired he was.

Amero had arranged for them to meet some old Academy friends later in the evening, but he would have time for a nap between the two events.

Bigger arenas drew larger crowds and higher profile duellists. Bryn hadn't recognised the name of Mistria's opponent, but in this arena there would be no ambitious thugs or double-jobbing soldiers. They would all be bannerets. It seemed that there was a young generation of duellists starting to come to prominence. During his time at the Collegium, Bryn had been far too busy to keep abreast of who the promising up-and-comers were, so there were few names on the billing that he did recognise, all bannerets who had been a few years ahead of him at the Academy. The prospect that they might all be as good as Mistria whetted his appetite for the spectacle to come, and he hadn't felt that excited about attending a duel in some time.

Mistria's duel was the second on the billing. The first was impressive; both swordsmen knew what they were about and were hungry for the victory. There could only be one winner however, and the match ended in a three touches to two score. It made him regret that he would not be able to stay any longer than Mistria's duel, knowing that he would need at least an hour's sleep if he was to make it back out to meet his friends that evening.

The arena's stands were full by the time Mistria walked out onto the arena floor. There was a strong response to his appearance, and he was definitely the man Bryn had passed on the stairway at Valdrio's salon.

The Master of Arms raised his hands and lowered them to hush the crowd. 'Banneret Mistria of Maestro Valdrio's Salle, and Banneret Aureo of Maestro Cavzanigo's Salle. Banneret Mistria has achieved a perfect score in his last fifteen duels.'

Bryn raised his eyebrows at the announcement. Mistria's opponent was from Cavzanigo's, one of the salons he and Amero had looked at and one he had immediately dismissed as being a vanity salon. He was curious to see what Banneret Aureo was made of.

The second reason for his interest was Mistria's track record, and the explanation it gave for his appearance in the small arena. A duellist's previous twenty-five matches were counted for his Ladder ranking. A perfect score, where the duellist did not concede a single touch, earned five points. It was not unheard of for a duellist to inflate his score with a few easier matches with low-rank opponents in back street arenas. To do it too often would draw the ire of the Bannerets' Commission, though. It was crafty, but it was accepted within reason.

It was rare for a duellist to achieve the maximum one hundred and twenty-five points, but it did happen. To do so was to be numbered among the greats, and have your banner hung in the Bannerets' Hall in pride of place. It was a huge achievement and a lofty dream. Thinking about it made Bryn's heart race.

On the Master of Arms's signal, Mistria took the initiative. He danced forward with his quick, light-footed grace, and thrust. Aureo was no slouch. He parried and riposted, but Mistria had already moved back to a safe distance. Bryn felt a tingle run along his spine when he heard the first clash of steel. Excitement coursed through his veins, tempered only by his jealousy that it was them on the arena floor and not him.

Bryn was still elated later that evening as he headed to the tavern in Docks to meet with Amero and his former classmates. He had not managed to sleep at all, despite telling Amero to go on ahead and that he would join them later. The duel had energised him and filled him with confidence that he had made the correct career choice. He wanted to take his place amongst the duellists in the arena more than anything.

The Sail and Sword was a dump, but it was an Academy favourite and the tavern keeper generally turned a blind eye to the students' excesses—and was even known to allow them out the back way in the event of a raid by the City Watch.

Students at the Academy proper were not supposed to be out in the city after ten bells. It was an accommodation reached between the Master of the Academy and the Captain of the City Watch centuries before, due to the danger of having so many trained swordsmen carousing around the city drunk out of their minds as young men were wont to do when at their liberty. It was a concession to nostalgia that the Sail and Sword was the chosen venue that evening.

The others were all there when he arrived, propping up the bar and laughing raucously. Bryn was well known enough to be acknowledged by the tavern keeper when he entered and to have a mug filled for him without having to ask. He walked up to the others and slapped Amero on the back.

'What are a bunch of upstanding gentlemen like you doing in a place of ill repute such as this?' he said.

'Waiting for your sister,' one of the others said, to a chorus of laughter and baiting.

Caught without a comeback, Bryn nodded, acknowledging his defeat to the smiles of his opponent.

They hadn't seen each other in several weeks, so the banter continued hard and fast along with rounds of drinks until the early hours. They had each taken a different career path since leaving the Collegium, and it was strange to think that after so many years in each other's company—they had all entered the Academy together as Under Cadets, what seemed like a lifetime ago—it was unlikely that they would all be together at the same time again.

Two had joined the army, and one was due to leave

Ostenheim the following week to continue his studies at the Academy in Humberland, on the other side of the Middle Sea. The conversation turned to what Bryn was doing.

'I'm training for the arena,' he said, wishing he had at least one duel under his belt at that point. It wouldn't seem real until he had. 'So's Amero here. Hopefully it'll keep him from mischief.'

One of the others, Barago, laughed. 'I thought after the Academy you'd have retired to the family estate to chase the maids and farm girls until your dotage.'

'I thought you'd have realised swordplay wasn't for you and answered your true calling as a rent boy,' Amero said.

They all fell silent. The banter and ribaldry had been non-stop all night, but it had all been in good humour. There was venom in Amero's voice now though. The uncomfortable silence continued until Bryn broke it.

'Well, I think we've all had our fill of booze for one night,' Bryn said. 'Perhaps this's a good point to call a halt.' He smiled, hoping the tension would diffuse, but his words and friendly manner had little effect.

'Indeed,' Amero said. He took a long drink from his mug, slammed it down on the bar and with a mock salute, stumbled out of the tavern.

When he was gone, the others all looked at Bryn. He shrugged his shoulders.

'Sorry,' he said. 'He's been acting a bit tetchy ever since he visited home when we graduated. I'm sure he didn't mean anything by it. Just a few too many drinks.'

'Too flashy! Too flashy!' Bautisto shouted. He paced around Bryn and Amero as they sparred, hands on hips and his brow furrowed.

'Too flashy' was a phrase that Bryn was hearing all too often, but thankfully it was never directed at him. For Amero, it was not just the result of a bout that mattered. The look of how he got there was just as important to him. Unfortunately, the punishments that his flourishes brought were equally shared.

Bautisto had a distinctive technique; Bryn had noticed it the first time they had sparred. It was the Estranzan style, characterised by economy of movement and precision. There was nothing flashy about it and if he was being honest with himself, it wasn't particularly interesting to watch. There was no sustainable argument to be made against its effectiveness however, and Bryn could certainly appreciate that. He would take whatever advantage he could with him into the arena.

Amero was of a differing opinion. He had always revelled in the flourishing style of some of the old Ostian masters; sweeping cuts and extremely angled thrusts mingled with spins and twists that when properly executed were a joy to watch. It was something that Amero excelled at, and with their new trainer espousing a different approach he was finding it difficult to adapt—or he was not willing to try.

Amero lowered his sword and stepped back. 'Who gives a damn if it's flashy if it works?'

'I didn't tell you to stop,' Bautisto said.

It was the first time Amero had clashed with Bautisto head on and Bryn was curious to see how it turned out.

Amero glared at Bautisto for a moment before taking his guard once more. Bryn was a little surprised that Amero backed down so quickly, but thus far it was difficult to find fault with anything Bautisto had done in their training. They were both greatly improved since they had started working with him; even Amero could not deny this despite their philosophies of swordsmanship running contrary to one another.

'Good. Continue,' Bautisto said as he recommenced his slow circling.

Amero came at Bryn with a wide cut that Bryn was easily

able to parry. His counter, a quick thrust that was more akin to the Estranzan style than the Ostian one failed to find its way through. So the exchange continued.

'Cardolo,' Bautisto said without breaking step.

At first Bryn couldn't work out what Bautisto meant. Cardolo was one of the Estranzan fencing masters, one that Bautisto had him studying.

Amero came at him again with a sweeping cut, one of his favourite attacks and one that he always executed to perfection. Bryn parried with one of Cardolo's favoured guards and countered with the appropriate thrust. A touch.

Bautisto stopped walking. 'I think that will be all for today.'

CHAPTER SEVEN

THE ARENA WAS small and quiet, but that was very much as Bryn had expected for his first duel. At capacity the low circular stand enclosing the sandy arena floor could have accommodated three or four hundred people, but if there were more than a few dozen there that day, Bryn would have been surprised.

The audience that were there were bored. They expected to see three types of swordsmen duelling that day. First, there were those like Bryn who were starting off. They had no name or reputation and most of them never would. The second type had once been able to draw a larger crowd, deserving of their place at a larger venue, but now were either too old or too broken to remain there. The final group had never amounted to anything but couldn't accept the fact and were still eking out a meagre existence pursuing the deluded hope that they might still make it. They were the ones that Bryn felt the most pity for, and whom he most feared becoming.

There was also the chance of a predatory high-ranking duellist hunting in shallower waters, as Mistria had been doing that first day Bryn saw him duel. It was an unlikely, but unnerving possibility. He had no desire to be made to look a fool in his first duel by a far more experienced swordsman. Entering the Ladder marked as 'one duel—no points' would be a disaster and a huge embarrassment.

He was scheduled to fight first, a lower billing to the matches that would follow. He wondered if the crowd was small only because of the early hour and the arena would fill up later, when the main duels were scheduled. It didn't matter; he wouldn't be there to find out.

Despite the humbling size of the crowd, he was glad of having first billing. He hadn't given much thought to fencing before an audience, in spite of the Major's warning on his last day at the Academy. The prospect of fighting in front of those there to be entertained made him anxious. That the arena was all but empty gave him some small comfort.

Both Amero and Bautisto had gone with him, Bautisto out of professional necessity and Amero out of friendship. He knew his mother, and perhaps with more reluctance his sister, would have been there, but he had not told them that his first duel was coming up. He wanted to have a win or two under his belt before he added the pressure of having relatives in the audience.

The three of them sat in silence until the steward approached and told Bryn to ready himself. Bautisto jumped to his feet and began to direct Bryn through a sequence of attack and defence patterns intended to loosen him up and focus his mind on the task at hand. Bryn fought to concentrate. All he could think about was the significance of the occasion. It was the realisation of a dream that had begun so many years before, the pursuit of which had placed enormous financial burden on his family. He felt guilty about not having told them he was finally stepping into the arena, but once he had fought his first few duels and gotten past the initial nerves, he would.

With his mind skipping in every direction but the one in which it needed to be applied, Bryn knew his patterns were mechanical and imprecise, the type of swordplay that would ordinarily warrant a tirade of abuse from Bautisto. The sharp tongue was absent that day, surprisingly. Bryn moved from a high guard to a low and then moved as though to counter an imagined attack. He was slow, sloppy and—if honest with himself—a long way from his best. His hands were shaking, something he could not conceal.

'Good,' Bautisto said. 'Smooth, controlled, precise.'

It was the mantra he repeated each time they began to learn something new. The words had a calming effect on Bryn, the familiarity sending him back to their shabby little salon in Docks rather than the small arena tucked away off a side street in the Cathedral quarter. Bautisto acknowledged a signal from the arena floor and fixed his gaze on Bryn.

'Breathe and concentrate. The rest will follow. There is no one here today who can beat you,' he said.

Bryn nodded, not able to think of anything to say. He struggled to keep his mind focussed. Amero gave him a nod and Bryn turned to walk into the centre of the arena. The Master of Arms was there, waiting by the black mark that would divide the two duellists before the match began. His opponent appeared a moment later, walking across the sandy arena floor toward him. As Bryn watched him approach he could feel his heart race and his mouth suddenly became very dry. Was it too late to go back to Bautisto for a quick gulp of water?

Bryn's opponent took his place on the other side of the black mark. He was about the same height as Bryn, slender and with dark hair but several years older. He wore a beige duelling uniform that contrasted with Bryn's dark blue kit. He seemed overly confident, while Bryn felt it was all he could do to try to hold down the contents of his stomach.

Bryn knew little about the other man. The billing was only published a few days before the match, not giving Bryn the time to study his form. His name was Nava Nozzo, a banneret who had done much of his duelling on the regional circuit. He had a single scar on his face, below his left cheek, one of the defining marks of a swordsman. It could mean many things; that he was a poor fencer, that he had a large amount of experience, that he was sloppy with his razor in the morning—there was no point in trying to read anything into it. It was only another distraction. Bryn closed his eyes and took a deep breath.

The Master of Arms was speaking, but it took Bryn a moment to notice him. He felt so desperately thirsty, but there was nothing to be done about it now.

'…salute and begin.'

Nozzo saluted with the thoughtless and practised manner of one who has done it many times. Bryn hurriedly mirrored the gesture. He had done it many times also, but never before in the arena, and never before when there seemed to be so many other things to take in. It felt awkward and unnatural, as though he had never held a sword before.

As soon as Bryn made his salute, his opponent dropped into a low guard. He would have known that Bryn was a Banneret of the Blue and even if this was his first time in the arena he was not a threat to be quickly dismissed. Bryn took two steps back, not committing himself to any form or guard. Nozzo made two probing strikes, beating on Bryn's blade with his own. They were either taunts or invitations, but Bryn would not be drawn. He would dictate his own actions.

The first contact of steel against steel settled Bryn's nerves. Gone were the thoughts of the audience, the heat and dust of the arena, the oppressive thirst he had felt. Now there was just him, his opponent, and their weapons—a situation he had been in more times than he could recall. If Nozzo was content to wait for the fight to be brought to him, then bring it Bryn would.

He lunged forward. It was an obvious attack, but a feint. He hoped his inexperience in the arena might lead Nozzo to be less suspicious of deceptive swordplay. He made to parry Bryn's thrust, but by the time his sword was where the strike had been aimed, there was nothing there. Bryn had quickly changed direction, the tip of his sword flicking through clear air and into the chest of his opponent.

There was not enough force behind the attack to puncture the thick material on the front of his opponent's doublet with the rounded, dull tip, but that was not necessary. A touch was all that was required, and it had been obvious and spotted by the Master of Arms. A ripple of excitement ran through Bryn's chest. He had scored his first point in the arena.

There was some applause from the stands, but so little that it was possible to identify each individual clap. Bryn didn't care; all he was interested in was the reset and the chance to score a second touch in the best-of-five duel.

The Master of Arms brought them back to the black marker and they saluted once more. Bryn's opponent seized the initiative this time, coming at Bryn straight away. Bryn danced back, parrying effortlessly with his rapier, not needing to use his dagger. He felt light on his feet as he moved, the reward of the hours of nausea-inducing training that Bautisto had forced on them.

Nozzo would be more wary now; if he had any brains at all he wouldn't succumb to underestimation again and see a novice mistake where there was none. Bryn had only used the trick because he wanted the easiest way to get his first touch out of the way and calm his nerves. It wouldn't work again, so the true test was to come.

Bryn allowed Nozzo take the initiative, defending as he considered what to do next. He threw in the occasional riposte to keep Nozzo on his toes, but wanted time to find his rhythm. Bryn was revelling in the duel, but the sense of occasion made it difficult to concentrate. So many years watching, yearning. Now he was doing. There was something about it that made it feel far more real than any of the training, examination or competition duels he had fought. It seemed as though he had spent his life up to that point reading about a subject but was now, for the first time, experiencing it first-hand.

Bryn shook all the nonsense from his head. He parried the attacking sword and dagger and launched into a blistering series of attacks. He pressed forward with speed and intensity, raining in strikes, none of which were intended to score a touch. He knew he was fitter, and wanted to take advantage of it. He kept up the intensity until he could see that it was beginning to have an effect. Nozzo was labouring for breath, strain showing on his face. Every moment of Bautisto's punishing training was now paying dividends. To be able to drive up the pace of a duel to exhaust a more experienced swordsman without any detrimental effect to himself was an asset beyond description.

When his opponent was red-faced and gasping for breath, Bryn fired in a scoring touch that the man didn't have the wind to defend against. As they both returned to their places, Bryn could hear Bautisto's applause standing out from the other more muted displays of appreciation. By now Bryn was tingling with excitement. He was on the verge of winning his first duel in the arena. Despite his nerves and the spectre of self-doubt lurking in the back of his mind, he had been in complete control from the outset. He had been foolish to get so nervous. This was what he was made for, what he had spent his life preparing for.

They reset and Bryn went straight at his opponent. Nozzo was still fatigued after the previous point; the brief respite of the reset had not been enough for him to catch his breath. Bryn had no intention of allowing him to do so now. He pressed in, sure that the duel was all but over. He had proved to himself that Nozzo couldn't keep up with him. So focussed was he on his attack that it wasn't until he could feel a point pressing against the material of his doublet that he realised he had been an overconfident fool. He hadn't even noticed his opponent's attack. He bit his lip to stifle his anger with himself.

He cursed himself as he walked back to the line, furious at his stupidity, but also realising that an important lesson had been learned. As they saluted and took their guards, Bryn could see that his opponent was still tired. Bryn had lost the previous point rather than Nozzo having won it. There would be no over-confidence this time, no mistakes.

The Master of Arms gave the command and Bryn went forward. Smooth, controlled, precise; just as Bautisto always said. A feint with his rapier and a thrust with his dagger was all that it took. A resigned look fell over Nozzo's face as he was forced to accept defeat at the hands of a debutant. He displayed good grace in their final salute before Bryn hurried off the arena floor to talk with Bautisto and Amero. Every fibre of his being was electrified by the experience, but he could not shake the lingering disappointment of having conceded that point so foolishly. Few of the spectators paid him any attention, but he did not care; he was now a duellist.

'It's good to see you, Renald,' Kristo dal Ronvel said.

Renald nodded and smiled, but did not get up from his seat in the Bannerets' Hall lounge. 'Likewise.'

'What brings you to the city? You're hardly ever here, even when the parliament is in session.'

'Some business to attend to,' Renald said. 'I thought it would be nice to catch up with some old friends while I'm here. I'm not likely to be back before the next session in autumn.'

'Well, I'm glad you got in touch. It's been too long.'

Renald was too experienced a soldier to launch straight into his true purpose; he would manoeuvre first. He allowed the conversation to flow along, pandering to dal Ronvel's overly nostalgic disposition. They had been friends once, comrades in arms. Renald supposed they still were, but he found as he got older he had less time for friends, only for those who could be of use to him. He gently steered the conversation along, until when dal Ronvel finally asked him about Amero, it seemed as though it was his idea entirely.

'Oh, you know how young men are,' Renald said. 'I still remember all too clearly what we were like at that age.'

Dal Ronvel smiled in agreement. 'Fighting, boozing, and whoring I expect, if he's anything like my two lads. Has he joined a regiment yet?'

'Sadly not,' Renald said. 'Young fool's taken it into his head to enter the arena.'

Dal Ronvel raised his eyebrows. 'How do you feel about that?'

'How do you think I feel? He's a Banneret of the Blue, so he must have some skill. However, I won't have him making a public spectacle of himself, or making a mockery of our family name.'

'So that's what you wanted to meet me about.'

Renald nodded. Dal Ronvel had never been a fool, but he was disappointed that his subtlety had gone to waste. 'Not entirely, but I'd be very much obliged to you if you could help me knock this whole ridiculous charade on the head, sooner rather than later.'

'What would you have me do?' dal Ronvel said.

'You still have influence with the Bannerets' Commission, don't you?'

'I'm not on it anymore, but yes, I'm still involved.'

'I want Amero's first fight to be a mismatch.'

'I can't do that,' dal Ronvel said, his voice hushed despite the lounge being otherwise empty. 'Arranging for your son to win his first duel goes against everything the Commission was established to do.'

Renald laughed. 'You misunderstand me, Kristo. I want Amero to be outclassed, defeated and made to feel like a fool. But I want it done somewhere discreet, where there won't be many to see it happen. One good, sharp kick to his pride should knock this nonsense from his head before he draws too much attention to himself.'

'Even still, Renald. You're asking too much. The only way I can see of doing it is to have him placed high on the Ladder before he starts, so he meets an experienced, successful duellist first time out. Tampering with the Ladder though…'

'I seem to recall you once telling me you were in my debt. I think I was pulling you out from under a dead horse at the time.'

Dal Ronvel flushed. After a moment he shook his head and sighed. 'I'll see what I can do. But I can't promise anything. How good is he?'

Renald smiled. 'He got his Blue, but he's young, inexperienced, headstrong. Nothing someone with a few tricks up their sleeve couldn't handle, I expect.'

CHAPTER EIGHT

THERE WAS NO fame, no glory and—contrary to what Amero seemed to believe—no adulation from a horde of beautiful women for victory. There was, however, a purse of silver florins that now hung from Bryn's belt, the weight of which could not have felt more satisfying were it stuffed to capacity with gold crowns.

It was the first time that he had money earned by his own hand, and small sum though it might be, that in itself brought an extraordinary sense of accomplishment. That he had earned prize money from duelling in the arena was almost beyond his comprehension. There were too many years of dreaming and too many hours of training for him to be able to fully take that in.

Now that he had fought a duel and won, there was only one thing on his mind. Even a day after the event his name would be on the Ladder, and he had waited a lifetime to see it there in black and white.

'I'd like to see the Ladder please,' Bryn said. It was early and the Bannerets' Hall was empty but for some staff.

The clerk looked at Bryn with sleepy eyes before shuffling away from the counter and into a back room. He reappeared a moment later with a leather folio bulging with sheets of paper. He dropped it down onto the counter with a thud and returned to a stool by the doorway to the back room.

Bryn felt his skin tingle with excitement as his hand hovered over the folio. He had promised himself that he wouldn't come to the Bannerets' Hall to look at the Ladder until he had several winning duels under his belt, but he hadn't been able to stop himself. His name was in there now, inked onto the same pages as the duellists he had supported obsessively in his youth. Great men, men he very much admired had done as he was now doing; opening the Ladder to see their name contained within for the first time.

The leather folio—the Ladder in its physical incarnation— contained a listing of every registered duellist in the city and their ranking. It was updated regularly, and Bryn fully expected that his name would now be included in it.

Being in the Ladder was a rite of passage for any aspiring duellist. Baldario, Rosetto, Calduro; the names of all the greats had been contained within at some point, with all of the retired pages stored within the Bannerets' Hall's archive. All of his life he had dreamed of having his name join theirs within. Now it had.

He flipped open the leather cover to reveal the first page. He knew his name would be far from it, but he wanted to savour the moment, to allow his anticipation build until finally he came upon his own name, contained somewhere toward the back.

There were several columns written in black ink in a neat, uniform hand; rank, name, year of graduation from the Academy, number of duels fought, points scored, and an arrow with a number beside it, indicating their position in the previous edition and whether they had moved up or down. Number one was Panceri Mistria. In the excitement and fuss of preparing for his own duel, Bryn had missed Mistria's most recent matches. Eighteen perfect scores. It seemed that he was destined to hit the magical one hundred and twenty-five. No one could stand in his way. In his most ambitious flights of fancy, Bryn saw himself stopping that meteoric rise, although he realised it was unlikely they would meet in the arena for months or perhaps years, if ever.

He flipped to the next page and scanned it briefly, some familiar names, some not so. Unable to contain his curiosity any longer, he flipped all the way to the last page. He ran his eyes down the list quickly until his heart leaped before his brain had the chance to register what his eyes had seen. There, five lines from the bottom of the last page, was his name. It had a star beside it indicating that he was a new addition to the Ladder. The rank didn't matter to him, only the fact that there, in black, waterproof ink, was his name. Bryn Pendollo.

He felt an enormous sense of satisfaction as he stood staring at the page for what must have been an inappropriately long time. The clerk cleared his throat, still looking at Bryn with his languid eyes.

Aside from fulfilling the lifelong ambition of seeing his name on the Ladder, he did have another purpose in visiting the Bannerets' Hall. The Ladder would also give him an idea of who his next competition would be. Tearing his eyes away from his own name, he ran his finger up the page, reading each name and trying to remember them.

As with the first two pages there were names that he recognised because they were his contemporaries. Two had been with him at the Academy, but had not gone on to the Collegium as Bryn had after graduating from the Academy. They had spent two years on the duelling circuit but had clearly not prospered if their names were so close to Bryn's. At the bottom of the page was Nava Nozzo's name.

He felt conflicted by the sight, both guilt and pride in the knowledge that he was responsible for the small downward pointing arrow next to his name. He flipped through the next few pages, wondering how many matches it would take him to reach and pass the familiar names on them. Again he ran his finger along the list, recognising a name here and there, until he stopped at one that he was very familiar with. Amero dal Moreno.

He turned back to the page that his name was on, checked the number and went back to Amero's listing. He was ranked two hundred and forty places higher than Bryn, despite not yet having fought a duel. Where the number indicating his duels fought and points won should be, there were the letters 'FR'. Bryn stared at the listing in bemusement, again for what must have been too long as the clerk cleared his throat once more. 'FR' meant 'foreign ranking'. When a duellist from another country travelled abroad to test his skill, he could, with the appropriate letters of reference, be admitted to the foreign Ladder at a place commensurate with his home ranking. To the best of Bryn's knowledge, Amero had not been out of the country in years. Having seen all he needed to, but no closer to understanding, he closed the folio and slid it across the countertop toward the clerk.

The next major event in their schedule was Amero's first duel. Bautisto had decided to refine his approach to how he would prepare them both for their matches. He intended to alternate their fixtures, so that he could tailor their training to address the needs of the one with the impending match for the few days leading up to it.

The system made sense to Bryn; it would allow each of them to focus on their own weaknesses and the strengths of their opponent in the run up to any individual duel. It wasn't possible with Bryn's first match as being a new entry, it was impossible to tell who he would be paired with. That would be different for his next match, but Amero's rank meant they could narrow the list of potentials to five or six men.

Bryn was still confused about how Amero had been able

to take his place on the Ladder but he kept the fact to himself. Bautisto had no reason to suspect there was anything unusual, or if he did he was too circumspect to comment. To anyone else asking, it would not be difficult for someone with Amero's resources to fabricate documentation of a foreign ranking. It was also not that unusual, some men preferring to make their name elsewhere before coming home to compete. He recalled how Amero had been able to circumvent the complicated process of being registered as a duellist and realised that it must come down to his family's position and the connections that brought with it. Drawing attention to the issue would not do Bryn any good, even had he wished to injure Amero by so doing. Putting the matter aside, Bryn was happy to help his friend prepare for his duel.

CHAPTER NINE

WHILE BRYN HAD fought his first duel in a nondescript little arena, Amero would not suffer any such indignity. His first duel was in one of the small boutique arenas in Lowgarden. It was only when Bryn saw the venue that he fully appreciated the reason behind the phoney entry on the Ladder. By starting where he had, Amero would be spared fighting in the grottiest of the city's arenas; the fictitious ranking being the minimum needed to get him to Lowgarden's arenas.

The audience would be small, but they would all be wealthy and there were some decent swordsmen on the listing that evening. This type of arena was one that Bryn would hope to reach after perhaps two or three months of successful competition. Amero was starting there, and Bryn could not help but feel a tug of jealousy. A higher ranked swordsman at the salon would increase its profile and benefit him though, so he swallowed his feelings.

As Amero had done for him, Bryn attended the duel. Sitting next to Bautisto he noticed all of the differences between that arena and the one he had fought in. Stone steps formed the tiered stands surrounding the arena that Bryn had duelled in. They were covered with wooden planks; faded, worn and splintering.

The crowd had been small and all of the competitors undistinguished. Here, the benches were covered with padded leather and were particularly comfortable. The most expensive seats had silken cushions. The sand of the arena floor was immaculate. It had been raked so that it was perfectly flat, with no ruts or holes that might cause a trip or fall.

There were two names on the list for that night that Bryn immediately recognised; both held high rankings on the Ladder. The others, though unfamiliar, would have all occupied respectable positions within it and it was beyond doubt that Amero, even with his artificially high position, was the lowliest ranked duellist there that day.

His rank was not going to be the talking point in the audience though; it was his name. His grandfather had been Duke of Ostia. His father was an elector count. He was the heir to one of the twelve most powerful families in Ostia, the closest thing to royalty that the city had.

Bryn realised how much hard work it was going to take him to get to an arena like that. He felt the rumbling of jealousy stir within him again. He took a deep breath and tried to push the thoughts away. He didn't get to attend duels as often as he liked, so it was a treat to get to spend an evening at such a comfortable arena. The bonus of being part of a competitor's entourage was that there was no admittance fee, which in that plush arena was extortionately high.

He could feel Amero's tension from several feet away. There were two small areas where the swordsmen sat in wait for their duels, the opponents being separated. It was in marked contrast to the arena that Bryn had fought in, where he had to wait for his duel in the stands with the rest of the crowd.

The quality of the swordsmanship on display was the other remarkable factor of that small arena. It was exceptional. The first duel was over quickly, the speed and precision with which the swordsmen fought doing good service to the reputation of all that held a sword.

Amero was to fight in the third duel of the evening. Each duel that preceded his had been a model of gentlemanly conduct, a factor that attracted the polite appreciation of the equally genteel crowd. As a child and youth, Bryn had attended the Amphitheatre many times. It was the largest of the arenas in the city and was famed for the heights of passion that the audiences reached. Raucous shouts and jeers occasionally made themselves heard over the general noise of a crowd of tens of thousands and it had an atmosphere so pronounced that it was almost palpable.

The citizens reached such fervour that fights were known to break out within the audience. The most famed swordsmen attracted devoted followings and their legions of fans occasionally boiled over in their enthusiasm to the point of riot.

Here the atmosphere was significantly more subdued. Muted applause with the occasional hushed comment of appreciation was all that a swordsman could expect from a crowd such as this. The contrast amused Bryn. It seemed more like a library than a duelling arena.

Amero's duel finally came around and he walked from the waiting area out onto the perfectly manicured sand. Between each duel, several men rushed out to rake smooth any of the imperfections that had been caused by the previous fight, ensuring it was pristine for each subsequent match.

Amero's opponent was called Arno Banda. He had graduated from the Academy five years before they entered, so he was something of an unknown. He was coming into what many would consider the prime years for a swordsman and would have to be taken seriously.

Amero looked incredibly alone as he walked out to the black line in the centre of the arena. Whereas Bryn had been able to fight his first duel in relative anonymity against a swordsman that he knew to be inferior, with no pressure other than his own expectations, Amero carried the weight of his family name out onto the sand and every eye in the arena was fixed on him.

Up until that moment, Bryn hadn't fully considered the effect all that additional pressure must have. He thought of his own nerves in the lead up to his first duel, and he wondered if he wasn't the luckier of the two. A great many of those in the audience would probably be known to Amero's family and those that were not would know who he was. This was confirmed by the whispers that Bryn could hear being exchanged among the crowd behind him. None of them were kind. That it was a small arena with only a few dozen spectators must have been little comfort for Amero.

As if all this were not enough of a burden, Amero didn't have the advantage of crossing blades with an inferior swordsman. His opponent had a solid record and a respectable ranking that was testimony to his ability. He would be a hard challenge and would not give up touches without a fight. Bryn pitied Amero his position.

Amero took his place at the black mark and Banda did the same. The Master of Arms gave his instructions, inaudible to those in the audience and the duellists saluted one another.

'Ready? Duel!'

Amero danced back several paces quickly, causing Banda's initial attack to meet nothing but thin air. Undeterred, Banda pressed forward until the blade of his rapier connected with steel. There was a flurry of clashing metal, none of it dictated by Amero. Bryn could feel his heart race and realised that he was holding his breath as he tracked every move Amero's opponent made, watching for any of the traits that they had identified in training and worked so hard to take advantage of.

Eventually Bryn spotted one; Amero did also. He thrust low, angling his blade up, trying to weave it past his opponent's defence. Banda was good though; too good to be taken in so quickly. He parried and moved back, allowing Amero to seize the initiative and dictate the next few clashes of blades.

Unable to find a way through, Amero dropped back to catch his breath. He appeared to be fitter than Banda, which was the only advantage that Bryn was able to identify. Giving his opponent any opportunity to rest was a mistake.

Amero lashed forward with sudden speed that Bryn had rarely seen from him, catching Banda still enjoying the breather. He was unable to defend against it, and Amero's sword struck home on the left side of his chest.

'Still too bloody flashy,' Bautisto said, louder than was appropriate for the otherwise subdued environment.

Bryn hoped that Amero was too far away to have heard it.

The duellists both returned to their respective sides of the black mark and took their guard. Amero was visibly more relaxed having scored his first touch, but Bryn was curious to see how his opponent reacted to having conceded a point to an arena novice.

As soon as the bout restarted, Banda fired in two quick thrusts, both striking at Amero's sword and both intended as a challenge rather than attacking swordplay. Amero was playing a clever game though, and would not be baited by it. Cunning had always been a strength of his swordplay.

They circled one another for what seemed like an age. Bryn could feel the tension build in the audience. From the mutters he had heard when Amero first walked out onto the sand, it was obvious that he was expected to fail. It was also obvious that there were many sitting in the arena that would have delighted in seeing it happen. It was probably the only reason they were there.

Banda exploded into motion. After so long a lull in the fighting, everyone in the audience was caught off guard. As was Amero. He made a valiant attempt to defend but he was driven back across the arena floor struggling to keep up with the deluge of steel.

Bryn felt his heart leap each time Banda struck. He sighed with relief when Amero managed to get one of his blades in the way. The emotional turmoil was almost too much to bear. Bryn wanted to jump to his feet to shout out in support of his friend, but he knew it wasn't appropriate in that arena and might result in him being thrown out. He wouldn't have cared were it not for the fact that he was there as part of Amero's entourage, and it would reflect badly on him, rather than Bryn.

As each one of his attacks was foiled, Banda followed in with a second and then a third. The intensity of the exchange was showing on both men, their gasps audible and unrestrained. Loud and overly emotive swordplay was considered crude and it would only be overlooked in the most extreme of circumstances; nobody took any notice of it now.

Eventually the inevitable happened; Amero was too slow, his opponent too fast. The previously restrained audience sighed in unison as Amero conceded a touch. Banda returned to the black mark without a pause, a look of satisfaction on his face. Amero's face was a picture of frustration as he followed, his head down. There was nothing more that he could have done; he had been thrown into deep water and it would be a challenge for him to stay afloat. Bryn could see that Amero was rattled by losing the point.

The Master of Arms reset them and Banda, buoyed by his success in the previous point, came at Amero right away. Amero's face was set with grim determination and Bryn found himself wondering if he would have been able to beat this opponent.

Amero showed true class fending off the attacks, working at his limit just to hold his own. He moved backward, slowly. He flicked his wrist to parry a strike, but it was a feint, and he realised too late. He couldn't even react to the true strike, and stood dumbly as it hit him, knowing it was coming, unable to do anything about it.

Bryn's heart was in his throat. Amero returned to the black mark trailing one touch to two, and Bryn feared that the match was all but over. One more touch and his opponent would win.

Banda wasted no time after the reset. Attacking quickly and aggressively, it seemed that he wanted to teach this young upstart a lesson; to show him that his name, and nothing else, had earned him his place in the arena that day. At first it looked as though Amero was being forced into the same situation that had cost him a point. Bryn could see that there was something different this time, however. Instead of the strained look that had been on his face previously, there was a focussed, calculating expression.

Just when it seemed as though his defence was going to falter—an opinion shared by the audience who were starting to whisper to one another that it was all over—Amero twisted out of a parry, locking both of Banda's blades together and countering with his dagger. Banda was unable to get his weapons free in time enough to defend, and Amero scored his second touch.

As they both walked back to the black mark, Amero cast a brief glance toward Bryn and Bautisto. There was a hungry, predatory look on his face. The next touch would win it, one way or the other. Amero's face said he had the measure of his opponent. His swordsmanship and experience might not yet be the match of Banda, but his cunning was superior and he would use this to his advantage.

They reset, but this time Banda looked doubtful, hesitant. He clearly didn't know what to make of Amero. He must have known that he was a novice in the arena, that he was most likely there due to his being the heir to an elector count rather than having the experience of many foreign duels under his belt. Banda had expected an easy fight of it, or as easy a duel as can ever be expected when facing a Banneret of the Blue. Conceding the first touch might have just been a fluke, something he had probably felt was confirmed by the way he was able to take back the next point. But despite his greater experience, he was on the verge of losing the duel.

Banda resorted to his previous tactic, a furious and intense attack intended to wear down his opponent. It was foolish; it was already clear to everyone watching that Amero was the fitter of the two. Bautisto's vomit—inducing sessions were paying their dividends yet again.

Amero was better prepared for Banda now; he had seen this approach once already, and while it had worked against him that time, Bryn was confident that it wouldn't a second. Amero dropped back as he had before, but his face betrayed no strain. He was focussed and thinking; despite Banda appearing to dictate matters, Bryn knew his friend well enough to recognise that was not the case.

Amero put a foot wrong and stumbled. Banda saw his chance and moved to take advantage of it, a smile spreading across his face as he lunged forward to take the match. Amero danced out of the way, his stumble merely a ruse, and executed a quick thrust to his opponent's midsection. The winning touch.

CHAPTER TEN

THEY WENT OUT after Amero's victory to celebrate. Bryn thought that Amero would be in high spirits after his win, but he was sullen and moody. Bryn was beginning to wonder if there was anything that would satisfy him. He had won a difficult fight, and his career was starting at a level many duellists would never reach. The change in Amero since leaving the Academy was marked, but Bryn was puzzled. All things considered, he saw no reason for it.

After Amero's outburst on the previous occasion in the Sail and Sword their other friends had all coincidentally found themselves to be busy, but Bryn was able to rally up a few who hadn't been there and had not heard about Amero's behaviour.

Bryn and Amero arrived before the others, and Bryn ordered a round of drinks. Amero had said hardly a word all evening, and when the two mugs of ale arrived he leaned against the bar, staring into the glass.

'You won. You should be happy,' Bryn said. 'He was tough opposition. You did well.'

'I was lucky,' Amero said. 'I might not be the next time. I need to be better then. All those bastards sitting there, waiting for me to make a fool of myself. A fool of my name. A fool of my father.'

Was that it? If so, Bryn thought Amero was being a little too sensitive. The crowd adored it when a duellist made a fool of himself in the arena. It was the same for everyone, Bryn included. There were even those who went purely in the hope that they would see a swordsman killed—an infrequent, but not unknown occurrence.

'Ho there, gentlemen Bannerets,' came a voice.

It was Rofier Cando and two others from the Academy, the sum total of friends that Bryn had been able to gather up for the evening.

In the instant of their arrival, Amero's demeanour changed from dark to light. It was as though he put on a mask and became an entirely different person. Bryn was surprised but said nothing, joining the conversation with the others. He was bemused by what he'd just witnessed, never having seen anyone change their mood so quickly or convincingly before. Anyone seeing Amero now would think he was walking on air after his victory in the arena. One face for himself, one for everyone else. It was jarring.

'So where're you living now that they've turfed you out of your room at the Academy?'

Bryn was so caught up in his thoughts it took him a moment to realise the question was directed at him. His delay gave Amero enough time to answer for him.

'He's enjoying the hospitality of the House of Moreno. And a lucky fellow he is too. I brought one of my father's cooks back, one of the better ones.'

Bryn flushed with embarrassment. Amero was still talking, light-hearted, jovial, and entertaining, but with Bryn as the butt of his jokes. It was the condescending, dismissive way he said it that irked Bryn most. Amero had asked Bryn to stay with him, and there hadn't been any discussion on the topic of rent since Bryn made it clear he would pay when the offer was first made. He didn't like their friends thinking that he was a charity case, or that he was dependent on Amero's goodwill.

He had enough money to rent his own apartment now. There was no need for him to be in a position where he could be condescended to. He would get up early the next day and look for one.

'And you're both duelling now?' Rofier said.

Bryn's attention returned to the conversation. 'Yes,' he said, his voice tinged with pride. 'First match under the belt. A three-one win. Finally on the Ladder.' He intended to show he was not sliding into the role of Amero's retainer.

'And how about you, Amero?' Rofier said.

Bryn cringed, hoping that Amero wouldn't be provoked into another outburst. They would quickly run out of friends if he kept that up.

'Had my first duel too,' Amero said.

He was still cheerful, upbeat. If it was an act, it was a convincing one. From moody to top of the world in a heartbeat.

'How'd it go?' Rofier said.

'Three-two win, so I'm happy enough. Against Arno Banda. He's well thought of by all accounts. It was a tough match. Tougher than Bryn's at any rate. Can't remember that fellow's name. He was a bit of a hack and slasher, wasn't he, Bryn?'

'Nava Nozzo. He knew what he was about,' Bryn said, his tone making it clear he wasn't happy that the skill of his opponent was being called into question. It was bad manners to publicly disparage another Banneret's skill in any event, but to do it now, to a friend was insulting, hurtful, and on the fringes of what Bryn would tolerate.

'Yes, but he wasn't a patch on the chap I fought. I mean, you don't exactly get the cream of the crop in that dump you had to fight in, do you.'

Bryn couldn't quite believe what he was hearing, but Amero seemed completely oblivious to the offence he was causing. Oblivious, or he just didn't care.

'Well, I think I'm going to call it a night,' Bryn said.

He'd had enough, and ignored the moans of him being a lightweight and a boring git, but he wasn't going to stand there while Amero continued to talk himself up and run him down.

Bryn got up early the next morning and went out to look at apartments. While the comforts on offer at Amero's apartment in Oldtown would be hard to give up, he found their situation claustrophobic and after the way Amero had behaved the previous night, Bryn couldn't even bear to look at him. Spending all day training together at the salon and then the rest of the day at the shared apartment was too much. He needed his own space; somewhere that he could be alone with his thoughts and somewhere that was his, not dependent on the goodwill of someone else. Particularly not if they were going to be in the habit of pointing that fact out.

Perhaps he had been getting on Amero's nerves, and that, coupled with the pressure he was obviously under, was what had motivated his behaviour. One way or the other, if their friendship was to survive Bryn had to move into his own place.

Now that he had a victory under his belt, he could expect his career to get underway properly. He didn't think it was expecting too much to have a duel at least every couple of weeks. He would still have to work his way up through the dross, so it would be some time before he could expect large prize purses, but a victory every two weeks would bring in more than enough to support himself, pay his rent and salon fees and have enough left over to put aside or enjoy.

The only issue that remained was a tricky one. How would he broach the issue of moving out of the apartment with Amero without causing irreparable damage? He felt less concerned about the sensitivity of it after the previous night, but it was best not to burn any bridges. One way or the other, he needed to find somewhere to live first.

He couldn't afford to be extravagant, so Oldtown and the other more fashionable parts of the city were out of the question. Considering that Bautisto's salon was in Docks and that he was always utterly exhausted leaving there, somewhere nearby seemed to be the most sensible idea.

Living in Docks itself was something he wasn't willing to do. It was a hardworking and rough part of the town and definitely not somewhere he wanted to make his home.

Docks was sandwiched between the two rivers that ran through Ostenheim, the Westway and the Eastway. The Westway separated it from Oldtown, Highgarden and Castle Hill, while the Eastway did the same with the industrial parts of the city, most immediately where the shipbuilders and all of the related business were located.

Moving farther into the city, there were the four quarters that surrounded Crossways. Bankers and Guilds were the first quarters that one came to, sitting on either side of the main road that bisected the city from the docks in the south to the city wall in the north. Prices there for anything he was willing to live in would be higher, perhaps more than Bryn could afford.

Bankers was home to many of the counting houses and banks of the city, and also the Great Exchange where much of the city's trade was arranged. It was also home to a great many people, living in apartments above the businesses. Of the four quarters, it was one of the wealthier ones, the better parts at least comparable to Oldtown and Lowgarden.

Guilds contained not only the institutions it took its name from, but also the homes of guild members. It was unusual for anyone not working in a trade represented by a guild to live there, and he would be an outsider in a close knit community were he to rent there.

All Bryn wanted was somewhere safe, convenient to the salon and reasonably quiet that fell within the rental bracket he had budgeted for.

He left Oldtown, passing through the ancient walls that marked the city's original boundary and walked over the bridge that crossed the Westway. Turning left, he made his way along the embankment until the warehouses along the edge of Docks gave way to the four and five storey buildings of Bankers.

At various intervals along the embankment there were circular stone buildings that emitted a dull mechanical noise. They were the tow-houses, where great cranks turned all hours of the day without any intervention, a left over machination from the days before magic was outlawed. They were connected to heavy chains that pulled barges back up the river and away from the harbour. Once they were clear of the city walls, teams of horses pulled them to their destinations, but within the city there was not the space for the constant traffic on the embankment road.

Barges passed up and down the river day and night and the dull rumbling from within the tow-houses would only seem louder when the background noise of the city faded with the light. He had no desire to lie awake at night listening to it. In any event, Bautisto's salon was toward the centre of Docks and he wanted to be closer.

Although Bryn had grown up in Ostenheim, it was a large city and surrounded on all sides by tall buildings. Once away from familiar areas and the main streets, it was easy to get lost. For natives, the warren of streets and alleys could be confusing—for a stranger, a nightmare. Bryn headed into the city to begin his search properly.

The first place that he looked at was small, dark and damp. If that wasn't enough to put him off, the landlord looked sinister. Bryn didn't have an especially active imagination but it did not take much to feel extremely uncomfortable in his presence. He excused himself politely and moved on.

Three more apartments fell short of the mark, but the fourth appeared to be exactly what he was looking for. It was small, but he really only needed somewhere to sleep. It was less than half the distance to Bautisto's salon than Amero's apartment, which he would be grateful for many times over. He signed the lease there and then, paying a deposit and his first month's rent to the landlord.

$$\circlearrowleft$$

Amero did not consider himself the pensive type. He had no quiet place that he would go to be alone with his thoughts, nor had he ever felt the need for one. The Academy might have been the reason for that; there was always the common room or the training halls to spend time in, thinking things through or thrashing them out while surrounded by noise and activity.

It was thus he found himself wandering the streets after Bryn had gone out that morning, trying to put his thoughts in order, losing himself to the city's constant commotion. He knew how it all must seem to others; the privileged rich boy landing on the middle of the Ladder before his first duel with dubious foreign ranking points. They must all think him lucky, spoiled, not having to drag himself up through the rankings like everyone else. He knew damn well what the reality was, but no one would ever believe it. This was all meant to be a burden on him, one that would break him.

He knew his father too well to have thought the matter was settled that morning in his office. He had not expected this to be the answer though, a high Ladder ranking and a fight that he was unlikely to win. One that would most likely end in Amero being beaten, humiliated even, and left wanting no more to do with the arena or a career as a duellist.

It was one of Renald's more subtle efforts of manipulation, and Amero had to hand it to his father; it was quite a feat to pull off, even for an elector count. Altering the Ladder rankings was a criminal offence. Amero laughed at the thought of his father being arrested for it. There was no way that would ever happen though. He was far too powerful, far too influential, as his ability to have the Ladder doctored showed.

He laughed too when he thought of how his father must have reacted when he heard his plan had backfired, but knew he wouldn't have long to enjoy his victory. Amero felt sorry for the inept idiot who had arranged the whole thing; Renald was unlikely to be pleased with them. Amero knew only too well what his father's displeasure could be like. There was something very satisfying about the thought of provoking more of it.

The duel had frightened Amero, however. It had taken everything he had to win, and even then he knew it was luck that Banda had fallen for his tricks. His duels were only going to get harder. He would not get the chance to ease into professional duelling and find his feet with a few less challenging matches. It was just a matter of time before his father got his wish, and saw Amero humiliated in the arena.

There was only so much punishment that his body could take each day before it needed rest. Even the training regime they had now was exhausting him. Each morning when he woke, he felt like he had been charged over by a stampeding bull. Given time—the year or two most fledgling duellists would have before they faced their first high ranked opponents—he knew he would be able to cope. He had the natural talent and the physical competence, just not the time to develop it. There was no point ruing the situation he found himself in; there was no way around it. How to deal with it and come out on top was the challenge.

CHAPTER ELEVEN

BRYN HAD ONLY found the time to make a couple of brief visits home since leaving the Academy. He knew he was neglectful, and determined to call more often when time allowed. While at the Academy he had called home at least two or three times a term. He knew his mother had been expecting to see more of him since he had left, but if anything he had been busier.

His sense of familiarity grew as he made his way through the streets that led him home until he was finally standing at its front door. He knocked and had to wait only a moment before the door opened and he was greeted by the sight of his sister. She looked at him for a moment, her expression changing from surprise to haughty indifference.

'And you are?' she said.

Bryn smiled. 'It's nice to see you too, Gilia.'

'Mother was beginning to wonder if you'd forgotten where we live.'

'May I come in?' Bryn said.

'I suppose so.' She stood aside and let him pass through.

His family home was an apartment on the ground floor of a building in Barons, a few streets back from the Blackwater Road. It was larger than his new apartment, but it couldn't be described as spacious. It had never seemed too small when he was growing up and the advantage of being the only boy in the family was that he had a room to himself, while his two sisters had to share one. After Amero's apartment though, he wondered how a family of five had lived there for all those years without driving each other mad. He supposed that at times they had.

Gilia led him into the living room and the table around which they had eaten all their meals together. His mother, Isotta, had come out from the kitchen to see who was there.

They knew that he had started his career as a professional duellist, but he had not told them about his first match. Telling them would be awkward, but unavoidable.

His mother said nothing but made her way across the room and embraced him. Gilia watched, still displeased by Bryn's lack of contact but her countenance had mellowed a little.

'Sit,' his mother said.

Never one to disobey her, Bryn sat.

'Are you eating properly? Are you still living in Oldtown with your friend?'

'Yes, and no,' Bryn said, interrupting what would have been a continuing stream of questions.

She was already moving in the direction of the kitchen by the time he spoke. She stopped when he answered.

'Where are you living?'

'I've taken a small apartment in Bankers. It's close to the salon I'm training in. Closer to here also, so I'll be able to call home more often.'

Gilia snorted in disbelief. Despite being younger than him, both she and his older sister had mothered him up until the point he had left for the Academy. She sat down at the table. 'You've settled on the arena then.'

'Yes, it seemed like a better option than the army. I'll give it a year or two and if it doesn't work out I shouldn't have any difficulty in securing a commission. Bannerets of the Blue are always in demand.'

'And when will we see you fight your first duel?' his mother said.

Bryn grimaced. There was no delicate way of putting it.

'I've fought it already,' he said. He could see his mother's face drop. 'It was in an awful little arena. I just wanted to get my first one out of the way before I told anyone about it. I'll be sure to let you know when my next one is coming up.'

Gilia scowled. 'Be sure you do. I'm just sorry Father didn't live to see it. He dreamed of watching you in the arena.'

Bryn felt his spirits drop, but still thought his decision was for the best. He had seen the pressure that Amero had been under for his first duel and he was glad that he hadn't been subjected to anything similar. It had never been his intention to hurt or offend his family. He wondered if he would have been better off lying about the duel.

'It really was just a case of getting it out of the way. It was a long way removed from the Amphitheatre, or even the arena on Carinale Street.'

He was trying to downplay the importance, but you only ever had one first duel. He was all too well aware of the sacrifices his family had made to provide him with the training and education needed to get into the Academy, and Gilia mentioning his father tugged at his heartstrings. He'd wanted his father to see him duel just as much.

They had never been wealthy; his father had been a clerk at Austorgas' Banking House, a respectable middle class profession, but one which would struggle to pay for someone to get to and through the Academy. By rights Bryn should have left as soon as he had earned his banner to start contributing financially, but when he was able to get a scholarship to remain on for the two years required to achieve colours at the Collegium—the right to be called Banneret of the Blue—he had jumped at the chance. The long-term payback would be greater but income would be a longer time coming. He suddenly felt very guilty, and determined to change the subject.

'How's Lena?' he asked.

'She's well,' his mother said. 'I had a letter from her only a week ago. She enjoys life in Tanosa. She's settled in well there. I don't think that we'll see her back in the city though. Business seems to be going well for Nicolano so I expect he'll wish to remain there.'

'I'm glad,' Bryn said. Lena's husband hadn't had much luck in business in Ostenheim, so he was glad to hear that their move to the regional city had proved to be a wise one.

It was only now that he noticed something different about the house, or rather an absence. There had always been the ticking sound of a clock in the apartment, a family heirloom that hung on the wall beside the door to the kitchen. It was gone.

'Where's the clock?' he said.

His mother looked away as she answered. 'It's being repaired.'

She was lying. Bryn looked at his sister, who also avoided his gaze. He said nothing, hoping that an awkward silence would elicit more information, but he already knew what was going on. He needed to get money to them soon. His mother disappeared into the kitchen and Gilia fidgeted with a saltcellar that was sitting on the table.

'I've written down my address,' he said, finally breaking the silence. 'I'm out most of the day, but I wanted you to have it so you know how to get hold of me.'

'That's good, just leave it on the table,' his mother said from the kitchen. She popped her head through the open doorway. 'I haven't been to the market yet, but there's some bread and salt beef if you want a sandwich.'

'That's all right, mother,' Bryn said. 'I've already eaten.'

'You're eating right?' she asked. 'With all that training you'll need to make sure you do now that you can't just call into the dining hall at the Academy.'

Bryn smiled at her concern. 'I can't really stay any longer I'm afraid, but I'll try to call in more frequently now that I'm settled and have a regular routine. I'll let you know when my next duel is.'

Bryn felt unsettled as he walked home. Guilt at not having visited more often was one part of it, as was the fact that he had not told them in advance about his duel. Being home had reminded Bryn of how much he had wanted his father to see him in the arena. The apartment seemed empty without him. He had died suddenly, when Bryn was away across the Middle Sea taking part in the Competition in Humberland. His father was long buried by the time he got home. Their trips to watch the duels had been a regular, and favourite, part of Bryn's youth. His father had at least seen him graduate from the Academy. That was something. The look of pride on his face would never leave Bryn.

That was not the main cause of his unsettled feeling, however. The missing clock bothered him. His mother had very obviously been lying when she said it was being repaired. They must have been very hard pressed if they had been forced to sell it. Clocks were expensive, and good ones were difficult to come by. He would replace it though, with something even better.

The fact that there was little food in the house also concerned him. His mother always kept the pantry well stocked; too well stocked if anything. Now that only the two of them were there, it was understandable that there would be less. Bryn himself had eaten nearly as much as all three of the women of his family when he had lived there, so his absence was one possible explanation. He could not explain it all away so easily though, and the feeling in his gut would not go away. He wasn't in a position to help yet, but that would change. He would make sure of that.

Amero had thought long and hard about what he could do to survive the next few months of duelling against skilled, experienced opponents. He was already training at the limit of what his body could endure, so increasing his workload was not an option. In any event, quantity did not mean quality and extra hours were of no use if his body was too fatigued to train effectively. It occurred to him that he should drop out of the arena for a few months, but that would be counter-productive; in order to improve, he needed the fitness and sharpness that only came with fighting regular competitive duels.

An idea had lurked in the back of his head for several days. It had not been one that he was willing to give attention to initially, but as he circled his problem over and over and continually failed to find an answer, the idea solidified and became more tempting.

There were people in Ostenheim who could help with problems; unwanted pregnancies, injuries and illnesses. Practitioners of magic still lived in the city. It was illegal, and they were few, but they could be found when needed. None were as powerful as the mages of old; the city's Intelligenciers saw to that. Amero had heard gossip of duellists seeking out magical aid when he was at the Academy. They were always scurrilous rumours, never naming names or saying what benefit they sought or whether they received any.

He did not like the idea of letting one of these backstreet magic practitioners anywhere near him, but he wondered what they could offer. There was risk involved, and not just the potential of some feckless sorcerer blowing him up or turning him into a goat, ridiculous as the notion seemed. If it were to be found out that he had received some sort of magical assistance, the disgrace would be far greater than any he could earn in defeat on the arena floor. It could also land him in the city dungeons, son of an elector count or not. He could imagine many risks and consequences, but no benefits. Anything he considered seemed like foolish speculation. He thought of his father, of how smug he would be to see Amero made a fool of, then of having to scurry off to Breganzo's Regiment of Medium Horse.

The decision to make enquiries caused him anxiety, but the temptation to know what he might gain was too strong to suppress. He would be careful and discreet—and might not go through with anything. He just wanted to know. The best solution to a problem was always found when all options were considered.

They trained as usual the next day, although Amero was quiet and edgy throughout the entire session. He didn't grumble, but there were none of his usual wisecracks or tongue in cheek moans when Bautisto subjected them to something particularly difficult. He seemed tense; his swordplay was tight and lacking in the usual fluid grace that characterised his style.

Bryn had been friends with Amero long enough to know better than to try and talk his spirits up, and that it was not the time to broach the matter of him moving out. He had never seen Amero like this before and his moods were becoming harder to predict. When Bryn was in a bad humour, he was best left alone to come out of it in his own time.

When Bautisto was satisfied that he had tortured them enough for one day, he let them go. As they were packing up their training swords Amero spoke for the first time that day.

'Lunch?'

'Absolutely,' Bryn said. It would be the ideal opportunity to tell Amero he was moving out, but he was relieved by the fact that the invitation suggested Amero's mood might be improving.

'I really don't fancy having to deal with that prima donna cook today. Let's just find a tavern and get something simple.'

Amero's cook was wasted in a private apartment and was quite extravagant. Asking him for a simple sandwich would result in something that although technically a sandwich, would be far more elaborate. The only reason he put up with the indignity of such an anonymous position was that he knew if he stuck with Amero, even in the obscurity of an Oldtown apartment, he would one day head the kitchen of perhaps the finest house in Ostenheim and would cater for dukes and princes. Even if tending toward the overly dramatic, Bryn had to credit that he was certainly patient. All he had to do was stay on Amero's good side, something that wasn't the easiest thing to do those days.

Bryn was disappointed at not getting one last meal from the cook; he would be living on his own culinary disasters soon enough, or more likely whatever slop the nearest tavern served up. Nonetheless, for the sake of a peaceful life he didn't argue.

They walked in silence to the tavern, a short distance from the salon along Harbour Road in the direction of Crossways. When they got there, they ordered and sat in silence until the food arrived. It was a little awkward, but being as tired as he was, Bryn didn't mind.

'I envy you, you know,' Amero said, finally breaking the silence.

No money, no estates, an uncertain future; there was much to be envious of, Bryn thought. 'How do you mean?'

'The only expectations weighing on you are the ones you've put there yourself. That must be nice, following your own goals and setting your own standards.'

It gave Bryn a strong hint as to what was causing Amero's moods, but there must have been more going on behind the scenes. He wasn't sure how to respond. He would have given both arms to swap places with Amero, no matter what pressure of expectation was on him.

'It's not all it's cracked up to be,' Bryn said. His thoughts returned to the clock, and the bare patch on his mother's wall.

Amero didn't seem to be listening to him. 'I've always been aware of what's expected of me, but it only struck me how bad it is the other day in the Arena. All those stuffy fuckers sitting in the audience passing judgement on me; what a scandal it is for the son of the Count of Moreno to be in the arena. I could feel their eyes burrowing into me the whole time I was out there. And I could tell most of them wanted me to fail. What a wheeze it would be for the grandson of a duke to be made to look a fool in the arena. I nearly did, because that was all I could think about for most of the duel.

'I'm sure you don't think it's fair that I got a mid-ranked opponent first time out, but you don't know what I would give to have no-namers in a grotty little arena for my first few duels to get some experience under my belt before having to deal with all those beady little eyes and big opinions. It was intended that I fail.'

'I know it must be hard,' Bryn said. 'I certainly didn't envy you having such a difficult opponent first time out, but don't you think you're being a little paranoid about it?'

Amero smiled in a way Bryn had never seen before, cold, empty of any sentiment. 'You have no idea.'

Bryn shrugged. 'Sometimes we just have to take the situation as we find it—particularly if there's nothing we can do about it. All you can do is train hard and do your best. People are always going to have their opinions, and by the time we're in the Amphitheatre there will be tens of thousands of them, and most likely half of them'll want you to fail. It'll get easier, I'm sure that it will.'

He hoped the mention of a successful future in the Amphitheatre might cheer Amero up a little but all he got was a resigned sigh and a change of subject. Bryn needed to steer the conversation to the matter of his moving out.

'There's something I need to talk to you about,' Bryn said.

'Oh?' Amero put his fork down. 'What?'

'Well, now that I've got money coming in, I'm going to take an apartment of my own.'

Amero said nothing for a moment, and then continued eating. 'Of course. That was always your plan, wasn't it?'

Bryn nodded.

'Give me the address and I'll have my man bring your things over,' Amero said, without looking up from his plate.

CHAPTER TWELVE

WITH LUNCH EATEN and paid for, they left the tavern. Amero hadn't said much since Bryn broke the news he was moving to his own apartment. With his mood so changeable, Bryn wasn't sure what to think. Someone called out from behind them.

They both turned to face the source of the shout. It had come from a young man called Thadeo dal Strenna, who had been at the Academy with them but who Bryn only knew passingly.

'Hello, chaps,' he said, as he approached them. 'Long time no see.'

'Indeed, how have you been, Thadeo?' Amero said. There was no enthusiasm in his voice.

Bryn felt a flash of alarm at Amero's tone. The fact that he reacted that way was as big a cause of concern as the alarm. Was he so worried by Amero's moods? Was it now him being paranoid?

'Well, thank you,' he said. 'I hear you've taken to a career in the arena.'

'Just something to pass the time,' Amero said. 'What are you doing with yourself these days?'

Thadeo ignored the question, ploughing on with jovial bluster. 'Heard you had a bit of a close run thing the other day. I always thought you Bannerets of the Blue were supposed to be indestructible.'

It was the type of friendly banter made by someone who was trying too hard to fit in, and the unfortunate fact was he didn't know either Amero or Bryn well enough to talk like that to them, and their shared history at the Academy was too tenuous to make up for the fact. To make matters worse, it was the wrong day to expect Amero to dismiss the comment with good grace, if that was possible any more.

'Were you there, Thadeo?' Amero said.

'Well, no, but I heard about it. One of the other chaps—'

'Well, why don't you shut the fuck up then and limit yourself to things within your knowledge. Quite a narrow field I dare say,' Amero said.

Bryn cringed but was still hopeful that the conversation might come to an end before it grew any more acrimonious. If Thadeo had any sense he would make his excuses and leave.

'I'm not sure I like the tone of that,' Thadeo said in indignation, puffing out his chest as he did. 'I think you should apologise.'

Bryn couldn't remember much about Thadeo from their time at the Academy, which didn't bode well; it meant he had not stood out as a quality swordsman, and he was now demonstrating that he lacked the intellectual capacity to identify and then extract himself from a rapidly deteriorating situation.

'I think you should take your half-baked opinions and shove them up your arse,' Amero said, smiling viciously.

Bryn noticed that Amero's hand had drifted to the hilt of his sword. Amero wasn't just being insulting any more, he was trying to precipitate a fight.

'Now, gentlemen,' Bryn said, feeling as though he was stepping into the path of a charging bull. 'There's no need to continue with this conversation. I think we should all be on our way.'

'No,' Thadeo said, his face flushing red with anger. 'I won't be spoken to like that by anyone, son of a count elector or not.'

'I'll speak to you any way I please, you bloody oik,' Amero said. He made to draw his sword and Thadeo took an abrupt step backward, his eyes widening.

There was no stopping it now. The opportunity for Thadeo to get out of this mess was now long past.

'Gods alive,' Bryn said, 'what the hell are you thinking of? What's going on with you?' He put out a hand to stay Amero's sword arm. He could feel the tension in it ease and began to hope that the situation could be salvaged.

Amero took a deep breath. 'Of course, it really isn't the place.' He reached inside his doublet and took out a small, cream-coloured piece of card.

Calling cards were a standard accessory for the aristocracy and since becoming a Banneret of the Blue and a member of the gentle classes, Bryn had been meaning to have some made.

'Have your second call on me at the soonest opportunity,' Amero said, holding the card out to Thadeo.

Thadeo took it with slight hesitation. His honour had been wounded and he was angry at the fact. Being faced with a duel put a different perspective on things, particularly one with a Banneret of the Blue. To try and make amends now would do nothing more than mark him out as a coward.

'You'll hear from him directly,' Thadeo said. He gave a curt nod to Bryn before turning and walking away.

'That could have been dealt with differently,' Bryn said.

'To hells with him. Maybe the rest of them will learn to keep their idiot gobs shut from now on.'

They walked in silence for the remainder of the route that they shared. They stopped when Bryn indicated that he needed to head in a different direction.

'You'll stand for me, won't you?' Amero said.

He said it in a way that Bryn was unsure if it was a question or an order. It was irrelevant of course, Amero was his friend and of course he would stand for him; he just didn't like the way it had been put.

'Yes, of course,' Bryn said. 'I suppose I'm going to have to get some bloody calling cards made up now.'

Amero laughed and his hard countenance softened a little for the first time that day, or for weeks.

Bautisto called Bryn aside after training the next day. At first he thought it was to discuss Amero's attitude, but when he became slightly cagey Bryn realised that he would be the subject of the conversation.

'I haven't been able to find another duel for you yet,' Bautisto said.

'It doesn't need to be particularly fancy,' Bryn said. The bare patch on the wall flashed into his mind. 'Until I get a few more wins and move up the Ladder, I'm happy to take anything that's available.'

'Yes, I realise that, but even finding you another match like your last one is proving more difficult than I would have expected. It seems there are a great many low ranked duellists around at the moment, and not very many people who wish to see them duel.'

'Ah,' Bryn said. There wasn't much he could add. He had known that it would be difficult to get matches when he started off, but had hoped that being a Banneret of the Blue would make him a more attractive proposition to duel organisers. Sadly it didn't seem to be the case. It made Amero's anger at his ranking stick in Bryn's craw all the more.

'It will only be a matter of time, I'm sure. Quality such as yours won't go unnoticed for long. I must also admit that the fault is not entirely yours; I don't have many contacts in this city, and you Ostians don't always think that highly of Estranzans.

My salon doesn't have the reputation to bring promoters to my door. Something will come along soon though, rest assured that I'm doing everything I can to get you a match.'

It was disappointing news, but Bryn didn't see what he could do about it. He had known that Bautisto was something of an unknown when deciding to train with him, so he had to accept the consequences of that decision. He couldn't see the situation lasting for long though.

'Thank you for letting me know.'

'That brings me on to the other thing that I need to discuss. Amero has another duel scheduled so I hope you won't be annoyed if we maintain our focus on him until your next one is coming up.'

'It stands to reason,' Bryn said. It was infuriating, frustrating. Bryn wanted to break something, but to go looking for matches himself was just not the done thing; it was seen to be beneath the dignity of a banneret so he had to rely on Bautisto. In any event, turning up looking for a duel in person smacked of desperation, and that would do him no good. If Amero won his next duel, it would give Bautisto's salon a higher profile, which would in turn benefit Bryn. He would have to content himself with that thought for the time being.

Amero felt naked without his rapier. He had carried one every time he stepped out in public for years. It made him wonder how ordinary people got by. A rapier at his waist marked him out as a banneret, however, and that day he wanted to look like everyone else. He complimented his swordless appearance with his oldest, worst suit of clothes; he looked as ordinary as he possibly could.

Some carefully placed questions had given him a name, and the address where the person could be found. 'A healer of bones and solver of problems' was how they were described. Amero had no broken bones, and his problem was not the one he imagined was being referred to, but if they could mend bodies they might be of use to him.

He found the address; a doorway in a tight alley in Artisans. He paused before knocking, but pushed his doubts aside. His decision was made.

'Who is it?'

'I've hurt my hand,' Amero said. 'I'm here for your ointment.'

There was a scraping sound from behind the door and it opened. An old man stood in the doorway. He scrutinised Amero.

'Let me see your hand,' he said.

Amero held both up.

'Nothing wrong with those.' The man's eyes narrowed and he gave Amero another intense stare. His eyes worked over Amero, his face, his clothes, his boots.

'You're too well dressed for an Intelligencier,' the man said. 'Come in.'

Amero stepped inside. 'How can you be so sure I'm not one?'

The man looked at him and smiled. 'I'm sure, and it's not just the clothes, if you're thinking I'm some sort of idiot. What are you really here for?'

'Can you make a man stronger? Faster?' Amero asked. He felt foolish saying it, but he had no idea what magic could do.

The man laughed. 'Of course not. You been reading fairy tale books? No one can do that type of thing anymore. I fix bones and help women with their troubles is all. Your bones look fine to me, and you're not a woman. You're welcome to waste my time, but you'll have to pay for it.'

'My work takes a heavy toll on me,' Amero said. 'I'm tired and sore all the time. Can you help with that?'

The man raised his eyebrows. 'Maybe. There's only one way to find out. What is it you do? Soldier of some sort by the look of you.'

Amero smiled, but said nothing.

'If that's the way you want to play it, it's fine with me,' the man said. 'I'll see some coin first, though.'

'How much?' Amero asked.

'Gentleman like yourself? Five crowns.'

Amero laughed and looked around the small, shabby room. 'One, and you're lucky to get it.' He took a gold crown from his purse and flicked it to the man.

The man caught it and turned it over in his fingers. 'Come closer,' he said.

Amero stepped forward, feeling his heart accelerate.

The man held out his hands. 'Tired and sore?'

'Tired and sore,' Amero said. It was the truth. He had trained all morning and wanted nothing more than to crawl into bed. His joints ached and his muscles burned; even standing still was a strain.

The man held his hands over Amero's chest and closed his eyes. Nothing happened, and Amero felt ridiculous. The whole thing was a farce. He had always scorned the idea of anyone being able to do anything worthwhile with magic. No one had since the days of the Empire—

A chill flooded though his entire body, so strong that it caused him to shiver uncontrollably. 'Wh— what are you doing to me?'

The man said nothing, but the cold became worse, penetrating every part of his body. Amero was about to order him to stop when the man slumped into a chair. The freezing sensation started to fade.

'Is that it?' Amero asked, indignantly.

'That's it.'

The feeling of cold was almost completely gone, and Amero realised he did not feel nearly so tired. Far from it. He felt more rested and refreshed than he could remember. He stretched his arms and shoulders. All of the ache, fatigue, and stiffness was gone. 'Astonishing. How often can you do this?'

'Often as you like,' the man said. 'Within reason. I need rest myself after doing it. Once a day maybe.'

'I'll be back every day,' Amero said. 'Same time, and you keep this to yourself.'

'I will,' the man said. 'But it'll be five crowns the next time.'

'That won't be a problem,' Amero said, revelling in the fresh sensation that filled every limb.

CHAPTER THIRTEEN

BRYN RETURNED HOME from training to find a letter pushed under his door. The address was in Amero's handwriting. He broke the seal on the letter and shut the door behind him, pausing to take in the first few lines. There was a second note contained within. In Amero's scrawling handwriting, he explained that the other letter was from Thadeo dal Strenna's second, a banneret by the name of Giaco dal Barraco. Bryn wracked his brains in an effort to remember the name, but he couldn't. It didn't matter; it was rare that seconds were ever required to fight each other.

The second letter contained all the formalities required to start the organisation of a duel. After the introduction it went on to point out that at this early stage of proceedings an apology would still be satisfactory. Bryn had expected that this would be the case and had broached the matter with Amero in anticipation of the offer. Amero's response had been couched in similar terms to his original statements. Bryn saw nothing to be gained by putting the matter to him a second time now that the offer had been formally made. Blood would be shed and no amount of talk would change that fact.

He moved farther into his apartment and sat on the stool beside his small writing table before continuing to read the note.

The remainder was sketchy on detail and Bryn couldn't help but get the impression that the injured party was still hopeful that an apology would be forthcoming when cooler heads prevailed. He was sadly mistaken if that was the case. Bryn pulled a sheet of paper from a tray on the desk and flipped open the lid on the bottle of ink sitting in its recess. He tapped the end of his pen on the desk as he thought, then started, disappointing dal Strenna's hopes of avoiding the acquisition of a new scar.

Dal Barraco's note had said that in the event of an apology not being made, the injured party—dal Strenna—chose to fight the duel with sword alone, to the usual rules, meaning the duel would cease after the first wound causing blood. Date and location were all that remained to be decided upon.

Bryn sighed as he read back over his note, sadly all too familiar with the process of setting out the details of a duel and fulfilling the role of a second.

With the duel scheduled for two days hence, Bryn took the time to return to the Academy to collect some things that had been left behind in the confusion of his move down to Amero's apartment. He had a full day of training scheduled, so had gotten up earlier than usual in the hopes of collecting them and being back at the salon on time. His hopes took their first blow when he arrived at the Blackwater Bridge and was presented with a large number of people gathered at the bridge's end.

As he grew closer he spotted a member of the Watch standing and holding the crowd back. Bryn pushed his way through the crowd, the rapier at his waist marking him as a man of status not to be obstructed.

'What's the problem?' Bryn said.

'A steelwood barge hit the bridge during the night,' the watchman said. 'The engineers've restricted access until they've had a chance to give it a proper look. Foot traffic only, and no more than ten people on it at any time. If you want to cross, you'll have to join the back of the queue.'

Bryn thanked the watchman and joined the queue as instructed. It was something of a haphazard queue at best, more of a mob surrounding the end of the bridge. The watchmen blocking access to the end of the bridge had to use the butts of their halberds to clear enough space to allow the people coming over from the other side get through.

Once the bridge was clear, the watchmen shepherded ten people through their picket and on toward the other side. The undisciplined crowd pressed forward a little farther, and the wait continued. There seemed to be regular movement, and Bryn wasn't yet in any hurry so he decided to wait.

The Blackwater Bridge was the main crossing point of the Westway River, although there were others, and it was not long before a substantial crowd had gathered behind Bryn. There was little difference in terms of distance with the other bridges over the river from his apartment, and he was beginning to regret not having chosen to go with one of the others. Not only did the crowd at his end of the bridge have to be allowed across, so did those gathered on the other side, doubling his initial estimate.

Slowly but surely, the crowd in front of him diminished while that behind him grew. Eventually he found himself at the picket—a couple of barrels and halberds manned by four members of the Watch. They counted off ten people before preventing anyone else from going onto the bridge.

Bryn came toward the front of the crowd, gently pressing his way forward in an effort to ensure he was in the next ten chosen to cross. The watchmen were nearing the end of their count as he came to the front. A watchman beckoned to him to come forward, which Bryn did eagerly. As he passed through the picket he could hear a woman's voice remonstrating with the watchman. He cast a glance over his shoulder to see a young woman who had the look of a lady's maid about her beseeching the watchman to let her through to join her lady who was already on the bridge.

The difficulty, as was bluntly stated by the watchman, was that there was no more space to pass across in that batch. He was in the process of pushing the lady's maid back into the throng when Bryn was struck by a sudden notion of chivalry. It was no doubt compounded by the fact that the lady standing on the bridge waiting for her maid was one of the most beautiful women he had ever seen.

'Please,' he said. 'I'm not in any hurry.' At this point it was something of an untruth. 'I'd be happy for you to take my place.'

The maid nodded to him in appreciation and pushed away the watchman's restraining hand.

The lady stepped forward. 'How very gracious of you, sir. Thank you very much.'

She held his gaze for a moment and Bryn felt as though he had been completely robbed of his wits. It was all that he could do to doff his hat in a gentlemanly fashion; speech was completely beyond him.

The lady continued on her way, leaving him to wait at the picket a little while longer, but she cast a glance back at him as she went that set his heart racing.

Bryn was nearly a full hour late by the time he got back to the salon. He had often wondered how Bautisto would deal with a breach of salon discipline. He had some inkling of it from Amero's initial wilfulness when they started training there, but it had not betrayed the extent of the brutal training Bryn was subjected to when he had eventually turned up. Lateness was a mark of disrespect, something he would not forget in the future.

He was utterly exhausted by the time he got home. With each step, he felt as though he would be unable to take a single one more. His legs burned and his shoulders were so strained that he couldn't lift his arms. The effort of breathing almost seemed too much. The only thing that kept him going was the thought of collapsing into his bed after he had finally made it up the flight of stairs to his apartment. The benefits of a ground floor apartment seemed all too evident now, and he regretted his frugality in taking the cheaper option four floors above. Never before, not even in his first days at the Academy, had he found a flight of stairs so daunting.

When he got to his building's doorway he found his sister, Gilia, sitting on the step before it. For a moment, his fatigue was forgotten and replaced by concern.

She stood when she saw him appear and brushed down her skirt with her hands.

'What is it?' Bryn said. 'What's wrong?'

'Don't worry, it's nothing that can't wait until we get inside,' she said.

'Come up then,' Bryn said, feeling a wave of relief pass over him.

Bryn struggled to hide his exhaustion from her as he climbed the stairs, and breathed a sigh of relief as he reached the top. He unlocked the door and led her into his sparsely furnished apartment. He looked at her face as she entered and caught the briefest hint of the disapproving look that he had seen so often. Were it not for his concern at her being there at all, it would have made him smile.

'Please, sit,' he said, gesturing to the solitary chair beside his writing desk. 'I'd offer you tea but I'm afraid I haven't brought up any water.'

'That's all right,' Gilia said. 'I'd rather just get to what I'm here to talk to you about.'

Bryn sat on the foot of his bed, glad of the relief on his legs but concerned by what she had to say.

'The other day when you called, you noticed that the clock was missing.'

Bryn nodded.

'It isn't being repaired. It had to be sold, but I think you already worked that out for yourself. The fact is Father didn't leave us with very much, and things have been difficult.'

'Surely there's still enough to live on?'

'There would be,' Gilia said. 'If it weren't for the debts.'

'Debts?'

'How do you think all of those fencing lessons were paid for? The years at the Academy before you got your scholarship?'

Bryn felt his stomach turn. 'Father said that his manager at Austorgas' had agreed to put up most of the money in patronage. The bank's well known for sponsoring students at the Academy.'

Gilia shook her head. 'No. He told you that because he knew you'd refuse to go if you thought that he had to find the money himself. Which is exactly what he had to do.'

Bryn rubbed his brow. The fees at the Academy were enormous. In theory, admission was open to any citizen of Ostenheim. It was the great social leveller and something the people were fiercely proud of, even if in reality it was far beyond the grasp of most of them. Some wealthy individuals and organisations sponsored promising young men of limited means to allow them to attend. This was not at all uncommon, and as one of the wealthiest institutions in the city, Austorgas' Banking House was a prolific sponsor. When his father had told him that he had managed to convince one of the managers to put his name on their sponsorship list, he hadn't given it a second thought. Questioning good fortune always seemed like such an ungrateful thing to do. He had been too excited in any event.

'How did he get the money?' He wasn't sure if he wanted the answer.

'How do you think?'

She could only mean one thing. Moneylenders. Aside from Austorgas', there were many reputable banks in the city, although none quite as large. Convincing any of them to give a loan to pay for a son to go to the Academy would be a difficult sell; there was no real collateral involved as there would be in the purchase of a house or some land. A swordsman in training was too nebulous a thing for any of them to take a gamble on, even on the signature of a man of respectable position and career such as his father. If the young swordsman were to be injured or were to fail and be thrown out of the Academy, he would be of no value and the loan moneys would have been squandered. It was a bad investment for any responsible banker.

The moneylenders who kept their shops on the back streets of Bankers were not so discerning. With a home and a good job, Bryn's father had plenty of value that an avaricious money-lender would have no compunction in taking in payment. Their rates were also higher, reflecting the greater risk they were tak-ing in making the loan and also factoring in their greed.

There was little need to ask who the moneylender was as there was little to distinguish them; one was just as bad as another. Bryn couldn't help but wonder how his father must have felt when he had announced that he would be continuing on to the Collegium, making it another two years—perhaps lon-ger—before he would be earning money. He hadn't complained or made any mention of Bryn going out to find work. He had just beamed proudly at his son's achievement. Bryn wanted to throw up.

'How bad is it?'

'Bad, but not impossible,' she said. 'We're not in default, but the repayments take such a large amount of the pensions left since Father died that any time there's anything else that needs paying for, we're short.'

'So there's something else that needs paying for?'

'Yes, nothing serious, but it needs to be dealt with. Mother hasn't been feeling well and needs medicine. It's only a mild ill-ness but if it isn't dealt with now I'm afraid it might grow into something larger.'

'And there isn't the money to pay for both medicine and the loan.'

Gilia shook her head. 'Each time anything like this happens, something has to be sold. The difference is there's nothing left worth selling.'

It made Bryn guilty to the point of self-loathing to think of the sacrifices that his family had made to give him a life of privilege. His sister was old to be unmarried. He had always thought that it was because she was proud to the point of haughtiness, but clearly there had been no money for a dowry. He'd been so focussed on his own career and the rewards it would bring to all of them that he hadn't stopped to think of what they would do in the interim.

He reached for his purse and felt his heart drop when he realised how light it was.

'Take this,' he said. 'It's all I have at the moment, but there should be more coming in now that I'm duelling.'

Gilia said nothing, but took the purse.

He could see how difficult it was for her to accept it, and knew how hard she must have found it to come and ask for help.

'I'm going to help with this,' Bryn said. 'I want to take care of the repayments. How much time is there until the next one is due?'

'Next week.'

'Give me a day or two. I'll do what I can.'

CHAPTER FOURTEEN

BRYN MADE SURE to be at Bautisto's salon early the next day—not only to make up for his previous lateness, but because he needed to talk to Bautisto about getting a duel. He chose to do it early so that they could speak without Amero there. He suspected that if Amero knew of his situation he might offer to help, which was something that he wanted to avoid. He did not want to be in Amero's debt. Not when he was being so moody.

'I need to get a duel as soon as possible,' Bryn said.

'I'm doing everything I can,' Bautisto said. 'It's just difficult right now. I'm hoping that there will be something for you soon.'

'I can't wait for something to come along. There are some debts that I need to pay, for my family.'

Bautisto regarded him carefully. 'There are always ways for a swordsman to make money quickly. It all depends on what you are willing to do; how low you are willing to sink, although I could not permit you to fight on the Black Carpet.'

'Nothing untoward,' Bryn said quickly. He didn't want to end up on the illegal duelling circuit, the Black Carpet, nor did he want Bautisto to think that he was willing to consider the idea. 'I just need a legitimate duel, and soon. I don't care who it's against or where it is.'

Bautisto nodded. 'How soon is soon?'

'Before the end of next week.'

'Leave it with me. I'll do everything I can.'

Bryn's family troubles were weighing on his mind and he found it difficult to concentrate on training that day. He felt that Bautisto was not as hard on him for his mistakes as he usually was, and that irritated him. In addition to all of the other things playing on his mind, he had received a reply from Thadeo dal Strenna's second. The duel was to be fought the following morning, their next day off from training. The last thing Bryn needed was to have to clear up Amero's mess.

Bryn thought it wise to keep the matter from Bautisto. He was unlikely to be supportive of the matter; older, more experienced swordsmen were rarely in favour of duelling outside of the most extreme circumstances despite the fact that there were few who had not fought at least one in their youth.

Amero seemed completely unperturbed by his impending duel, although he did apply himself with more focus than usual and he was consistently getting the better of Bryn. His ability to push his worries from his mind and continue as though he didn't have a care in the world was quite impressive—assuming he was worried at all. If anything he seemed more relaxed than he had been in some time.

Once training had finished for the day, Bryn had to call on the physician that had agreed to attend the duel to pay him and finalise the time; dawn of the next day.

There was something of a romantic cliché about fighting a duel at dawn, the time they were almost always fought if not immediately after the insult causing the duel was given—but there was good reason for it.

Duels of honour, despite being very common in a city full of men trained in the use of swords, were technically illegal.

THE FIRST BLADE OF OSTIA

By fighting at dawn when there were still few people about, there was a greater chance of being able to complete the matter unnoticed and not be bothered by the City Watch. This was also the reason for the duels being fought outside of the city walls. Although the standard format for the duel was to the first blood, people were occasionally killed. When that occurred, it was always sensible for the surviving duellist to retreat to the countryside for a few weeks until the matter had blown over. As the participants in duels were usually aristocrats, this was no great imposition on them as they would simply remain at their country mansions until a dispensation was granted for them to return to the city.

Being already outside of the city walls made this easier for the authorities. If the Watch were aware that there had been a fatality in a duel inside the city walls, they would be obliged to arrest all those connected to it—if only to pay lip-service to a law that was not held in any great esteem—and lock them up for a few hours until the appropriate bribes were paid. It was another example of the practical application of the law deviating from its written form in Ostenheim. So long as appearances were satisfied, an aristocrat could get away with a great many things.

As he passed through Crossways on his way to the surgeon's, Bryn could hear the city crier's voice rising above all the noise of the busy marketplace.

'Panceri Mistria defeats Juan Aubero, and retains the honour of being the First Blade of Ostia! Former great dal Errio proclaims Mistria to be the finest blade of our times!

'Banneret-General dal Sharnhome leads punitive raiding parties into Ruripathia! Duke assures citizens that there will be no war!'

The news continued, but it was the mention of Mistria that Bryn was most interested in. Mistria certainly was the man of the hour, getting precedence over the brewing conflict in the north. Bryn supposed that petty wars with Ruripathia were so common, and so little came of them, that Mistria's achievements probably were more newsworthy. He had remained undefeated for some time and many of his fans seemed to believe that would continue to be the case. The lofty goal of a perfect one hundred and twenty-five points was growing ever closer for Panceri Mistria.

Bryn returned his thoughts to the task at hand. Finding physicians who would attend duels was not difficult; there were many around the city who were happy to provide the service. This was despite the tacit illegality of the enterprise, and due to the extortionate rates they could charge. As Bryn handed over their share of the fee, it occurred to him that it would have been more than enough to satisfy his family's creditors for the next few months. Perhaps he had chosen the wrong career path.

A light mist hovered over the ground of the chosen duelling field, lifted from the grass by the warming air. It was early, but already Bryn could feel the temperature starting to rise even though the summer was all but over. Bryn's eyes were heavy and he hadn't slept well the night before. Amero looked relaxed and refreshed, clearly less nervous than his second.

All of the previous duels that Bryn was involved in had taken place when he was at the Academy. They usually occurred during the darker days of winter when people had less to do and boredom led them to poor choices. That meant dawn happened several hours later than that day, and Bryn rued having had to get up so early.

The rules were simple. At the first sight of blood, both combatants ceased fighting. It was this standard, accepted rule that Bryn and Thadeo's second, Giaco dal Barraco, were there to ensure was followed. There was no rule to dictate how or from where that blood would be drawn and overzealous strikes could cause far greater injury than was required. That was what the physician was there for. Even a simple cut could go septic, lead to blood poisoning and kill if left untreated, an eventuality that was not in anyone's interests.

The duellists were informed of the rules, limited as they were, and faced one another waiting for the instruction to begin. Dal Strenna looked as though he would rather be anywhere else. Amero looked raring to go. Bryn checked with dal Barraco and then, with a sigh, gave the command to begin.

The reason for Bryn not having any recollection of dal Strenna's ability despite his best efforts to remember was quickly exposed. He was a middling swordsman at best, by Academy standards. Bryn could see right from the off that the duel would not last long and that there could only be one result. Dal Strenna was a perfect example of the aristocratic type who attended the Academy for no reason other than it being expected of them because of their position. He was not bad—no one who managed to graduate from the Academy was—but Amero was in an entirely different class.

Amero danced forward with three fast cuts, right-left-right, none of which were intended to strike home. He was far lighter on his feet than dal Strenna, who didn't seem to have maintained a rigorous training regime since leaving the Academy. At best he could have been one of the idlers lounging around on a sofa in one of the more expensive salons like those Amero had initially been keen on. Bryn's insistence on choosing a salon of substance rather than style was certainly paying off now.

Amero allowed dal Strenna to take the initiative for a moment, for nothing other than to exercise his back leg it seemed. He danced backward as fluidly as he had forward, effortlessly parrying away dal Strenna's comparatively clumsy strikes. Amero had a broad smile on his face as he toyed with dal Strenna. Bryn looked to his opposite number whose face gave away the fact that he was all too well aware how this duel would end. All he could hope for now was that his friend would not be too badly injured.

Amero held his ground and parried away a thrust that left dal Strenna so open Bryn would have had enough time to walk over and put in a cutting strike himself. Bryn expected he would make a quick cut to one of dal Strenna's shoulders, or if he felt particular offence, to a cheek. Instead he whipped his sword across dal Strenna's face in a vicious cut that opened it from jaw to opposite temple.

Bryn's jaw dropped in surprise and horror as dal Strenna shrieked in pain and dropped his sword. Both of his hands went to his face and blood flowed from between his fingers. Dal Barraco and the physician rushed forward to dal Strenna while Amero turned and began to walk toward Bryn. He nonchalantly inspected the tip of his blade as he went, and smiled to Bryn when he arrived.

'Glad that's dealt with,' he said. 'I think I owe you breakfast now.'

Bryn didn't know what to say. The viciousness of Amero's behaviour was unwarranted and utterly shocking. The calm and detached way he spoke about it was equally so. The young man was maimed for life over a foolish and unintended insult, and Amero didn't give a damn. Bryn wondered if this was what he had intended all along, and felt ill at the thought.

CHAPTER FIFTEEN

BRYN WOKE TO the sound of shuffling and scraping. It was still dark outside, although the warm orange glow of a mage lamp out on the street cast enough light through his window blinds to create harsh shadows in his small apartment. It took him a moment to go from sleep to awareness and his heart began to race as he realised the sound was coming from his door.

There was no reason he could think of that anyone would be at his door in the middle of the night, unless they were there for nefarious purposes. He had heard few enough instances of arrests being made over duels, let alone any of the City Watch turning up at a participant's home in the middle of the night. A moment's consideration was all it took to dismiss that possibility.

He had no enemies, so it would have to be a case of robbery. Any would-be robbers had made a poor choice in coming to his apartment. He took his sword from the hook on the wall beside his bed as quietly as possible and slowly sat up, swinging his legs out from underneath his blanket. He placed his feet on the bare floorboards as softly as he could and stood, hoping they wouldn't creak and betray his movement.

The door to his apartment was still bolted. He padded towards it as silently as he could manage, carefully stepping over the one floorboard he knew to have a particularly bad creak. He pressed his ear to the door but of the sound that had woken him he could detect no trace. He felt his foot brush against something on the floor.

Satisfied that his door was not about to be kicked in he knelt down and fumbled around in the darkness to find the object his foot had brushed against. It was a small fold of paper. It seemed that someone had felt the need to push a note underneath his door in the middle of the night.

He returned his sword to its hook and went to one of the windows. He opened the window blind, allowing more of the light from the mage lamp on the street to get in.

The lamps were something of an anachronism. They were one of the few objects that had survived down to the present time from the days of the mages. It was difficult for Bryn to imagine just how old they must be. Each lamp was a thick glass sphere that contained some form of enchanted magical energy. Each evening as the light of the sun waned, the lamps would wax. By the time full darkness had fallen they would reach the peak of their illumination, casting a warm orange-yellow light all around them. There were thousands of them all along the streets of Ostenheim, ensuring the major thoroughfares were illuminated every hour of the day.

To steal or tamper with a mage lamp would invite the attention of the headsman's axe. The reason for their harsh protection was simply down to the fact that there were no more of them being made. The last true mage had been put to death the better part of a thousand years before and no more magical items could be created. They were said to have not dimmed an iota in all the years of their existence, so the only danger was theft and vandalism. Such was the way of things that this rarely, if ever, occurred.

Bryn broke the wax seal on the note and unfolded it. He had to angle it to cast some of the light coming through the window onto the paper. It was from Bautisto. He was intrigued to see what information needed to be conveyed to him in the small hours.

In a neat and austere script—much in keeping with his swordplay—Bautisto instructed him to bring his full fighting kit along with clothes and other necessaries for several days away from the city the next morning. There was no other information and Bryn's curiosity was piqued. What could Bautisto have planned?

Bryn had struggled to get back to sleep after reading Bautisto's note. He yawned repeatedly as he leaned against one of the posts supporting the roof of Bautisto's salon as he watched through the skylight his second sunrise in as many days. Finally Bautisto appeared out of the back room with a travelling bag slung over his shoulder.

'Where are we going?'

'Tanosa,' Bautisto said. 'I heard of a match becoming available there, but the duel is tomorrow evening. We'll need to travel hard to get there in time. If we catch the morning express carriage it should have us there by late tomorrow afternoon.'

'Is that the best that's on offer?' Bryn said, disappointed by the reality behind the mysterious note.

'At such short notice it is. But believe me when I tell you that it is a good option. Better than I had hoped for, merely less convenient. It is against a decent regional duellist and there are Ladder points to be had if you win. I sent word that we would accept the match last night and at such short notice I was able to command a high price. Twice your usual purse. No one else was available so we must count ourselves lucky.'

Other than the inconvenience of getting to Tanosa by the next day, it didn't sound bad. He needed the money and would have taken it anyway, but the Ladder points were an added attraction.

In essence, the match would be no different to a duel in the city. His initial reaction was born from snobbery. The swordsmen who populated the regional circuit were often looked down on as being second rate, for no reason other than that they were not in the city. Many of them were Bannerets, so they had the same Academy training most city duellists had. When Bryn thought about it he realised that the scorn was foolish, but nonetheless felt uncomfortable with the notion that a regional duel was the only one he could get.

While most of the money and glamour was to be found in Ostenheim, and it was certainly where the very top tier of swordsmen were, there were several small cities and large towns dotted around Ostia that also had a demand for the spectacle offered by the arena. While none were big enough to sustain a large and diverse pool of competitors, between all of them it was possible. For those who found it difficult to make a living in Ostenheim it was an alternative, but not one Bryn was initially interested in. It was usually a more attractive proposition for Bannerets who were originally from the provinces and wished to return there after leaving the Academy.

For Bryn, born and bred in the city, the thought of traipsing around the country from town to town leading a nomadic life was not appealing. Ostenheim was the centre of the world as far as he was concerned.

They walked from Bautisto's salon to the eastern gate of the city. There was a passenger coach station outside each of the city's gates where private individuals could pay for passage to any of the other cities and towns of the Duchy. Tanosa was one of the largest, perhaps the largest in the Duchy after Ostenheim. It was also the home seat of one of the twelve elector count families of Ostia, where his elder sister lived and hopefully the location of a successful duel and good payday.

The express carriage would travel through the night, changing horses at various way-stations along the route, thus allowing them to make the best time possible; better even than they would have been able to manage pushing hard on horseback. The carriage would also give him the best chance of arriving in Tanosa in a condition to fight a duel. If Bryn was lucky, the early departure hour might mean they were the only ones on the carriage. That would allow Bryn to stretch out and sleep as much as possible. The more relaxed and rested he was on arrival, the better a chance he would have in his match.

Bryn and Bautisto's sudden trip out of the city was perfectly timed for Amero. With all that was going on—having to deal with the dal Strenna idiot chief amongst it—he had little opportunity to take full advantage of his new-found energy. At first he had not known how much benefit he would derive from it, but the results were almost immediately visible. Being so much fresher made everything else easier, and had instantly closed the gap between him and Bryn.

The extra speed that came with a well-rested body was only one of the advantages. He could push himself harder for longer when they were training, could wear Bryn down with less detriment to himself. Where before he had hobbled out of Bautisto's salon at the end of every morning's training, now he felt well-worked and nothing more. The daily visit to his secret friend on the way home alleviated even that.

After a few days, Amero started to feel lazy. It was the same sense he used to get in the Academy when he knew he was letting his training slacken in favour of other pursuits. The difference now was that he was training as hard as ever. It was only that his capacity was greatly extended. It struck him as foolish to sit around and enjoy his new-found energy, and be content with the edge it had already given him.

He could happily put in several more hours of work a day, and the advantage that could give him was tantalising. It would be difficult to explain how he was suddenly able to do another session in the afternoon however. Bryn and Bautisto being away gave him the chance to put everything in place without being noticed. A private and very expensive tutor to train against, and a small warehouse in Oldtown that still smelled of the exotic spices it had once housed were his solution.

CHAPTER SIXTEEN

I T WAS LATE the following afternoon when Bryn's carriage clattered up to the gates of Tanosa. It had been filled to capacity, and the journey was far from comfortable.

The small city sat overlooking what would become the Eastway River farther downstream, but here it was called the Whitewater. The river's source was well away to the northeast, past the Silver Hills and up in the southern reaches of the Telastrian Mountains. The water was a cloudy white colour as it churned its way past the city; very different to the dark and not particularly inviting shade it took on by the time it reached Ostenheim.

As in Ostenheim, the carriage depot was outside the town walls, so they had to walk from there. When Bryn exited the carriage, he could feel all of his joints pop and click. His muscles were stiff and his back ached from the cramped conditions on board. There had been several opportunities to get out for a brief walk while the horses were being changed, but it wasn't enough to prevent the discomfort he was now experiencing. He worried about his duel later that evening— leaving the city for a duel was humbling enough, losing it would be downright embarrassing.

They unloaded their baggage and made their way into the town. In many ways it appeared to be a smaller version of Ostenheim. There was little difference in terms of the style of architecture and the building materials used and as they walked down the street, between tall buildings on either side, Bryn thought one could be forgiven for mistaking the place as Ostenheim.

'Do you have any idea of where we're going?' Bryn said, after they had been walking for a few minutes.

'In a manner of speaking. I have the name of an inn where accommodation has been arranged for us. Once we're there, I have the name of a man to contact. The duel is not for several hours yet, so there's no hurry and hopefully you will have time to rest.'

It appeared that Bautisto was not the type of man to ask for directions without very good reason and they continued wandering for several more minutes before Bryn finally demanded the name of the inn from him and asked a passer-by himself.

That done, it didn't take long to find their way to The Five Coronets. The inn was named to commemorate the fact that the counts of Tanosa had been dukes of Ostia on five occasions, more than any of the other elector count families.

The inn was much like any other that Bryn had happened to visit. There was nothing about it, or the town itself, that justified the snide contempt those from Ostenheim often held the provincial towns in. He could see why his sister was happy there and wondered if there would be time to call on her and Nicolo. Probably not, which would no doubt draw his mother's ire when he got home.

There were a number of patrons in the taproom, eating, drinking and chatting. Bautisto instructed him to sit while he went to attend to the details with the innkeeper. Bautisto was insisting on taking care of everything, for which Bryn was glad. The journey had drained all the energy out of him, and he had no idea how he was going to reinvigorate himself before his duel in a few hours.

The arena in Tanosa was far larger than Bryn had expected, far larger than the one he had fought at in Ostenheim. He was even more surprised to learn that it was one of several there. He had felt humbled by having to come to the small city in the first place, but now he felt humbled by his foolishly preconceived arrogance. There was a capacity crowd and he felt a flutter of nerves at the thought of competing in front of so many people. What made it worse was that he was duelling a local banneret and it was unlikely the crowd would give him a warm welcome.

He had slept for a couple of hours, but it hadn't been enough to entirely undo the effect of all those hours in a carriage bumping along rough roads. His aches and stiffness were supplemented by the dullness of thought brought on by a lack of sleep.

His duel was second on the bill, so he had the opportunity to watch one match to get a feel for how things worked in the provinces and inject some energy into his mind and limbs. The crowd was far more vocal than in even the most raucous backstreet arenas in Ostenheim. The arena in Lowgarden that Amero had fought in was like a graveyard by comparison. How the duellists managed to maintain their concentration was anyone's guess.

The standard of fencing left nothing to be desired. The duellists were competent and wouldn't have disgraced themselves in the arenas of Ostenheim. The condescension city duellists held their rural brethren in was entirely undeserved and reflected badly on the city swordsmen, highlighting their arrogance. Bryn had to admit he'd been guilty of it, but wouldn't be any longer.

Any hopes that Bryn might have entertained about having an easy evening's work were scotched by the display. Although Bryn understood there were more non-Bannerets on the regional circuit, both of the men now duelling had been to the Academy.

It was clear that the choice to duel on the provincial circuit was dictated by reasons other than a want of ability. He felt foolish for thinking that he was going to be bringing a taste of city sophistication to the proceedings, and hoped the evening wouldn't end in humiliation.

The enthusiasm of the crowd had already set him ill at ease, but his nerves were positively rattled by the reaction of the audience to the announcement of his duel. Bryn had known that his opponent was a local man and that this meant the crowd would likely be hostile to him. He had harboured the faint hope that his opponent was one of those duellists that attracted the loving hatred of the crowd, but that certainly was not the case.

Bryn's opponent appeared to be the darling of the Tanosa audience. When his name, Chalmo Capani, was announced, they became hysterical. Bryn's heart sank and he walked from the warm-up area toward the arena feeling as though his boots had been filled with lead.

Capani was three years ahead of Bryn at the Academy. He had been duelling on the provincial circuit ever since and appeared to be something of a rising star, not to mention a crowd favourite.

Bryn paused and took a deep breath before stepping out onto the arena floor. As soon as he did, a stream of vitriol hit him with such force it felt as though it were actually physical rather than simply sentiment. He gritted his teeth to steady his nerve and concentrated on maintaining as blank an expression as possible. The only benefit of attracting so much hostile attention was that its full weight blotted out any of the individual catcalls and insults.

Bryn faced Capani across the black line, with the Master of Arms standing between them. His voice was barely audible over the noise from the crowd as he outlined the rules—a standard list that both duellists knew by heart. The formality was required nonetheless.

Capani looked loose and confident. Bryn didn't feel that way. He tried to forget everything he might remember about his opponent, which was little anyway. Much could have changed since Bryn last saw him fence at the Academy. He needed to take the match as he found it, and be prepared for anything. The atmosphere generated by the crowd felt as though it was closing in around him, like great walls that were getting ever tighter. He tried to blot out the noise, to focus only on the sound of his breath and the sight of his opponent.

'Duel.' The Master of Arms's voice cut through the oppressive noise and all of the other distractions.

His opponent lunged forward, and for Bryn everything else ceased to exist.

The carriage didn't feel nearly so cramped on the way home to Ostenheim. That had something to do with the pleasant flush of victory and the purse of silver coins inside his doublet. The victory meant two things. First and by far the most important, he would be able to satisfy the imminent payment required on his family's loans. Secondly, he was taking home five Ladder points, and the knowledge that he had taken an important step forward in his career.

They would be enough to facilitate his jump up the Ladder, probably onto the next page—perhaps even higher. While winning was the primary goal of every match in the arena, the margin by which one was victorious was important for the effect it had on the Ladder ranking. A victory by three touches to two would earn the winner one point toward his Ladder ranking. A victory by a three to one margin would earn two points, while a win without conceding a touch granted five.

With five points to be added to his ranking, he found it difficult to think of Tanosa with anything other than affection, in spite of the hostility with which he had been received. Indeed, as the duel had gone on the crowd started to show their appreciation of his skill and effort, the sign of true fans.

He relaxed back into his corner of the cramped carriage, feeling an enormous sense of satisfaction. He closed his eyes and let his mind run over the numbers, but he couldn't escape the feeling of guilt at not having called to see his sister, Lena. It was unlikely he could get away with it. His name would be listed in the newssheets that reported the duelling results, and perhaps also by the town criers. His focus on career was time and time again causing him to neglect his family.

The first thing that Bryn did when he got back to Ostenheim was call to see his family. He knew that his mother was proud and wouldn't accept the money from him. She would be mortified to find out that he even knew of the difficulty they were in. When he had the chance, he took his sister aside and gave it to her.

Once that was done there was little left over and he was essentially back in the position he had been before rushing out to Tanosa; broke and looking for another duel. He hoped that having the extra points would stand in his favour and something would come along soon. It was an unpleasant feeling, like waiting for divine intervention to sweep in and solve his problems.

CHAPTER SEVENTEEN

EACH YEAR, AS the summer cooled into autumn and green faded to yellow then golden-brown, the great and the wealthy of Ostia flocked back from their country estates to Ostenheim to spend the winter months in the city. Where there were aristocrats there was also society, and the finer aspects of the city came to life with their return. The theatres and opera houses began to show new works and the wealthier parts of the city were filled once more with the sounds of music and revelry. Aristocratic families held balls, each trying to outdo the others in terms of extravagance and luxury.

Bryn didn't like being thought of as part of anyone's retinue, and everything he had done in recent weeks had been intended to prevent that. He couldn't deny that it had been the de facto situation ever since he and Amero had established their friendship in the first few weeks at the Academy, but there was a difference between being a supporter of a powerful aristocrat and being his retainer. He wanted to be thought of as his own man, but despite his distaste at the concept there were some benefits to close association with the son of an elector count. One of those was access to the more enjoyable aspects of fine society.

Bryn was never directly invited to any of these events; his anonymous presence was merely accepted as part of the invitation given to Amero. This was not unusual however; few aristocrats attended without a group of their friends or supporters.

Balls would never lose their novelty for Bryn. The music was the part he enjoyed the most, as he never got the opportunity to hear it otherwise. Full orchestras were not uncommon if the house was large enough, as was the case with the first ball of the season that Amero asked him along to. The food and drink were always excellent—a welcome change to tavern food or his attempts at cooking—and there was always plenty of both.

He would usually have looked forward to a ball without reservation, but he felt a sense of dread that evening as he walked to Oldtown to meet Amero. The last few occasions they had socialised had been unpleasant experiences, and Bryn could not put from his mind what Amero had done to Thadeo dal Strenna. Leaving the Academy was a big upheaval, and Bryn realised Amero was dealing with the strain of carrying his family name into the arena, but there was only so much latitude that could buy him. A duel was a duel, and people got cut badly—but Bryn knew Amero had intended to cause that injury, even if the others did not realise it. It was time for Amero to settle into his new life or consider an alternative. Bryn tried not to dwell on it further in the hope of enjoying the evening.

Bryn couldn't help but notice that the composition of Amero's party had changed since their Academy days. Back then, when he had a ball to attend, he would usually bring along whoever was in their house's common room and free to go. Now, however, Bryn hardly knew any of them. They were all aristocrats, and from their family names Bryn recognised them all as being from families that were in some way allied to the House of Moreno. These were the young men who would, in the future, provide Amero with his base of support when the considerations of duty and politics caught up with him and he took his family's seat in the Barons' Hall.

They had arrived fashionably late, so there had not been any time to make small talk with the other ball-goers until after the meal was finished. Amero seemed to be in genuinely good form, with no hint of trouble lurking beneath the surface. Bryn's relief was enormous, and it shocked him just how tense he had grown on the walk down to Oldtown. Perhaps the couple of rest days while he and Bautisto were in Tanosa had done Amero good.

Bryn was content to sit and listen to the orchestra, but there were social conventions that he couldn't avoid, and one of those required him to wander about with Amero, chatting with others. There were many there that Bryn knew from the Academy, some of whom he had not seen in the months since he had left.

One of the other attractions of the balls was the fact that they were also attended by many of the city's single young women. Amero drew quite a bit of attention; with his wealth and position he was one of the most eligible bachelors in the Duchy. Bryn was hopeful that as a Banneret of the Blue he made for an attractive prospect himself.

He was chatting to someone that he had been in the Academy with while Amero talked to a group behind him. When he turned, he was taken aback to see a familiar face.

'Ah, Bryn,' Amero said. 'This is Lady Joranna dal Verrara; my lady, this is Banneret of the Blue Bryn Pendollo.'

Bryn nodded his head in deference to her. She was not just familiar; her face had been burned onto his mind since he had first seen her, that day on the bridge.

She looked at him curiously for a moment before her eyes widened and she smiled slightly. 'Why, I believe that the banneret and I have already met.' She bowed her head in response to him.

'Really?' Amero said.

'Ah, yes,' Bryn said, feigning that he had only now realised who she was. 'I believe it was on the Blackwater Bridge, wasn't it?'

'Yes, it was,' Joranna said. She turned to Amero. 'The bridge had been damaged by a barge during the night and the City Watch were restricting the number of people who could cross. Banneret Pendollo was kind enough to give up his place in the queue so that my maid and I could cross at the same time.'

'Banneret Pendollo has always been the consummate gentleman,' Amero said, giving Bryn a sideways glance and a mischievous smile. 'He won the sword of honour at the Academy too. And again in the Collegium. That was shortly after he had represented Ostia in the Competition.'

Bryn blushed, and Amero's smile widened.

Joranna raised an eyebrow as she turned her attention back to Bryn. 'I only hope that it didn't cause you any delay.'

'Oh, no, it was no trouble at all.'

Amero snorted in amused disbelief. 'No trouble? Our maestro gave us the grilling of a lifetime after Bryn turned up late for training. I could hardly walk the next day.'

'Training?' said Joranna.

'Yes. Bryn and I are competing in the arena. I'm surprised you hadn't heard I was doing it; it seems pretty much everyone else has.'

'Now that you mention it, I think I did hear something about it. You thrashed some fellow in Lowgarden not so long ago?'

Bryn felt himself tense—this was dangerous ground—and breathed a sigh of relief that she had put it in better terms than dal Strenna or any of the others had. He really didn't want to have to deal with Amero in another foul mood.

'Indeed I did,' Amero said, with cavalier charm.

Joranna smiled tactfully. 'Well, perhaps I shall talk to you again later.' She held Bryn's gaze for a moment longer before leaving them.

Bryn and Amero walked toward a group of

bannerets—classmates of theirs when at the Academy—who were standing next to the table from which drinks were dispensed.

'Not bad looking, is she,' Amero said.

'No, not at all bad.'

'Very chivalrous of you to let her cross the bridge like that.'

Bryn knew when he was being baited. 'Oh, piss off.'

Amero burst into laughter. 'She's not the best catch, I'm afraid. Her family don't have a penny. A mouldering old mansion on the edge of Moreno and a few acres that aren't much better than swamp. Still, there are titles to be had if you're willing to earn the coin, I suppose. She'll be looking to attach herself to a good prospect. Not sure I'd advise an advance in that direction though.'

Bryn watched her as she moved between groups on the other side of the room. She was utterly exquisite; graceful and elegant with thick curls of blonde hair perfectly shaped around her head. 'Perhaps,' he said, absently.

Amero watched Bryn's eyes follow her across the room. 'Don't want to rain on your parade or anything, but seriously, I wouldn't get too caught up in her if I were you.'

'Why?' Bryn said sharply, returning his focus to Amero. 'Is there something wrong with her?'

Amero laughed. 'No, nothing like that. I know where you're coming from, Bryn, and I haven't seen you look at a girl the way you look at her before.'

'Just looking is all,' Bryn said.

'Yes, and just going all dreamy eyed while you're at it too,' Amero said. 'If you're going to set your sights on someone, go for the daughter of a burgess, or grand burgess if you can hook one. Plenty of money, and being a Banneret'll carry more weight. I know girls like Joranna. You'll be far happier if you take my advice. She's a shark, that one. Titles and no money is always a dangerous combination if you're looking for more than a bit of mischief.'

'I'm never averse to a bit of mischief,' Bryn said, casting his gaze back across the ballroom to where Joranna stood with a group of ladies. He felt indignant at Amero's crudely veiled suggestion that he was setting his sights too high, and wanted her all the more for it.

CHAPTER EIGHTEEN

AMERO RAN AN oily cloth along the length of his rapier blade. The arena was all but empty and he was alone in the Bannerets' Enclosure. He liked the peaceful atmosphere; so different to the emotionally charged one that had prevailed a short time before. He checked the mirror finish of the blade's surface in the light to make sure there were no droplets of sweat or blood remaining, anything that could cause the blade to rust while in storage until his next duel.

A lower ranked opponent usually followed a match with a higher ranked one, which was what he had faced that evening. He smiled as he thought of the five points he had just won. It was another step toward silencing the whispers and gossip. He was not just the Hammer's son, and he was going to prove that to anyone who thought to the contrary.

'You're going to continue with this farce?'

The smile dropped from Amero's face. 'Looks that way.' He did not look up from his sword case.

'I watched, you know,' Renald said.

'That must have been painful.' Amero snapped the catches on the case shut.

'Yes and no. I think you're above this prancing about to

entertain the masses, but you do have form. You made that other fellow look like a donkey.'

Amero raised his eyebrows. It was the closest thing to a compliment his father had ever paid him.

'It's form that would be put to better use in a regiment, though.'

'Now we come to the core of it,' Amero said, not to anyone in particular.

'I wanted to try and make you see sense one more time,' Renald said. 'The grandson of a Duke should not be making a spectacle of himself in the arena.'

'Yes, slaughtering peasants by the thousand in the southern passes is a far better use of one's time,' Amero said.

'I've said what I came to say,' Renald said. 'It's not the time or place to say more. Think on it. I've asked, and I won't do that again. Rest assured, this isn't the end of it.'

Bryn had trained alone with Bautisto that day. Amero had fought another match the day before so had taken a day's rest. With the winter social season moving into full swing, Amero had another ball to attend and as usual asked Bryn to go along. It was in one of the mansions of Highgarden so Bryn had to rush back to his apartment to wash and change after training. They agreed to meet at the venue at eight bells, knowing it was unlikely he would be able to call down to the apartment in Oldtown early enough.

As usual he wore his dark blue Academy doublet. Without a military commission and the uniform to go with it, it was the only thing that he had which marked him out as being a member of the finer classes. He knew it was time to get something more suitable now that he was no longer a student, but there were more important things that needed the money.

He found himself unusually excited by the prospect of the

ball, and it was not the music that was causing it. He did not like to get too caught up in anyone or anything, but he could not help but hope that Joranna dal Verrara would be there. He remembered Amero's words of warning, but found himself unable to give them any credence.

The chime for eight bells rang out from the cathedral's campanile over on the far side of Crossways, the time he had arranged to meet Amero. He cursed and hastened the speed at which he was buttoning up his doublet. He charged out of his apartment and down the stairs two at a time, trying not to get his sword tangled between his legs. He burst out onto the street and abruptly slowed to a normal walk. It wasn't the done thing for a banneret to be seen running through the streets.

It was completely dark when he arrived at the gates to the mansion. Large mage lamps held within ornately decorated metal frames illuminated the gateway and several liveried men stood there checking the invitations. Bryn approached them and one held out a hand, a polite smile on his face.

'I'm afraid I don't have an invitation,' Bryn said. 'I'm here in the party of Amero dal Moreno. I think he's already arrived.'

'I'm afraid I'll have to ask you to wait a moment, sir, I'll have someone go and find him.'

'That's all right,' a voice from behind Bryn said, a woman's voice.

'Very good, ma'am, might I see your invitation?'

Bryn turned to see Joranna dal Verrara standing behind him, along with several other ladies and the chaperones of her party.

She smiled demurely at Bryn and reached forward to hand her invitation to the servant.

He stepped back to allow them all to pass. 'Enjoy your evening, my lady.'

After they passed into the courtyard Bryn stopped and turned to Joranna. 'Thank you for that, gods only know how long it would have taken them to find Amero and bring him out.'

'You're very welcome,' she said, and then more quietly so that no one else could hear her, 'at the very least you had better offer me a dance this evening.'

'I… Yes, of course.'

'Well, you better go on ahead, it wouldn't be seemly for us to go in together.'

'Yes, of course, thanks again,' Bryn said, realising that he had repeated himself. He turned and began to walk toward the house.

'Don't forget now,' she called out after him.

He cast another glance over his shoulder to look back at her, but she had already returned to a conversation with her companions.

As soon as he got inside, he could hear music drifting out from the back of the house. It lifted his spirits, if they could be lifted any further after his brief exchange with Joranna and he felt the excitement of the night ahead flush through him. It was something he had never felt at a ball before.

He walked through the house, being discreetly directed by more servants until he reached the ballroom. It ran the length of the back of the house and overlooked what he imagined to be an ornate garden, although it was too dark to see anything beyond the glass of the large windows. Half the room was filled with tables fully decked out with glassware and cutlery and it was something of a relief to Bryn that he hadn't missed the start of the meal; he was starving. The other half was clear to allow for dancing later in the night, while the orchestra was set up at that end, still only playing quietly to allow for conversation.

Bryn had never been in this house before, and the features that particularly caught his attention were the three ornate chandeliers that were suspended from the high ceiling. Each was a masterpiece of intricately cut crystal and home to what must have been hundreds of tiny mage lamps, each no bigger than the end of his thumb. They bathed the room in a warm, decadent light that shouted opulence and wealth as clearly as though the city criers in Crossways were announcing it.

It only took him a moment to find Amero, propping up the bar at one end of the room with several other bannerets, all of them the new additions to his retinue.

'I thought you'd decided not to come,' Amero said as he approached.

'It takes longer than you'd expect to look this good,' Bryn said, eliciting a slight chuckle from the other bannerets.

'No,' Amero said. 'I imagine it takes you *quite* some time. How'd you get in anyway?'

'I have my methods,' Bryn said. 'Now, I'm parched, what's good to drink?'

'Dal Bragadin piss from the shores of the Blackwater is all, I'm afraid,' Amero said. 'Can never understand how they charge so much for a bottle of it. Compared to the wines from home, it's not much better than vinegar.'

Bryn raised an eyebrow. Blackwater wines—produced by the Elector Count Bragadin family—were amongst the most expensive available, and another one of the subtle statements of effortless wealth aristocrats liked to make at their balls. There was no love lost between the Moreno and Bragadin families though; they had long been political rivals. Bryn was delighted to get a glass or two. For him it was an unexpected, and rare, treat.

The bar behind them was laid out with dozens of glasses filled with sparkling wine. Bryn took one and joined the others in their disinterested, yet surreptitiously watchful pose. It was only a moment or two later that Joranna and her group came into the ballroom.

'The evening's looking up,' one of the bannerets said, and all the rest laughed, including Bryn.

Seeing Joranna walking into the ballroom reminded him of his promise to ask her for a dance, which served to eradicate the relaxed feeling his glass of wine had been imbuing. Dancing lessons were given at the Academy in an effort to ensure all of the graduates would be able to function in polite society. Bryn had always appreciated that dancing and swordplay were not all that far removed from one another, but despite his love for music, the practical utility he saw in it and the effort he had made in learning, he had never taken to it particularly well. He felt nervous not just at the idea of dancing with her, but having to formally approach her in front of her chaperone to ask to sign her dance card. He had done it only rarely in the past, and never with an aristocrat and the additional formality that went with one of that station. All things considered he realised that it was unlikely she would turn him down; nonetheless, he felt little different than he had in the moments before stepping into the arena in Tanosa.

'Is everything all right?' Amero said.

'Yes, fine, why?'

'You're sweating.'

Bryn realised that his forehead was covered in a wet sheen. He took a handkerchief from his pocket and wiped it off. 'It's just the walk up the hill.'

It looked as though half of the intended guests had arrived before Bryn. The room continued to fill until the gong was rung to call everyone to their tables for the meal.

He found it hard to concentrate on the conversation at the table, or the meal itself. By the time it was finished he felt more nervous than he ever had when faced with an impending duel. One by one the other bannerets at the table began to disperse to track down the young women they wanted to ask for a dance. This was usually the point where Bryn made himself comfortable with a bottle of wine to listen to the music.

It was not long before he found himself alone at the table and felt the sheen of sweat return to his brow. As circumspectly as he could, Bryn scanned the room for Joranna. He didn't want to have to wander around the room like an idiot trying to find her, so he decided not to make his move until he spotted her.

When he did eventually see her, he hesitated a moment too long. She turned and caught his gaze. He completely lost his nerve and looked away. In that moment the prospect of being run through in the arena felt a lot more comforting than the idea of walking up to Joranna and, in front of dozens of other people, asking to sign her card. Nevertheless, that was what he had to do. He took a fortifying breath, stood and walked across the room to her with as much confidence as he could muster.

'I was wondering if I might have the honour of a dance,' he said, his delivery not nearly as authoritative as he had imagined it would be.

Joranna's expression changed as she regarded him, but she said nothing. Bryn flicked his eyes to the older woman standing to the side, whom Bryn took to be Joranna's chaperone, before flicking back to Joranna. She held out her card, cream with gilt lettering at the top and a small pencil attached by a piece of crimson ribbon. He took it and flipped it open, casting his eyes down the list. He felt his face flush as each line his eyes passed was already filled in. He breathed a sigh of relief when he realised there was one dance, the last, still free. He signed his name.

'I was beginning to run out of excuses,' Joranna said, as Bryn handed her back the card. 'That last spot has been much in demand.'

'I hadn't thought that it would fill so quickly,' Bryn said, realising the implication as soon as the words had left his mouth and wishing he could pull them back in.

'My, my, you are the charmer.' She smiled with mock indignation. 'See you for the last dance.' She turned and walked away in the company of her chaperone, leaving Bryn standing alone feeling more than a little foolish.

Bryn knew it was foolish putting all of his eggs in one basket by not bothering to ask anyone else to dance that night, and letting Joranna see that he wasn't interested in anyone else, but he did so regardless. As the dancing began he idled around the bar chatting with the other bannerets he knew, much of which revolved around making amusing, but disparaging, remarks about those gentlemen present who hadn't been to the Academy.

Eventually the time came for his dance with Joranna. As her card had suggested would be the case, she had not left the floor since the dancing had begun. Bryn had found it difficult to take his eyes off her all night. She moved with practised grace and elegance as though she was floating across the floor in her pale blue gown, and he couldn't help but think she would make a superb duellist, were the sport open to women.

When his turn arrived, he made his way over to her and took her hand.

'Ah, Banneret,' she said. 'From the amount of time you've spent at the bar this evening, I'm surprised you're still able to stand, let alone dance. But it is a little flattering that I'm the only one you've chosen to dance with.'

He hadn't realised that she'd noticed him, and although he'd been far more moderate in his drinking than the others he had been talking to, he was feeling a little more relaxed than he might have otherwise.

'Dancing with anyone else seemed pointless,' he said, trying to sound tongue in cheek.

She smiled and looked at him with teasingly indignant eyes. 'It's an improvement on your last effort, but you're going to have to do better than that.'

Bryn smiled as the music began and he led her in the dance. She was far better than he, but the basic classes he had taken, along with the agility imbued by countless hours of swordplay allowed him to acquit himself reasonably well. However the conversation was stilted, as Bryn needed most of his concentration to keep up with Joranna's greater skill. It was a relief when the music finally ended.

'Thank you for the dance,' Bryn said.

'Thank you, sir,' she said, in the formal fashion. She cast a quick glance at her chaperone who was standing to the side of the dance floor, no doubt ready to drag Bryn away by the ear like a naughty schoolboy if one of his hands wandered too far for propriety.

She produced a small card from somewhere and handed it to him. 'Call on me if you wish. I'll be in the city all winter.'

He went back to the bar where Amero and the others had gathered, feeling very pleased with himself. The ladies at the ball would start to filter away now that the dancing was finished, but some of the men would remain drinking until dawn.

Amero watched him as he approached, a wolfish expression on his face that made Bryn think he was about to be on the receiving end of a ribbing.

'That looked like it went well,' Amero said.

'Reckon so,' Bryn said. He was still waiting for the teasing to start, and didn't want to say anything that would give Amero an opening.

'Courting a girl like that will hit your purse pretty hard, you know.'

'Well, hopefully the five points I picked up in Tanosa means that will no longer be a problem,' Bryn said, still watching Joranna on the other side of the ballroom out of the corner of his eye.

'You never did tell me why you charged out of the city like that with Bautisto,' Amero said. 'The first I knew of it was a note under my door telling me to take a couple of days off.'

The topic surprised Bryn. 'It was last minute. I needed to get a duel and a good spot came up. I didn't really think about it, we just went.'

'All the way to Tanosa? Could you not just have waited until something came along in the city.'

'No,' Bryn said. 'I needed to get one quickly, and it was the first that came along. There was extra money because it was last minute.'

Amero raised his eyebrows. 'Money problems?'

'Nothing serious. I just needed to send a little coin back home.' Bryn felt that he had already said more than he was comfortable revealing. 'Let's have another drink.'

CHAPTER NINETEEN

'I'LL COME RIGHT to the point. I'm still having difficulty in finding you a suitable duel,' Bautisto said.

Bryn felt his heart drop and his muscles tighten with frustration. With the points he had earned in Tanosa he thought he would be able to get regular placings. His disappointment was tinged with anger. What more did he have to do? 'Is there anything on offer at all?'

'Yes, but they're of a lower rank than you now, and the prize purses are low also. The only option that I can think of for you is to take these matches whenever they become available and bide your time until your rank increases to a point where you will have to be offered something better.'

Bryn took a deep breath. He felt a flush of anger, but knew it was not Bautisto's fault and that taking it out on him would be senseless. While the idea of the Ladder was egalitarian and merit based, arena owners were not. All they were interested in was filling seats, and a low ranked, no-name duellist wouldn't do that. He had to build a reputation to get duels, and needed duels to build a reputation. He wanted to scream; not just from rage and frustration, but impotence. What could he do to get his career moving?

Amero on the other hand had a name, and that was drawing

attention from duellists ranked well above him. He might think that a poisoned chalice, but it was one from which Bryn would gladly drink.

'I don't care who they are,' he said. 'I'll fight them. I'll beat them, and I'll force the higher ranks to take notice. Try to get me into as many as you can and I'll rack up enough points to get out of the mire. If that doesn't work, I'll just have to give more serious consideration to going out on the regional circuit. If the schedulers won't take notice on their own, I'll make them.'

Bautisto nodded and smiled at him reassuringly, but it wasn't much consolation. Bryn wondered if it would have been more sensible to take Major dal Damaso's advice after all, and stayed away from the arena altogether.

Amero fought another duel in a boutique arena in Lowgarden, matched against a swordsman of a far higher rank. It seemed the thought of embarrassing the son of an elector count was a very attractive proposition to hard working swordsmen, as it was to promoters seeking to draw a crowd. There was also the added bonus for his opponents of knowing that the crowd Amero drew would ensure a healthy prize purse if they won.

Amero won again, but the victory didn't come easily. Despite being a Banneret of the Blue, there was no substitute for experience in the arena and Bryn had to give credit where it was due; Amero was holding his own in waters that would drown many of his peers. It didn't make his own lack of success any easier to bear, however.

As they left the arena to walk back down toward Oldtown, Amero limping slightly from an unlucky thrust to the thigh, Bryn noticed a vaguely familiar face following them a few paces behind.

'I think there's someone following us,' Bryn said.

'I know. It's Emeric, my father's lap dog.'

Bryn instantly recognised the name, which explained the familiarity. He had been at the Academy under the sponsorship of Amero's father, a senior student—they were known as 'Adepti'—while Amero and Bryn had been Under Cadets. He had been expelled after killing another student in a duel. Some said Emeric was hard done by, others said he had gotten what he had deserved, and the same was said of the student who had been killed. It was one of those things that everyone had seemed to have a different opinion on. Expulsion was the ultimate dishonour for a student, and for many it would be a taint that they would never recover from. Bryn recalled Emeric as being good with a sword—confirmed by the reason for his expulsion—so Amero's father must still have found a use for him, which for the time being was following Amero, presumably having been instructed to keep him out of trouble.

He had aged a little since Bryn had last seen him and taken to shaving his head, but his face was still the same: hard and ruthless. Almost all of the younger students had been terrified of him, Bryn included.

'Why's he following us?'

'My father found out about the duel with dal Strenna. No doubt his father whined that I'd spoiled his idiot son's dashing good looks. Emeric's here to make sure that I don't get myself into any more trouble.'

Bryn could not help but feel relieved by the proposition.

By the arena's door, a group of men had gathered. They were chatting animatedly, about the evening's duels most likely. One of them spotted Amero and must have said something, as the conversation stopped and they all turned to look.

Despite standing more than a foot away from Amero, Bryn could feel his tension increase. The memory of the day that they had met dal Strenna on the street flashed through Bryn's mind and he was suddenly glad of Emeric's glowering presence. He felt his grip tightening on the hilt of his sword. With that many men, if insults were exchanged it was as likely they would fight there and then as deal with things in a civilised manner and postpone it until an appropriate time.

One of them passed a comment, not loud enough for Bryn to hear, but obvious in its content. It was enough to set Amero off. What Bryn did hear was the sound of steel being pulled from its sheath. A hand stopped him from drawing completely. Emeric had covered the distance between them took a firm grip of Amero's arm.

'Now, now,' he said.

His voice was level, but cold and gravelly. Bryn could feel some of the terror that he had inspired in all of the younger students once again.

'This one'll be too messy for it to be worth the effort, and we'd see the inside of a dungeon before the day's out.'

Bryn could see the strain on Emeric's arm as he ensured that Amero did not draw. Finally Amero relaxed, as did Emeric. Amero cast the assembled men a filthy glance and they continued on their way. Bryn breathed a sigh of relief.

'I'm sick of them passing judgment. Everywhere I go it's "ooh look, it's the Count of Moreno's son. Bored and spoiled and making a fool of himself in the arena". Fuck them.'

Bryn had bided his time for what he thought was a sensible period before calling on Joranna, neither wanting to seem too keen nor disinterested. He felt nervous as he hopped up the steps to knock on the door of her family's townhouse and was beginning to wonder if it was all worth the stress. It was the first time he'd had a real interest in the girl he was courting, or seeking to court, and it added a level of pressure that he wasn't comfortable with. He would have been far happier if he was able to maintain a distant lack of concern, but there was no chance of that.

For one who had grown up in an apartment in the centre of the city, her house was an opulent and impressive building. However, sitting on the edge of Highgarden and—as some of the more elitist in Ostenheim put it—precariously close to Lowgarden, it wasn't nearly as grand as the mansions that occupied the higher part of the hill. Lowgarden tended to be the domain of wealthy merchants, professionals and some poorer nobles, and as such was looked down upon by the high aristocracy in Highgarden, both figuratively and literally. Snobbery was rampant in Ostian society and permeated every level of it—Bryn had heard it said the beggars in the Cathedral district were venomously scornful of those resident in Docks, an absurd thought but apparently true nonetheless. Despite it all, Bryn would be very glad if he were ever able to afford to live in Lowgarden.

He waited for a moment after knocking before a servant opened the door.

'I was wondering if Lady dal Verrara was at home today?'

'Senior or junior, sir?'

'Junior, I presume,' Bryn said. 'It's Lady Joranna that I'm looking for.'

'Junior it is, sir. Might I ask who is calling?'

'Banneret of the Blue Bryn Pendollo.'

Bryn raised his eyebrows in surprise when the door was closed. It was usual convention for a caller of rank to be allowed to wait in the hall and Bryn began to wonder if he was being punished for not calling sooner. A few minutes went by before the door opened again.

'My lady will see you, sir. If you would come this way please.'

The servant led him through to a parlour where Joranna was sitting on a sofa, looking slightly flushed, betraying the rush and fuss there must have been when it was announced that there was a gentleman calling for her. Bryn had to suppress a smile at the thought of having won back some of the initiative in their fledgling courtship.

The same older woman that had been with Joranna at the ball sat in the corner of the room, ostensibly reading a book but glancing in his direction as discreetly as she could every few moments.

'Good afternoon, Banneret,' Joranna said, without standing. 'Please sit.' She gestured to the sofa opposite her.

He did as he was bade.

'I was beginning to wonder if you were ever going to call,' she said.

'Well, I've been very busy with training.'

'Ah yes, you're in the arena, I'd almost forgotten. It must be a very exciting lifestyle.'

He wasn't sure if she was teasing him or putting on the display of rigid formality for her chaperone.

'Well, that's what I'm hoping for,' Bryn said, his eyes drifting inquiringly toward the chaperone. 'Right now it's something of a struggle. Getting duels when you're starting off is harder than I thought it would be. I'm hopeful things will pick up though, sooner rather than later.'

She smiled and cast a furtive glance in the direction of her chaperone, giving Bryn reason to believe his second opinion was the correct one.

'I'm afraid that I have other engagements to attend to this afternoon, but I thought that if you were free tomorrow you could call and we could go for a walk.'

'That would be very nice,' Bryn said. 'Tomorrow then.'

'That was well fought, well fought indeed, Banneret.'

Bryn looked up from the leather case that he was putting his duelling sword into. The arena's owner was standing next to him with a broad, toothy smile.

'Thank you.'

'I was speaking with your trainer a little earlier. He mentioned that you've been finding it difficult to get matches.'

It was late in the evening, and Bryn was tired. He was in no mood to speak with anyone, much less make pleasantries with an arena owner.

'It's certainly been more difficult than I was expecting,' Bryn said.

'Yes, that's often the case these days. No one's particularly interested in watching the lower ranked swordsmen duel. That means owners like myself can't afford to host many lower ranked matches.'

'It's unfortunate, but if that's the way things are there's little I can do about it,' Bryn said. There was something about the owner that he didn't like; there was something insincere about him.

The promoter smiled again, confirming Bryn's dislike.

'That might not be entirely the case,' the promoter said. 'I've been thinking for some time about what might bring more people in to watch lower ranked matches, and then something occurred to me.'

Bryn couldn't quite work out what the owner was playing at, but he could tell that he was trying to draw Bryn into the conversation, to pique his interest. He wasn't willing to play along, so he remained silent and stared at the man.

'Well, when I heard from your trainer how eager you are to get more matches, I thought perhaps we could help one another to solve our respective problems.'

Bryn continued to stare.

'The last occasion that this arena was regularly filled was in the period following a death.'

So that was it. The weasel of a man wanted him to kill an opponent. 'If you're still within arm's reach by the time I stand up, there will be a death in this arena, this very evening,' Bryn said, giving the promoter the most venomous look he could muster, while pausing in closing his sword case.

'Now, there's no need for that, all that I meant was that—'

'I'm standing up now,' Bryn said, tensing his legs and making to stand.

The owner scurried away leaving Bryn alone once more. He sighed and slumped. He looked around at the grotty arena as the last of the patrons filed out of the stands toward the exits, not that there had been many present even during the height of the evening's entertainments. Had it really come to the point that he needed to kill someone on the arena floor to get ahead? He had another five points to add to his tally after that evening. Surely that would be enough to improve things?

CHAPTER TWENTY

THERE WAS A slight chill in the air as Bryn strolled with Joranna through one of the parks in Highgarden. Her chaperone, the woman who had been her childhood nanny as it transpired, followed a short distance behind them. After the long, hot summer, the crispness of the early winter evenings was a novel experience. It was dry and made for the perfect evening; many young couples had taken advantage of it.

As they walked, Bryn found it difficult to believe this was his life. He had never been poor, but the parks of Highgarden, the status of a duelling swordsman, and a beautiful aristocrat on his arm represented the culmination of a dream and a lifetime of hard work. It was almost too much to believe. All he needed were regular fixtures, and his life would be perfect.

Joranna was an only child. If Bryn were to marry her, their eldest child would take her family's title. The thought made Bryn want to laugh out loud. He wondered how his father would have reacted if told his grandchildren might bear titles of nobility. It was a gigantic step up the ladder of Ostian society, but Bryn took none of it for granted. It had been earned with blood, sweat, and coin that his family had little enough of. He deserved it, and felt as though his reward for all of that sacrifice was so close, he could almost reach out and touch it.

'So, when will I hear your name mentioned by the criers in Crossways?' Joranna said.

'Ha! Possibly never,' Bryn said. 'Progress is proving to be extremely slow.'

'But you've won all your matches so far. Haven't you?'

Bryn nodded. 'Yes, but there's more to it than that. There're a lot of duellists on the Ladder these days, and half of them are winning their matches. I'm beginning to realise that the crawl up through the bottom ranks is going to take longer than I thought, or I'd like.'

'Oh,' Joranna said, a hint of concern in her voice.

Bryn smiled. 'There's no need for you to give it a second thought though; I'll get there eventually. It'll just take time.'

'I just know how hard you've been working for it,' she said hastily.

It reminded Bryn of something that Amero had said to him, about Joranna's family being poor. He was sure that was of a comparative nature to other aristocrats, but it occurred to him that she might be less than inclined to step out with a penniless swordsman.

Bryn pressed Amero back across the floor of Bautisto's salon, mixing cuts with thrusts, none intended to strike, merely to pressure Amero and tire him. He might be getting choicer duels, but Bryn wanted to constantly assert his skill and make it very clear who the superior swordsman was.

'I hear you were out with Joranna dal Verrara the other night,' Amero said.

If he was hoping to break Bryn's concentration, Amero was labouring in vain. 'How'd you hear about that?'

'I have my sources,' Amero said, dodging Bryn's blade and countering. 'I did mention that her family don't have a pot to piss in?'

Bryn smiled, parrying and retaking the initiative with a riposte. 'Yes, you did.'

They had to speak loudly to be heard over the thud of leather boot soles on the wooden floor and the clash of blades.

'That's all right then,' Amero said. 'I wouldn't want you to get the wrong idea about her.'

Amero came forward with two swipes that Bryn stepped back from. Bautisto had left them to spar while he was out running some errands, trusting them not to slack off.

'Does your mother know you're stepping out with a penniless aristocrat?'

Bryn laughed. 'No, not yet. I wonder if Joranna's parents know she's stepping out with a penniless swordsman.' He lunged forward in riposte to Amero's attacks but was parried away. He hadn't expected Amero to catch it.

'A penniless swordsman with prospects,' Amero said. 'I heard that Mistria was paid a thousand crowns for his last duel. Two more wins with no conceded touches and he'll hit a hundred and twenty-five points.'

Bryn raised his eyebrows at the size of the prize purse and was almost caught off guard by Amero's next attack. His boots thumped out on the wooden floor as he moved abruptly, and more heavily than he would have liked, the sound echoing around the empty shell of a building.

'I expect I have a while to wait before I can demand that size of a purse,' Bryn said.

A thousand crowns was an enormous sum. Not even a drop in the ocean for a wealthy aristocrat, someone of Amero's stature for example, but it was an unimaginable amount for only one duel. Mistria fought at least once a month, usually once every two weeks. Earnings of that amount were verging on being overwhelming to think about. A house in Highgarden, an estate in the country, titles; all of these things were possible with regular earnings like that. The money Bryn had made for his last duel wouldn't even have paid Mistria for the first step he took on his way out to the black line for the start of that duel.

'Probably never if you keep fighting like this.' Amero parried and lunged, following up his barbed comment with another attack.

Bryn forced himself to concentrate and parried both before dancing back out of the way, focussing on staying light on his feet. 'It's enough to keep you on your back foot,' Bryn said, launching into another series of attacks and taking back all the ground Amero had made. 'I hope she isn't counting on me pulling in money like that, though. Setting herself up for a big disappointment if she is.'

Amero attacked with a three-stroke combination. Bryn stepped back, parried twice, dodged and countered. He put a touch on the centre of Amero's chest. Amero acknowledged and they reset to begin once more.

Bryn enjoyed those lazy mornings of swordplay. There was no pressure, no scrutiny, commentary, or verbal abuse from Bautisto. It was swordsmanship plain and simple; in those moments nothing else really mattered. Above all, it was fun.

'What about you?' Bryn said. 'I saw you dancing with some fairly attractive types at the ball last week.'

Amero said nothing for a moment, starting their next bout with two neatly executed thrusts. Bryn could not help but notice how over the past weeks his swordsmanship had really benefitted from Bautisto's tuition.

'I've my mind on someone else right now.'

Intrigued, Bryn raised his eyebrows, but Amero dismissed it with a wave of his hand.

'Nothing but a little trifle,' he said. 'It's not like I have any real say in who I end up with anyway.'

Amero's face darkened. It was something Bryn had noticed happening more and more often. He found it just as unsettling every time.

'My future in that regard has been long since planned out for me. I've been betrothed since the moment they knew I was a boy,' Amero said.

'Really?' Bryn said, lowering his sword. 'You've never mentioned that before.'

Amero shrugged, but his face turned melancholy. 'My mother made the match. It's a good one, and I'll abide by her wishes.' His face brightened again, but it looked forced. 'Not to worry though, I've a couple of years left to enjoy myself before then!'

He continued his attack, fast and determined and Bryn strained to defend. So much of Amero's life was dictated to by expectation and it was clear how much he hated the fact. All the same, with the wealth, titles and privilege that would be his, it was difficult to pity him his situation. However, none of it managed to distract Bryn from his surprise at how much better Amero was getting.

In the days that followed, Bryn began to see less and less of Amero outside of the salon and more of Joranna. For the most part they went their separate ways each day after training instead of spending several hours enjoying a lazy lunch and chatting as they had in the past. On the occasions they did, Amero seemed distant and was poor company.

Each evening, which ordinarily would have been spent reading in his apartment before an early night, Bryn now called on Joranna and spent the time walking with her in Highgarden or taking tea at her house, all under the watchful gaze of her former nanny.

He fought another duel, one that would have been as unremarkable as his previous were it not for the fact that it put him within reach of a tally of twenty Ladder points, the level at which he hoped his advance would quicken. As he was walking back to the Bannerets' Enclosure, he had spotted someone sitting in the audience who seemed peculiarly out of place.

A bald man with a neat beard had been watching him. He was sitting too far away for Bryn to be able to make him out during the duel, and was obscured from sight when Bryn was sitting in the small enclosure. It seemed almost too much to believe that the star of the moment would deign to visit a small, out of the way arena to watch unknown duellists, but Bryn would have sworn the bald man was Panceri Mistria.

CHAPTER TWENTY-ONE

BRYN LOOKED OVER the family accounts one last time in the forlorn hope of seeing something different. The numbers were depressing. His mother worked as a seamstress, and Gilia was a governess to a wealthy family in Highgarden, but their income was consistently below their weekly expenses. Even with a duel on the level he was getting intermittently, every week, there would not be much left over to live on. His own expenses—salon fees, entry fees, maintaining his equipment—were not insubstantial, and the money he could add to his family's accounts was not enough to cover all the expenses.

He took a deep breath to calm himself and looked around. There was nothing in his tiny apartment to distract him from his worries for even a moment. No matter what way he looked at it, the problem seemed insurmountable. The fat, greasy promoter who suggested he kill someone in the arena popped back into his head. People died there from time to time; it was a risk every duelling swordsman accepted when going into the arena. He pushed the idea from his head, disgusted with himself for giving it even a moment's consideration. Unintentionally killing a man in the heat of a duel was one thing, walking into the arena to kill a man to further his career was a stain on his honour he would never be able to erase.

There was a knock at his door. He was glad of the distraction and got up from his desk to see who it was. He opened the door to a cloaked and hooded figure, and suddenly regretted not having his sword closer to hand. Ostenheim was a dangerous city; robbery and murder were common.

'Can I help you?' he said.

'I certainly hope so,' a feminine voice said. Joranna cast the hood back and smiled mischievously. 'Aren't you going to invite me in?'

'I'm not sure that's proper,' he said. 'I've my reputation to think of.' He feigned as self-righteous a pose as he could. Then it occurred to him that trying to be funny could cause more problems than it was worth, so he gestured for her to enter.

She walked around looking at the bare walls before turning to him and smiling. 'The luxurious life of an arena star.'

'I haven't really been here all that long, there hasn't been time to—'

'That's all right,' she said. 'Boys are rarely good at making their domains look any better than a cave. I have three cousins in the city. Their apartments make this one look like a palace.'

'I'm afraid that I don't have anything to offer you to drink; I'm not accustomed to visitors.'

'No, that much is obvious,' she said. 'I'm not thirsty though.'

'No chaperone tonight?' Bryn said. He was unsure of what she was doing there, and was trying to tread carefully. He had sneaked girls back to his room at the Academy on occasion, but then, the worst an unwanted suggestion had garnered was a slap in the face. He didn't want to make a mistake with Joranna.

'No, I'm in disguise. Hence my rather lovely travelling cloak.'

She swirled it about and Bryn wondered how she had come by such a mouldering old rag. He also wondered what possessed

her to allow it anywhere near the rest of her clothes, which were
of a far finer order.

'So,' he said, letting the word hang on the air for a moment.
'What brings you to my cave-like dwelling at this late hour?'

'No chaperone. In disguise. What do you think?'

Amero was alone in the salon; Bautisto was out arranging a
match and Bryn had scuttled off as soon as training had finished to spend time with dal Verrara. His own matches had been
growing increasingly difficult, but he was coping—and doing
better than he had expected. The daunting prospect of fighting
far more experienced duellists had passed and the odds against
him no longer seemed insurmountable.

On graduating from the Academy, he had felt as though he
knew everything. He had finished second in his class, the highest ranking that any member of his family had ever managed
to achieve, and was one of very few who had gone on to take
the Blue. He had no doubt that if he had applied himself a little
harder, he would have taken that year's sword of honour for
graduating first, an accolade that had gone to Bryn. The amount
he had learned since leaving astounded him. The sessions with
the mage allowed him to train longer and harder, to pack years
into months.

He realised now that the Academy was only a beginning.
The true learning came after, and he felt that the quality of his
opponents had accelerated the process. He knew that Bryn
thought himself the better of the two. Even his friends thought,
deep down, that he was nothing more than the product of a fortunate birth. It was difficult to remain friends so long as Bryn
held that opinion, but Amero knew that he would not be able
to do so for much longer. Each day their sparring grew closer.
There was little to separate them now, if anything.

He knew that his father expected him to have long given up

on the idea of duelling. They had not spoken since Renald had appeared at the arena that evening, and that bothered him. He knew that Renald had not let the matter go, and it worried him that he had not encountered his father's involvement. Renald was planning something, and the not knowing was worse than having to deal with it.

All he had planned to do was express his independence. The Academy had shielded him from his father's control for so long, but he always knew it would be waiting for him when he graduated. Defying Renald had felt good, but that was all it had been about. At first.

Now, there was far more to it than just the opportunity to assert himself. Amero had gotten a thrill from duelling, a rush of excitement that was both intoxicating and addictive from the outset. The fear of making a fool of himself—the danger of being considered an idiot, an idler and a wastrel—had stirred him like nothing before. He was hungry for the chance to stick it in the face of everyone who tittered behind their hands at the idea of an elector count's son making a spectacle of himself like a common banneret in the arena. It fuelled his desire to succeed. That initial thrill faded with familiarity, but it was replaced with something far more enrapturing. Power.

Many duellists spoke of the effect a crowd could have on them. How their support could lift them to snatch victory from the jaws of certain defeat, and fill them with such energy that they kept coming back to the arena for that reason alone. It was always what former duellists said they missed the most.

What none of them ever commented on, at least not to Amero's knowledge, was the power. A truly talented swordsman, one with flair and a sense of the dramatic, could grab hold of a spectator and take them on an adventure of every emotion. He could inspire such love or hatred that they would fight in the stands, riot on the streets, and murder each other in tavern arguments. The boost their passion could give in the arena was all well and good, but it was inspiring that fervour that caught Amero's imagination. It gave him a hold over people. Control. With it, a man could do anything.

He thought of the powerful men of the city, the Duke, the Master of the Guilds, the head of Austorgas' Banking House. Could any of them incite tens of thousands of people to the heights of passion in a few moments? He knew that they couldn't. He also knew that he could. He thought of his father, running all across the Duchy at the Duke's command like a faithful hunting dog, convinced of his infallibility but never seeing that he was merely a servant himself. With the arena, Amero could wrap the mob of Ostenheim around his little finger. The man who could control the masses had the real power. What would his father, with all his schemes and plots and intrigues in the corridors of the Barons' Hall, think of that?

He smiled and went through the movement he had been working on again. He could only practice it in private, when neither Bautisto nor Bryn were around. Bautisto would lambast him for being too flashy, and Bryn would tut at him for not doing as he was told. Both would question how he was able to cope with the additional workload.

Bautisto's technique might be effective, but it was dull. His swordplay would never inspire the passion of a spectator, probably the reason he was reduced to teaching two students in a rundown little salon thousands of miles from his home. It might win duels, but winning alone was not enough. Not for Amero.

He took from Bautisto what he thought was useful: economy of movement, superb fitness and a ruthless approach to taking points, and blended them with ideas of his own. Sweeps, flourishes, twists and spins could all be injected if a swordsman was clever about it. There was no need to mire himself in stolid swordplay so long as he was careful. A flourishing follow through after a scoring touch did nothing but inflame a crowd. He just needed to be sure of the scoring touch first.

Leaving himself open after a miss would quickly lead to disaster. Everything needed to be perfect before he could risk using it. That was the reason for his secret, after-hours practice.

Amero heard a knock at the door, but was so focussed on what he was doing it had opened before he had the chance to react. He expected Bautisto to walk in, so he immediately reverted to the economical movements the Estranzan espoused; anything like what he had just been doing would attract heavy criticism. It was not Bautisto however, but a man Amero could not recall seeing before.

'I'm looking for the maestro of this salon,' the man said.

Swordsmen, young or old, always had a particular bearing about them—good posture and an expression that some might call haughty—and this fellow was no different. The man's hair and moustache were both salt-and-pepper grey, but there was no mistaking that he had once been, and perhaps still was, a regular practitioner of swordsmanship. He had the athletic bearing of a man who spent little time at rest and the confidence of one who knew how to handle himself.

'I'm afraid he's not here,' Amero said.

'Ah. A shame.' The man looked around the warehouse that passed for their salon, but his face didn't betray what he was thinking. He nodded to Amero before putting his wide brimmed hat back on and making to leave.

'Perhaps I can be of assistance. I could pass on a message if you like,' Amero said, intrigued by what might bring a man like that to Bautisto's all but anonymous salon.

'Yes, that would be kind of you. I am Banneret of the Blue Arfeni Caxto, I'm an assistant to Maestro Valdrio, trainer to Banneret of the Blue Panceri Mistria.'

Amero nearly dropped his sword. What was this man doing in Bautisto's dump of a salon?

'A student of this salon has come to Banneret Mistria's attention, as has the Estranzan style he uses. The Banneret would very much like to test himself against this technique. The swordsman I'm looking for is Banneret of the Blue Bryn Pendollo.'

For a moment Amero had dared hope that it was he who Caxto was looking for. A fight against Mistria would be of massively high profile. To win against him would be momentous. In one duel, he could achieve what would take him a year or more otherwise. There would not be a single person, aristocrat or commoner who could lay a single valid criticism against him after that. The mob would be speaking his name for weeks. How in hells had Mistria spotted Bryn fighting in rural and back alley rat-pits?

'I'm afraid that Banneret Pendollo no longer trains here,' Amero said. 'He's moved out onto the provincial circuit. I'm sure with a little effort he could be tracked down...'

'No, I don't think time would allow for that. It's a pity. Banneret Mistria was hoping to make the duel something of an exhibition of the disparate styles shortly after he achieves one hundred and twenty-five.'

'Well, I'm trained in the Estranzan style. Until recently Banneret Pendollo was my training partner.'

'Really? Your name?'

'Banneret of the Blue Amero,' he hesitated before saying his surname, 'dal Moreno.' He expected to feel guilt grow inside him, but he felt nothing.

Caxto's face didn't show any sign of reaction. 'I believe I've heard your name mentioned. I shall have to consult the Banneret, but that might be acceptable. He's eager to show how the Ostian style of swordsmanship is superior to all others. An Estranzan style is the only one remaining for me to find, and there seems to be a dearth of Estranzans in the city. I'll call again with the Banneret's response, one way or the other.'

Amero thought fast. 'As no doubt you can see from the state of the salon, we're in the process of moving to new premises. It might be easiest to contact me at this address.' He walked forward quickly and proffered one of his calling cards, which would direct Caxto to his Oldtown apartment.

Caxto took it and gave the card a cursory glance. 'Very well.' Caxto clicked his heels together and nodded. 'Good day.'

As he exited, Bautisto arrived. He nodded politely to the departing man before entering the salon.

'Who was that?' Bautisto asked.

Amero hesitated for a moment. 'Just someone looking for directions.'

CHAPTER TWENTY-TWO

'HAVE YOU HEARD?' Bautisto said, his voice filled with a giddy excitement that Bryn had never encountered in him before.

'Heard what?'

'Mistria's trainer contacted Amero. Mistria wants to fight an exhibition match with someone trained in the Estranzan style.'

'Really?' Bryn was too surprised to say anything else. Amero was lurking at the back of the salon, working against a practice dummy, so focussed that he hadn't even looked up when Bryn arrived.

'Indeed. Quite a thing, wouldn't you say?' Bautisto said.

It was an astonishing development. He thought immediately of the man he had seen at the arena, the one he thought to be Mistria. Had he been wrong about that? He preferred to think that he was mistaken rather than that Mistria had chosen Amero over him, but deep down he knew he wasn't. Had Amero surpassed him in the time since they had left the Academy? Or was it his name, once again? The news felt like a kick in the stomach.

'It's fantastic news. Not just for Amero, but you,' Bryn said. 'You'll have students flocking to your door after this.'

'Ha. Assuming Amero acquits himself well. We'll have to make sure that he does. Good news for you too, though. Every promoter will know of this salon and its style, and will want someone who can duel in it for their billings.'

Bryn felt his heart sink a little farther. With this match looming on the horizon, the focus of their training would all be on Amero; it had to be. As much as he wanted to help, it would be to Bryn's disadvantage. There were a great many things he needed to focus on, but once again, dealing with them would be put off.

'I want you to take the rest of the day off,' Bautisto said. 'Be back at eight bells in the morning. We've a couple of hard weeks ahead of us. This might be an exhibition match, but we will treat it as the opportunity it is. Don't forget, if Amero does well, you will benefit also. Everyone will want to fight a student of the Estranzan School. And of this salon.'

'He will have fought between three and five exhibition bouts before he gets to you. Even a man like Mistria will be starting to fatigue at that point. Speed and movement will be the key to beating him,' Bautisto said.

'I don't think I'm supposed to beat him,' Amero said.

Bryn smiled, but knew what the reward for laughing out loud would be so he bit his lip to stifle it.

'If you walk into the Amphitheatre without the desire to win and the complete commitment to achieving that, then you have no right to be there. Win or lose, no matter. You are only truly beaten when you do not try your hardest.'

It was decent advice, and toned down from Bautisto's usual attacking attitude, perhaps conceding the unrealistic quality of expecting victory. The momentary display of sensitivity did nothing to soften what Bryn knew was coming next. If Bautisto wanted Amero to try and tire Mistria out, it meant he would drive them into the ground over the coming days to make sure Amero could grind Mistria down.

Bryn had arranged to meet Joranna and her chaperone by the entrance to one of the parks in Highgarden. He waited by the wrought iron gates and stared at the swirling light of the mage lamp on the gatepost opposite him. He drummed his fingers against his thigh and leaned against the gatepost as couples passed by, entering and leaving the park. Still he waited.

The sound of the cathedral bell chiming eight times drifted across the crisp evening air, and that was enough for Bryn. It wasn't especially cold, but he had been waiting there long enough for the tip of his nose and fingers to feel it. Puzzled, he started for home.

Bryn sat at the desk in his apartment, staring at a blank piece of paper, his pen poised to strike. He was angry, and knew it was never a good idea to put pen to paper when in a bad mood. There was also a lurking sense of worry. He hadn't known Joranna all that long, but he felt he knew her well enough to be concerned by the fact that she hadn't shown up.

He had thought about calling at her house, but decided against it. Nonetheless, he couldn't let the matter go unaddressed—it was dominating his thoughts, and try as he might, he couldn't push it from them. He was sure she had a good reason for standing him up, but somewhere in the pit of his stomach, doubt lurked. He grimaced, and set pen to paper.

Bryn didn't know how Amero was feeling, but in the days leading up to the Mistria exhibition duel he felt virtually indestructible. The intense days of training had left them lean and finely tuned. Muscles that had been coated with a cushion of fat were now sinewy and defined. He had never felt as light on his feet or as fast in his reactions. He only hoped that he had a duel of his own soon, so he could take advantage of his superb conditioning, which he knew would be impossible to maintain in the long term without burning out. Amero had gained so much from his regular matches, far more than Bryn would have thought possible, so he knew training could never match the real thing. He needed regular duels of his own if he was to keep up, and soon.

As well as his concern about his professional prospects, Joranna standing him up was still playing on his mind. He had only sent her the note the day before, but had yet to hear anything back. Her behaviour came as a confusing surprise, and he could not help but wonder if the novelty of stepping out with an impecunious banneret had worn off.

CHAPTER TWENTY-THREE

THE ATMOSPHERE IN the Amphitheatre was electric. With all the additional matches being fought that evening, admittance to the enclosure was limited, meaning Amero had only been able to take Bautisto in with him. It meant Bryn had to sit in the crowd with the other spectators, but he was enjoying the experience—the Amphitheatre was such an energising place it was difficult not to get carried away by the excitement.

The early arrangement of the exhibition match did not prove to be premature, as Mistria had achieved his one hundred and twenty-five points the week before it was due to take place. He had rounded up a half dozen proponents of different styles, the plan being to fight them one after another in a gala spectacular. It sent a tingle down Bryn's spine to think that in a few moments he would watch a close friend step out into the Amphitheatre, the greatest of all the arenas in Ostenheim, perhaps even the world, and face one of the greatest swordsmen to have lived.

Mistria had already fought a Mirabayan, a Ruripathian, and an Auracian by the time Amero's turn came. He defeated them all in fine fashion but in a way that made it clear this was an exhibition rather than a competition.

Bryn watched Amero and Bautisto go through their

warm-up routine, keenly feeling left out. As cool as he had been up to that point, Bryn could see Amero's face grow pale and his movement gave away how tense he was getting as his match drew closer.

The final match was to be the true highlight of the evening's entertainment, the one after Amero's. Mistria would face a Shandahari, from the exotic country far to the south. It had never been part of the long defunct empire that the other nations around the Middle Sea had once formed, and maintained a mysterious curiosity as a result. Bryn had never seen a Shandahari swordsman before, although he had read about them in his studies. Despite the fact that his friend was due to fight in what would perhaps be a career highlight, Bryn was looking forward to that final display the most.

Large and well built, Mistria was an imposing figure, even from the distant seat Bryn occupied. He stood alone in the centre of the Amphitheatre—as comfortable there, the centre of attention of tens of thousands of people, as he would be in private. He was the epitome of a champion.

Bryn glanced at the seat next to him, which was conspicuously vacant—he had considered inviting Joranna to come along, but decided against it at the last moment. He had still not received any response to his letter. It made him angry to think about it, and threatened to spoil the evening for him, so he did his best to forget about her.

The Amphitheatre's atmosphere was always as much of an experience as the duelling itself. To see so many people in one place could be overwhelming. He couldn't begin to imagine what it was like to be out there in the centre of it all, with every pair of eyes fixed on you. He wondered how Amero would cope.

The noise was also something to take in. In the small arenas that Bryn had fought in, one could generally hear an individual's voice. Here, with so many thousands, they blended into something entirely more potent. At times the sound was so powerful and so tangible it felt like a great wave rushing through the air. As the crowd waited for the next duel, their voices dropped to no more than a subdued murmur, like the sea receding from the shore in preparation for the next great wave.

When Amero took his first tentative step out into the sandy oval in the centre of the Amphitheatre, the volume and focus of all of those murmurs began to change, the energy behind them gathering like the heat of the morning sun.

He looked so lonely making his way out to Mistria who remained where he was, standing tall and confident, basking in the adoration of his audience and the success of his victories. The distance was more than twice that of any of the arenas either of them had previously fought in, and with each step Amero took, Bryn could feel his heart pound. It was a particularly warm evening, but that wasn't the cause of the sweat on Bryn's brow. He realised that his knuckles were white where he had been gripping the edge of the bench, as he lived each moment with Amero.

Finally Amero reached the black line, the Master of Arms, and Mistria. There was the usual brief discussion as both men were told the rules. Then they were facing one another opposite the black line, saluting. Bryn's heartbeat hastened once again. It felt as though it was straining against the confines of his chest.

'Duel!'

Mistria danced forward, his blade flashing in the evening sunlight. It was clear he intended to put on a good show, and Amero was able to move backward—a little heavy on his feet, Bryn thought—and parry the challenge with no difficulty. He made a tentative riposte that Mistria seemed happy to encourage; swordsmen in the arena were not just warriors, they were also showmen. The accommodation seemed to give Amero confidence. His movement grew lighter, more fluid.

Mistria burst into a flurry of action. Fast, aggressive,

dazzling; it was everything that he was famed for. Somehow Amero managed to avoid his blade, stepping away or parrying with aplomb. Bryn hardly recognised him as he dealt with everything Mistria had to throw at him. It was not the tight, economical movement that Bautisto had been beating into them for weeks. Far from it. There were flourishing follow-throughs and elaborate feints. It was something that Bryn had seen glimpses of when Amero was messing about, but never in such a polished form.

The engagement ended in stalemate. From Mistria's movement it was clear that he had expected to score a touch and was both disappointed and surprised. The crowd seemed to feel likewise, their collective sound shaped into a puzzled murmur. Amero hung back, wary of his famous opponent but not appearing in any way unnerved by the intensity of the onslaught he had just been subjected to.

Mistria came at him again, stamping forward hard with his front foot as he cut at Amero with speed that was almost impossible to follow. His attack spoke his intention as clearly as though he had said it aloud. He would put manners on this young upstart. Bryn couldn't hear the sounds of the blades clashing over the noise of the audience, but he knew it was there and his imagination filled in the missing pieces.

They locked blades, pressing against one another for a moment before pushing apart. Amero pounced; a leap forward brought him back within striking distance and he thrust. A touch. The first point conceded by Mistria in over twenty-five duels. Bryn had to remind himself to breathe.

The crowd gasped, as did Bryn. He couldn't believe what he had just witnessed. The match was an exhibition—the scores didn't count toward the Ladder—but that did nothing to lessen what Bryn and the tens of thousands there that evening had just seen. There were many swordsmen considered great in their own right who had not managed to do what Amero had just done.

Mistria himself didn't seem to be able to believe it. He stood motionless for a moment, before the Master of Arms gestured for him to take his place at the black line once again. They saluted and restarted.

Mistria pushed Amero back a dozen paces or more, attacking high and low, a deluge of steel that would overwhelm a lesser swordsman. From the intensity of the way he fought it was clear that Mistria no longer considered this to be a simple exhibition match. A low ranked swordsman had affronted his honour and he couldn't let that stand. Bryn grimaced as he watched the exchange; Amero was running backwards as he attempted to stay out of the way of Mistria's blade.

It wasn't enough. Mistria's sword found its way through and the score was one touch each. The crowd roared in appreciation as both swordsmen walked back to the black line. The audience was getting far more of a show for their admission fee than any of them had expected.

Amero still held his head high. What he had already achieved was beyond all expectation and surely the cruel whispers would be quelled now. As they stepped up to the black line they were both animated, gently bouncing on the balls of their feet. Both men wanted the win, and it was obvious they both thought they could get it. The Master of Arms spoke to them briefly and they were off.

Mistria didn't seem content to let his young challenger have any respite. Once again he pressed Amero back the length of the sandy oval in which they fought. Amero didn't retreat as quickly this time. His face was a picture of concentration as he parried Mistria's blade each time it came for him.

His style came as the biggest surprise to Bryn. Amero had shown hints of it clowning around after training, but here it was in a complete and usable fashion. It was sweeping and flamboyant but at the same time there seemed to be nothing that was wasteful or without purpose. There was little Amero could do with it under such an intense barrage of steel, however. His defence faltered. The third touch of the match came and it was two to Mistria.

Amero wore a white doublet with gold embroidery. It looked dashing, but too ostentatious for Bryn's taste. Amero's concern for styling seemed to be greater than for function. The material looked too light to provide the protection a duelling doublet ordinarily would, and he was now enjoying the reward of that choice. The white cloth had parted, showing a red line of blood on his left breast. It required some effort to make an arena duelling blade draw blood; its tip was dull and rounded like a butter knife, but in a heated exchange it was possible to cut with one, intentionally or not, and even kill.

Bryn strained his eyes to see how severe the wound was, but Amero was too far to be sure one way or the other. The way he was moving suggested that it was little more than a graze, but as Bryn squinted in the evening light he could make out the expression on Amero's face; the same twist of rage he had seen on it so many times of late. He was hurt, and that angered him.

As the Master of Arms reset the duel, Bryn could feel the tension in the audience ease. After the first touch, they had been agitated to a near frenzy. Now, however, the duel was falling into line with everyone's expectations and the emotion waned. Mistria had retaken the initiative, and everyone expected the result to be a foregone conclusion.

It seemed as though Mistria thought the same as the crowd. There was less purpose in his movement when he made his way over the black line after the re-start, pushing Amero back with more showman-like blade work. Bryn watched Amero's face, still unchanged from a moment before. Harsh. Against the flow of play, Amero struck, tight and precise, nothing showy—far more characteristic of what Bautisto was teaching them. Bryn felt his heart leap. Amero held the pose of a perfectly executed thrust, hand high, blade angled down. Mistria stood, looking down, his sword arm slowly falling.

Amero took a step back and returned to his guard position. Mistria fell to the ground. Only now did Bryn notice that the crowd had fallen silent. Utterly silent. He could hear the wooden bench beneath him creak as he shifted around to get a better view. The Master of Arms rushed forward to Mistria's fallen form. Amero remained stock still, watching.

The Master of Arms gestured to the Bannerets' Enclosure and several men ran out. One of them Bryn recognised, Caxto, a trainer he had spoken with the day that he had called at the salon Mistria trained in. Still the crowd was silent, everyone straining forward in the hope of being able to identify the gravity of the wound. No one could quite believe what they were seeing; the greatest swordsman of his generation, Mistria of One Hundred and Twenty-Five, the First Blade of Ostia, lying on the sand of the Amphitheatre having not just conceded a touch, but also a wound that had dropped him to the ground.

Unable to contain himself any longer, Bryn rushed down to the Bannerets' Enclosure. Amero began his walk back there, casting looks back over his shoulder to the drama on the arena floor, uncertain as to what was happening or what he should do.

Bryn got to the boundary of the Enclosure where a guard barred his entry. Over the man's shoulder he could see Bautisto, staring intently out at the commotion in the centre of the Amphitheatre.

'Maestro Bautisto,' Bryn shouted.

Bautisto looked toward the shout, audible against the backdrop of silence, and walked over. He spoke with the guard, who let Bryn through. Together they stood watching and waiting for Amero to get to them. Mistria had not moved since Amero stepped back, still lying on the sand, surrounded by his attendants. Gradually the noise in the Amphitheatre began to build, as people started to suspect the worst. All of those who had been lost for words found their tongues once more. It was not Mistria's name on their lips, however. A great swordsman was loved by many; a great champion was loved by more, but one who would kill in the arena thrilled them all like no other.

When Amero reached them, Bautisto immediately went to examine the wound on his chest. Amero stood with casual indifference and allowed Bautisto to inspect the rent in his doublet without even so much as a look over his shoulder. His face had grown cold and impassive. A steward handed him a beaker of water. Amero handed his sword to Bryn with a nod of thanks and took the beaker, otherwise ignoring the steward. He took a long drink, gulping down half of the beaker's contents. Only when a stretcher was brought out from the enclosure did he turn to take another look at what was happening on the arena floor.

'Not much more than a scratch,' Bautisto said. 'You were lucky. Mistria, it seems, was less so. A damnable shame.'

His words were harder than Bryn would have expected. There was no hint of congratulation.

Amero was completely unperturbed by the scene unfolding out on the arena sand. Bryn was unsure if it was genuine insouciance or feigned out of a sense of professional experience. Swordsmen died in the arena; it was not the first time and it would not be the last. That didn't make it any less tragic in Bryn's mind. Amero's countenance made him wonder if it was an accident or intended, though.

There was little sympathy on display from the audience as Mistria's body was carried from the Amphitheatre floor. Conversation carried on as normal, and Bryn could have sworn he heard one person ask a steward if the final fight against the Shandahari would be going ahead now with Amero instead. It made Bryn feel sick. Moments before, Mistria had been their hero. Now he was a prone, covered shape on a stretcher and nothing more. A defeated hero was just defeated. An announcement had yet to be made to the audience, but there could be little doubt in anyone's mind by now that Mistria had met his end on Amero's blade.

Bautisto took Amero away, thinking it better that he was quickly gone in the event of the crowd turning nasty. Mistria's body was brought though the Bannerets' Enclosure, where those present showed their respect, all knowing that on a different day any one of them might be leaving the arena floor in a similar fashion. The audience on the other hand merely grumbled that their night's entertainment had been cut short.

CHAPTER TWENTY-FOUR

AMERO WAS LYING on his living room couch, his eyes closed as he visualised a combination of feints and attacks that he wanted to practice later that day. He swished his hand through the air, pronating and supinating his wrist to follow the imagined movements.

'Is this how you spend your day?'

Amero opened his eyes with a start. He had been so caught up in his thoughts that he hadn't heard his father come into the room. Amero would be sure to have words with his butler for allowing Renald in unannounced.

'That was how I plan to win my next duel,' Amero said. He stood and straightened his clothes, the skin across his chest still tight from the partly healed wound.

'Any hope I had for keeping that carry on quiet has well and truly vanished. It almost amuses me, the lengths you will go to defy me.'

'Is there a point to your being here? I would have thought it abundantly clear by now that I'm not leaving the arena until it suits me.'

'You're my only heir, so I can't disinherit you, but if you stay in the arena it will be without my money. You'll have to wait till I'm dead before you see another penny of it.'

'You can stuff your money. I'll be able to name my price in the arena now.'

Amero could see the vein in his father's head pulse. He was furious, but there was nothing he could do. The threat of cutting off his allowance had come far too late.

Renald pursed his lips and took a deep breath. 'What is it that so attracts you to the arena? There are plenty of other less public ways to defy me. If only you knew what was being said in the Barons' Hall.'

'If only I cared,' Amero said. 'Although I wonder how many of *them* are the topic of conversation for every man in the city? Imagine what could be achieved with that kind of influence.'

'And how long do you think that will last?' Renald said dismissively.

'For as long as I keep winning.'

Nobody could have predicted what the next few days would be like for Amero. He had gone from being talked about as a spoilt rich boy who was getting duels far beyond his worth to being the giant slayer, the most dangerous young blade to arrive in the arena since… ever. While he had been known among the elite of Highgarden for some time—the subject of conversation at expensive coffee houses, card tables, and brothels—beyond that, his profile had been low. To the crowd, the mob, the city's masses, he had been an unknown. People would be aware of the name dal Moreno, some might even remember that there had been a duke by that name some decades before. Few if any would have known that the current heir of that family was making his way in the arena.

Now all of that had changed. Bryn thought it unlikely that there was a single person in the city who had not heard his name and what he had done, even if they wouldn't have been able to put a face to it. There was a constant stream of callers to the salon and Bryn had to fight his way through a crowd of them—young women mainly—to get in each morning. Amero had been forced to sneak in through the back alleys and a window to avoid them, and for the sake of convenience Bryn was considering starting to do the same.

As well as the star-struck, there were also a number of serious individuals who condescended to pay a visit to the shabby salon in Docks. The first of these was the promoter from the Amphitheatre. Usually only those who graced the first few pages of the Ladder would ever have the chance to meet Ricoveri dal Corsi, a burly old banneret with a bushy white moustache and a waistline that in circumference appeared likely to exceed his height.

Not a week after Amero slew Mistria, dal Corsi breezed into the salon as though his arrival would be greeted with the same joy as one hundred beautiful women bearing pots of gold.

He walked a few paces into the salon, stopped and looked about, no doubt thinking that he still cut a dashing, youthful figure—if indeed he ever had—while in reality he appeared ridiculous, stitched into a civilian outfit of martial cut, as often favoured by those bannerets who had never gravitated toward military service. The sword strapped around his waist looked pathetically small in comparison to his significant rotundity.

Two assistants followed on his coattails, both unremarkable in all regards other than bearing the appearance of those who have had any notions of independent thought beaten out of them.

'I am Banneret Ricoveri dal Corsi. Where is the Maestro of this salon?' He addressed Bryn as though he were talking to a disliked servant. 'And the hero of the hour, dal Moreno? Where is he?'

His demands placed, Bryn held no more interest for him. He continued to look about with apparent disdain, no doubt expecting that his words would be acted upon with haste. Bryn did as he was requested grudgingly, aware of the fact that rubbing dal Corsi up the wrong way could negatively impact his own career. Amero had yet to arrive at the salon; since the fêted day, he had been making his appearance at increasingly late hours. When he did arrive his eyes were red and carried black bags beneath them. He stank of smoke and booze, and on more than one occasion Bryn was confident that he was still wearing the clothes that he had been in the day before.

All of the old aristocratic friends that had been too busy to see him after his bad behaviour were suddenly available once again, and the resulting contact with their idle and decadent ways appeared to be having an impact on him. It seemed that the very habits he had declared himself to be going to the arena to avoid were those that he was now increasingly drawn to.

Bryn fetched Bautisto from the back room where he was going through some paperwork.

'I am Maestro Bautisto.' He wiped ink from his fingers with a rag as he walked toward the new arrival.

'Ah, the Estranzan, good. I want to discuss appearance terms with your protégé. Get him into the Amphitheatre regular.' Dal Corsi spoke in the clipped sentences favoured by the older generation in Ostenheim, but that style of speech had long since fallen out of fashion and Bryn found it difficult not to see him as a parody of a bygone generation. At his weight and age, it was something of a wonder that he was not bygone himself.

Bautisto gestured to Bryn, who stood to his right. 'I appreciate your offer, but I think my protégé here would benefit from a little more time and experience at modest venues before making that step.'

It took dal Corsi a moment to realise that Bautisto was referring to Bryn. It took him a moment longer to realise that Bautisto had known that it was Amero he was referring to, and that Bautisto was trifling with him.

'Not him, you bloody fool. The giant killer: dal Moreno. I

don't appreciate being toyed with. You'll get the same rates that I offer all newcomers to the Amphitheatre, and less if you try and lead me a merry dance. Now where is he?'

There was something innately unpleasant about those accustomed to always getting their own way. This was all the more so when that individual held too much influence to be told where to stick their demands, as Bryn would be sorely tempted to do were he in Bautisto's position.

The window rattled as it was opened and Amero stumbled through, bearing the same bedraggled appearance that he had each morning since fighting Mistria. He walked toward them and looked to Bryn with raised eyebrows and bloodshot eyes.

'This is he,' Bautisto said.

Dal Corsi stepped forward, clicked his heels and bowed his head, the mark of respect a banneret made when not holding a sword, and the first social grace displayed by him thus far. 'Pleased to meet you, young man. I am Banneret Ricoveri dal Corsi.'

It seemed that he felt that this was all the introduction that was necessary. Granted Bryn had recognised the name; Amero on the other hand did not.

'So?' Amero said, looking to be caught somewhere between puzzled and irritated.

'Banneret dal Corsi is the scheduler for the Amphitheatre,' Bryn said, quietly.

Not missing a beat, Amero picked up the cue, his demeanour changing instantly. 'A pleasure to meet you, Banneret. How may I be of assistance?'

'It is I who will be of assistance, young man.'

Dal Corsi clearly saw gold coins fluttering through the air each time he looked at Amero. Bryn felt his loathing for the man grow.

'After your magnificent show the other day the duelling committee at the Amphitheatre are in agreement that it would be a frightful waste for you to have to return to backstreet arenas until you've worked your way up the ranks of the Ladder. Already there are many top tier swordsmen clamouring for the chance to face you. I think they're worried people will think them afraid of being shown up by a young upstart.' He chortled, sounding and looking very like one of the walruses at the city menagerie.

'That's a very attractive prospect,' Amero said. 'The terms?'

'Ha! Straight to business. Excellent. It's always easier to work with a swordsman who knows business is as important as steel.'

Dal Corsi beckoned to one of his assistants, who scurried forward and took a page from his satchel. Amero took it and began to scrutinise it with his red, tired eyes. The smell of alcohol, smoke and the crumpled clothing seemed to have had no impact at all on dal Corsi. Amero's potential to generate money outweighed any other considerations.

Bryn tried to catch a glimpse of the terms without being too obvious. He caught himself mid breath when he saw the figure being paid for an appearance. He didn't even have to win to earn it; a winning purse would be greater still. Money like that would solve a great many things for Bryn and he would have taken an offer like that with such enthusiasm that he would have ripped off the proffering hand.

Amero looked up from the page and smiled. 'I'll think on it a while.'

Bryn clenched his teeth to stop his jaw from dropping, but realised that Amero had never been in this for the money. Dal Corsi was surprised also; it seemed he was not often given this answer, which was understandable enough.

'Don't think on it too long, lad. There may be hordes of young females outside clamouring to get in today, but tomorrow? Memories are short in this city. Just ask someone who Panceri Mistria was.' He whirled around, his cloak billowing out about him and headed for the door, followed by his assistants without so much as a by your leave.

Bryn watched them go before turning to Amero. 'Do you really need to think about it?'

'Of course not, but I'm not going to jump onto the fat old fart's lap like a grateful puppy. I'll sign it and have it sent over in a day or two. Otherwise, I'm going back home, I feel bloody awful.' Without another word he stuffed the contract into his doublet and made for the window through which he had entered.

When he was gone, Bautisto turned to Bryn. 'Be patient. Luck doesn't favour us all, but hard work and ability earn their rewards eventually.'

Bryn looked at Bautisto, a man on the other side of middle age, and then at the salon in which he eked out a living with only two students. Those rewards seemed far less certain than he would have liked.

CHAPTER TWENTY-FIVE

AMERO DIDN'T SHOW for training at all the next day, and Bryn was concerned. An increasingly bad temper, heavy drinking and a sword close to hand were not a healthy combination. Bryn worried his behaviour was leading him toward trouble. Emeric was still around, so Bryn was confident that any trouble would not be severe, but his current lifestyle would lead him to ruin of one sort or another if not knocked on the head soon.

After training, he decided to call at Amero's apartment and give him a talking to. He didn't look forward to Amero's reaction but it had to be done, and Bryn was the only person to do it. They were still best friends after all.

The door opened the instant he pulled on the bell-rope, and Bryn's initial reaction was surprise at the speed of the servant's reactions. The door wasn't being opened for him, however. A lady was departing; Amero's most recent conquest no doubt, and probably also the reason for his absence from training.

When his eye's fell on Joranna's face, Bryn was unable to contain his surprise. Her face was flushed—not from the surprise of seeing him—and her hair was not quite as neatly styled as he would expect if she was out making calls on friends.

'Bryn... I. What are you doing here?'

Bryn said nothing and pushed past her, taking the stairs up to Amero's apartment two at a time. He burst in through the door, where Amero was lounging on his armchair, wearing nothing but his britches, smoking a twist of tobacco. There were several empty bottles of wine sitting on the table.

'Back for more?' Amero said, in response to the sound of the door opening. Only then did he look over and see Bryn standing in the doorway. 'Ah. Bryn. What brings you over?'

Bryn said nothing, trying to separate rage from his decision-making.

'Oh. You saw her then,' Amero said.

'I saw her,' Bryn said, in as measured a tone as he could manage.

'Well, I did warn you about her.'

'You utter bastard. Why did you do that?'

'Did you a favour, if you're asking. She's just like all the rest of her type. I warned you, and this is proof that I'm right. The first chance of a step up the social ladder and they drop their skirts. Told you to go after the daughter of a burgess or such like.'

'You utter bastard,' Bryan said again, unable to think of anything else.

'Now listen here,' Amero said. 'You're a bank clerk's son. What were you thinking getting mixed up with a nobleman's daughter anyway? Did you really think that would ever work out?'

Bryn thought about drawing his sword. It was the way swordsmen settled things like that, but Amero's words rang true. Bryn *was* the son of a bank clerk. Whatever the result of a duel between them, or a fight there and then, it would end badly for Bryn. If he killed the son of an elector count he would be in the city dungeon or on the headsman's block before he even had his sword sheathed again. Reason had to prevail. He had to be responsible and provide for his mother and sister. He couldn't do that incarcerated or dead. The whore wasn't worth it. Neither was Amero. He took a deep breath and swallowed his anger.

'Fuck you,' Bryn said, before turning and leaving.

Bryn was amazed when Amero turned up for training the next day. He looked healthier than he had in some time; clean clothes, no bags under his eyes, and no stench of booze.

'Surprised you're showing your face around here,' Bryn said.

'It's where I train, isn't it?'

'Warm up quickly please, gentlemen,' Bautisto said. 'We'll start with some sparring when you're ready.'

Bryn started into his warm up routine, glowering at Amero, who ignored him. Whenever he looked at Amero, all he could think of was Joranna and her deceit, and Amero's arrogance in the way he just took whatever he wanted with no thought for others. Bryn couldn't think of ever hating anyone more. After years of friendship, that was what it had come to; Amero's blatant lack of respect for Bryn. The thought made him light-headed with rage, and he struggled to maintain his control.

'That will do, gentlemen. Take your guards please,' Bautisto said. 'We'll start with basic patterns. I don't plan on anything too strenuous today.'

They began without another word, and Bautisto regarded them both curiously. As they worked their way through the basic parries, disengages and attacks, Bryn found himself striking with more force than he ordinarily would in those exercises. He could tell by Amero's expression that he noticed it.

'That's enough,' Bautisto said. 'Normal sparring now.'

Amero did nothing to disguise the new style he'd used against Mistria. He had proven it now, and obviously no longer cared about Bautisto's reaction. He came at Bryn much the same way he had with Mistria. The attacks were fast and precise, with flourishes, sweeps and just enough showmanship to make it visually appealing to the untrained eye. Far more so than Bautisto's workmanlike functionality.

'Rubbish!' Bautisto shouted.

Bryn felt incredibly satisfied at Bautisto's criticism and pressed Amero a little harder to see if he could provoke more of his ostentatious swordplay.

'If you wave your sword about like that, it will be the end of you! A waste of time!' Bautisto shouted, his voice laced with a rare show of anger.

Amero responded to Bryn in kind, ignoring Bautisto's commentary. Bryn pressed harder again, relishing the tongue lashing that Amero was getting and giving in to his own desire to cause his former friend physical harm. He upped the tempo and attacked aggressively. His move could not be mistaken by anyone with even the slightest knowledge of swordplay, and once again Amero responded.

Were it not for the fact that they were using blunt swords, there was nothing to differentiate their sparring from a serious duel. Try as he might, Bryn couldn't find a way through Amero's defence. One good, hard whack was all he wanted. That would be enough to demonstrate his feelings on the matter. Once he had that, he wouldn't train with Amero again. Ever. He attacked again, but Amero parried and riposted, taking the initiative and pressed Bryn back across the floor behind a blur of clashing steel.

Bryn hadn't expected such a quick turn around, and realised that he had allowed his anger to cloud his swordplay.

'Enough!' Bautisto walked between them as soon as the blades stopped moving. 'I don't know what's going on, but I said spar. Not try to kill one another. And you.' He turned to Amero. 'What have I said about the flourishes?'

Amero shrugged obstinately.

'They'll get you killed. And you'll look like an idiot in the process,' Bautisto said.

'Worked well enough against Mistria,' Amero said.

'Well,' Bautisto said. 'Perhaps Mistria wasn't all he was made out to be.'

Amero lowered his sword and turned to face Bautisto. His face twisted in anger. It had been some time since he had spoken back in the salon.

'I'm sick of your fucking criticism. Do this, do that. The same old shit every day. The same old hackneyed swordsmanship. Some of the crap you're peddling should be gathering dust by now. What I'm doing is new. No one's seen it before. I know it's far from perfect but you've already seen what it can do. Imagine what it will be like when I have it down. I won't have a greasy little Estranzan prick like you talk down to me any longer. Who the fuck do you think you are anyway? If it were up to you I'd still be nothing more than a circus attraction to be mocked in Lowgarden. Well no more.'

Amero was still holding his sword, but somewhere in the midst of his tirade he had raised it again. Both Bryn and Bautisto's eyes were locked on it.

Amero realised what they were both looking at and his face relaxed a little. 'Oh really. As if I'd waste the effort on either of you.' He flung the practice sword across the room where it clattered into a wall and fell to the floor. Gathering up his things, he stormed out.

CHAPTER TWENTY-SIX

THERE WAS A knock at his door, but Bryn was in little mood for company. There were few people who would call on him at home though, and in each instance it could be important. He opened the door to a slight figure in a dark travelling cloak.

'What do you want?' he said.

'Can I at least come in?' Joranna said.

Bryn didn't want to let her in, but if there was going to be an argument, he preferred that it be conducted in private. He stepped back from the door to allow her past, but other than Amero, he couldn't think of a person he wanted to see less.

'Say what you've come for, and be quick about it.'

'I wanted to apologise,' she said.

'Fine. Accepted. Leave.'

'Look. I didn't realise you'd react that way. I just thought it was a bit of fun. You bannerets are always chasing after girls, and I didn't think this was any different.'

'Well, you thought wrong,' Bryn said, gesturing toward the door once again.

'I'm sorry,' she said. 'For what it's worth, I won't be seeing Amero again. You have to understand, when a future elector count showers you with attention it's difficult to ignore. My family might have titles, but we don't have much else. I made a bad choice and I'm sorry for that.'

As hurt by her behaviour as he was, Bryn found it difficult not to see some reason in what she was saying. In spite of that, he couldn't find it in himself to forgive her; the hurt was still too fresh.

'I think you should leave.'

This time she said nothing, but nodded, and did as Bryn said.

Bryn sparred with Bautisto in the absence of a proper training partner. Having the full attention of a fencing master was of benefit, but something about the situation felt artificial. There had been a number of inquiries from people hoping to train there since the Mistria duel, but word of Amero's departure was not long in circulating through the gossip channels of the duelling community, and the majority of those inquiries were not followed up.

Bryn felt bad for Bautisto, and the role he had played in inflaming Amero, which undoubtedly contributed to his angry departure, but one of them would have left the salon that day and not returned. If not Amero, then Bryn, and even taking into account the extra business Amero would have brought, Bryn reckoned that Bautisto was far happier having Bryn there than Amero. Bryn was confident that Amero would not have stayed there much longer, one way or the other.

Amero had already won another victory in the Amphitheatre since leaving Bautisto's and had another match scheduled, which was receiving a great deal of promotion around the city. His name was mentioned by the city criers in Crossways regularly, and Bryn had heard him being discussed by people on the street.

Although he had paid little attention to Amero's movements

after storming out of Bautisto's, Bryn had heard that he had gone to Cavzanigo's, the plush salon that exemplified everything Bryn loathed about how the profession of being a banneret mingled with high society. He was welcome to the place as far as Bryn was concerned—and they were welcome to him.

A few days later Bryn was making his way through the city toward his mother's house. He had fought another unremarkable duel the previous evening, in an equally unremarkable arena tucked away in Guilds, unfortunately conceding a touch in a moment of foolishness. He was still distracted by everything that had happened over the past couple of weeks and focus was not coming easily. To further darken his mood, that same evening Amero had won another duel in the Amphitheatre without conceding a touch, a fact that was being announced by the criers on Crossways nearly every hour.

Nonetheless, Bryn had won another few crowns to give to his sister to keep the debt collectors from their door. It continually pained him to only be able to give them so little. That would change soon, he kept telling himself. It had to.

The route that he took brought him past Maestro Vaprio's salon and he paused with a sense of regret when he reached it. As much as the crowd relished the morbid spectacle of a man being killed on the arena floor, the notion always pained Bryn. It was a risk that they all shared and each time it happened that fact was made unpleasantly fresh in his mind. Happily it was not often.

As he was about to move off, the door to the salon opened and a man that Bryn recognised stepped out. He held the man's look for a moment longer than he would have had there been no recognition, and in that time the man spotted him. Seemingly the recognition was mutual.

'Banneret Pendollo, isn't it?'

Bryn was surprised that the man recognised him at all, more so that he could remember his name. 'Indeed. You have an excellent memory, sir. We've only met once, and that was quite some time ago when I called on the salon to enquire about training here. Banneret Caxto, isn't it.'

'Yes, Banneret Arfeni Caxto. I've actually seen you duel since the day you called. Have you been back from the circuit long?'

How had Caxto known that he had fought a duel out on the circuit? 'Some weeks now,' Bryn said. 'I want to say how sorry I am for the loss of Panceri Mistria. He was a truly great blade.'

'Yes, he was. Tragic. Not a day goes by that I don't wonder if things would have been different had you fought that match against him as was intended. I can't help but feel a degree of responsibility for how he ended up fighting Banneret dal Moreno. Still, there's nothing that can be done now and such is the risk that...'

Caxto was still talking, but his words faded into oblivion. Bryn was supposed to fight the match against Mistria? What could Caxto be going on about? Was he cracked in the head?

'I'm sorry to interrupt, but you said that it was intended that I fight that match against Banneret Mistria, and that you've seen me duel?'

'Yes, Panceri came from Tanosa; he still has family there. His brother wrote to him about an excellent Ostian swordsman who fought in the Estranzan style. Panceri had been interested in doing some exhibition matches against practitioners of foreign styles for some time, so we both went to watch you duel. That confirmed his brother's opinion and it was decided that we'd invite you to take part in the event. However, when I sought you out I discovered you'd left the city to go out on the duelling circuit. At the time I counted myself lucky that there was another swordsman close at hand who also fought in the Estranzan style, although I can now see how it was very definitely not Divine

Fortune whose gaze was upon me that day. I'm sorry to be abrupt, but I really must go. I've delayed too long already. Good day, Banneret.'

Bryn was too bemused to press Caxto with further questions; there was too much for him to take in. He said a distant good bye and continued on his way, all the while trying to make sense of what he had just been told.

After his conversation with Caxto, Bryn was in no mood to attend to family matters. He gave the money to his sister and made his apologies, before wandering the streets of Ostenheim for several hours, trying to make sense of what he had heard and then wondering what to do when he finally accepted that someone must have played him very cheap indeed. Bautisto? Amero? Both of them? He couldn't believe that Bautisto would do something like that to him. With Amero, after what had already happened, it was very much the opposite.

Eventually he found himself standing outside Bautisto's salon. He was reluctant to go in, to push the matter any further, but there was no way he could let the matter lie. He went in and called out for Bautisto. He appeared a moment later, a curious look on his face; it was unusual for Bryn to return in the afternoon with training finished for the day.

'Did you know about it?' Bryn said.

Bautisto looked puzzled. 'Know about what? Have you been drinking?'

'The Mistria duel. It was supposed to be given to me.'

Bautisto continued to look puzzled. 'What are you talking about?'

His confusion seemed in earnest. Bryn mellowed his approach. 'I bumped into one of Mistria's trainers today, Arfeni Caxto. He told me that Mistria had been looking to duel against someone who fought in the Estranzan style and that my name came up. He watched me and decided I was the right fit for the match. At some point after that, the match went to Amero and I want to know how and why.'

'This is all news to me,' Bautisto said.

'So it seems.' Bryn was satisfied that Bautisto was being honest with him. 'How in hells did that happen though?'

'I can only think of one answer. He stole it from you. I don't know how, but there can't be any other explanation.'

'He was my friend for years. I wish I could say I didn't believe that was possible, but I don't have any difficulty believing it now.'

'The reason for your heated sparring the day he left?'

Bryn nodded, but Bautisto didn't press him for any more information.

'Nothing that can be done about it now,' Bautisto said. 'At least you know you can't trust him. You are the better swordsman. Other opportunities will come.'

For a man making his living in a dingy warehouse in a bad part of the city, a long way from family and home, Bautisto had a remarkable ability to remain positive. Bryn could not. He wouldn't forgive, or forget, so easily.

CHAPTER TWENTY-SEVEN

BRYN WALKED SLOWLY all the way from his apartment to Amero's new salon. The conversation he intended to have was one that he really didn't want to, but he would never respect himself again if he did not confront Amero. He hadn't slept much the previous night, and had grown angrier and angrier as each sleepless hour had gone by. No matter how hard he tried to put it from his mind it refused to leave. When sleep finally did come, it was fitful and his dreams were filled with betrayal and anger.

When he arrived at Cavzanigo's, Bryn hesitated before going in. Freshly decorated and clean, it admittedly looked like a far more pleasant place to spend time than the dingy salon in Docks, but hardship bred toughness and pampering the opposite.

There was more activity than there had been on the occasion of his previous call, probably having to do with the fact that it was now home to the fastest rising star on the city's duelling circuit, and he was making all the regulars look bad.

He looked enviously at the training equipment, all of which looked new and well maintained. There was a comfortable-looking rest area that Bryn had to admit would be welcome after some of the sessions that Bautisto put them through, and instead of lounging wastrels talking nonsense, it was now populated with exhausted men, red faced and dripping with sweat.

Looking at the place and seeing how new it all was made Bryn wonder if Amero had simply bought it and fitted it out with both equipment and students to cater to his suddenly thriving career. There was still the faint smell of fresh paint in the air, which only firmed up Bryn's suspicion.

He didn't go unnoticed long, lurking near the doorway. As Bryn looked around to see if he could spot Amero, a member of the staff approached him.

'Good morning, sir, I'm afraid the salon is closed to new applicants.'

'I'm here to see Banneret dal Moreno,' Bryn said.

'The Banneret is very much in demand. I'm afraid he's very busy right now, sir, perhaps if you leave a note he might be able to reply to you later.'

Bryn felt his temper begin to rise, but he knew the man was doing his best; if the hordes of fans outside Bautisto's salon when Amero was still there were anything to go by then there must have been a steady stream of potential interruptions flowing through the door he had just come through.

'I think if you let Banneret dal Moreno know that Banneret of the Blue Bryn Pendollo is here to see him, he will not be displeased with you.' At least not at first, Bryn thought. He added his title to give his request further weight. Bannerets of the Blue were never to be dismissed lightly and the title at least indicated that he was not simply a fan looking for an autograph or a handshake, if his appearance had not done so already.

The man hesitated for a moment and Bryn fixed him with his most glowering stare.

'Very well, sir, if you'd wait a moment.' He walked through the rest area and around a corner, from where Bryn could hear the faint sounds of sparring. A moment later Amero appeared around the corner, a smile on his face. Someone handed him a glass of water as he passed, which Amero took without acknowledging it.

'Finally come to your senses? There's no need to worry, I won't hold a grudge against your overreaction. She's a pretty thing, and I've known fellows to lose their minds over far plainer. No hard feelings. What do you say?' Amero held out his hand, a smile firmly fixed to his sweaty face.

Bryn swallowed hard, forcing away the urge to draw his sword and commit murder.

'I just want to know two things. Why you did it, and how you managed it?' Bryn said.

'The why surely doesn't need explaining, does it? The how? Well, I rather hope you already know how that part works.' He laughed out loud, but stifled it when he saw the expression on Bryn's face. 'What are you talking about?'

'What do you think I'm talking about?' Bryn said. 'The Mistria duel. His trainer told me that I was supposed to have it, not you.'

'That's absolute rubbish,' Amero said. He cast a slightly nervous look behind him to where the others were standing. 'I don't know who told you that, but they played a nasty trick on you. Probably someone who doesn't like me. Gods know there're enough suspects to choose from.'

Bryn remained silent, teeth gritted.

'How long have we known each other, Bryn? Do you mean to say you believe some complete stranger over me?'

'Now?' Bryn said. 'Without hesitation.' His suspicion was confirmed beyond doubt by Amero's demeanour. He had indeed known Amero for a very long time, more than long enough to know that he was lying. 'You just take whatever you want, don't you? You couldn't give a damn about anyone else.'

'I'm not sure I like your tone,' Amero said, the genial quality of his own now replaced by a cold edge.

'You knew how badly I needed the money,' Bryn said. 'How

could you take something like that away from me?' As he spoke he found his anger was replaced by something else, the great hurt caused by the betrayal of someone he had once trusted absolutely.

Amero remained silent for a moment, then changed tack. 'It's all for the best really. Mistria would have just made a fool of you in front of all those people. Just like the girl. I did you a favour really. Again.'

His arrogance brought Bryn's anger back with vengeance. 'A favour? You son of a whore. A favour? You stole that fight from me.'

Everyone else in the salon turned and stared, if they had not been already.

'Watch. Your. Fucking. Mouth,' Amero said, his eyes blazing with anger. 'This is a gentlemen's salon. If you can't behave like one, you should leave.' His voice was quiet, laden with threat.

'What? You're afraid your new lickspittles there will find out you're a lying, cheating piece of shit who steals duels from his friends? And women? You know I'm better than you; you know I'd not have made a fool of myself against Mistria.'

'Better than me?' Amero said, his voice rising now for the first time. His face twisted in anger. 'You uppity little prick. Who the fuck do you think you're speaking to? I'm not some common little street urchin that you can order about as you please! You don't come in here and speak like that to me.'

He flung the glass of water across the room, where it smashed against the wall, splashing water all over the fresh paintwork. Bryn knew that had Amero been carrying a sword, they would have gone to blows at that moment.

'Fine,' Amero said. 'If you think you're better than me, and you're so eager to have a fool made of yourself in the Amphitheatre, I can arrange that. You can fight me. I'll be only too happy to put you back in your place.'

'Perfect,' Bryn said. 'Nobility might not bestow manners,

but I'll be happy to put some on you.' He felt ridiculous saying it, but he had let it out before thinking it through.

'I'll have my people attend to the details and get in touch. I presume I can still find you in that dump of a salon?'

Bryn nodded, not willing to risk saying anything else that would make him feel foolish. He gave Amero one final glare before storming out.

Bryn returned to Bautisto's. Bautisto was sitting in the centre of the salon on the sole wooden chair, a rapier between his knees, its point in the wood. He was idly spinning the hilt between his hands and looked up when Bryn stepped through the door.

'I presume your lateness is the result of a call to Cavzanigo's?' Bautisto said.

'It is.'

'He admitted to stealing the Mistria duel?'

'No. Not in so many words. But he didn't need to.'

'And you are still alive. Might I assume that he is not? Or do I hope for too much?' Bautisto said.

'We didn't fight.'

Bautisto frowned. 'A shame. He has it coming. A little younger and I might have considered doing it myself.'

'We will, though,' Bryn said.

'Have arrangements been made?'

'Amero said he'd send word.'

'I would consider it a privilege to stand second for you,' Bautisto said.

'No. It's not going to be like that. We'll fight in the Amphitheatre.'

'Good,' Bautisto said, standing up, allowing the rapier to sit balanced on its tip for a moment before picking it up with a sweeping movement of his arm, perhaps the most flamboyant that Bryn had ever seen him make. 'You will be able to win back everything he has taken from you. Now, we'll train.'

True to his word, on this occasion at least, Amero sent someone to Bautisto's to outline his proposal for the duel. It would be a normal match, taking part during a regularly scheduled list of fixtures. It wouldn't stand out as anything special, not like Mistria's exhibition match, but that suited Bryn perfectly. He sent his acceptance to the terms back immediately, by the same messenger.

The arrangements gave Bryn three weeks to train. After so long training with Amero, Bryn knew he ought to feel confident of what to expect, but that was not the case. Amero was almost an unknown quantity now. He had all the advantages. He knew exactly how Bryn fought. Amero's new technique and style was a surprise to everyone, and even in the short time since revealing it against Mistria it had evolved considerably as he became more practised and confident with it.

Amero wouldn't fight again before their duel, so there would be no opportunity to have a look at him. What made it worse was that Bryn had not watched any of his duels since the Mistria fight. Bautisto had, by coincidence, been to one and was able to report the further development of Amero's new style, but Bryn would be going into the match all but blind.

Not knowing had never bothered Bryn before. If Amero had been a complete stranger, it was likely that Bryn wouldn't have given a new and exciting style a second thought. Knowing that they were closely matched, and that Amero was as familiar with how Bryn fought as anyone alive gave Bryn great cause for concern, though. Three weeks wasn't long enough for him to adopt something new and expect to be able to use it effectively.

Training progressed as well as could be hoped. Bautisto tried to change things up as much as possible to keep Bryn on his toes and ready for whatever new tricks Amero had to throw at him. It was far from perfect, but it was as much as they could do.

Every aspect of his life was carefully considered. What he ate, when he ate, how much he slept, when he slept; it was all planned down to the last pea and the last minute. Each day on his way home from training he called by Crossways to buy fresh fruit, vegetables, and meat for the coming day. If there had been any more than three weeks to prepare for the duel, he would have likely bankrupted himself with his food bills alone.

As he left the salon, Bautisto shouted a list of the groceries he was to remember to buy, which made Bryn laugh. He was feeling good about things for the first time, partly a consequence of his excellent diet and the quality rest. It was also due to how pleased he was with his swordplay.

When he got to Crossways he wandered around looking at the different stalls. He tried to vary things, and different vendors had different produce from different regions. The trick was finding one who would sell the freshest he had, rather than try and mix a little that was over-ripe into his parcel.

He was paying for a selection of apples and oranges and was trying to keep a careful eye on the vendor's assistant as he paid when he was distracted by the voice of the nearest crier.

As always, the crier's voice lifted up over the noise of the crowds on the square. There were several of them there at any time, one at each corner and another in the centre standing atop large stone pulpit-like edifices. From dawn until dusk they announced the news of the day, mainly for the benefit of those who could not read—a large proportion of the population—but they also included morsels of gossip and scandal that tended to be absent from the printed news sheets sold throughout the city, which was of interest to everyone.

Once the news and scandal were dealt with, they usually addressed some of the highlights of the previous duels at the

Amphitheatre and some of the upcoming matches to whet the citizens' appetites. Bryn heard Amero's name being mentioned, which was not all that surprising; it was becoming a more regular feature. His meteoric rise in fame and popularity was something of a phenomenon. Bryn presumed, fairly or not, it was simply a demonstration of the mob's thirst for blood and hope that he might kill someone once again.

Hearing his own name mentioned came as a complete shock. He flushed with mild embarrassment before he realised that no one would know he was the person the crier was talking about. As nonchalantly as he could, he finished paying and, taking his parcel of fruit, walked toward the crier, straining to pick out every last word.

'A tragic tale, good citizens, of friendship destroyed by greed, jealousy and ambition. If I didn't know it to be true, I would not believe it myself! It promises to be one of the most epic battles and tragic tales to unfold in the Amphitheatre, as Amero, the Giant Slayer, the most dangerous young blade in the city, makes one last gesture of friendship to a bitter, jealous and utterly deadly rival!'

Bryn was flabbergasted. He stood there, jaw agape, trying to take in the sensational and false light in which he was being presented. At first Bryn found it hard to believe that the story of how Amero had behaved had gotten out, but his heart sank as he realised that the greed and jealousy the crier spoke of were in reference to him and not Amero. He was beyond disbelief. He couldn't even begin to understand what Amero was about, but Bryn was the one painted the villain.

Part of him wanted to walk away and ignore it, but a morbid curiosity locked him in place and compelled him to listen.

'Friends from their earliest days at the Academy, they chose to train together when Banneret Pendollo followed his friend Amero into the arena. However, Banneret Pendollo grew jealous at his lack of success and it was not long before he began to resent his former friend. Now good citizens, we shall see that jealousy and resentment take its place on the arena floor where it will be tested against bravery, skill and daring. Yes, good citizens, it promises to be the duel of the century. Tickets are available from reputable vendors here in Crossways or from the Amphitheatre itself. Prices from only one shilling!'

Bryn felt sick.

CHAPTER TWENTY-EIGHT

THERE WAS ONLY one way for Bryn to deal with Amero's slander campaign: to try to ignore it. It was difficult to avoid Crossways, but it was the only way to remain out of earshot of the criers, who were enthusiastically painting him as the worst villain in Ostenheim. When Crossways was unavoidable, as was unfortunately the case on a couple of occasions, he felt as though every eye was on him as the criers waxed lyrical about the upcoming duel and how Amero, now being called 'the Lightning Blade' had been so wronged and injured by his friend that a duel was the only option left to him. He wondered if there was any way to correct the falsehoods, but short of having a very public disagreement with a city crier nothing jumped to mind.

There were many inconsistencies in the tale as it was being recited, but no one was bothered to stop and think about it. It was sensational, it was black and white and it involved the current darling of the city. It gave them someone to love and someone to hate, and that was all they wanted. He dreaded to think of how his mother would react when she found out what was being said.

Bryn focussed on training, but it was not possible to dismiss it entirely. Each time his mind drifted toward it he could feel his anger grow, and he knew this wasn't the state of mind to fight a duel in. As well as anger there was another new sensation he had to deal with. The deluge of hatred directed at him was oppressive. It felt like a great weight pressing down on top of him, threatening to crush him. There were moments when he feared that it would.

When he left the salon one afternoon, there was a group of boys gathered on the other side of the street. As Bryn pulled the door shut behind him, one of the boys called out.

'Hey, are you Bryn Pendollo?'

He hesitated, not knowing whether to answer, then decided ignoring them was the best option.

'Yeah, I reckon you are!' shouted another one of them. 'You're a right bastard!'

The rest of them took this as a cue to start throwing things at Bryn. It wasn't until one of the objects actually hit him that he realised it was rotten fruit, the same variety of object favoured for use against those unfortunate enough to find themselves in the stocks in Delinquents' Square, beside the City Watch barracks. He shielded himself with his arm as he walked away from the salon. He was thankful when the boys stopped following after he had gone only a few yards. Perhaps the window at the back of the salon would be a better choice in the future.

He felt his chest falter as he took a breath. He knew in that moment that even if he beat Amero in the Amphitheatre, Amero had already won. If Amero offered to make it all go away, he would have gladly accepted.

Amero stared out the window of Cavzanigo's, the only one that allowed a glimpse of Crossways. He knew the town criers were there painting Bryn as the worst villain in history. It was an unkind thing to do, but no one knew the truth of it, and having been so thoroughly indoctrinated the crowd wouldn't believe anything to the contrary. It was unfortunate that his old friend should bear the indignity of it all, but the opportunity it gave Amero to enhance his standing was too good to pass up. It made him look like the tragic hero of legends, scorned and betrayed by the friend he trusted most.

It occurred to him that it might be worth bringing the Verrara slut into the story; that Bryn stole away his one true love while he was training hard and living the honest, pure life of a hero-banneret. He dismissed the idea. Losing a woman to Bryn might make him look weak, and it was not worth taking the chance.

If everything went to plan, he would come out of this duel with greater fame and status than the top five ranked duellists put together, even though he was still some time away from sharing the same page in the Ladder with them. He would be untouchable. He just needed to make absolutely certain he won the duel. Even now, after all the extra training and improvement he had made, Bryn was still the person who had bested him each year at the Academy, and that spectre was a difficult one to disregard.

'I was in Crossways today,' Joranna said.

Her arrival at his door came as a surprise. Hers was not a face he expected to see.

'I wanted to see how you are,' she said.

'I'm fine.' It was a lie, but she was the last person he would bare his soul to.

'Is this over me?' she asked.

Bryn laughed sardonically. 'No. There's a lot more to it. Maybe a little.'

She nodded. 'I hope you make a fool of him.'

'I hope so too,' he said.

She stood before him silently for a moment, as though she

expected him to say something else or invite her in. When he didn't, she smiled sadly, turned and left.

The day before the duel, Bryn felt utterly miserable. He was sneaking in and out of the salon via the back window like a criminal. Avoiding Crossways was no longer enough to keep from hearing the constant hype about the duel, as it seemed to be all anyone was talking about in the city. Tickets had sold out and despite having done nothing, Bryn's name was as well known in the city as Amero's, but for all the wrong reasons. The only saving grace was that there was hardly anyone who could put his name to his face. Bryn was surprised Amero hadn't had likenesses of him made and posted all over the city to make sure his campaign of mud-slinging was complete. Clearly Amero wasn't as thorough an assassin of character as he might have thought.

The stress of it all had been affecting Bryn's sleep for days; at night all he did was toss and turn, getting angrier one moment and wishing that none of it had happened the next. He should have left Amero to his deceit and gotten on with things. It would have been a bitter pill to swallow, but it had to be better than what he was going through.

He was sitting in his apartment reading a book, trying to put any other thoughts from his mind when there was a hammering at his door. With his notoriety at an all-time high, the way the door was being pounded gave him cause for concern. His immediate thought was that there was someone there at the very least wanting to give him an earful, at the worst, to do him harm. He had long since taken to leaving a sword hanging by his doorway. Ostensibly it was there for decoration and he had positioned it in line with his notion of how best to achieve decorative effect, but it was a sharp and functional weapon that was always close to hand any time he opened the door.

He opened the door as abruptly as he could, hoping to

surprise whoever was on the other side. His sister stood there, distraught.

'Bryn, they're trying to throw us out of the house. You have to come quickly.'

He grabbed his sword belt from the wall and strapped it on, before hurrying out of his apartment behind his sister. They rushed through the evening streets of Ostenheim as the mage lamps were beginning to illuminate, but Bryn wasn't able to enjoy the magical quality to that hour of the day as his sister continued on with unabating pace.

The door to his family's apartment building was open, and there was a commotion coming from inside. He could hear his mother's voice and those of at least two men.

'Wait here,' he said to Gilia, before going in.

'What's going on here?' Bryn said, loudly enough to be heard over the noise, and loudly enough to achieve his desired effect as the three men standing there turned to face him.

Bryn's mother looked furious but desperate at the same time. Two of the men were tall and rough looking while the third, of average height, had a shrewder look about him and was obviously the brains of the operation.

'This is none of your business,' the shrewd looking one said.

'That's my mother, and this is very much my business. I'll ask again. What are you doing here?'

On Bryn's words, the two larger men moved closer to their boss and puffed out their chests.

'Everything's legit, friend,' the shrewd one said. 'We're just here settling a debt. I have the papers here, you can take a look if you want.' He rapped a fold of papers against the knuckles of his other hand.

Bryn stepped forward and held out his hand. There hadn't been a single missed payment on any of the loans his parents had taken out. They had been close on a number of occasions, but Bryn had managed to ensure they had never fallen from good standing in regard to their debt.

The shrewd man flicked his eyes nervously to one of his companions, but Bryn's hand didn't waver. With resignation he handed the papers over. Bryn snatched them and scanned through their contents. He had never taken out a loan in his life, so he had no real idea of what he was looking for, but perusing their credentials seemed to be the appropriate thing to do.

'Why are they being called in now?' Bryn said, as he read.

'Not for me to say, sir, we just do the collecting,' the shrewd one said.

Bryn kept flipping through the pages until he finally came to what appeared to be the answer to his family's current predicament. The loans had all been purchased by one individual, several days before. Sadly, the name of that individual was not mentioned. One of the larger men started to move forward, slowly.

'Who purchased the loans?' Bryn said.

The shrewd looking man smiled and shook his head. 'None of my business. We just do the collecting.' He emphasised each word.

'Well, you'll have to do it another time. I'm going to have my lawyer take a look at these. Until then, you can tell whoever it is you work for to tell whoever it is that bought the loans, to piss off.' Bryn's eyes involuntarily flicked to his mother, and even under the circumstances he could see the look of disapproval on her face over his choice of words.

'We don't want no trouble, but we're here to do a job and we're gonna do it.'

'It'll end badly for you if you try,' Bryn said.

The man nodded in resignation. 'The boss said that might be the case.'

A man appeared at the doorway, immediately behind where Bryn was standing. It was luck as much as anything that Bryn caught the movement out of the corner of his eye. He must have been lurking in the shadows outside, unseen when Bryn went into the apartment.

The fourth man lunged through the doorway with a dagger. Bryn's fortuitous glimpse gave him enough time to duck out of the way, but it still caught him a glancing blow on the side beneath his right arm, neatly slicing through cloth and into flesh.

He gasped in pain but had enough wits about him to defend himself. He grabbed the dagger-bearing wrist as it passed him and pulled forward hard, hauling the man completely into the apartment and hurling him across the room. Bryn drew his sword. He needed to reduce threats quickly. He ran the man he had just thrown against the wall through the chest. His mother had had the sense to duck into the kitchen and neither of the other thugs had the opportunity to grab her. The shrewd looking one had taken a step back from the danger, behind the screen of his two remaining men.

Bryn's mother was the main weakness in his defence. He had to get between her and the men as quickly as possible, and hope that his sister remained safely outside.

One of the big men yelled in anger at Bryn, having just seen his comrade slain in front of him. He hurled the table over and both he and his mate came forward, drawing cudgels from under their robes. The shrewd looking man remained with his back to the wall, seemingly confident that his minders would be able to take care of the trouble.

The minders were wary though, and didn't throw themselves at Bryn. Bryn worried that the shrewd one might get it in his head to go after his mother, given the time.

Since he wore a rapier within the city limits they knew he was a banneret, and that was likely the reason for their caution. If the new owner of his family's debts was Amero, as he suspected, the men would have been well briefed and the best available. If they were hesitant, Bryn would make their choice for them.

He thrust forward with blistering speed, running the rough to his right through the belly. Pulling his blade free he whipped it to the left, slashing the other rough's midsection. The men's screams of pain mingled as Bryn looked to their leader, satisfied that neither minder any longer posed a threat.

The shrewd man was slumped in the doorway to the kitchen. His mother stood over the body, looking down, a large frying pan in her hand.

Bryn breathed a sigh of relief. 'Are you all right?'

His mother nodded. 'Where's your sister?'

Bryn groaned and turned, jogging out the door onto the street.

Gilia was slumped against the wall, her head lolling on her chest. Bryn rushed forward and knelt beside her. He checked her over for wounds, but could see none. It seemed the thug who had come in after Bryn had some semblance of propriety and had just given her a knock on the head. Bryn picked her up and carried her inside. His mother replaced the table in the centre of the room and Bryn laid Gilia down on it.

His mother tended to her while Bryn dragged the bodies out of the house. He was pulling the shrewd man out—the blow to the head had been fatal—when the City Watch arrived. The commotion had inspired someone to send for them, but only after it had ceased rather than when they might have been of use in throwing the bailiffs out.

The Watch lieutenant gave Bryn a very suspicious look. Backed up by a half dozen watchmen, he had every right to feel confident.

'What's happened here?' he demanded.

'These men were debt collectors, forcing payment on a debt that wasn't outstanding. They became violent when I brought that up and attacked. You can see my sister inside if you like. One of the bastards cracked her over the head.'

The lieutenant nodded to one of his men who went inside to verify what Bryn had just said.

'And the four bodies, sir?'

'Like I said, they became violent and I defended myself, my family, and my property.'

'As you say, sir. And the sword? Are you a banneret?' This question was asked with the most suspicious tone so far.

'Yes, I am. Banneret of the Blue as it happens. I believe my mother still keeps my parchments framed on the wall inside if you'd like to take a look at those too.'

The lieutenant gestured to another one of his men who also headed inside. He came out a moment later and nodded to the lieutenant.

'Right enough, lieutenant,' he said. 'Banneret of the Blue Bryn Pendollo.'

The lieutenant's eyes widened in recognition. Bryn cringed on the inside, but puffed out his chest defiantly. It was a bad time to be the owner of his name.

'Well, sir, I'm sorry for the trouble. We'll take care of the bodies and see that an investigation is opened into why they were getting rough if there was no default in payment as you say.'

The lieutenant chewed at his lower lip and continued to stare at Bryn. As an officer of the City Watch, he could not say anything improper and would most certainly lose his commission if he insulted a banneret. However, it was clear that he wanted to say something, just that he felt he could not. He maintained his gaze a moment longer, until he was sure that Bryn had taken its meaning, before getting his men to take care of the thugs heaped on the side of the street.

Bryn went back inside where his sister was waking. His mother held her head gently and looked up to Bryn.

'We can't have any more of this,' she said. 'I want these debts cleared and your sister married with a good dowry. We've given up far too much to hear your name being called out like a curse on the streets. After tomorrow, when you've beaten that Moreno bastard and shown him up as the liar that he is, it's the army for you. A regular wage to support your family isn't too much to ask, is it? No more of this duelling rubbish.'

He sat down in the wreckage of their living room, his sister barely in charge of her wits and his mother dealing with the emotion of just having killed a man. She was right. It was all too much. His foolish dream had brought all this misery to their doorstep. There was no reason good enough for all of this.

Once he was done with Amero, he was finished with the arena. There were other ways to make his living, ways beyond the filthy tarnish of life as a duellist.

CHAPTER TWENTY-NINE

BRYN AWOKE WITH a jolt. He wasn't sure how late it had been when he'd finally fallen asleep, but he had tossed and turned for hours. His side burned and throbbed. He should have attended to it properly the night before, but with his sister's injury and the rest of the commotion he hadn't given it any thought. He'd been cut a number of times by blades in the past, and the wounds always healed quickly. However, those cuts were made with clean, well maintained blades. The debt collector's thug who cut him the night before was probably less particular in keeping his dagger clean.

He touched the flesh around the wound, which wasn't deep. It was hot and tender, and Bryn cursed. He sat up and the movement revealed a slight headache. He rolled his right shoulder around and grimaced. The skin on the right side of his torso was tight, and his arm ached. The situation wasn't serious and he knew that it could be treated before the duel, but it was going to be a hindrance when he had to fight. Not only had Amero managed to rob him of several nights of decent sleep, he had nobbled him physically. Bryn had never appreciated Amero's capacity for capriciousness before, but it seemed to have no bounds.

Bryn was certain that Amero was behind the events of the previous night. It was all too convenient to be merely coincidence. It would never be possible to prove it—Amero was both too clever and too powerful for his involvement to be brought out into the open—but after all that had happened, suspicion was all that Bryn needed to be convinced that it was him.

He dressed quickly, gathered his things and left. The walk from his apartment was the longest and loneliest that he had ever endured. He had arranged to meet Bautisto at the Amphitheatre, preferring to be alone in the final few hours leading up to the duel. He walked there with the hood of his cloak pulled low. His face was still not recognised by many and it was his intention that would remain the case even after the duel. At least the size of the Amphitheatre meant the majority of the crowd was quite a distance away. Even those in the most expensive front rows were too far away to make out every detail. He hoped that time would wash his name clear eventually.

People were most likely to get a good look at his face when he left or arrived. He hoped that the large hood would solve this problem. The memories of the citizens of Ostenheim were short lived. While foul deeds tended to live on in their recollections longer, there was always another foul deed, or glorious one, to take its place. He was comfortable that whichever way things went, in a few months it would all be forgotten and he could get on with life as normal; a private one, as far from public scrutiny as he could possibly get.

He slipped in through the competitors' entrance, unnoticed by anyone other than the guard who took the identification token Amero had sent to the salon a few days previously. People were unaccustomed to swordsmen competing on the premier stage of Ostenheim to be shy of the attention of the mob; anyone who avoided their attention was most likely unworthy of it. He walked through the labyrinth beneath the Amphitheatre until he reached the Bannerets' Enclosure, where Bautisto was waiting for him.

'I was expecting you earlier.'

It was an attempt at humour, but during his time under Bautisto's tutelage Bryn had been constantly made aware that the Estranzan sense of humour was very different to the Ostian. Bryn forced a smile. He wasn't feeling very chatty.

'Let's get you warmed up,' Bautisto said, as he removed Bryn's cloak from his shoulders. He unintentionally pulled on Bryn's arm.

Bryn grimaced and let out a slight groan. Bautisto furrowed his brow and gave Bryn an inquisitive look.

'It's nothing,' Bryn said. 'I just slept awkwardly on it.'

Bautisto wasn't convinced. He probed under Bryn's arm gently with his fingers. Bautisto's jaw dropped when his fingers came away tipped with fresh red blood. 'What in hells is this?'

'It's just a cut. Nothing serious,' Bryn said, stepping back out of reach of Bautisto's red fingers.

'Rubbish,' Bautisto said. 'Your doublet is soaked through. A "nothing" cut doesn't bleed that much.' He stepped forward and put his hand on Bryn's forehead. 'You're warm. Too warm. Now, are you going to tell me what happened, and what we have to deal with here before the duel?'

'I got cut last night. There was some trouble at my mother's house—'

'Your mother did this?'

Bryn laughed, a first for an Estranzan joke, although he wasn't certain it was meant as a joke. 'No, she didn't. My family has some debts. Mysteriously, they were all called in last night. The bailiffs were turning over my mother's apartment look- ing for anything of value. I stopped them, and took a cut in the process.'

Bautisto looked at him suspiciously.

'Don't worry,' Bryn said. 'I had right on my side; the Watch are looking into it, and they aren't going to come crashing in here halfway through the duel to arrest me.'

'That's something at least. Hold on while I try to find

somewhere discreet to treat that wound. I don't want anyone knowing about it.'

Bautisto wandered off and came back a moment later. 'There's a room we can use. Come this way.'

Bryn followed Bautisto to a small room intended for the treatment of wounded swordsmen. Bautisto told the steward they just wanted some peace and quiet to prepare. Being seen going into a treatment room without explanation was likely to achieve the same effect as telling Amero in person that Bryn was wounded.

As soon as the door was closed, Bryn sat down on the examination table and removed his doublet. The right side of his white shirt was soaked through with blood. He removed that also, trying not to cover himself in blood in the process. He had done his best to cover the wound, wrapping lengths of crepe bandage around his chest enough times to cover the width of the cut, but to little effect.

Bautisto grimaced as he saw the mess of blood and bandage. He started peeling back the layers and grimaced even more when he revealed the wound beneath. There were medical supplies on a shelf in the room. He picked through various things and placed some of them on the table beside Bryn. He took a bottle of alcohol spirits and poured a large splash onto a wad of cloth. He gently began wiping away the dried and still wet blood, revealing the clean skin beneath.

'It's infected,' he said, pointing out the angry red edges of the wound, which was already becoming covered by the fresh blood oozing out. He pinched both sides of the wound together and frowned.

Bryn winced in pain.

'It's all the way through the skin. It will need stitches,' Bautisto said, 'but I can't do that here or now. After the duel you will have to get it properly tended to. For now all that we can do is clean and bandage it up as best we can. If you're lucky, it won't burst open again while you fight.'

He worked as he spoke, splashing more of the alcohol onto the wound causing Bryn to flinch from the intense stinging. Bautisto then set to wrapping lengths of the linen bandage around him.

'You cannot favour this side in any way. If Amero gets any sense that you're carrying an injury, he'll exploit it for everything it's worth.'

Bryn nodded his head. It was pointing out the obvious, but was at least taking his mind off things.

'You suspect that Amero had something to do with this?'

Bryn grunted as Bautisto cinched the bandages tight. 'I don't really see any other answer; it's too much of a coincidence.'

'Well, now you have the opportunity to repay him.'

CHAPTER THIRTY

THE AMPHITHEATRE COULD be filled and emptied in a matter of minutes, an impressive feat considering it held over fifty thousand people. When Bryn had left for the treatment room, the first spectators had been gathering in the stands. There was a huge sense of expectation as they started to take their places, but it was eerie when there were so few people there. Even the slightest sound seemed to echo across the great space.

Now, only a few minutes later, there were thousands upon thousands of people sitting along the benches and the air was filled with the excited hum of their voices. The contrast was startling. The first of the evening's duels was soon to begin, but the crowd would continue to grow over the course of the early matches, fought by lower ranked swordsmen who were never as interesting to the crowd as those involved in the later, higher profile matches.

'There's little point in doing your usual warm-up routine,' Bautisto said, breaking Bryn from his thoughts.

'Limit yourself to whatever stretching you feel comfortable with and warm yourself up to the point of perspiration, but no further; we must marshal every ounce of your strength and hope that the bandages hold your wound closed.'

Bryn knew that the moment was coming, but it did not stop the furious fluttering of nerves in his stomach when he saw the steward come to talk to Bautisto. The steward whispered in his ear for a moment, as they always did, and Bautisto turned to Bryn. Their eyes met and Bautisto nodded.

The first few steps out onto the arena floor were daunting. He listened for the sound of his footfalls on the sand, but could hear nothing over the electrifying noise of the audience. He had gone a few paces before they realised the man they had come to hate had stepped out of the Bannerets' Enclosure. In that instant noise erupted from the crowd like a winter gale. Walking out onto the Amphitheatre's sand was the realisation of a lifelong dream for Bryn, but it gave him no joy.

He had wondered how he would react when this moment finally came. He had to stifle a laugh as the tens of thousands all began to roar at him. He couldn't make out any of the individual insults; they were absorbed into one wave of noise. It wasn't nearly as bad as he had been expecting.

They reached the black mark and both stood on their respective sides waiting for the Master of Arms to give them their instructions. They didn't exchange any words, and Amero barely gave Bryn a glance. He took a few moments to wave to the crowd and they responded instantly. Bryn had to hand it to him; he really had taken to the celebrity with aplomb. It was as though he was born for it. Bryn stood waiting, no doubt looking every part the sullen, jealous villain that he had been painted as.

Finally the Master of Arms walked over and explained the rules. Bryn didn't pay any attention. He knew them by heart. All he wanted to hear was one word.

'Begin!'

Bryn couldn't hold himself back. He lunged forward as soon as the word left the Master of Arms's mouth, venting all the pent-up anger that had accumulated over the past few weeks. Amero was prepared for it. There was no way he could not be expecting it. After all he had done—stealing the Mistria fight, promoting a campaign of hate against Bryn, trying to have his family thrown out on the street and possibly even him murdered or at least badly beaten—he must have known how much anger Bryn would be channelling toward him.

Amero danced backward, parrying delicately but stylishly as he went. His mastery of the new technique was near complete; his movements were as well executed as any that Bryn had seen. The crowd were enthralled and even out in the centre of the arena floor Bryn could sense the tension they felt at seeing their darling being beaten back across the sand.

He pressed forward as hard and fast as he could. The more opportunity for attack he gave Amero, the greater the chance he would surprise Bryn with something he couldn't deal with. He paid no thought to the wound across his ribs; he needed every ounce of his concentration directed at achieving his goal. He forced Amero left and right as fast as he could—faster, he hoped, than Amero was ready for. Finally he saw a gap and he lunged. As he stretched forward, he felt a tearing agony in his side. Amero's eyes widened. Bryn's sword continued forward unimpeded. A touch.

The entire crowd went silent. As he walked back to the black line, Bryn heard a woman wail in anguish. More cries of disbelief and shouts of anger followed. If they thought Amero was that wonderful, then to hells with them.

The combined relief and joy of having scored the first touch was overwhelming, but still not enough to block out the pain in his side. He felt like someone had thrown a pan of boiling water over his torso. He wished he'd been able to drive his attack home hard enough to hurt the bastard and even things between them. He took a deep breath and readied himself for the next point, pushing the crowd's noise and movement out of his head. Bryn remembered Amero's wide eyes. It wasn't an expression of surprise, it was one of realisation. He knew that Bryn was in pain.

The Master of Arms reset the duel but this time Amero took the initiative. He rained a barrage of strikes at Bryn's right side, forcing pressure onto the weakened muscles. Bryn's face must have begun to show strain, as Amero smiled. Bryn could feel his strength fade under the press of attacks and knew that his only chance was to regain the initiative—to fight the duel on his terms.

He backed away quickly, hoping that by putting some distance between them he would be able to dictate the next exchange. The crowd started to boo and jeer. Amero relaxed for a moment, standing up straight and regarding Bryn. He was clever enough to realise that Bryn was not simply falling back from fear or an inability to keep up. He wasn't going to plunge blindly in.

Once again the character of the noise changed; the jeers and taunts became supportive and encouraging, willing Amero on to even the match. Finally he came forward, directing himself at Bryn's right, as Bryn knew that he would. He quickly sidestepped to receive the attack on his left side and parried it away, hoping that the shift in position would leave Amero's left exposed. He thrust quickly more out of a desire to capitalise on the possibility than on any perceived weakness. Amero's sword was there, however. Bryn reacted too slowly and Amero was quick to take advantage. He flicked his blade in, slapping it against Bryn's side.

Bryn shut his eyes and grimaced, recoiling at the stinging pain. Amero didn't wait and was already walking back to the black line when Bryn opened his eyes. When he breathed, his side raged in pain and brought tears to his eyes. He steadied himself and tied to conceal as much as he could. Amero might know that he was hurt, but he didn't know how much and Bryn needed to keep it that way.

Bryn reeled in pain as he followed Amero back to the centre of the arena. There was only so much he could do to hide it, and Amero smiled as they looked at each other across the black line. His smile was predatory and knowing. He had the advantage and would use it. Bryn tried to focus on taking long, slow breaths in an effort to control the pain. He wasn't sure if he was imagining it, but it felt as though the fresh bandage was soaked through. All he could do was try to push the things he could not control from his mind and focus on those that he could.

The Master of Arms restarted them and again Amero charged forward, confident now that Bryn was struggling and that victory was within his grasp. Bryn worked back across the sand parrying as he went, keeping his movements tight and precise, not overstraining his flank. Amero thought he had the match in his grasp, and Bryn was more than happy to encourage his overconfidence. Bryn's breath whistled from between his teeth as he fought to suppress the feeling of pain and weakness that was engulfing his entire body. If he was to win the next point, he would just have to accept how much it hurt and get on with it.

If Amero was so fond of deceit, perhaps Bryn could play him at his own game. Bryn let Amero drive him back across the sand, and at a moment of his choosing, he allowed his face to display the pain he was feeling. He tightened on his right side and drew his sword arm back, extending his left hand and dagger as though to compensate. Amero went straight for Bryn's weak side, but Bryn was ready and parried, with a fast riposte following. So convinced was he of victory, Amero had over extended himself and had no way to get back to defend. Bryn's riposte met no opposition. A second touch to him, and once again the crowd erupted with indignation and anger. The satisfaction almost made the pain worth it. He thought of taunting Amero on the way back to the black line, perhaps make him think the injury was a complete ruse, anything to try and unsettle him, but the pain was pressing on his thoughts too heavily. Breathing was enough of a struggle.

A trick was only likely to work once, but with luck Amero would be wondering if Bryn was indeed carrying an injury that could be capitalised on, or if it had all been a deception—if Bryn had been willing to concede a single touch in order to put him within reach of victory. Amero liked to play mind games. Now he would be wondering if Bryn did too.

Bryn tried to focus, to rally his thoughts on the positive to escape the pain. Amero would not have orchestrated the hate campaign, nor the attack the previous night if he had believed that he could beat Bryn in a fair fight. He wasn't as confident in his new technique as he might like people to think. It could be the only reason. All Bryn had to do was hold himself together for one more point.

Amero was more cautious when they restarted. Gone was the blustering confidence that had led him to concede the second point. Instead he reverted to safe, testing swordplay. Bryn worked hard, both to defend and to make it seem like he was uninjured. His right side felt wet, but he dared not look down to see if the blood was showing through his doublet. He was also starting to feel light headed.

Amero fired in a quick thrust that caught Bryn off guard. He didn't have a chance to react. He had allowed a distance to form between his mind and the duel, and his anticipation of what was happening to drift away. Another touch for Amero. A moment before, Bryn had been holding his own, but now it was slipping away from him. He was in serious trouble, and whoever scored the next point would win.

They began again; too quickly for Bryn's liking. There was barely enough time for him to catch his breath let alone prepare himself to fight for the next point. He tried to draw Amero in again, letting him press forward but always staying just out of reach in the hope that Amero would overextend and lose his balance. Bryn felt as though the action before him was receding farther and farther into the distance. It seemed like he was sinking deeper and deeper into cold water.

He was already falling to the ground when he conceded the third touch. The roar of the crowd became nothing more than a distant sound and Amero no more than a shadow standing above him.

High above, he could see the beams of the Amphitheatre's sun awnings, bare with their covers drawn back to allow the evening light in. Bryn could feel delirium take hold, so much so that he thought he could see a small boy clinging onto the end of one of the beams. His last thought before darkness swallowed him was of what a ridiculous notion that was.

CHAPTER THIRTY-ONE

BRYN CAME TO in the recovery room where Bautisto had bandaged him up before the duel. It took him a moment to recognise where he was, and a moment longer to remember what had come before. His heart sank. Bautisto was sitting on a stool next to the wall; otherwise the room was empty. Bryn tried to sit up but was quickly persuaded not to by the pain in his side. He noticed that someone had removed his doublet and the bandages were fresh.

Bautisto reacted to his movement and stood up. 'How are you feeling?'

'Not really sure. How long have I been here?'

'A little while now. The surgeon stitched your wound. It was far larger than before, but he thinks it will heal well.'

'That's something,' Bryn said.

'Do you remember what happened?'

'Some,' Bryn said. 'I remember the reset for the last point, dropping back, then... nothing.'

'You stumbled onto Amero's blade. He couldn't believe his luck. You're fortunate to be alive. The mob wanted him to finish you. When he declined I was worried they might charge down onto the arena floor to do it themselves. If he hadn't been so surprised by the way he won it, he might have given it further consideration.'

Bryn sighed. 'I suppose we should get moving.'

'It would be better to rest a little longer. You could use it, and I want to wait until all of the crowd have left.'

'They were that bad?'

Bautisto nodded. 'Yes, but they will forget before long.'

Bryn felt like he had woken up from a nightmare, only to discover it wasn't a nightmare. 'I'm done with this.'

Bautisto nodded. 'I thought you might say that, but perhaps you should take a few days to consider it. It will be difficult to get duels for a while, but when the vitriol fades the notoriety will stand in your favour.'

'No, I don't need any more time to think about it. I had my mind made up before today. This whole experience has killed it for me. I don't want fame or fortune; after all of this I'll just be glad to be unknown again.'

'And for money?'

'Duelling hasn't exactly been the best source of that. I need regular income. Part of this whole mess,' he gestured to the bandages, 'is because my family had to take out loans to put me through the Academy. It's a foolish way to make a living. There are far better ones.'

'Yes. Baking, brewing, carpentry. They would be a waste of your skills though.'

'The Master at the Academy said he could arrange a commission for me. I think it's time I took him up on his offer.

Bryn's sister took charge of his care while he was recovering. Both she and his mother had witnessed his debacle in the Amphitheatre, the only time either of them had seen him duel as a professional swordsman. He found it difficult to quell his anger at the whole experience as he lay on his sickbed. It made him wonder what he could have done to so anger the gods to ignore all of his hard work and hopes and bestow their rewards on Amero. Perhaps they had simply abandoned him.

Gilia diligently called each day to make sure that the wound and bandages were clean and that he had decent food to eat; even fully fit, his own culinary offerings were less than attractive so he appreciated this above all. However, having her selflessly tend to him like that made him feel worse about things. The only consolation behind his experience in the Amphitheatre was the purse. When duelling there, a swordsman got paid whether he won or not. If the debt collectors came calling again, there would be enough to get rid of them; unfortunately there wasn't enough to pay them off once and for all.

Someone knocked at his door and he moved to answer it. Gilia held out her hand before standing and walking to the door and opening it.

She was blocking the door and Bryn couldn't see who was there. He tried to catch a glimpse without straining too much. If he opened his wound, he knew he would incur Gilia's wrath, and the expense of another doctor's visit.

'He doesn't want to see you,' Gilia said.

Bryn felt a flush of panic at the thought it might be Amero, there to gloat. He couldn't make out what the other person was saying, but it was a woman's voice. That could only mean one person.

'It's all right, Gilia,' Bryn said. 'Let her in.'

Joranna walked into the room, followed by Gilia's disapproving gaze.

'You've looked better,' Joranna said, smiling.

'Felt better too,' Bryn said, wondering what she was there for.

'Are you all right?'

'I will be,' he said.

'I'm sure you'll be in greater demand now that you're the most infamous swordsman in Ostenheim.'

'You always see the positives, don't you?' Bryn said.

'When you're broke and you've a position to maintain, you have to,' she said, smiling wryly.

Bryn gestured around at his sparsely furnished apartment. He noticed his sister had tactfully stepped outside and closed the door behind her. 'I'm not planning on going back to the arena.'

'What will you do?'

'I'll scrounge up a commission with a regiment most likely, if I can't find anything better.'

'From penniless duellist to penniless officer. At least you'll have a nice uniform…'

'Always with the positives,' Bryn said.

'Like I said.' She smiled, then hesitated for a moment. 'I should go.'

Bryn knew it was foolish after all that had happened, but for some reason he felt as though there was something worth salvaging.

'I take it that an officer isn't enough either,' he said, rhetorically.

She smiled and shook her head. 'If I had a choice, it would be.' She left, giving Gilia a polite nod.

When Bryn's sister finally agreed that he was well enough to go out of the apartment without opening his wound again, he headed straight to see Major dal Damaso at the Academy.

The combination of the wound and several days of inactivity meant that the walk up the hill felt harder than it should have. He was sweating and out of breath by the time he got to the Academy's entrance gates. It was a harsh reminder of the past few weeks, but it was a relief to know they were now behind him. He hadn't heard a single mention of his name on the way there, the first time he could say that of a trip through the city in quite a while.

The adjutant sitting outside dal Damaso's office immediately recognised Bryn; he had passed by often enough over the years and was still a recent enough graduate to be fresh in his memory. He went into the office to check with the Major before bringing Bryn in.

'I've seen you better,' dal Damaso said.

'I've been better.' Bryn had to stop himself from adding sir, as had been his habit for all his years at the Academy, remembering the last conversation that they had.

'Nasty business with the Moreno lad. Never liked him, but could never put my finger on why. I don't imagine much of what's been touted around the city over the past couple of weeks is true, is it?'

'No. I could go into it all but it's not a particularly enjoyable story. Suffice to say it's all rubbish.'

'Bad business all the same. Not a good choice of someone to cross, although I never imagined he'd make much of a friend either unless you had something he wanted.'

It was only now, after his falling out with Amero, that people were revealing what they truly thought of him. It seemed that he was someone that everyone knew, but nobody actually liked. Bryn was disappointed that he had been such a bad judge of character for so long.

'Anyway,' the Major said, 'I'm sure this isn't a social call. What can I do for you?'

'When we last spoke, you mentioned that you'd be able to arrange an infantry commission for me. I'm not going anywhere near the arena again after last week, so I need to find something else.'

The Major shifted uncomfortably in his seat. 'I don't doubt anything you've said to me, Bryn, not for a moment. I've known you since you weren't much more than a lad and that's long enough to know the things being said about you aren't true. Sadly what I think doesn't count for very much.'

This wasn't going how Bryn had expected it to. He could see what was coming.

'The long and short of it is,' the Major said, 'the regiment won't have you. It'll just embarrass us both to ask now. Your name has been dragged through the mud and true or not, it's all too fresh for them to take you on as an officer. I'm sure that will change with a bit of time. If you were to come back in a few months, once it's all blown over, I don't foresee a difficulty.'

Bryn pursed his lips and nodded. There was nothing to say, and profound disappointment didn't come close to how he felt. There was a time when a military career would have been disappointing to him. Now that option wasn't even available. Amero had turned him into a pariah.

'It's one of the reasons I counselled against the arena in the first place,' the Major said. His face softened when he saw Bryn's reaction. 'Look, memories are short in this city. There's always a new hero to love, a new villain to hate. Come back to me in a few months' time, I'm sure I'll be able to place you after that.'

CHAPTER THIRTY-TWO

WAITING A FEW months for his infamy to fade would have been all well and good if Bryn had enough money. He didn't, and the bills facing his family would not wait. He could cover them for a few weeks, but no more. After leaving Major dal Damaso's office he wandered back down the hill into the city, not heading anywhere in particular. It was probably habit that brought him to Bautisto's salon in Docks. Seeing that Bautisto was there, he decided to go in.

He had only been away a week, and although Bautisto had called on him to see how his recovery was progressing, it felt far longer. A gulf had opened between him and the life he had led only a handful of days earlier. As he opened the door, he was greeted by the sound of clashing blades. Bautisto had already found his replacement.

He shut the door and waited by it for the swordsmen to finish. The salon was no different than before—still grotty, in need of painting and looking as though it might fall down in the not too distant future—but he felt like a stranger there.

Bautisto stopped and saluted his sparring partner, who looked to be about eighteen, the right age to be preparing for entry to the Academy.

'Thank you, Brevio, that will be all for today.'

The lad quickly gathered his belongings and made his way out, nodding to Bryn as he passed.

'Good to see you on your feet again,' Bautisto said.

'Good to be up and about. I was getting bored lying around at home all day. I see you've found some new students.'

'Yes, four in total. All preparing to sit their entrance tests for the Academy so they won't be here for long, but I'm happy to have the work nonetheless. A couple of duellists have expressed an interest too, but nothing certain yet.'

'I'm glad to hear it, you deserve the business.'

'Yes.' Bautisto shrugged. 'The only reason they're here is because I used to train Amero. Still, I'll take their money.'

'Might as well,' Bryn said. 'A bit of coin never hurts.'

'How is your search for new employment going?'

'Badly. Apparently my name is too tarnished for a commission right now. The Major said I should wait a few months and he'd be able to find me something, but I need to make money now.'

'I'd offer you work here, but you know how it is. Four students is still not enough to pay to have the place painted, and they'll be gone by the end of the month.'

'That's all right,' Bryn said. 'I was just wandering around and ended up here without really thinking about it.'

'I can't offer you much advice on how to live your life. I wouldn't be living in this city if I'd made all the correct decisions. The only one I can advise you against making with any confidence is the Black Carpet. Stay away from it. There are always better ways to make money.'

In truth, Bryn hadn't even thought of the illegal duelling clubs, named after the patch of black painted on the ground where the matches were held. There was decent money to be made and regular matches, though not as good as in the arena and only then if you weren't killed first, which happened as often as not. With his new found infamy, he'd probably be able to command a higher than average price, but contemplating it made him feel nauseous.

'No, I hadn't even considered it. I've farther to fall before I end up there.'

☾

Rejection followed rejection as Bryn searched Ostenheim for a job. He looked at tutoring and body guarding, the two main city occupations for bannerets. Despite the damage done to his name, it was his firm desire to stay in the city. He wanted to be close to his family, both to protect them from another episode like the bailiffs, and so that he could ensure they were properly provided for. He couldn't do that if he was traipsing around the countryside as a mercenary, never knowing when he'd be able to send money home.

The Bannerets' Hall kept a list of vacant positions in the city for the benefit of its members, but Bryn had exhausted the list of suitable jobs quickly. Everyone knew his name and didn't want anything to do with him. Becoming a mercenary and leaving the city looked like the only option when, on his last visit to see if anything new was available, he spotted something. It would never have been his first choice, but he was long beyond that point.

The headsman dealt with the ordinary citizens of Ostenheim who were convicted of crimes that warranted the death penalty, which were surprisingly numerous. A member of the gentle classes, a banneret or an aristocrat—the higher echelons of the merchant class, the burgesses, were considered commoners—would only meet with the headsman's axe if found guilty of treason, again something that came in numerous forms and was far more regularly committed as a result than one might think. Otherwise, the gentle classes had the right to choose trial by combat.

In order to facilitate this right, the city magistrates had to

234

maintain a panel of swordsmen to represent the Duke in these matters. It was not a sought-after job. The judicial duels were always fought to the death. If the accused killed the city's appointed swordsman they were free to go. It was rare; hardly any were skilled enough for the duel to give them a better chance of survival than the headsman's block.

Few swordsmen saw the job as being anything other than an executioner with a fancier title. It was well paid however, and was certainly better than the Black Carpet, Bryn's only other alternative if he wanted to remain in the city.

With no particular enthusiasm, Bryn called to the Palace of Justice located beside the Barons' Hall on Crossways. He announced himself as a banneret and was led through to see the magistrate in charge of the judicial swordsmen, who resided in a small office tucked away in the back of the building.

'I'm told you're a banneret,' the magistrate said, when the clerk led Bryn in.

'Yes, Banneret of the Blue,' he said, sitting in the chair the magistrate gestured to.

'Fantastic.' The magistrate had a ruddy, fleshy face, but intelligent eyes behind a pair of wire framed spectacles. The rim of white hair around his otherwise bald head was messed by the black felt magistrate's hat that now resided on a wooden stand on his desk.

'What's your name, Banneret?'

'Bryn Pendollo.'

The magistrate's face fell, the change from animated to taciturn very pronounced. Bryn wondered if he was as good guarding his thoughts when hearing trials.

'Is that a problem?' Bryn asked.

'No, no. Not at all. Just recognise the name is all. None of that's important here. We haven't had a Banneret of the Blue apply for a position in all my time as a magistrate. You know what the job entails?'

'Representing the Duke and the city when someone accused of a capital offence chooses trial by combat.' He would have said something glib were it not for how much he needed the job.

'That's exactly it,' the magistrate said. 'You understand that you will be expected to kill without compunction. I know bannerets have moral considerations, honour and what not, when it comes to killing.'

'I realise that,' Bryn said.

'The best way to think of it is upholding the city's honour. The Duke's. You are comfortable with fighting to the death? You must remember that you might also be killed. It's rare, but it has happened.'

'I can reconcile myself to what needs to be done, and the risk it involves.'

'Excellent. Sign this warrant and you will be the newest of the Duke's Judicial Swordsmen. Before you do though, there is one other thing. If you fail in your duty to the Duke, and refuse to carry out your charge while in the court, you will be guilty of an offence against the state. Treason.' He slid a piece of parchment covered with ornate script across the table to Bryn, and handed him a pen.

Bryn thought for a moment, and signed. He didn't bother asking what the pay was.

'Excellent,' the magistrate said. He took the parchment back and blotted Bryn's signature before adding his own and repeating the process.

'The aristocracy aren't quite as riddled with criminals as one might expect, or they don't get caught that often, so your services will only be required once a month or so. The payment is fifty crowns per trial.'

It was a good living for very little work, distasteful though it was.

'It just so happens that there's a trial next week in which

the Duke needs representation. Are you comfortable starting so soon?'

'I don't see why not,' Bryn said.

'You'll need to be properly equipped. Plain, black duelling clothes. An undecorated sword, and dagger if you choose to fence with one. They'll all be provided if you speak with the commissary on your way out. A level of... solemnity needs to be maintained, if you follow.'

'Of course,' Bryn said.

CHAPTER THIRTY-THREE

BRYN'S HANDS WERE cold as he waited to get called in to the judicial arena. He'd been shown around the Palace of Justice earlier. Unlike the open-air duelling arenas, the judicial one was indoors. It was similar to the salons in the Academy, but without the mirrors lining the walls. There was a gallery where the magistrate sat watching to ensure everything was conducted in full accordance with the law, with two bailiffs on the floor to carry out his instructions.

One of them opened the door to Bryn.

'We're ready for you, Banneret.'

Bryn nodded, stood and walked out into the salon. He was greeted by a musty smell. It was simply the hallmark of a poorly ventilated room, but it made him think of death. His sword was still sheathed, a plain, army issue hilt mounted on a light duelling blade. It was sturdy and functional, but there were no concessions to style or artistry. He felt sinister in his completely black duelling clothes, but they fit well and were practical. No matter how many positives he tried to cling to, he felt as though a dark cloud loomed low over his head.

A moment later a man was led into the salon from a different door. Bryn was surprised. Short, overweight and with a flushed, nervous face, he was as unlikely a candidate for trial by combat as Bryn could imagine. He would have had as good a chance of surviving the headsman's block, and Bryn doubted he had held a sword in his life.

As well as making an unlikely looking swordsman, he didn't look like a criminal. If anything, he bore the appearance of a serial victim.

'For the crime of defrauding the taxes of the county of Lloedale, you are sentenced to trial by combat. If you are successful, this court will deem you as having satisfied justice and you will be released,' the magistrate said.

The man nodded eagerly, as though still entertaining the notion that this was a possibility. He had started sweating heavily.

'Banneret, are you ready to carry out the requirements of justice as prescribed by His Grace, the Duke of Ostia?'

Bryn nodded. 'I stand ready to do the Duke's bidding, Magistrate.' It was the formal response required. He drew his sword. He had an uneasy feeling—this was an execution and bore no resemblance to a duel—but he'd known what he was getting himself into when he signed the warrant. Now was not the time for second thoughts.

One of the bailiffs undid the manacles binding the accused's hands, and handed him a sword. Bryn's suspicion was confirmed from the way he took it, allowing the point to drop as soon as he took the weight. He put his second hand on it and raised the blade, which betrayed the shaking in his hands. He looked utterly pathetic.

The bailiffs stepped back, leaving Bryn to be about his job. He reminded himself that the man was a criminal, there because he had broken the law. He had stolen from the state, and by corollary from Bryn and his family. He had no idea what drove that short, sweaty, pathetic little man to do what he did, but the prospect of killing him affronted Bryn's sense of honour in every way imaginable.

'Begin.'

Bryn felt his stomach twist with disgust, but at least he could be merciful about it. Bryn thrust. In one movement he knocked the man's blade out of the way and ran him through the heart. He pulled his blade free, turned and walked back to the waiting room. Judicial Duellist was not the job for him.

Bryn used the mundane task of cleaning and oiling the blade of his sword—he found it difficult to think of it as anything other than an executioner's blade—to take his mind off what he had just done.

There was a knock at the door and the magistrate entered. 'That was very well done, Banneret. I've not seen anyone dispatch an accused as efficiently, although he admittedly wasn't the most challenging of defendants. You Bannerets of the Blue really are a class above. The precision of that thrust. First class. You'll be in demand here as soon as the other magistrates hear about it.'

Bryn grunted in appreciation but said nothing. He had to sign a new warrant for every trial—they were specific to each accused. There was no way he would sign another one or fight another duel like that, even if it meant starving in the street. In choosing never to do it again, Bryn knew he was finally acknowledging that he had exhausted the potential for work in Ostenheim.

A lack of work within the city did not mean Bryn's search there ended. Many jobs that would take him out of the city were recruited for there. The guilds regularly hired in this fashion, and Bryn hoped that he would find something that way. They hired swordsmen to escort transport wagons, work that was said to be dull, and would take him away from the city for long periods, but paid well.

As with all things in Ostenheim, Crossways was the place to begin his search. The square was filled with market stalls, and those for every other type of business imaginable. Like businesses tended to cluster together, and one section—tucked away in the shade of one of the arcades lining the square—was given over to mercenary companies looking to hire swordsmen, thugs, brawlers; anyone who could hold a weapon. There were wars all over the world at any given time, large and small. There was almost always trouble in the Free Principalities of Auracia to the south and there was the recent eruption of hostility with Ruripathia to the north, which had escalated far beyond a punitive border raid. If he felt the need to go farther afield to escape the spectre of his duel with Amero, he was sure there was fighting that needed doing elsewhere too.

The difficulty was going to be finding something that was acceptable to him; what he wanted, and what wanted him had so far run contrary. His name was dirt, and he had no desire to make it worse by signing on with the type of mercenary company that gave all the others a bad name.

Every young swordsman had heard tales of the duplicity and avarice of mercenary companies, raping, pillaging and cheating their way from war to war. There were as many stories of heroism, sacrifice and honour, but they were told with less frequency. Heroic tales were usually reserved for soldiers in the regiments of some great lord. After what he had already been through, he felt he could do with more of the latter than the former.

The companies' recruiters set themselves out with little stalls—usually no more than a table draped with a banner in the colours of the company. Their colours were often gaudy eyesores that were an ostentatious attempt at a statement by their leader that his company was superior to any of the others. Most of the stalls were manned by maimed men, a missing arm here, a missing eye there, missing teeth almost everywhere. It was not a positive advertisement for the work, but Bryn realised it showed that they made an effort to look after their comrades who could no longer fight.

Years of training imbued one with a bearing and physique that were as strong a sign of one's profession as carrying a notice stating the same. Bryn sought out the men with this soldierly look, rather than those bearing the hallmarks of thieves, murderers and rapists pretending to be something they were not.

The companies were always hungry to fill out their recruiting quotas, and Bryn began to attract attention as soon as he walked into the arcade where they gathered.

'Sign on with the Company of the White Cockerel, friend,' called one, a fellow with a tatty looking patch over one eye.

The name wasn't particularly attractive to Bryn, so he shook his head and continued.

'Bonuses and a share of any plunder. Join the Band of Bladesmen,' another implored. He had the appearance of a recent resident in the city gaol, and the only type of blade he looked familiar with was a stiletto. Not someone Bryn had any interest in marching with. Whoever had chosen the name had a decent sense of alliteration, but nothing else of positive note. Bryn shook his head again and moved on.

They were all the same; gaudy, flamboyant and exactly what sprung to mind when Bryn cast his thoughts back to the stories of mercenary bands laying waste to entire swathes of countryside and putting villagers to the sword over a chicken or sack of vegetables.

Finally he passed by one that made no effort at all to attract his attention, which piqued his curiosity.

'What are you hiring for?'

'Escort work.'

That was all he said; the recruiter went back to a close inspection of something he had just picked out of his nose, behaving as though Bryn were not standing there watching him.

'Escort work for what?'

The man looked up at Bryn, not pleased by the disturbance to what he clearly found to be a fascinating study. 'Supply wagons to the army up North.'

'What's the pay?'

The man seemed surprised that the questioning had gone any farther than the disclosure of the fact that the work was watching over supplies being pulled slowly northward. He sat up and leaned forward, showing interest for the first time.

'You a banneret?'

'I am,' Bryn said.

'Fourteen florins a day. Round trip takes about forty days.' He stopped at that point. The pay wasn't bad for the work, but unlike the other recruiters this man didn't have the luxury of being able to add in the promise of booty, which could be substantial. Bryn expected that most potential recruits walked away at this point, if they had not done so already.

Forty days out of the city with decent pay was an attractive proposition. All he wanted was enough to be able to keep the bailiffs from his mother's door, and his belly full until his reputation had been sufficiently weathered to make him palatable for a regular commission. One trip might be sufficient for the tarnish to wear off his name.

'When do the wagons leave?'

'Every few days. There's a train leaving tomorrow and we're still short on numbers. The Duke isn't providing enough men; that's why the guilds have chosen to take on extra at their own expense. They don't get paid for the wagons they send, only the ones that arrive. You interested?'

'I am,' Bryn said.

'Sign the ledger then, and you'll be a proud member of the Guilds' Company.'

'You're getting better at this,' Amero said, as he felt the cold flush through his limbs and ease the fatigue, aches and stiffness.

'Practice,' the old man said. 'And you're the only person I work for now. Don't need anything else, and there's no point drawing attention to myself for no reason.'

Amero nodded. It was wise advice indeed, advice it occurred to him he should take heed of. His profile in the city was growing by the day. While there were still relatively few who could match his face to his name, that number was growing with each match he fought. It was only a matter of time before someone spotted him on his way to this daily appointment, and it wouldn't be long before they discovered what it was for. That would be the end of it all. Disgrace would follow. He had to prevent that from happening, but there was only one way he could see doing that.

He had only ever gone to the mage to help him get up to the standard required to prosper in the arena in as short a time as possible. He was there now. He was the one who did all the hard work. The skill was all his. Now that he had reached and surpassed that level, did he really need to continue seeing the mage? Was it worth the risk, when he knew he was better than any of his peers? He didn't need to work that hard any longer to maintain what he had acquired.

There was only one obvious answer. The risk was too great, and the benefits were no longer enough. The old man always slumped into his seat, exhausted after their session. Amero looked at him as he sat there, expecting Amero to leave the payment and go without another word. He didn't expect Amero's dagger in his eye. Amero held it firmly as the old man's body twitched several times before eventually remaining still.

CHAPTER THIRTY-FOUR

BRYN WALKED TO the depot to report for work with a sense of purpose, the travelling bag slung over his shoulder containing, he hoped, all that he would need for the trip. He had spent the previous evening with his mother and sister, and while they weren't happy about him having to leave the city they realised it was the only option for all of them.

Bryn was confident that he was leaving them with more than enough money to get by. There was the money left over from the duel, his pay for the judicial work and an upfront payment of a quarter of his wage for the escort work. It wasn't a fortune but it meant there was enough in reserve to pay any bailiffs that came knocking on their door. Bryn didn't think there was any risk of that, however. Amero had already achieved all he wanted from taking over the debt; he had no reason to press it farther. In all likelihood, he had already written it off. It was too insignificant for him to waste any more time on it, just as Bryn was. He felt his temper flare when he thought of it, but forced it down. Amero didn't care; the anger only ate away at Bryn.

With each familiar sight, sound and smell, Bryn felt a tumultuous mix of emotion, hate, betrayal, disappointment, heartbreak and shame. There were also the remnants of Amero's hate campaign to contend with. Occasionally someone recognised him and felt it their responsibility to let him know what everyone thought of him. With luck, that would have subsided by the time he got home. He wondered which unfortunate would next fall foul of Amero's meteoric rise.

As bad as all of that made him feel, it wasn't the worst part. It was the shame that was the most difficult to bear. It was hard to put the blame for all of his miseries on Amero. He bore a great part of the responsibility himself. Pride, ambition, stupidity. He couldn't blame anyone else for that.

The depot was a hive of activity when Bryn arrived. Gangs of men hauled sacks and crates from the warehouses and loaded them onto the waiting wagons. The guilds that had the contract to supply the army made a fortune doing it but, as the recruiter had pointed out, they were only paid for the wagons that arrived. They wanted to ensure every single one that left the city reached the army intact.

Bryn made his presence known and was directed to speak with the escort's captain, a banneret called Deverardo.

As he wandered around looking, he had to dodge between the teams of brutish looking oxen that were being led out of the depot and hitched to the wagons, four to a team. The wagons themselves were flatbeds, loaded high with whatever it was they were carrying and then covered with grey oilskins and strapped down securely. Despite the early hour, the depot was buzzing with the energy of the final preparations for departure.

Eventually Bryn came to a group of men, one of whom had a rapier strapped to his ample waist.

'Banneret Deverardo?'

'Yes?' he said.

Deverardo was not at all what Bryn expected. Usually a banneret still actively employed needed to maintain a certain physical competence. Deverardo had given up any effort in this regard some time before. He looked as though he liberally helped himself to the provisions on the wagons as they travelled north.

'Banneret of the Blue Pendollo,' Bryn said.

'Ah, excellent. I've been expecting you. The rest of the lads are former soldiers for the most part, know their stuff, but it's nice to have another banneret along. Have you done this type of work before?'

'No, first time,' Bryn said.

'That's not a problem; there's not much to it really. The bandits tend to stay clear when they can see armed escorts… Wait, Pendollo you say?'

Bryn nodded.

'Well, I've heard the name and more besides, but I don't judge a man until I've known him a while. I know the duelling promoters like to spice things up a little for the crowd, so do right by me and I'll do right by you.'

'I appreciate that,' Bryn said. 'You won't have any problems with me.'

'Good. We leave in twenty minutes. You can take your pick of the riding horses over there. The guilds kit us out pretty well—want to make sure their wagons arrive—so most of them are decent beasts. If there's anything else you need, talk to one of the guild commissaries, they'll sort you out.'

Bryn nodded and went to look at the horses. Despite his poor physique, Deverardo seemed to be a decent man.

The horses were much as Deverardo had said. None were outstanding, but they were all healthy and reliable looking. He chose one and led it back toward where Deverardo was in discussion with one of the wagon drivers. Bryn was relieved by Deverardo's reaction to his name. He hoped the other men were either similarly open-minded, or better yet, completely ignorant of it.

Up until meeting Deverardo, Bryn had a nagging fear in the back of his head that he would be stuck for forty days taking the orders of a man with a preformed opinion. With that in mind, he could forgive corpulence, incompetence or pretty much anything else. Perhaps he should follow Deverardo's example and not pre-judge someone. Not maintaining a fighting physique didn't nec-essarily speak of anything other than a fondness for food and a job that placed him in no danger.

The guilds were well practised at getting the supply wag-ons underway; as the recruiter had mentioned they sent them out every few days. A hungry army is an unhappy one and the con-tracts were far too lucrative for the guilds to risk losing them to a rival. They made sure that the supply was regular and reliable. Bryn had barely chosen his horse and stowed his belongings on one of the wagons when Deverardo gave the order to move off. The air filled with the shouts of the wagon drivers, the cracks of their whips and the creaking groans of the wagons' axles. It was exciting, the start of a new adventure, and the chance to leave the misery of the past months behind him. Was it hoping too much that it would all be forgotten when he returned?

What Deverardo had said was fresh in Bryn's mind, and he was determined to prove his worth. He did his best to appear alert and vigilant—even with the city only barely out of sight, the roads grew dangerous—but it was difficult. The monotony of the task wore away at him, and even the excitement of a new experience and the best of intentions could not keep him focussed for more than a few hours.

It did not appear that he was the only one. Several wag-ons ahead, Deverardo lounged back reading a book. It had not occurred to Bryn to bring one and he was rapidly beginning to regret the oversight. Each time he allowed his mind to drift, Amero appeared. Bryn focussed on the horizon. The journey would be a difficult one if he was plagued by unwelcome thoughts.

CHAPTER THIRTY-FIVE

BRYN HAD NEVER been near a war before and beyond the tales of fluttering banners, heroic deeds and glory that filled the books on the subject, he knew little of it. Those stories had always struck him as being unlikely, and he had no idea of what to really expect. When they moved from what was definitely Ostia to the region that was contested, there was no mistaking the fact.

The land gradually took on a look of depredation. Fields didn't seem as well tended, nor did the roads, something his back could testify to, jarred as it was by the frequent potholes that the wagon now encountered. There were not as many people. Indeed, potholes were the only things he saw with any increasing regularity. The land seemed to have been stripped of anything of value—foodstuffs, building material; anything that could be carried away.

Seeing the first body came as something of a shock. No one else on the convoy paid it any attention, but it was the first Bryn had seen under those circumstances. He'd seen Mistria killed in the Amphitheatre, but that had been neat. Tidy almost. The men he had killed had seemed likewise. This corpse was anything but. It lay, crumpled, by the side of the road, what remained of the face twisted in an expression of pain and terror. It had been there for some time by the look of it; it was the stuff nightmares were made of.

He wondered why no one had collected the body and taken it away, family or friends perhaps. It didn't take long to realise that it was probably because they were all dead too. Bryn didn't notice any weapons. They could have been looted, but more than likely the person never had any to begin with. It was a grim introduction to war.

The army had moved on since the wagoners were last in the North. Deverardo had to send out scouts in an effort to find it, but a marching army was not a difficult thing to track. Bryn was hopeful he might be chosen to go—anything to break the monotony—but realised he was too new to be given command of the scouting party, and anything less would be an affront to a banneret. He remained behind with the convoy as it continued to wend its way north.

They were twenty days into their journey north—the point at which Bryn expected they would have completed their mission and be heading for home—and still waiting to hear back from their scouts when Deverardo spotted smoke on the horizon. He halted the wagons while he considered what it might mean. Bryn slipped from his wagon bench onto his horse and rode forward to Deverardo's wagon.

'Trouble?' Bryn said.

'Possibly. Hard to tell from here. With no sign of the army, any fighting should still be a long way north.'

'Bandits then?'

'Most likely. We've enough swords to scare them off. We'll continue on. No need to be concerned yet.'

The smoke grew less as they moved toward it, the fires that caused it dying out. When they arrived at its source, they were greeted by the burnt out husk of what had once been a small village—probably as recently as that morning. There was no sign of any life.

Deverardo clambered down from his wagon and surveyed the destruction. 'A quick stop to check for survivors and then we move on,' he said.

Bryn nodded and fell in behind him. They walked toward the charred ground, and the rest of the escort men followed after them. The wagoners took the chance to unharness their oxen and water them.

No one said a word as they walked into the village, surveying the devastation. Bryn had only taken a few steps onto the blackened ground when he saw the first of the former inhabitants, a blackened husk that bore little resemblance to the human being it had once been. The features were so badly burned that it was impossible to tell whether it had been a man or a woman. As they moved farther in, bodies became a frequent sight. They were all burned; the entire village had been torched, but from the position of the bodies it looked as though they had been killed before the flames got to them. Bryn felt the bile rise in his throat and he struggled to stop himself from vomiting.

In one or two places there were still fires burning, but there was no sign of anything living or any trace of the men that had caused the devastation. Bryn felt a mix of anger and revulsion. It was difficult to separate the romantic and honourable notions he had of soldiering from the reality he was faced with. He couldn't understand what would drive men to such barbarity.

Deverardo approached and saw the look on Bryn's face. 'First time you've seen something like this?' he said.

Bryn nodded.

Deverardo grimaced and looked around. 'Best get used to it. You'll see plenty more like it in this line of work. Always what's left behind after the fighting. People who can't take care of themselves usually end up dead. Just be glad it's not anyone you care about.'

'What drives men to do something like this? They were just village folk. They can't have had anything worth stealing.'

'Not a whole lot. I've passed by this village before. There wasn't much here to begin with. But I've seen men kill each other over a chicken, so it doesn't need to be much if the want for it's great enough. We'd best get back to the wagons and be on our way. If anyone survived this, they're long gone.'

Deverardo shouted to the other men and they turned and started back toward the wagons. The sound of approaching horses joined his voice. Some of the more alert men drew their blades and Bryn thought it was prudent to do likewise. Considering where they were, there was no way of knowing if the approaching horsemen were friend or foe. Deverardo looked to Bryn with a spooked expression that said Bryn drawing his sword was the correct reaction.

The horsemen came into view, all wearing the grey uniforms of Ruripathian soldiers. On foot, running away wasn't an option; they wouldn't have gotten far before the horsemen were on them. When Bryn cast a glance back to the wagons, he could see another, smaller group of grey uniformed horsemen approaching them. Each group outnumbered the men of the Guilds' Company; there was nowhere to run.

'Who commands here?' the leader of the horsemen said.

They had the look of regular soldiers, rather than bandits. Bryn was hopeful that their behaviour would be more measured as a result. That they had not charged in and attacked was a positive sign; perhaps Deverardo could talk them out of the situation, but probably without the contents of the wagons.

'I do,' Deverardo said, after a moment's hesitation.

'I am Colonel dal Ewalt. In the name of the Crown of Ruripathia I place you under arrest for the pillage and destruction of the village of Grelitz.'

'Now listen here,' Deverardo said. 'We've only just gotten here ourselves. This destruction had nothing to do with us. We're not even soldiers. We're just escorting the wagons north. We wanted to see if there was anyone left we could help.'

The Ruripathian colonel sneered. 'A likely story. You are Ostians, yes?'

'We are,' Deverardo said, puffing out his chest in what struck Bryn as a rather ridiculous and futile demonstration of bravado, as though being Ostian meant his word was beyond reproach. 'This could as easily have been done by Ruripathian brigands.'

'No. This was done by Ostians,' dal Ewalt said, gesturing to the charred remains of the village and its citizens. 'You are Ostians. In the absence of any others, the guilt seems most likely to lie with you.'

Bryn could see they were getting the blame no matter what. The Ruripathians wanted heads for what had happened to the village, and so long as those heads were Ostian, guilt was unimportant.

Surrender was not an option as far as Bryn was concerned, although he worried that Deverardo's nerve would not be up to starting a fight. If they were to lay down their arms, immediate execution seemed the most likely outcome. The Ruripathians wanted Ostian blood, one way or the other.

There was a moment of quiet where both sides regarded each other. Several of the Ostians, including Bryn, had weapons drawn while all of the Ruripathians still had theirs sheathed. If there was to be any hope for them, taking the initiative seemed to be it. Deverardo was proving himself to be completely unable to make a decision; years of easy wagon duty had dulled his reactions, and Bryn was unwilling to squander this single advantage.

'At them, lads!' he shouted.

They rushed at the Ruripathians before they had a chance to draw their weapons. Bryn was so caught up in the moment that he didn't have time to think about the danger. The sounds of shouts, whinnying, and clashing steel filled the air as Bryn traded a couple of blows with a Ruripathian trooper before pulling him off his horse and running him through.

Deverardo was in the middle of it all, roaring and hacking like a man possessed. He was not a bad swordsman, despite his physique and his initial ambivalence was forgotten.

Bryn cut down a second Ruripathian and pulled another from his horse, ducking a blow aimed at his head in the process. Caught up in the centre of things it was difficult to see which way the fight was going, but outnumbered as they were, Bryn didn't get his hopes up. There was nothing for it but to fight as hard as he could and hope for the best. So much for simply going along to frighten off bandits, Bryn thought.

He clashed blades with another man, knocking his guard to one side and prepared for a killing strike when there was a bright flash behind his eyes, and then nothing.

Coming back to one's senses after an injury was not pleasant, and something that Bryn seemed to be doing all too often for his liking. As was always the case, it took a moment for memory to return as he looked around trying to fend off the feelings of anxiety that accompany such confusion.

He was sitting with his back against a tree. His hands were tied behind him, uncomfortably crushed between his body and the trunk. He tried to lean forward a little to take some of the pressure off them, and his movement attracted attention.

'Colonel! He's awake!'

A group of men made their way into Bryn's field of view, one of whom he recognised as the Colonel of the Ruripathian horsemen. They stopped in front of Bryn, draping him in their shadow.

'You are a banneret?'

Bryn looked up at the silhouetted shape above him. 'I am.'

'Your men said as much. That's why you are still alive.'

'Banneret Deverardo?' Bryn asked.

'The fat one?'

Bryn nodded.

'Dead in the skirmish.'

Bryn didn't feel one way or the other about it; it was to be expected. The only real surprise was that he was still alive.

'Your wagons have been seized and your men have been executed for what happened here. As a banneret you will be held to a higher standard however.' He turned back to his men. 'Hang him!'

The sun rose, signalling an end to a hellish night and the start of what would be an even worse day. The rope suspending Bryn from the tree swayed gently from side to side in the breeze, and each time it tugged on his shoulders agonisingly. The Ruripathian understanding of hanging differed from the Ostian, theirs being a far more brutal experience. They had tied his hands behind his back, and suspended him from the branch by his bound wrists. He had lost the feeling in his arms at some point, as his body weight pulled him down, slowly tearing his shoulders from their sockets. He found it difficult to breathe. All things considered, a further deterioration in that regard was probably a blessing.

As the sun grew stronger, he could feel it sear his bare skin; the Ruripathians had been charitable enough to spare him his dignity and leave him in his britches, but the bare, stretched, red skin of his chest and shoulders stung furiously.

He rotated slowly one way before the tension in the rope built and twisted it back the other. The slow spinning made him dizzy and nauseated. He didn't have the strength left in his shoulders and neck to lift his head, but he could hear birds on the branch above him. His imagination filled in what his eyes could not tell him. He pictured a flock of evil looking carrion birds, patiently waiting for their chance to get at him without interruption. He wished more than anything he had fallen during the fight like Deverardo. It seemed that in this, as with everything else, Divine Fortune did not favour him.

CHAPTER THIRTY-SIX

BRYN COULD HEAR a crackling noise and the faintest scent of smoke tinged the air. He realised he was lying on his back rather than hanging from a tree. He tried to open his eyes, and they did so only grudgingly. Darkness and flame were all he could see. One of the Three Hells perhaps? His first emotion was indignation. Had he not already suffered enough in life only to be punished further in death?

He shifted a little, but that small movement was enough to make him gasp as his shoulders screamed in pain. He had never been a particularly diligent student of theology and could not recall which of the Three Hells tortured its inhabitants, but he would no doubt discover sooner rather than later. His skin felt as though it had been roasted, and he couldn't even begin to describe the pain in his shoulders. He had never experienced anything like it, and it made him wonder at the nature of the injury they had sustained. His hands and arms were numb, but he wasn't sure if that was a blessing or a cause for concern.

'You're awake.'

A woman's voice. An unusual accent, not Ostian, not Ruripathian. A Borderlander? Unfortunate enough to be joining him for an eternity in this awful place? He tried to speak, but no words would come, only a dry and painful croak.

'You shouldn't try to talk yet. Drink first.'

The teat of a water-skin was pressed to his lips and he felt cool liquid spill into his mouth. It made him realise how thirsty he was and he gulped at it greedily. It was an instant relief to his swollen tongue and dry throat. He tried to speak again. The result was no more successful than his first effort, but there was less pain in his throat.

'Don't talk. Just rest. You're safe now.' The same female voice. He didn't feel as though there was any possible alternative to simply complying with her instructions. His head still felt like it was spinning as it had been when he was suspended from the rope. He tried to relax and closed his eyes. Sleep followed swiftly.

When he next woke there was less pain when he moved. The raw feeling on his skin had lessened, but the agony in his shoulders had not. As he shifted his body awkwardly, his arms dragged behind. He tried to move them, but there was no response and, just as worryingly, no feeling. The pain from his shoulders more than made up for it though.

The fire was still there and he could see a dark shape moving around on the other side.

'I can't move my arms,' he said. At least his voice was working.

The dark shape stopped moving and he thought he could make out a pair of eyes twinkling in the firelight. The fire crackled and popped and filled the air with smoky warmth.

'You were hanging from them for at least a day, maybe longer. They were both out of their sockets when I cut you down.'

As best he could tell, they were both back where they should be now. Had she done that? 'Who are you?'

'My name's Ayla. I lived in the village.'

'I'm Bryn. Do you have any more water?'

She shuffled around the fire and put the teat of the water skin to his lips again. As he drank he wondered why she had cut him down and kept him alive.

'Thank you for cutting me down,' he said, when he had finished drinking.

'Nearly didn't, but I reckoned that you were strung up for what happened to the village and I know you aren't responsible. The ones that did it were long gone before the flames had died. With the state you were in when I found you, I didn't see much point binding your hands, so don't go thinking that was me being soft. I've a knife and a sword and I've no problems using either if you don't behave.'

Bryn tried moving one of his arms again, to no effect. He hoped he was not imagining it but the pain seemed a little less. Not pleasant, but encouraging nonetheless. 'Who did do it?'

'Doesn't matter. This year it was Ostians; last year Ruripathians came close to doing the same. Soldiers are never good for ordinary folk. Doesn't matter who they fight for. It was only a matter of time before something like this happened.'

Bryn thought he heard her voice catch a little toward the end as she spoke. 'Where are we?'

'An old hunting shack. I've been here ever since they burned the village. I don't think anyone else managed to get away. I've been looking, but I can't find anyone.'

'What happened to the others who were with me?'

'Dead. Some were in the ashes of the village, more were behind the tree where you were hanging. Friends?'

'No, just men I worked with. I hardly knew any of them really.'

'Why didn't they kill you too?' she asked.

'I'm a banneret. They thought I deserved worse than a quick death.'

'Well, joke's on them then. The gods must have been smiling on you.'

Bryn laughed sardonically. 'What are you going to do now?'

'Don't know. I was looking for anyone else who got away, but I suppose that if anyone did they'll have gone somewhere else by now. Nothing left to keep them in Grelitz now except burnt bodies. If it hadn't been for finding you, I'd probably be gone by now myself.'

'Where?'

'Don't know. All my kin and everyone I knew were in Grelitz.' Her voice faltered again as she spoke.

'Grelitz is the name of the village?'

She nodded. 'Was the name.'

It was only now that Bryn realised that he still had no idea what she looked like, whether she was old or young. The only light in the shack came from the fire, and that left plenty of shadows. He would have tried moving to get a better look, but his shoulders hurt so badly the thought of moving made him want to vomit.

'You from Ostenheim?' she said.

'Yes.'

'You're not a soldier. What brought you all the way out here?'

'I needed work. Escorting supply wagons was all I could get. Doesn't seem like such a good idea now though.'

She let out a staccato laugh. 'Plenty of things are like that.'

It only took a couple of days cooped up inside the shack before Bryn felt strong enough to venture outside again. In truth it was as much boredom as recovery that encouraged him to try. He was still not sure that he would make it farther than a few paces. He was weak and unsteady on his feet, and wasn't able to put his hand out quickly to grab onto something for support, which made his efforts perilous.

Ayla watched him warily. Despite the hours that they had

spent talking, and the many more that she had spent caring for him, feeding him, it was obvious that she didn't trust him. For the first few days she had appeared to him only as a shadowy figure in the gloomy hunting shack. He had come to know her by the sound of her voice alone, his imagination creating an image of what she looked like. Fair hair and skin were common in the north, and that was how he pictured her. Her voice was always tense, strained, so it was impossible to tell how old she was. It could be a sign of age, or as a result of recent events. Each time she spoke he changed his mind.

When he first saw her out of doors, he smiled with satisfaction at the accuracy of his prediction. She was fair skinned, with hair the colour of wheat at harvest time. She was no older than he although, like her voice, her face showed the stress caused by the destruction of her village and it added years to her. Bryn couldn't even begin to imagine what it must be like to lose everyone you know and care about. His own troubles paled in comparison.

On his first attempt at going for a walk, Bryn was able for little more than limping outside and sitting on a tree stump a few steps from the door of the shack. Ayla had to leave him to his own devices when she went to fetch water or look for food—something she had previously done when he slept, which was most of the time.

After a few more days, he found that he could walk farther, and that some of his old stamina was returning—far more quickly than if building it from scratch. He slowly made his way toward the remains of the village, for no more reason than it was the only destination in the area that he knew of. The pain had started to fade from his shoulders—there was also an element of him growing accustomed to it—but his hands and arms were still numb. He couldn't feel anything at all. He didn't know what that meant, but it was difficult not to be concerned.

Ayla had gone off to look for food earlier and had yet to

return, so he decided to take another walk. Each day he set himself a more ambitious goal. The shack was not far from the village, but it was far enough that Bryn was beginning to wonder if he had pushed himself too hard when it finally came into view. It looked much the same as it had when he had first encountered the place, little more than a black stain on the landscape with charred pieces of wood occasionally hinting at where a building had once been. The only difference was a solitary figure standing amidst the ash.

Ayla stood motionless, staring at a patch of charred ground, oblivious to everything around her. Abruptly, she walked forward quickly and bent down to examine something on the ground. She stood again after a moment, not having picked anything up. Watching her felt like an invasion of privacy, so Bryn backed away. She had been so diligent in caring for him, so attentive, he hadn't thought of how much she must have been hurting. She had done so much for him; he didn't have the first idea of what he could do for her.

He hobbled back to the shack and was well and truly exhausted by the time he got there. Ayla was clutching a small cloth parcel of food when she returned. She dropped it down on the table in the corner before sitting down in the shadows, beyond the light of the small fire.

'Foraging's getting harder,' she said.

Having seen her standing in the village, so sad, he felt he needed to make some gesture toward her, but didn't know what form it should take or how to put it. It occurred to him that her loved ones probably still lay where they were killed and that just didn't seem right.

'I was thinking,' he said. 'I know your loved ones must still be in the village. I thought maybe when my arms are better I could go down and help you bury them.'

'Unless you plan on digging more than two hundred holes there's not much point,' she said, bitterly. 'I can't tell who's who.

They're all too badly burned. I didn't see where they fell; they weren't in our house. Anyhow, who knows when your arms will start working again?'

She got up and walked out of the shack.

Bryn sighed. At times he felt like he was an idiot. At times he knew he was one.

CHAPTER THIRTY-SEVEN

AMERO SAT IN his apartment reviewing the Amphitheatre listings for the coming month. His name featured frequently on the long sheet of parchment— too frequently, some might say. It came as a surprise to him that the benefits of the old man's healing would linger. Even without the regular sessions, he found that his recuperation was far faster than it ever was before. He did not expect that to remain the case for very long, and decided that it would be foolish not to take advantage of it so long as it lingered.

A duel a week was unusual, but not unheard of. Two or even three in a week was something a duellist might manage once, with a long break afterward. Amero planned on keeping up that pace for several weeks. With the inhuman load of training he had subjected himself to over the previous weeks, he felt invincible.

He knew his style was a part of that. It was mesmerising, and lethal. Thinking of the crowd reacting brought a smile to his face. It inflamed them and made fools of his opponents. He had taken the things he thought useful from others, but he altered, embellished and enhanced them all to suit himself. The magic may have helped him, but it only allowed him to realise his potential sooner. The victories, the style, that was all him. He knew nothing and no-one else could take credit for that.

All that remained for him to achieve in the arena was the legendary one hundred and twenty-five. He wanted it, and he wasn't willing to wait. Not only would he achieve that vaunted number, he would do it faster than anyone before him.

Bryn had been at the shack for ten days when the feeling started to return to his hands. It began with a tingling in his fingers and was followed by them responding slightly to his commands to move. He almost wept with joy as he saw his fingers twitch; a wave of hope flooded through his frustration and despair. The deadness had lasted long enough for him to fear that the feeling would never return. He lifted his hands to look at them and was cut down by the two stabs of pain that shot in from his shoulders through his torso. His stomach twisted and he thought he was going to be sick. More disappointingly, the sensation in his fingers was gone.

He continued to walk every day. He gently moved his arms as he went, testing them against the limits of pain, trying to push them more on each outing. Conversation with Ayla had been stilted since his suggestion of burying her loved ones. He knew that she returned to the village for several hours each day, ostensibly to forage for food. How she had managed to find enough to keep them going for as long as she had was something of a marvel, but it could only get harder in a region that had been stripped of so much. She had shown enough trust in him to give him the sword.

It turned out that it was his, driven into the ground beneath where he was hanging, to let everyone who passed by know the executed man was a banneret. If it came to it he doubted he would be able to do much with it, but it felt good to have at his waist nonetheless. With the fighting far away, and the village destroyed, there was no reason for anyone to pass through the area, but there was always the risk of a roving band of marauders happening upon them. Appearances alone often counted for a great deal, even if he couldn't pull it from the scabbard.

He tended to avoid going too close to the village after the previous time, wanting to respect Ayla's privacy as much as he could, and also not wanting to compound his previous clumsiness. She had saved his life, nursed him back to health, and he had nothing to offer her in return—not even a sensitively chosen word.

He reached the extremity of his day's exercise, a low hill that in other circumstances would have given a captivating view of the Telastrian Mountains to the east, but now did little more than showcase a desolated land. It was clear to him that he was ready to start thinking seriously about making the journey home. With no money and no realistic notion of how to come by any, it would be a very long walk. Until his arms were working reasonably well again, starvation was the only thing that awaited him on the road. That was of course only if he had to travel alone.

An idea had come to him of a way to repay Ayla's kindness and help to get her on her feet again. When Grelitz was destroyed and her family killed, she had lost everything. He didn't have much, but at the very least she could stay with his mother and sister until she found work as a cook or lady's maid, or any of the other jobs available to a single young woman in the city. If she could read and write the options would be even greater, as would the quality of life available to her. It wasn't much, but it was the best he could come up with. He decided to suggest the idea of her coming back to Ostenheim with him when she returned to the shack that evening.

Being fed was the most emasculating thing Bryn had ever experienced. He was grateful that Ayla did it without comment, but he was as hungry for the moment when he could do it himself as he was for their meagre meals. She gave him a mouthful of water to wash the food down. He made to wipe his mouth and his head throbbed with frustration when his arms remained still. What if they stayed like that? The last thing his family needed was an invalid to support. He pushed the thought out of his head as quickly as it had entered. There were other things he had to address. He cleared his throat, and started his pitch.

'I've been thinking,' he said. 'We can't stay here forever. There's nothing for you here now...' He realised how insensitive his words sounded, and continued in the hope he hadn't caused offence. 'You've been so kind to me. I want to repay that. I want you to come to Ostenheim with me. You'll have a roof over your head, people who will care about you, and the chance to start a new life. A good life.'

While he could not see her face in the shack's darkness, Bryn could tell by her body language that Ayla was uncomfortable with the offer. She said nothing, but set about clearing up the few utensils they used to eat with.

'Will you think on it, at least?' Bryn said.

She nodded. 'I'll think on it.'

Bryn stared south, roughly toward where he imagined Ostenheim lay, many miles distant. He couldn't deny that his motives had in part been selfish; without Ayla he had little or no chance of being able to make the journey.

In spite of her avoiding the issue, the idea grew on him the more he thought of it. She had nothing here and wherever she chose to go she would be a stranger trying to survive. She might as well be a stranger in Ostenheim, where at least there would be a couple of people looking out for her. Otherwise, pretty young women in her situation usually ended up doing only one thing, and after all she had done for him he refused to allow that happen unopposed. He would have to give her a little more time and try again.

He had turned the idea over in his head all night, and as he walked that morning he tried to work out how to demonstrate to Ayla that this idea was the best option for her. His legs were getting tired, so he turned around and headed back toward the shack, keenly feeling homesick and wondering how his mother and sister were doing. Would they have had word of the disappearance of the wagon train? Did they think he was dead?

His route took him near to the village. He knew that Ayla would be there and part of him longed to be able to do something to help her cope with the grief and shock of losing everything that she knew. Sadly it didn't seem to be that simple, and he knew he lacked the emotional subtlety needed in such situations. Most of the things he had learned in life were with a sword in his hand, which left him ill prepared for dealing with things that required sensitivity.

As he neared the village, he could hear noise. The sound was unmistakably that of a group of dismounted men. Whatever danger they represented to him, they were a far greater one to Ayla if they spotted her. He knew that she was smart and aware enough to stay out of their way, but he couldn't take the chance that she would spot their approach in time to avoid them. When he had seen her in the village that first time, she had seemed so lost in thought he feared she wouldn't notice them at all.

He broke into a steady run, little faster than a jog but the most that he could maintain for any length of time. As he had suspected, she was at the remains of the house she had been standing by the previous time. She was sitting cross-legged in the centre, her attention somewhere far away. She didn't seem to have noticed the sound, which was growing closer all the time.

'Ayla!'

She looked up, a puzzled expression on her face.

'Men are coming! We have to go!'

The tension in his voice had the desired effect and she stood, concern appearing on her face as she looked toward the source of the sound that was now unmissable. He rushed over to her with the intention of taking her hand and leading her in the direction of the shack, but in his haste forgot his injury and contorted in pain, his hand not moving from his side.

She took his hand and led the way as they broke into a run in the opposite direction to the sound. The had gone no more than a dozen paces when a crossbow bolt thudded into the soft turf at their feet, bringing them to an abrupt halt. There was a roar of laughter from behind them, a half dozen voices at least.

'Watch where you go there, friend!' called a voice.

Bryn turned to face its source, unintentionally letting Ayla's hand slip from his unresponsive fingers.

'No need to be in such a hurry. Not seemly to make such a lovely young lady run, no matter how impatient you might be to get her home.'

There was more raucous laughter.

The men spread out as they approached, forming a semi-circle in front of Bryn and Ayla. She remained silent, standing close by and Bryn could feel the tension in her body. She knew only too well what could come of a situation like this.

'We hoped to find a town hereabouts, friend. Any idea where it is?' More laughter.

'You can see for yourself,' Bryn said. He wondered if they were the ones that had caused the destruction, but it seemed unlikely that the perpetrators would return. They knew there was nothing left of value.

'No need to be rude about it, friend. You're from Ostenheim?'

Bryn nodded. The leader of the group, for the comedian was clearly the leader, reminded Bryn of every bully he had ever encountered. He was brave, swaggering and invincible so long as he had six men to back him up.

'I'm from Ostenheim too. Artisans, born and bred. What

brings you to the inhospitable North?' He stood arms akimbo, and although his words were addressed to Bryn, his eyes were firmly on Ayla.

His overt friendliness worried Bryn. 'Same as you I expect,' said Bryn.

The man nodded and rubbed at the several days of dark stubble on his chin. 'No uniform?'

Bryn shook his head. 'No, came up on private work with the wagons.'

'Don't see no wagons, friend.'

'I don't see no regiment,' Bryn said, trying to drag the man's gaze away from Ayla and back to him.

The man laughed and his cronies joined in. 'Guess you got us on that. We're not with a regiment anymore. That's a very pretty northern wench you've got yourself there.'

Bryn remained silent. There was nothing to say, but they were getting to the point of things nonetheless.

'Well? What do you have to say, friend?' the man said.

'You wouldn't like what I have to say, friend. She's mine.'

'Oh, come now.' He turned to his cronies for a reaction; they all oohed. He turned back to Bryn. 'We're all Ostians here, all friends. We just think you should share and share alike.'

The men all laughed, much to their leader's pleasure. Bryn willed his left hand to the neck of his sword scabbard, as though he was preparing the sword to be drawn. He tried not to show the strain he was under to make it do his bidding. 'You and your friends should move along. There's nothing for you here.'

'Not so sure about that, friend,' the man said, his eyes hungry, locked on Ayla. 'There's seven of us. Think we'll be doing what we like.'

If Bryn had the use of his arms, the man would already be dead. So too would his friends. 'There might be seven of you, and I might not be able to kill you all, but you, I will definitely kill.' One of the men behind the leader looked particularly confident. Bryn glared at him. 'You'll be the next after him.'

His face dropped a little, some of the bluster knocked out of him.

Finally the leader turned his gaze to Bryn. 'Nice sword.' He nodded his head to Bryn's blade. 'You a banneret?'

'Do you really want to find out?' Bryn felt his stomach clench. He couldn't even draw his sword, let alone use it.

The man smiled, but didn't turn to his cronies for support, he just kept his gaze fixed on Bryn, who returned it with as much steely determination as he could muster.

'Reckon I don't, friend. Not today leastways. Come on, lads, nothing here worth having after all. Not for that price anyhow.'

They moved off, grudging looks at Bryn intermixed with longing ones directed at Ayla. Bryn maintained his bluff, holding his body as erect as he could manage, his left hand at the neck of his scabbard and his right dangling uselessly, but he hoped appearing as though it was primed to draw his sword.

Bryn watched them carefully until they were out of sight, and then out of earshot. 'We need to get whatever we can carry from the shack and leave this place as quickly as we can. They'll be back tonight, if not before.'

Ayla remained silent, but nodded vigorously.

There was little in the shack that was worth taking; some food and water skins, but nothing else. They were heading south within the hour and Bryn pushed on as hard as he could—harder than he thought was wise, but he wanted to put as much distance between him and the deserters as he could while there was light enough to see by.

'There's a village not far from here,' Ayla said, when the sun was creeping below the horizon. They had not followed the road, striking out across country instead. He reckoned that if the deserters chose to pursue they would expect them to have taken the road. Bryn hoped they would be safe by the time they reached the village—the deserters struck Bryn as scavengers, an intact village being too much for them. In any event, none of them looked clever enough to track, especially not in the dark and Bryn expected that cutting across country would have thrown them off the scent.

'Fine, lead on and we'll stop there for the night.'

'That was brave of you,' she said. 'To stand up to them like that.'

Bryn opened his mouth to say something gallant, but found himself shrugging and saying nothing.

'You wouldn't have been able to fight them, would you?'

She knew well that he couldn't, and didn't wait for an answer.

'You could have given me to them. Joined them maybe. If they'd found out about your arms you wouldn't have lasted a second.'

He shook his head. 'They didn't find out.'

'No, they didn't. Thank you.'

They walked in silence until they reached the village, a collection of single storey wooden buildings clustered around a muddy road. There was not much to be seen in the village, and there was nowhere clearly identifiable as an inn. Despite not having any money, it was still Bryn's first thought on entering the town. Few didn't have an inn of some description; there were always travellers passing through looking for somewhere to spend a night, grateful for the opportunity to have a roof over their heads.

It was not late, but it was well past the hour when hard-working folk retreated to their homes for their evening meal and, in an agricultural community characterised by hard physical work, bed. Bryn stood in what seemed to be the centre of the village, looking around and wondering what to do next.

'I don't see an inn,' he said.

'How d'you plan to pay for it?'

'Good point.'

They continued on past the village until they spotted a hay-shed one field over from the edge of the road. They had been walking by moonlight, and neither of them had the desire to continue any farther.

The shed was a basic affair, four posts with a shallow apex roof of planks topping them, and no walls. The hay had been there for some time and smelt musty, but was dry. They ate the little food she had brought with her, and he fell asleep almost as soon as he had stopped chewing.

CHAPTER THIRTY-EIGHT

'THEY'RE SAYING YOU'RE going to be the fastest man to achieve one hundred and twenty-five,' Renald said.

'Nice to see you too, Father,' Amero said. He would love to tell his servant to turn his father away at the door, but Renald owned the apartment and also paid the servant's wages.

'Any hope I had of you putting this showboating behind you before too many people noticed is long gone,' Renald said. 'Which leaves me to wonder what to do now.'

Amero said nothing, but knew it was too much to hope for that his father would go away if ignored. His independent wealth was growing rapidly, so he could afford to be openly hostile to Renald without having to worry about the threats of having his allowance cut off. Unfortunately that did not completely free Amero of his influence.

'The fact of the matter,' Renald said, 'is that if you leave the arena now, it will likely cause more damage than remaining. They'll say you couldn't take the pressure. Don't have what it takes.'

'I assure you,' Amero said, 'I have what it takes, as I prove every time I step out onto the arena floor.'

'Be that as it may, you've brought far more attention to our house than I like. It's always been our way to serve the state with honour and fidelity. Any glory that we attracted was a consequence of that. Morenos do not seek glory for glory's sake. In that, you are, and will continue to be, a disappointment to me. There's little that can be done about it now however, and failing will bring greater shame on our house than continuing to prance about the arena like a prize horse.'

'Your point?' Amero said.

'My point is this. You now have my full support and all of the resources of our house. You achieve your one hundred and twenty-five, then you retire; attend to your duty as a leading son of Ostia.'

There were times when Renald spoke that Amero thought he could hear the blowing of trumpets and the screeching of eagles. There were few men alive who had not obeyed his every word, and he was unaccustomed to the alternative. He was the doyen of mindless patriotism, something Amero had always thought difficult to reconcile with his utter ruthlessness. Perhaps he simply enjoyed killing people more than he did politics. Doing it in the name of Ostia made it all legal.

If he was happy being nothing more than the duke's battering ram that was his business, but he lacked ambition. In any other country, the Morenos would have been kings. In Ostenheim they sat by waiting for their turn to be eligible for election to the ducal throne, and even then won it only occasionally. Amero wanted far more.

The offer left him suppressing a smile. It was a small, temporary victory, but a victory nonetheless. Not having to wonder what his father might do to nobble him was also one less thing to worry about. The deal suited him for now, even if it would not when it came to his turn to abide by it.

Ayla was already awake when Bryn emerged from a deep sleep. The sun was still low in the sky, so he had not over-slept. His first thought on waking was how hungry he was; his second was how stiff and sore his legs were. It was disappointing how far his condition had slipped from only a few weeks previously.

Once that brief but serene moment after waking when all in the world seems well had passed, his next thought was always of his arms. Had another night's sleep led to further improvement? He tried to flex his fingers and was encouraged by what seemed to be a greater amount of movement than the day before. It was still little more than a twitch though. He tried to flex his arms, gritting his teeth in expectation of the grinding pain, but it also felt less than before. When he let his palms rest on the ground, he was certain that he could feel the prickly ends of the straw stalks beneath them.

'You're awake,' she said. 'I need to go and find us something to eat.'

He struggled to his feet and looked over his shoulders at the various pieces of straw that had stuck to his clothes. He wanted to brush them off, but couldn't. Seeing them there was like having an itch that he couldn't scratch and the consternation must have shown on his face, for Ayla laughed. It was the first time he had heard her laugh and it brought a smile to his face. In that moment, for the first time in an age, it felt like everything would work out.

She wandered off to look for something to eat, telling him she would be back as soon as she found something. He sat in the shed and watched her go, wishing that he could be a help.

After facing Panceri Mistria, Amero doubted he would ever find an opponent daunting again. On that day, he had merely been confident that he would win; there was room for doubt. Today, however, he was certain that victory would be his. There was a sense of occasion that made it difficult not to feel a little nervous, though. Today, if Divine Fortune favoured him, he would reach one hundred and twenty-five. Even if she didn't, he would take the victory without her, and in so doing become the fastest swordsman to ever achieve the feat. He almost felt pity for Mistria. A few months before, he had been fêted as the greatest swordsman of the age. Now Amero's shadow had consigned his memory to obscurity.

The Amphitheatre was full long before his match was due to take place. Every person in Ostenheim wanted to be there, even those with little interest in the sport. They were there to watch him make history, and take his place as First Blade of Ostia. He showed his chit to the guard at the competitors' entrance, but there was no need; he was recognised immediately.

As he walked through the gate, a small boy of no more than five years charged past him and disappeared into the dark bowels of the Amphitheatre.

'Get back here, you little bastard!' the guard shouted. He made to close the gate and give chase.

Amero laughed. He was a quick little fellow. 'Leave him,' he said to the guard. 'What harm is one more little boy in the crowd? Here.' Amero flicked a crown to the guard. 'The price of his admission.'

The guard looked at the gold coin, far more than the cost of most tickets, and then at Amero. 'That's very generous of you, my Lord. May Divine Fortune smile on you this evening.'

'Thank you,' Amero said. 'I certainly hope she does.' He nodded his thanks and headed for the Bannerets' Enclosure. Small acts like that cost him nothing but a coin and a smile, and would win him loyal and passionate fans. That guard would tell all of his friends about Amero's generosity, and so his legend would grow.

Salvestre Besulto was the man who stood between Amero and the fame his achievement would bring. He was very good; but then every man whose name reached the first few pages of the Ladder was.

Amero's trainers spoke to him as he sat waiting in the Bannerets' Enclosure; words of advice and encouragement. Amero blocked them out. He blocked out all the noise, all the movement. All he thought of was his opponent. He had watched Besulto duel several times. Amero knew how he moved, how he thought.

The Master of Arms signalled for Amero to go out onto the sand. He stood and ignored the trainers. He focussed on the black line in the centre of the arena and started toward it. Out of the corner of his eye, he could see Besulto making his way out from the other part of the enclosure. Amero didn't look over, but he could tell Besulto was watching him. Amero saw it as a sign of weakness.

They took their places by the black line, and the Master of Arms started to outline the instructions. Amero didn't pay them any attention. He knew them by heart. Only now did he look at Besulto. He locked his gaze on his opponent and smiled. Besulto showed no reaction, but Amero knew it was going to be his day.

'Duel!'

Amero pounced forward, two sweeping cuts and a thrust, the combination he had decided on to open the duel. Besulto would have known that Amero would start fast, and parried all three strikes. He was unsettled though. Amero circled him like a cat toying with a mouse. Besulto watched him, a forced calm on his face. He might have been able to control his emotions, but having to do so at all weakened his concentration.

Amero attacked again, steel grating against steel as he tested Besulto's defence. It was good; Amero feinted twice and thrust. A touch. It was not good enough.

Amero smiled as he walked back to the black mark. The crowd could have been deathly silent, or they could have been screaming their lungs out; Amero could not hear them. All that existed was the victory that was about to be his.

Besulto attacked as soon as they restarted. He was First Blade of Ostia, not an accolade anyone gave up easily. He was fast, precise, and aggressive. Amero moved back fluidly as he parried each strike. It was testing; Amero preferred to be on the front foot rather than the back. Besulto thrust and Amero's sword was too far away. He sucked his belly in and twisted, watching as the blade passed him by no more than a hair's breadth.

Besulto followed up without pause, two attacks that were picture perfect, good enough to grace any printed treatise. Amero parried and riposted, seizing the initiative. He fired in a half dozen fast thrusts, pushing Besulto's blade wider to the left each time. He angled his wrist to the right with a beautiful flourish and struck Besulto on the shoulder. Two to nothing.

You are truly magnificent, Amero thought to himself as he walked back to the line. He wondered if Besulto would accept his fate, or if he would fight down to the last point. Some men knew when they were beaten, and had no desire to prolong the agony. Amero found himself hoping he would fight, for no other reason than it would allow him to further inflame the crowd.

Besulto was dangerous coming forward, as he had shown, and Amero had no desire to take unnecessary risks. He launched forward at the restart, taking the initiative without any intention of allowing Besulto to have it again. He could not afford to be as ostentatious as he would have liked. There was too much at stake. He recalled Bautisto's words; smooth, controlled, precise. It was good advice, even if he was a bore. Amero saw an opening. He saw victory. He struck. Besulto managed to get his sword in the way and Amero's heart leaped to his mouth as he felt his blade be diverted away. He had gambled everything on the strike; if it failed, he would be exposed.

He felt the tip impact, and the wave of relief that came with it. There was such force that his blunt tip cut through Besulto's thick doublet and across his upper arm. There was blood on his blade when Amero withdrew it. The match was won, but Besulto fixed Amero with a knowing look. The thrust had more than enough force to kill. He knew what Amero had intended.

Amero ignored him and turned to face the crowd. He opened himself to all the distractions of the Amphitheatre, which flushed away his anger at not having finished the match, and his historic achievement, with a kill as he had desired. He bowed, sweeping the tip of his sword out to the side, a movement he had prepared for this moment. The crowd roared. The sound reverberated in Amero's chest. It filled his head with so much noise there was no room for thought. Their passion was overwhelming. It was primal. It was his.

CHAPTER THIRTY-NINE

SOMEHOW AYLA MANAGED to keep them fed for the first few days of the journey. Each morning she would disappear for an hour and return, more often than not with a mischievous 'don't ask where I got it' look on her face. Small pails of milk, eggs, various items of fruit and once even a fresh loaf of bread. Quite how she managed it impressed and intrigued him. All things considered, they were eating well—certainly no worse than they had when they were at the hunting shack.

Each day he had a little less pain, a little more movement in his arms and a little more strength in his fingers. Each day brought him closer to home and each step raised his spirits a little higher. The end to the ordeal was in sight.

The weather remained fine until several days into their long walk. A light drizzle set in as a small town loomed into view. By the time they reached its outskirts it was raining heavily and they were both quickly soaked. Bryn had no idea how far they still had to go to Ostenheim as he hadn't seen a signpost in some time. Irrespective of how far it was, a rain-induced chill wasn't going to do either of them any good. They were unprepared for bad weather, and he wanted to get them out of it as quickly as possible.

Rather than go into the town itself—they still had no money—he skirted around its edge, along the low walls that marked out the gardens and yards of the houses. In a region used to the passage of armies and mercenaries, Bryn didn't think penniless travellers would be welcomed. Eventually, as darkness fell, he spotted a manger in the yard behind one of the houses. Doing their best to shield themselves from the rain they both charged into the manger—and into its sole occupant, a large pig. Its response to this intrusion was to start squealing as though a butcher's cleaver was being waved before its eyes.

It wasn't an ideal situation for either party, and Bryn was just coming around to accepting the fact that they would have to find somewhere else for the night when some noise came from the house at the front of the muddy yard. There was the sound of a metal latch scraping and the squeak of door hinges.

'Who's there? Piss off or there'll be trouble! If that's you, Arno, I'm telling your father in the morning!'

Ayla took his hand and they fled from the yard, laughing so hard it almost made him forget about the pain.

Bryn awoke first the next morning. It had been cold during the night, but at some point it had stopped raining. They had taken shelter under a tree a short distance from the village. He suspected that the cold, rather than the wet had been the greater influence on the fact that when he awoke, he and Ayla were wrapped together as tightly as could be. They were so close he could feel the warmth and touch of each breath that left her mouth.

He wasn't sure how they had ended up like that, and he didn't know how to react to it. He found himself wishing that she had woken up first and so have to deal with it rather than him. He was considering the possibility of pretending to be asleep when she stirred. Before he had the chance to shut his eyes and drop his jaw to mimic his version of deep sleep, her eyes opened. She smiled lazily and looked up at him, a reaction that came as a surprise, and one that filled him with an over-whelming sense of happiness. His heart raced as she quickly remembered where she was and he could feel her body tense.

'It was cold last night,' he said, a little too quickly, making it sound like an excuse rather than an explanation.

'I'll go and get some food.' She untangled herself and got up.

Bryn said nothing, just watched her as she made her way off to forage, feeling curiously alone without her next to him.

They walked in silence for much of that morning, neither men-tioning the embrace they had woken in. The sun had come out but the road was wet and muddy, and it was hard going. It wound its way down a gentle slope toward a wooded area and then disappeared out of sight. The journey was beginning to take its toll on Bryn, and he found himself wishing for the sight of Ostenheim every time they reached a rise on the road. His feet were blistered and his calves ached. Ayla hadn't uttered a single word of complaint though, and he was determined not to be the first to do so. He knew they still had a long way to go.

Concentrating on not slipping on the mucky road was fully occupying both of their thoughts, so the silence was not as awk-ward as it might have been otherwise. Bryn found his mind increasingly occupied by the way they'd woken. He couldn't recall ever having felt as content as he had for those few waking moments in her arms, nor as happy as he had been for the past few days. He was so caught up in his thoughts that it caused him to miss the figure standing at the side of the road just inside the tree line.

'Ho there!' the man called when they were no more than a few steps from him.

The road entered the forest at the bottom of the slope, and it was wetter and more churned up there. The voice came as a shock to both of them. Bryn looked up and they both stopped as the man stepped out from the verge onto the road, theatrically lifting his booted feet free of the sucking mud.

'Not the best day for walking the roads, is it?' he said.

'Indeed not,' Bryn said, trying to remain friendly. Deep down he knew any conversation with a stranger on the road was unlikely to remain friendly for long.

'I'm afraid for you, it's just gotten a good deal worse,' the man said.

Bryn moved for his sword, hopeful that his ruse would work for a second time, but the man brushed back his heavy black travelling cloak to reveal a small crossbow, loaded, primed and pointed at Bryn's abdomen. Bryn hesitated.

'We've got no money,' Bryn said.

'That might be the case,' the man said, 'but it's been a while since anyone has happened along, and I'm getting bored.'

'I hate to have to bore you further,' Bryn said, 'but really, we've got nothing. Do we really look like we're the moneyed sort?'

'It's a possibility that you aren't, I agree, but the last fellow I had make the same claim—dressed in tatters he was—turned out to have a belt of gold crowns strapped around his waist. It taught me that rags are often the best way to hide a fortune, and I cursed myself for all the beggars and vagabonds that I have allowed to pass unobstructed over the years. It's a lesson that brings bad news for you I'm afraid. And anyway, that pretty rapier there makes me think you're a liar.' Holding his bow steady and trained on Bryn's stomach in one hand, he drew his sword and pointed it at Bryn with the other, its length enough to span the distance between them. 'Now, remove your doublet and shirt, if you please.'

Bryn cast a glance to Ayla, who was a little farther from

him than he would have liked, and closer to the man. There was no way he would be able to get between them if things got any uglier than they already were. Would he be able to remove his doublet and shirt? Reluctantly, he began to undo his doublet. The feeling in his hands was still poor, and he fumbled with the buttons, his fingers clumsy, but he had regained enough movement to be able to carry out the task, albeit slowly and without grace.

'No games. Be quick about it,' the highwayman said. He dropped the cavalier, almost friendly tone.

Bryn could feel sweat break out on his brow from the effort and concentration this simple task required. His hand faltered and the highwayman's patience was exceeded. He drew his arm back to cut at Bryn. Bryn went for his sword, a task that had once required neither thought nor effort, but now felt like an impossible challenge. He had no idea what he would do with it even if he managed to draw it. As he moved, Ayla dropped to the ground. Bryn's heart jumped into his throat and his eyes instantly went to the highwayman's crossbow, but he had not fired; the bolt was still in place and the string still primed.

The highwayman ignored her and advanced on Bryn, who backed away as he struggled to draw his sword. Ayla leaped to her feet clutching a sizeable rock. She stretched full, using the momentum of standing up to drive the rock forward. She had been closer to the highwayman than Bryn, but their assailant had taken her for granted, seeing Bryn and his sword as the real threat.

She smashed the rock into the back of his head. It made a sickening crack and the highwayman crumpled to the ground without so much as a groan. His crossbow, aimed in Bryn's direction, went off as he fell with an audible click and thrum. Bryn dived for the ground as soon as his brain registered what was happening. He squelched into the mud and had the air knocked from his lungs. He heard Ayla cry out.

He lay still on the ground for a moment, trying to work out if he had been hit. Not feeling the intense pain he would expect from a crossbow wound, he tried to press himself up from the ground, but his arms were still too weak and he slumped back into the mud. He rolled over onto his back, and sat up. Ayla was over him in an instant.

'Are you all right? Did he hit you?'

'I'm fine,' he said. 'He missed.' Ayla helped him to his feet. He walked over to the highwayman and knelt down beside him. He stared at the highwayman's chest for a moment.

'Still breathing.'

Ayla said nothing and Bryn wasn't entirely sure if it was due to concern or disappointment.

'What should we do with him?' she said.

'Nothing. He'd have done us in so I'm not going to worry myself about leaving him here. He'll wake up in a while with a headache, but it's nothing more than he deserves. If we pass a town before nightfall we can tell any watchmen we come across that there's a highwayman out here, but he'll probably have woken and gone by then. We should move him to the side of the road so he doesn't get hit by a passing carriage, but that's all I'm doing for him. Help me drag him.'

Bryn looped his arms under the highwayman's shoulders, having just enough strength and mobility in them to manage it with Ayla's help, and together they dragged him to the verge at the side of the road. Bryn was terrified by how helpless he had been. Without Ayla, the highwayman could have killed him, and wouldn't even have broken a sweat. When were his shoulders going to get better?

Bryn grimaced with discomfort and frustration at his debilitation as he dumped the highwayman's body on the grass. There was a chink of metal as he did it. Bryn looked up to Ayla, who had also heard the sound. She frisked the highwayman and came away with a coin purse. It was small, and didn't look to contain that stash of gold crowns the highwayman had mentioned, but still held a healthy sum.

Ayla looked to Bryn and raised her eyebrows.

He shrugged. 'He'd have taken ours.'

CHAPTER FORTY

T HE HIGHWAYMAN WASN'T wealthy, but there was enough in his purse to ensure that Bryn and Ayla would be able to pass the remainder of their journey in relative comfort. It was too late to call on the town watch when they arrived in the next village, so they looked for an inn.

It wasn't until the warm, dry air of the inn hit him that Bryn realised how long it had been since he had been out of the elements. The shack had provided shelter, and the fire within some heat, but it was draughty and damp—and cold after the fire had died down. The prospect of a warm bed and a hot meal lifted a weight from his shoulders, not to mention the appeal of a wash and a shave.

The inn was crowded, busy and bright, a contrast to the dark, deserted street outside, and the change seemed to startle Ayla. At first no one took any notice of them, but gradually a number of the patrons turned and gave Bryn an appraising look. Bryn thought nothing of it, they were just strangers to the village, arriving late in the day, something that was always a cause for curiosity. He walked up to the bar enthusiastic at the prospect of a little comfort, but Ayla hung back nervously. It was her first time in a crowd since her village had been destroyed. He glanced back over his shoulder, took her by the hand and pulled her forward, which took a great deal of effort.

'A room, please,' Bryn said to the innkeeper. 'And food. Dinner with all the trimmings.'

The innkeeper looked at him suspiciously, then at Ayla.

'Two rooms. I meant two rooms.' Rural villages could have oddly conservative notions of propriety. He hoped his unintentional slip wouldn't result in them being run out of the town with pitchforks and burning torches.

He looked back at Ayla and gave her a reassuring smile. He hoped he hadn't offended her. He turned back to face the innkeeper and tapped some coins out of the highwayman's purse. Silver florins all, he reckoned there was enough to see them through the rest of their journey. The innkeeper gave Bryn two keys and led them over to a table in the corner of the taproom.

When the food arrived, Bryn stared at it with trepidation. Bring fed in private was humiliating enough. He would rather go hungry than suffer it in front of an audience. He slowly reached for the knife on the table, feeling the tautness in his shoulder as he did. No pain though, which was something. He realised Ayla was watching him in silence and had not yet touched her food, in spite of how hungry she must have been. With one last effort, encouraged by the smell of the hot foot, he grabbed at the knife and managed to get a firm grip on it first try. He took hold of a leg of chicken and cut a piece free, then slowly lifted the morsel to his mouth. The act of raising his hand was difficult, and he had to strain against the resistance from his shoulder. It was only stiffness though, not pain.

The flavour of the chicken flooded through his mouth and he smiled. He looked at Ayla before they both attacked their food with fervour, and didn't utter a word to one another until they had finished. It wasn't just his appetite that dictated his silence, it took whatever concentration he had left over to make his hands work well enough to ensure the food ended up in his mouth rather than down the front of his doublet or on the floor. It was a struggle, but he was determined not to suffer the indignity of having to have Ayla help him in front of the inn's patrons, who gave the pair regular and curious looks. It was a delight to manage it at all, but discomfiting that achieving something so simple should give him such satisfaction.

The pleasure of having hot food in his belly was difficult to describe, but from the expression on Ayla's face, he could tell that she felt it too. The innkeeper came to take away their empty plates, and must have noticed the way they had been wiped clean with crusts of bread.

'There's still some pie left in the kitchen. Apple.'

Ayla started to shake her head in the way Bryn had seen people act when refusing something they actually wanted.

'Two slices, please. Cream too, if there's any to be had.'

The innkeeper smiled and nodded, clearly happy that people were appreciating his food. Ayla beamed at Bryn. They could afford one decent meal, and still have enough left over for a carriage the rest of the way to Ostenheim, all thanks to the highwayman. Bryn wondered what had become of him, having had a taste of his own medicine.

They ate the apple pie much the same way as they had devoured their dinner. Bryn tried to slow down and savour each bite, but he couldn't help himself. He was sure it wasn't the best meal he'd ever eaten, but after all he had been through, it certainly felt like it was.

As the food settled in his stomach he leaned back in his chair to relax, trying to lace his fingers over his full belly and just about succeeding. His doublet was rough and covered in what he first thought were crumbs. Then he realised that his clothes were caked in dry mud. He tentatively put his hand up to his face and realised it was the same, many days of beard growth matted in dried clumps. It was from when he dived to the ground to avoid the highwayman's wayward crossbow shot. He must have looked a sorry state, and realised why he had attracted so many odd looks when they first arrived at the inn. All things considered, he was surprised they had been served at all.

He felt an impatient urge to get to his room and clean himself up, now that he realised how filthy he was.

'Time for bed, I think,' he said.

Ayla blushed, then nodded.

They walked up the stairs to the inn's rooms. Theirs were on opposite sides of the corridor. He gave her a key to one of them, wondering after he had if he should have let her take a look at them both before deciding. He had never felt responsible for anyone before, and never felt so indebted to anyone. He owed her his life many times over.

She took the key and turned to open the door to her room. She looked over her shoulder as she stepped across the threshold. 'Sleep well,' she said, before closing the door behind her.

It was the first time in weeks that they hadn't shared their sleeping space and as he stood there by his doorway, key in hand, he was filled with the most incredible sense of loneliness. Only then did he realise that he hadn't even remembered to wish her a good night's sleep.

Their journey had taken them well into what Bryn believed was the middle of nowhere. It took four different carriages to get them the rest of the way to Ostenheim, making Bryn concerned that they wouldn't have enough money to pay for their passage on each of them. He managed to stretch it far enough by sharing the box seat with the coach driver on two occasions, but there were no more extravagant meals for the remainder of the journey.

Bryn had mixed feelings when their carriage pulled up by the coaching stables outside Ostenheim's walls. He didn't know if his family had been told he was dead, or how they would react to his sudden appearance. He also wondered how they would feel about him arriving with a strange girl from the borderlands. It played on his mind during the inactivity of the carriage journey. When the idea of bringing Ayla south first came to him, it seemed like the only option. As the reality of bringing her into the city drew closer he started to worry. What if he couldn't find work? What if he couldn't provide for her? Take care of her the way she had taken care of him? The city was a dangerous place for someone not accustomed to it. He evaded the real cause of his concern, though he knew what it was. How would he take care of himself, let alone anyone else, without the proper use of his arms? Feeding himself was still his most impressive achievement. The feeling in his hands came and went, but he still couldn't even fully draw his sword from its scabbard.

Bryn alighted from the carriage and stretched stiffly, flexing his arms slowly and uncertainly. His shoulders felt tight and restricted, as though he was wearing a doublet several sizes too small. He tried not to dwell on it, and told himself over and over that more time would improve them.

'That's Ostenheim?' Ayla said, looking up toward the tops of the city walls as she followed Bryn out of the carriage.

'It is,' Bryn said. 'Home. For you too now, if you choose it.'

'It's big. How many people live there?'

'Over a hundred thousand. Near enough three times that, I think.'

Ayla's eyes widened. 'So many.'

As they passed through the city's north gate and into the city, she looked on with awe. They walked under the great stone archway and into wide streets lined with four and five storey buildings. Bryn found her sense of wonderment and curiosity warming, and forced himself not to continually smile at her barrage of questions and fascination.

'Where are we going?' she said.

'To my mother's home. It's not far from here.'

'Does she own the entire building?'

Bryn laughed. 'No, just an apartment.'

'Lots of people living on top of each other,' she said, her voice distant as she continued to take in all of the new sights, sounds and smells.

Finally they were standing outside the nondescript doorway to his mother's apartment. He hesitated before knocking, afraid that he would discover they had moved out. It hadn't been all that long since he left, but so much had changed for him, it seemed possible. They could have gone to Tanosa to be with his other sister and her husband. He knocked and waited.

When he heard the sound of the latch being opened he realised that he was holding his breath. The door swung open to reveal his mother standing there. She let out a gasp of surprise. She stood statue still for a moment, eyes wide, and then rushed forward and took him in her arms. He returned the embrace as best he could and his mother began to cry. A voice came from within the apartment.

'Who's that, Mother?'

'It's your brother. It's Bryn.'

His sister came into view, peering out the doorway. Her reaction of surprise was much the same as his mother's.

'Can we come in?' he said.

'Of course, of course,' his mother said. 'We?'

His mother released him and moved back. Bryn beckoned to Ayla to follow him and went in. She went after him hesitantly.

His mother was dabbing her eyes with a handkerchief.

'This is Ayla,' Bryn said.

His mother nodded to her and smiled, but seemed unsure how to react beyond this.

'We were told your convoy had disappeared. That you were probably dead,' Gilia said. She stifled a sob.

'I was lucky. The wagons were attacked, and I was left for dead, but Ayla,' he gestured to her stiffly, 'saved me.'

It was clear to Bryn that Ayla was uncomfortable with the situation. It would take his mother and sister a time to come to terms with the fact that he was home alive, and had brought a woman with him.

'Her village was destroyed before we got there. After the attack I was injured and she looked after me until I was up and about again. She had nothing left there, so I asked her to come back to Ostenheim with me. I said that we'd help her get on her feet.'

His mother looked at Ayla and smiled, her face a picture of gratitude.

CHAPTER FORTY-ONE

WHEN BRYN WOKE, it took a moment to realise that he was warm, and comfortable, and back in his old room in his mother's apartment. He enjoyed that moment, brief though it was. He was home and safe, but all of his other problems still existed. He had no job, no income, and couldn't use his sword. He flexed his shoulders, and grimaced at how tight and uncomfortable the movement was.

There wasn't any time to waste in getting back to normal life. He knew his mother and sister could support themselves—they had survived thus far—but he wanted more than that for them. They were the close relatives of a banneret, and should have better. There was Ayla to think about too. Finally, there were still loans that needed to be paid off. There was no time to feel sorry for himself, nor to allow his uncertain recuperation to run its course.

The first call he needed to make was to the Guilds' Hall. The mercenary company he had signed on with was bound under their contract, and after all he had been through, he very much wanted his pay. As a matter of courtesy, he felt he also needed to notify them of exactly what had happened, so the families of the dead men could have the bad news confirmed.

He left before anyone else woke, walking the short distance

to the Guilds' Hall in the crisp morning air. The market on Crossways was beginning to come to life, as traders set up their stalls and laid out their goods. Bryn bought an orange from one of them and ate it as he crossed the square.

The Guilds' Hall was a huge building, home to the Congress of Guilds, who oversaw all business in the city. The ground floor was a great open expanse in which each guild had a counter or alcove, the size depending on their power and importance. Most of them would have their own private house somewhere else in Guilds, the quarter of the city behind the Guilds' Hall, but all maintained a presence in the Hall.

Ostenheim's wealth was based on trade and enterprise, and that wealth was enormous. The Hall was a firm statement of that, and no expense had been spared in its construction or decoration. It was as grand as the Barons' Hall or the Cathedral, proclaiming that the merchant classes were every bit as important, wealthy and sophisticated as the church and the aristocracy.

There was an ornate counter just inside the door of wood so highly polished its surface was mirror-like. A number of clerks sat behind it, all waiting to deal with the enquiries of those who wandered in.

'Which guild deals with the shipment of supplies to the army in the North?' Bryn asked. 'The one that holds the contract for the Guilds' Company?'

The clerk smiled and referred to a large, leather-bound book. 'That would be the Mercers' Guild, the Wagoners' Guild and Co-operative Guild Number Forty-Seven.'

'Co-operative Guild?'

'Yes, a number of small guilds that combine to satisfy particular contracts of work. They usually only last for the duration of the contract.'

It was a large number of potential employers. 'I was, am, an escort with the Guilds' Company. Who should I speak to?'

'I believe the Wagoners' Guild usually takes responsibility

for the manning of the supply convoys. They're at Counter Ninety-Six half way down the hall. If there's no one there, their main house is on Eastbridge Lane.'

Bryn nodded his thanks and walked further into the hall, looking at the large gilt numbers painted on signs over each of the counters. Some of the larger guilds had impressive looking kiosks, but not all of them were manned.

Bryn groaned when he saw no sign of life at Counter Ninety-Six, turned on his heel and headed for Eastbridge Lane.

Eastbridge Lane wasn't far from the depot where his convoy had set off. It had seemed like such a mundane thing at the time. It was hard to believe everything that had happened—the fight with the Ruripathian soldiers seemed almost like a dream now.

The Wagoners were a large, wealthy guild and their private house was opulent. It was a microcosm of the enormous Guilds' Hall, and was somewhere its members could meet, dine, find accommodation and regulate their industry.

Bryn walked in, to find a far less formal atmosphere than in the Guilds' Hall. There was an open room with a large fireplace and a table surrounded by chairs. Several men were sitting there chatting. They ignored him when he first walked into the room.

'I need to speak to someone about the convoy that went missing in the North.'

One of the men turned to face him. 'Speak then, we're all guild officers.'

'I was with the Guilds' Company convoy, with Banneret Deverardo.'

'You're one of Deverardo's boys?'

'Was,' Bryn said.

'Where is that fat fucker? And where're our wagons?'

'He's dead. As best I know, all the men were killed and the wagons taken.'

'Reckoned as much. Expensive loss. Still, the underwriters've already paid out on it, so no harm done in the long run. How'd you survive?'

'Got lucky,' Bryn said, taken aback by the casual disregard they had for all the men who were killed. 'I'm here for the rest of my pay.'

All the men burst into laughter. 'You don't look like much of a runner, but I suppose you must be. We don't pay out on lost cargoes. We certainly don't pay the men who were supposed to be guarding them.' There was no levity in the man's voice.

'I've done everything I was signed on to do. I fought when we got attacked, was lucky to survive, and have had a miserable time trying to get back to the city. I want my pay.'

'You're not getting it. Piss off.' The man turned his back to Bryn.

'I'm a banneret, you bloody oik. Don't you dare speak to me like that.' He realised that he sounded exactly like Amero, but he needed the money, and the prospect of being bilked caused his temper to flare.

'I'll speak to you any way I like. Now fuck off.'

Bryn pushed his cloak back from his sword, an instinctive reaction. He was well within his rights to strike this man down for insulting him. He just didn't know if he could, not that he wanted to resort to violence. All he wanted was his pay. Was a threat going to be enough?

The guildsman looked at him and sneered. He turned his head to his colleagues. 'Fella who ran from a convoy thinks he can come in here and act tough. I reckon he's a coward.' He looked back at Bryn. 'Well then? Draw it. Draw it or fuck off.'

Bryn got his hand to the hilt of his sword. This was an insult that he couldn't let stand. He gritted his teeth. He drew it out part way and stopped. He knew he could draw it now, albeit awkwardly, but that was all he knew. He had no faith in

---

his ability to deal with the insult, or the guildsmen. He slid his sword back into its sheath.

'See lads. Yellow to the core,' the guildsman said.

They all roared with laughter, and Bryn was left with no option but to turn and walk out of the guild house, feeling more humiliated than he could possibly imagine.

He walked back to the apartment filled with a rage that he had no way to express. Crossways was full of activity when he passed back through it, the city criers had taken their places and they were starting to fill the air with the news of the day. Bryn tried to ignore it, knowing their reports would make mention of the arena, and the ascendant swordsmen of the day, the last thing he wanted to hear.

His previous experience of bad publicity had done little to improve his skill at blocking out things he didn't want to hear. He nearly made it off Crossways and out of earshot when he heard the words 'one hundred and twenty-five'. Then he heard Amero's name being called out. His sixth consecutive defence of his perfect one hundred and twenty five. Bryn wanted to vomit. His rage and frustration built so much that it felt like his head would burst. He tried to tighten his fists in anger, but could barely feel his fingertips pressing against his palms.

How in hells had Amero managed to accumulate such a tally in such a short period of time? It must have been the fastest one hundred and twenty-five in history. To get the requisite twenty-five matches in since he fought Bryn, Amero must have had at least two duels a week, and sometimes even three. However hard he worked for it, success still came far too easily for Amero.

He got home in time for breakfast with the others, but ate in silence. He could see it made Ayla uncomfortable. His mother and sister were doing their best to make her welcome, but his mood was so foul that he felt opening his mouth would make things worse.

Eventually his mother—never best known for her patience in dealing with his moods—broke the silence.

'You called at the Guilds' Hall this morning?'

Bryn nodded.

'And?'

'And nothing. I told them about what happened. They'd already written the convoy off as lost, and didn't seem to care.'

'Did they give you your pay?'

Bryn shook his head. 'They don't pay for lost convoys.'

'Can you— Are you going to do anything about that?' his mother said, an edge to her voice.

Bryn closed his eyes and took a deep breath. Standing and walking out of the apartment was the least damaging reaction he could think of, so that was what he did.

As he walked through the streets with no destination, he realised that his mother didn't know about the extent of the injury to his shoulders, or any of what had happened. All she knew was that bannerets didn't stand for sharp treatment from guildsmen, or anyone else. He didn't want her to know how bad the injury was, nor how enfeebled it had left him. She would find out soon enough if he had to keep swallowing his pride, but he didn't want her to worry and he didn't want to be a continued burden.

He racked his brains. What could he do to make a living? With his shoulders the way they were, there were few avenues still open to him. Teaching was all he could think of. His initial inclination was to go to the salons and see if they needed any additional trainers, but he knew how that would turn out. He'd been humiliated enough for one lifetime, and his name would still be mud in the salons.

That left private tutoring. There was plenty of that work to be had in the city, from children being taught the very basics all the way up to teenagers preparing for their Academy entrance tests. Bryn's natural inclination was to teach as high a standard of pupil as he could; his interest lay more with the exploration of advanced techniques, rather than the grating rote process of instilling the basic movements in younger pupils. He knew the reality was that he would have to take whatever he could get, and even then he wasn't sure if he could manage it.

'What do you mean there's no one willing to book me?' Amero said.

'You're a sure thing,' dal Corsi said. 'Everyone expects you to win.'

'What? You want me to lose?' Amero said. 'You'll have a hard time finding anyone who can beat me.'

Dal Corsi shrugged. 'Things always get quiet for the First Blade. Your duels are all challenge matches now, and only those in the top ten can make one. It's a bit harder for you though. No one believes you can be beaten. At least not by anyone around at the moment.'

'Well, find someone. Hype them up. Make people think he has a chance,' Amero said.

'Easier said than done,' dal Corsi said.

'Just do it. I want a match every two weeks. People forget fast, and I'll be damned if I let them forget me.'

CHAPTER FORTY-TWO

B RYN WAS DETERMINED not to go home until he had at least one job prospect lined up. He returned to the Bannerets' Hall to check on their register of situations vacant. Most often these tutoring jobs were from individuals hoping to get their sons up to the standard required for admission to the Academy. Occasionally they would be from those who needed assistance in preparing for a duel of honour, a not infrequent occurrence.

He browsed through the list, which was not quite as long or diversified as he had hoped. However, there were several tutoring positions available at addresses in Highgarden, where the remuneration would be the highest. He made note of them and then went into the lounge to sit and write letters to each of the people advertising the positions. That done, he paid one of the boys who worked at the Hall as an errand runner a penny to deliver them.

With that flurry of activity complete, he felt more positive. He didn't yet feel ready to go home though, and realised how unfair he was being to Ayla. In the North, and on the road, he had convinced himself that just getting home would be the answer to all of his problems, that he could... He wasn't sure what he had thought he could do for her. He knew he wanted to be with her, but everything that he had defined himself by, everything in him that he thought to be of value in his life was gone. What worth could he be to her now?

The Hall was well used and there was steady traffic in and out of the lounge where Bryn sat, but it had developed a reputation as being the domain of elderly bannerets who, with nothing better to do, congregated there to share old stories.

The lounge was a large room populated with comfortable chairs and small tables, with bay windows overlooking the street below. The University sat on the other side of it, where those destined for careers in law, medicine, bureaucracy and finance were educated. Bryn's father had gone there and lately Bryn often wondered if he would not have been better off choosing one of those paths. It had never even been a consideration for him though. His earliest memories were of his fascination with bannerets and duelling and, perhaps apocryphally, heroics. It was also the dream of every man who had worked his way up the social ladder to a profession to see his son attend the Academy, and it was always Bryn's father's dream for him. Bryn wondered if he would be disappointed in him now.

As he sat there, staring out the window, he knew that he should make use of the training hall. The truth of it was that he was afraid to. He had not done anything with a sword other than buckle one around his waist in the morning and take it off again in the evening since being strung up in the tree. He could move his hands, fingers and arms again and feel everything that he touched, to a degree. He had enough flexibility now to do all of the things that were needed to get through the day, but his movement was still restricted; there was stiffness, sometimes pain and no strength when he tried to move his arms too far in certain directions.

He kept telling himself they would get better in time, but it had been weeks now. What if the range of motion and flexibility that he needed to fence effectively never came back? He had to believe that it would. There was nothing else he could do. Each time he thought of it he was hit by a flash of panic.

Aristocrats were never ones to wait, and they expected their employees to be at their beck and call. A note arrived back at the lounge only a couple of hours after Bryn had arrived. He had spent the time staring out the window, watching students and academics pass in and out of the University. One of the Hall's ushers brought Bryn the note, startling him out of his stupor.

He was surprised to get something so quickly, and nodding his thanks to the usher, he broke the wax seal on the note. It was from an aristocratic banneret living in Highgarden who was looking for tuition for his son, a seventeen year old preparing for the Academy entrance exam. The job would be of limited duration as the next admission was only a couple of months away, but if he could secure the work, paid at three crowns a day, it would be perfect. It would only require his attention for a few hours a day, allowing him plenty of free time to…

He didn't really know what else there was for him to do. He kept feeling as though there was something more important out there waiting for him, and that everything else was just an interim measure to get him there. He couldn't understand why. There was nothing, and each time he reminded himself of the fact, his misplaced feeling of hope crashed.

There was no point in thinking any further about it. The aristocrat wanted him to call for an interview the following morning, and for the time being that was all that mattered. He had the possibility of well-paid work for the next couple of months, and that was enough to go home with.

His mother was there alone when he got home. 'Where have you been?'

Bryn had expected his mother to take a harsher tone with him for the way he had behaved that morning. The fact that she didn't suggested to him that Ayla had elaborated on his injuries, and of how they still caused him difficulty.

'Looking for work. I have an interview for a tutoring position in the morning. It'll only be for a few months, but it's a start.' He tried to inject some enthusiasm into his voice.

Ayla and his sister arrived back only a few moments after he did.

'Where have you been?' he said, realising that he was echoing the same question his mother had asked moments before.

'Looking for work,' Ayla said.

Bryn raised his eyebrows. She certainly hadn't wasted any time.

'Well, I need to find something. Why wait?' Ayla said.

'Find anything?' Bryn asked.

'Yes. Gilia knew a family in Lowgarden who need a governess for their daughters.'

'Governess?' Bryn said. He had assumed that having lived in a small, rural village, she wouldn't be able to read.

She looked at him curiously for a moment before his meaning dawned on her. 'Oh, of course, being a country bumpkin, I had to pretend to be able to read and write, but they seemed to fall for it.'

Bryn's mother gave him a clip around the ear, making him feel like a small child again. Everyone laughed, which completely changed the atmosphere in the small living room.

'We did have a church school in Grelitz,' Ayla said. As soon as she mentioned the name of her village, all of the levity dropped from her face. 'Had.' The mournful expression that had dominated her features while they were staying at the shack returned.

'I'm sure you'll be a fine governess,' Bryn's mother said, sensing that the mood had taken a turn in the wrong direction.

When Gilia and Ayla had both turned in for the night, his mother sat with him in the living room.

'Were you going to tell me?'

'Tell you what?' Bryn said, already knowing what she meant.

'About your arms. Ayla said you were hurt.'

Bryn nodded.

'That's why you weren't able to do anything about the guildsmen?'

Bryn nodded again.

'How bad is it?'

'Bad,' Bryn said. 'Bad enough that I worry if I'll ever be able to use a sword properly again.'

Even his mother, usually good at dealing with unexpected news, was visibly taken aback. His family had gone without for years to put him through the Academy, assuming that they would benefit from having a banneret in the family. It took her a moment to compose herself.

'How will you teach if you can't use your sword?'

'I'll come up with something. I have to. A critical eye and the ability to correct flaws is important. I can still do that. Perhaps it'll be enough.'

His mother nodded, but didn't seem convinced. 'You'll have to see a physician,' she said. 'There must be something they can do.'

Bryn had to admit that the time for hoping the injury would heal on its own was past. He didn't think they could afford the expense, but he was running out of options. He nodded. 'In the morning.'

'Hmm. Yes. I see.' The physician raised one of Bryn's arms again and studied his shoulder as he did.

He had done it a half dozen times, among other tests, but had not uttered a single conclusive statement, nor anything that gave Bryn any encouragement. Eventually he stopped, rubbed his chin and frowned. In that moment Bryn knew that whatever the physician suggested would be a complete waste of time.

'Still stiff and constricted despite several weeks of healing? And intermittent sensation in your hands?' the physician said.

'Yes,' Bryn said. It was the fourth time he had told the physician the same thing.

The physician went to a cupboard and took out a glass jar filled with a pale yellow substance.

'Apply this ointment to the affected areas three times a day until it's finished. If the symptoms haven't faded at that point, come back to me for another jar.'

Another jar. Bryn wondered how much they cost.

'That will be one crown,' the physician said, as though he had read Bryn's thoughts.

Bryn paid reluctantly, but waited until he got outside before opening the jar. He didn't even need to hold it up to his nose to catch the smell of its stench. Vomit, shit or rotting vegetables? He couldn't decide which came closest. He dropped the jar on a pile of rubbish at the side of the street and continued on his way, ruing the waste of time and money.

Bryn lay awake in bed, unable to sleep and wondering what the following day would bring. Doubt clouded his thoughts and he grew more agitated. He had to know what he could do before his interview. With no chance of getting any sleep until he did, he dressed and headed for the Bannerets' Hall.

Although it was late, the Hall was open every hour of the day. There would be few people around, which suited Bryn perfectly. It was unlikely anyone would walk in on him in the training hall and see him make a fool of himself.

The late-night attendant barely gave Bryn a second look when he blustered in. They were well used to the bannerets staying there coming in at all hours, often the worse for drink. Bryn gave him a curt nod and headed straight for the training hall.

It was huge, echoing and in the dark, cavernous. His boot falls thumped out like beats on a great drum. It took a moment for the mage lamps to react to his presence and illuminate, filling the hall with their warm light. The hall had a couple of drones, training tools filled with the same magical energy that powered the mage lamps. They responded to basic instructions, and Bryn had used similar ones many times at the Academy. They would be an ambitious start however. For that night, all he wanted to do was test himself against a stationary target.

His heart raced as he stood before one, a wooden mannequin with a number of targets marked on it. It bore far fewer signs of use than those at the Academy, looking almost unused. Bryn thrust tentatively at one of the targets, gritting his teeth in preparation for the pain he expected. He breathed a sigh of relief when there was none. He had completely missed though.

He tried again, slowly, willing his arm along the path he desired. The tip wobbled and he strained to control it, but it seemed to have a mind of its own. He felt tension spread through his body, a combination of fear and frustration. He took a moment and forced himself to relax and focus. He couldn't expect to pick up exactly where he had been. Only patience and perseverance would see him through.

He spent two hours standing in front of the wooden mannequin, slowly striking at each of the targets, training the movement back into his arm as though he was back at his very first lesson. There was little satisfaction to be taken from it though. That his shoulder only ached rather than hurt was something, as was the fact that he could move his arm through most of the basic positions. It was all well and good doing it against a wooden practice dummy, but against another person, even if they were only a student?

CHAPTER FORTY-THREE

BRYN DRESSED IN his best fencing clothes and made absolutely certain that he arrived at the address punctually. Ayla had left the apartment early to start her new job, and he had to admit a certain sense of rivalry. She had found a job almost as soon as she arrived in the city. He wanted to make sure he got one quickly too.

He knocked on the door and a deferential servant admitted him to the house, then led him through to a study to meet with his prospective employer.

'Banneret of the Blue Bryn Pendollo, sir,' the servant said, before leaving them alone.

'Good morning, Banneret,' the man said, standing. 'I am Banneret Ollo dal Rari. Pleased to make your acquaintance.'

'Likewise,' Bryn said, giving a curt bow of his head, the appropriate salutation to a banneret of lower rank.

'Please sit,' dal Rari said, doing the same himself. 'As my advertisement stated, I'm looking for a tutor for my son. He's seventeen, and will be making his first attempt for the Academy at the next admissions.'

'How long has he been training?' Bryn said, hoping that the lad had actually started in some fashion many years previously, or his job would be all but impossible. As a banneret, dal Rari should have a good idea of what would be required of his son.

'Naturally he's been taking lessons since he was old enough to hold a sword. He had three terms at Candario's and two at Birend's but now that we're getting so close, I wanted to engage a Banneret of the Blue to put the final polish on him, as it were.'

Bryn nodded, impressed at the names of two such prestigious schools being dropped so casually. If the young man had lasted for more than a term in each of them, he had plenty of talent and Bryn's task would be considerably easier.

'I think that should be possible. I'll have to assess him first of course. I couldn't take the position under the false pretence of promising the impossible.' Bryn had never been the most diplomatic, but even at the risk of offending, he had to make it clear from the outset. Not all young gentlemen were meant for the Academy; it was not unheard of for half of those that gained admission to fail at the end of their first year.

'Indeed,' he said. 'While having earned your colours speaks volumes for your ability, I will require a short demonstration from you. I need to be certain that your style will be compatible with my son's. At this late stage I don't want to expose him to too much new material. All we want is to enhance what he already has. The rest can come after he's admitted.'

'That's not a problem,' Bryn said. He felt the flush of panic again. What would the demonstration involve? Would he be able enough for it? Perhaps he should have been honest with himself and fully tested the extent of his ability at the Bannerets' Hall. He silently cursed himself for his stupidity. Bluffing his way past a nervous teenager while hiding behind his vaunted title of Banneret of the Blue was one thing, proving his worth to an Academy graduate was another.

'Excellent. We can use the gallery upstairs. Follow me,' dal Rari said, as he jumped up from his chair and set off with enthusiasm.

He led Bryn up a staircase carpeted in a thick red weave that his foot sank into with each step. The gallery was a long room that ran along the front of the house on the first of its five floors. Bryn had been in more impressive mansions in Highgarden, but the dal Rari family were obviously extremely wealthy.

Galleries such as this one often doubled as ballrooms in Bryn's experience. It had a polished wooden floor, a high ceiling and plenty of space. One side was lined with bay windows, while the other bore the paintings of what Bryn assumed were ancestors of the dal Rari dynasty.

Dal Rari took two training blades from a stand and offered one to Bryn. 'I value my blood,' he said, 'and would rather not have any of it spilled on the floor.'

Bryn forced a smile. It was meant as a joke, but he was too tense to take it that way. He inspected the sword dal Rari handed him. It was blunt and had a button tip, with a flexible blade and a good point of balance. As training swords went it was as fine an example as he could hope for. There could be no blaming it if things did not go well.

They both took their guard and dal Rari stood waiting for Bryn to initiate. Bryn went through the motions of a standard three stroke attack, the type that would be taught to a budding swordsman at an early stage. Dal Rari parried all three attacks, moving backward with each one.

His arm felt all right, and hope kindled within him. It had not been a taxing move, but he had felt nothing in his shoulder that hinted at trouble to come. It was better than he feared it might be.

'Come now,' dal Rari said. 'There's no need to go easy on me. It may have been a few years since I've trained in earnest, but I'm able for more than that.'

Bryn bowed his head and took a step back before launching into another combination, slightly more ambitious, but not something that would ordinarily have required any thought or much effort on his part. Again dal Rari parried with little difficulty. He raised an eyebrow at Bryn, who nodded once again.

This time he tried to push himself, nothing especially complex, but something that required precision, speed, and reach. It felt like the bottom fell out of his stomach as he launched into it. Of precision, there was little. His blade was wild and the tip bobbed about like a cork on rough water. Dal Rari parried his first attack. Of speed, there was none. Dal Rari parried the second, able to take his time. Of reach, there was not enough. As dal Rari moved back with each attack, Bryn's final thrust, the one intended to strike, fell short by more than a hand's span. Try as he might, he couldn't get his shoulder to move through the same range as it had before the tree. It was much as he had feared it might be after his session at the Bannerets' Hall the night before.

Dal Rari countered with a respectable combination that drove Bryn back and put him under far more pressure to defend against than he would like to admit. He only narrowly diverted the final thrust and felt beads of sweat form on his brow.

Bryn countered back and tried to push himself to something that could at least be called respectable for a Banneret of the Blue. The best he could describe it as was a shambles. His arm didn't move as smoothly as it once had; his joints seemed stiff and his movement mechanical. He couldn't extend his arm as far forward as he needed, nor draw it back as easily. His speed was something that he didn't even want to think about.

Bryn thrust, extending as far as he thought he could, and tried to press beyond that point. His attack stopped short, and he felt his grip loosen involuntarily. The sword dropped from his hand.

'I'm sorry,' Bryn said. 'I appear to have strained something in my shoulder.' He gathered his things as quickly as he could, and left.

Panic churned in Bryn's gut as he walked home. He had been a fool to seek out work so soon, but he felt under so much pressure to start earning that there had seemed little other choice. He had hoped that teaching might be the least taxing avenue open to him, but he was wrong. What else was there? Was there any job that he could bluff his way into, and then hide his restrictions for long enough to recover or find a way around them?

Everyone was sitting around the table drinking tea by the time he got home. They were chatting happily; Ayla's first day at work had gone well. He shuffled in and sat down with no more than a nod to them. Ayla mentioned two unfamiliar girls' names several times, her new wards Bryn assumed. His mother and sister were clearly delighted with how it had gone. After an awkward first couple of days, Ayla was fitting in well with them. His sister had gotten over her initial resentment of having to share her room once again, something she had not had to do since his elder sister had married and left the city, and now seemed to view Ayla as a replacement.

Bryn was happy for her, but so worried about his situation that it was difficult to think of anything else.

Later that evening, when both Gilia and his mother were in the kitchen, he was left alone at the table with Ayla. The distance he had tried to put between him and everyone else made things difficult between them. His mood had nothing to do with her, but he couldn't separate himself from the disappointment and fear of continued failure that dominated his thoughts. Making it all worse was the raw wound of the humiliation he had suffered from the guildsman. He felt as though he had promised her something that he could not deliver.

'Will you take me for a walk?' she said. 'There's still so much of the city I haven't seen.'

That at least was something he could do. He knew he

wouldn't make good company, but that he had to try his best. He told his mother and sister that they were going out and they headed in the direction of Highgarden.

They reached one of the parks that was popular with couples for romantic evening strolls. Were it not for the fact that Ayla and Bryn walked separately they would have appeared no different to anyone else there.

'Is everything all right?' she said.

'Yes, of course. Well, no,' Bryn said. 'I'm sorry if I've been distant, things are just difficult for me right now. It will be better once I've managed to get work.' It wasn't a good excuse for the way he was behaving, but he didn't see any way out of his problems, and try as he might, he couldn't put them out of his mind.

She nodded but said nothing.

CHAPTER FORTY-FOUR

EVEN THE THOUGHT of magic disgusted Bryn. Every child heard stories of how wicked the mages were in the days of the Empire. Tales of their evil acts were told to frighten naughty children, and when he grew older and read the histories himself, Bryn realised those tales only hinted at the true horror of their deeds.

The Mage Wars, how the Bannerets came to be and how they turned on the mages and rid the world of their foul presence featured regularly in the lessons at the Academy. Bryn always counted himself lucky to live in a time when they were long gone, and the practice of magic was highly illegal. The dark-cloaked Intelligenciers one could occasionally see about the city worked tirelessly to ensure that magery could never re-establish itself.

Nonetheless, there were those in the city who practised magic in a limited way—small tricks to entertain paying spectators, or help recovery from injury or illness. Bryn wondered how these people escaped the Intelligenciers' attention; if Bryn could find them, surely the Intelligenciers could too. The only conclusion he could come to was that these people were not seen as a danger and were thus ignored.

It didn't change the way Bryn felt when the idea of seeking

one out in hope that they might be able to help with his injuries came to mind. It nauseated him, but faced with no alternatives the temptation grew too strong to resist.

It didn't take much asking around. In a city like Ostenheim, there was always someone in the know. Bryn scraped together every last penny he could find—the mage's services did not come cheap—and spent several hours battling with himself as to whether this was really the option he wanted to take. Even the Black Carpet seemed more favourable, although he knew that he would in all likelihood be killed the instant he set foot on it. The Black Carpet was no place to try to earn a living while injured.

He hesitated every few steps on the way to the address he was given, and again when he arrived at the door. He hadn't told anyone about what he was doing, but convinced himself that it was the best choice. In his gut he couldn't shake the terror that the magic would do something to him, change him in some way or take something else from him. He was probably being silly—he knew of many people that had used a mage to help them with an ailment, including the neighbour who had given him this particular address. None of them seemed any the worse for it.

He knocked on the door and felt his heart race. There was a rattle behind it a moment later, and the hinges creaked as the door opened. Bryn almost jumped in fright. His jaw dropped when he saw what awaited him on the other side.

'Can I help you?' a woman said.

She was in later middle-age, well dressed and well presented. She looked not unlike someone who would be in his mother's circle of friends. Nothing like what Bryn had imagined.

'I'm not sure I have the right place,' Bryn said. 'Sylvester Tanzi gave me this addre—'

'Come right in,' the woman said, smiling warmly. She stepped back from the door and beckoned for Bryn to enter.

He did so, unable to conceal his reluctance.

'I take it this is your first visit to someone like me,' she said, as she led Bryn into her small, modestly appointed apartment.

'Yes,' he said, awkwardly.

'You've nothing to worry about,' she said. 'Now. Tell me what your problem is.' She gestured for him to sit, which he did.

'I injured my arms and shoulders. They've healed some, but my movement is restricted and I lose feeling in my hands sometimes.'

'I see,' she said. 'Before we start, there's something I need to explain.'

Bryn felt a chill run through him. He hoped she wasn't going to insist on him sacrificing anything. That would be too much for him, desperate or not.

'People often come to me with unrealistic expectations. All I can do is hasten a process that is already underway in the body, and even then only to a point. My help will only go so far, and in some cases it will stop the body's own healing.'

Bryn furrowed his brow.

'What I mean,' she said, 'is that sometimes it's better to leave things be and let nature take its course. That will be a decision for you to make once I've examined you.'

Bryn nodded, fear replaced by burgeoning disappointment. 'I understand.'

'Good. We can begin then. My fee is five crowns.'

Bryn pulled the coins from his purse, all that he had but one, and gave them to her. Then he started to unbutton his doublet, his fingers clumsy.

She smiled and held up her hand. 'There's no need for that.' She reached forward with her hand and held it over Bryn's shoulder for a moment, before slowly working down along his arm. 'How long ago did the injury occur?'

'Eight, nine weeks. The time immediately after is a bit of a blur.'

She nodded. 'There's already much healing here. I suspect

that's in part the cause of your trouble moving. The bad news is there's not much I can do for that. I can't undo what's already done.'

Bryn closed his eyes and cursed silently. There was a warm, tingling sensation in his right hand, more feeling than he had experienced in it in weeks. He opened his eyes and looked down. The woman held her hand over his, and for a moment he thought he saw a blue glow between them, but it seemed to disappear as soon as he became aware of it. She lifted her hand away and gestured for him to try his.

He lifted it and flexed his fingers. He could feel everything, the stretch and fold of the skin as the fingers bent, and the nails pressing against his palm. He laughed and greedily held out his left.

The woman smiled and held her hand out over that one too. There was the same tingling sensation, and the senses in his hand were reinvigorated. He held them both out in front, flexing and stretching, revelling in the sensations that had been lost to him for so many weeks.

'That's amazing,' he said, fixated on his hands. 'Are you sure there's nothing you can do for my shoulders?' He looked up at her.

She smiled wistfully and shook her head. Bryn's eyes widened as he saw how tired she looked, as though she had aged a decade in the last minute.

'If I interfere now, there will be no more healing in them. Nature may well do more for them than I can.'

Bryn nodded, concerned by how frail looking she had become. 'Are you all right?'

'I'm fine. I just need to rest.'

She let the comment hang in the air, making it clear to Bryn that it was time to leave.

⟨⟩

Everyone had left the apartment when he woke the next day. He lay in bed for some time, staring at the ceiling, flexing his hands. As happy as he was to have them feeling so much better, he rued the fact that nothing could be done for his shoulders beyond exercising them and hoping. He wondered how different things could be if he had seen the mage sooner.

He thought of the applications he had sent for the other jobs, and wondered if he should go to the Bannerets' Hall to see if there were any responses. There seemed little point in checking; he wouldn't be able to take on any jobs and would most likely end up embarrassing himself in an interview.

He started to feel claustrophobic cooped up in the apartment, so he went out in the hope that a walk would clear his thoughts and help him find an answer. He wandered the streets until he found himself standing outside Bautisto's salon. He strained to hear if there were any sounds of training coming from inside, tempted to go in, but holding himself back for some reason.

'Bryn?'

Bryn turned to see Bautisto standing behind him, carrying an armful of long, cloth-wrapped bundles, which Bryn took to be training swords.

'Maestro Bautisto,' Bryn said.

'I was told you had been killed.' Bautisto's voice was incredulous.

'You weren't the only one,' Bryn said. 'I wasn't though. Obviously.'

'Obviously,' Bautisto said, giving a rare smile. 'Are you coming in?'

'I suppose so,' Bryn said. He had nothing else to do, so why not?

He followed Bautisto inside. It was much the same as when Bryn had last seen it.

'When did you get back to the city?' Bautisto said, as he began unwrapping what were indeed new training swords.

'A couple of days ago.'

'What happened out there? We were told the supply convoy you were with disappeared, and everyone was presumed to be dead. Killed. I called on your family a couple of times to see if there was anything I could do.'

'That was good of you. I appreciate it. It's a long story. Not an especially interesting one. I was lucky is all. Maybe.'

'Maybe?'

Bryn walked over and picked up one of the new training swords. They were nice, better than Bautisto had when Bryn was training there, so he must have been doing well. Bryn was happy for him. He took his guard and made a thrust and parry.

Bautisto raised an eyebrow. 'Out of practice?'

Bryn shook his head. He raised the sword high. As his shoulder stretched, his grip became weak and it fell from his hand.

Bautisto frowned. 'What's wrong?'

'Who knows?' Bryn said. 'I spent a while hanging from a tree. That's as good as it's been since.'

Bautisto reached forward, picked up the sword Bryn had dropped and handed it to him. Puzzled, Bryn took it.

Bautisto picked up another. 'Take your guard.'

Out of habit, Bryn complied immediately. Bautisto attacked him. Nothing taxing, just the type of routine they would have used for a warm-up in the past. Bryn's arm was slow and stiff, but he was able to keep up. Bautisto came at him again, faster and more aggressive this time. As Bryn stretched his arm, he felt the sword slip in his grip on the second parry. On the third it flew from his hand. His shoulder was so tight that he couldn't maintain a hold on it.

Bautisto lowered his sword and put his hand on his hip. 'I see. Is it strength or feeling you lose when you move to extremities?'

'I just lose my grip when I stretch my arm. I can't move my shoulders nearly as well either,' Bryn said.

'Well. You can't fence the way you used to anymore, not unless the condition improves. We'll have to come up with something different until it does, or that will suffice if it doesn't. I'm busy today. Come back first thing in the morning and we will start.'

With that, Bautisto disappeared into the back room, indicating that their conversation was over. Bryn had never before felt so elated by Bautisto's brusqueness.

CHAPTER FORTY-FIVE

AMERO'S ULTIMATUM OF no less than one match every two weeks expired that day, and there was no sign of a match being arranged for him. The top ten seemed to be happy to jostle amongst themselves for second place. Amero was confident that eventually one of the cowardly curs would fancy their chances, but he wasn't willing to wait. Perhaps he had overdone it with the mage in the early days. He speculated that it had advanced his training by four, perhaps even five years. That was the point at which most swordsmen peaked, and it made Amero wonder what he would be capable of then. If the others were all so afraid of him humiliating them now, what would it be like then?

Perhaps it was time to consider bringing someone in from abroad, a foreign champion. He thought about what dal Corsi had said, calling him a sure thing. The old fart hadn't said it outright, but Amero could read between the lines. Ticket sales weren't the only thing that fuelled the duelling business. Gambling took pride of place in that regard, and if Amero was such a sure thing no one would take a bet against him. They were the ones holding back his career. He knew he could fill out the Amphitheatre just by turning up.

He had achieved the fastest one hundred and twenty-five,

and defended his title of First Blade a number of times. Perhaps he should lose. The shock it would cause would have the city talking about nothing else for weeks. His comeback afterward would fill the Amphitheatre. The thought galled him, having to pander to the whims of the filthy touts who lurked around outside the arena. A few large, but discreetly placed bets and then intentionally losing would ruin some of them, and that thought was very appealing, but Amero wasn't willing to let his winning streak come to an end yet, not until it was an unassailable record that would stand long after he had died. There had to be another way to draw so much attention to his duel that it could not be refused.

◯

'Again!'

Bautisto had not altered his approach to training during Bryn's absence. Brusque, harsh, dictatorial; Bryn hadn't realised how much he missed it.

He was exhausted and his limbs burned like they were on fire. He wanted more than anything to be able to be master of his sword again. Too many years and too many dreams had been devoted to it. He refused to give up, but each hour of agony tested his resolve.

'I can't,' Bryn said.

'Of course you can. You just won't.'

Bryn wiped the sweat from his brow and heaved his arm back up into the guard position. There was only so far he could move it, so Bautisto had focussed their efforts on improving his agility with blade in hand. His sword still needed to get to all the places his arm couldn't reach, so he had to compensate by developing greater forearm strength and forcing flexibility back into his shoulder. Bautisto's chosen method for achieving the former was hard training with a heavy sword and for the latter, hours of painful and mind-numbing stretching exercises.

Bryn hoped it was working; he even dared to think that it might be, but feared he was getting his hopes up unrealistically.

The style they were developing was different. It built on the economical Estranzan techniques that Bautisto had spent their first months together beating into him, dispensing with all unnecessary movement, creating something that was plain and workmanlike to the eye—ugly even—but it reduced the amount of movement required of Bryn's shoulder. It placed more strain on everything else, but it seemed to work.

As they slowly moved through the patterns that Bautisto had devised, he was able to cover far more space than he had expected. Bautisto was the first to acknowledge that his system was a work in progress but to Bryn, with all his fears, it seemed like a work of genius. For the first time in weeks he had hope.

When Bautisto's other students arrived, Bryn slipped into the background, tidied up, did whatever needed to be done to keep the salon clean and standing. It was the only way he had to repay Bautisto's kindness. He actually enjoyed having something to do when Bautisto's financial considerations dictated he work with paying students.

Bryn got home late every evening, exhausted but encouraged by the progress he was making. His style would change completely with the training they were doing, but he was convinced that it would be just as effective, and saw the hope of matching his old self as tenable. His shoulders felt looser as each day went by, and the new movement patterns came more easily.

The days stretched into weeks, and claiming that he was spending his time job hunting was quickly wearing thin. He wasn't convinced anyone at home believed him anyway. With all that had happened they were giving him space, but he knew that wouldn't last for long. The hours spent at the salon meant he hardly saw anyone at home, and Ayla was spending an ever-increasing amount of time at the house in Highgarden with her wards. They had barely exchanged more than a few words in some time, and Bryn had no idea of how to cross the gulf that seemed to have formed between them. At times he actually longed to be back on the road, or even in the shack, when it was just the two of them and nothing else mattered.

Faced with the prospect of regaining what he had thought lost to him forever, it was difficult to think of anything else, even eating. As hard as it had been to accept the idea that he might never be able to competently use a sword again, in his darkest moments he had. To have the prospect of being able to get it all back was intoxicating—but the requirements were a jealous mistress with whom there was room for nothing else.

There were restrictions on him now that Bryn was coming to realise would remain with him for the rest of his life. There were ways around this, however. It was merely a case of being willing to make the changes required. Few swordsmen would agree to erasing every trace of style and flair from their swordplay and fundamentally altering the movements ingrained by a lifetime of practice, but that was the challenge Bryn had to accept.

Every movement—even only so much as a hair's breadth— had to have a purpose, whether offensive or defensive. There would never again be room for flair or stylistic embellishment. His swordplay would never again inspire admiration, nor could it be called a thing of beauty, but so long as it worked, it could give him his life back.

He had taken to changing before and after training at the salon to help hide what he was actually up to, but the deceit was starting to weigh on him. Now that he had confirmed to himself that what he was doing was not a delusion or a waste of time, he wanted to come clean. He hoped they would be as enthusiastic as he was about it.

'How's the job hunting going, Bryn?' his mother said. It was her standard question every evening before they ate.

'I've stopped looking for the moment, actually,' he said.

Gilia and Ayla both paused mid-chew and looked at Bryn.

'I've been helping Maestro Bautisto out in the salon.'

His mother's face hardened. 'How is loitering around a salon going to help you get work? You said yourself that you can't use a sword anymore. Don't you think it's time to accept that and start working toward something you can do? There's no dishonour in a banneret working in the Chancellery. The pay is good too.'

Bryn swallowed hard, knowing how what he was going to say next would be received. 'Actually, Maestro Bautisto believes I might have been hasty in deciding that I can't fence anymore.'

'So you're training again?'

'Yes,' Bryn said.

His mother's face went from hard to dark. 'How long has that been going on?'

'A few weeks,' Bryn said.

'I knew you were up to something. But even I didn't fathom you could be that stupid. Haven't you had enough of all this yet? Can't you see the trouble it's caused not just you, but all of us?'

'I've spent my entire life training to be a swordsman. You of all people know the sacrifices that involved.'

'You trained to be a banneret. Playing with a sword isn't the only thing bannerets do. That's only for the ones too stupid to make a better career for themselves. I'd have thought you'd have learned that lesson by now. How much more misery will it take to beat that into your thick skull? Get a job. Stop being such a bloody fool.'

This time it was his mother who stormed out of the house. Bryn dropped his head into his hands. She was almost correct on one thing—some bannerets were drawn to the excitement and adventure of a life by the sword. Others were indeed not clever enough to earn their living any other way. His academic scores had long since told Bryn he was in the latter group.

The argument with his mother had hammered home the fact that he needed to get paying work of some description, but that didn't necessarily mean he had to stop training with Bautisto. The work they had already done had brought Bryn far. He still had a long way to go, but felt that lower level tutoring jobs were now a reasonable consideration. If he could get one, his mother would soften her position. It put him out of harm's way, would earn him an income and allow him to continue using a sword to make his livelihood. As he improved, he could look for jobs with more advanced students. It was not where he wanted to be, but it was a start that put him in the right direction.

Before heading to the salon for the day, he called back to the Bannerets' Hall and sent off another half dozen responses to the situations vacant register.

He returned on his way home that evening, pleased to see that there were two notes asking him to call on the senders at his earliest opportunity. One was from an aristocrat in Highgarden, the other a grand burgess in Lowgarden. He prioritised the appointment in Highgarden, for no other reason than he thought he would be able to charge a higher rate.

He wasn't sure what kind of reception awaited him at home, but armed with yet another job prospect, he hoped that he would be able to deflect some of his mother's ire.

Bryn felt nervous as he waited for his appointment in Highgarden. Memory of his previous interview flitted through his mind, as did the laughter of the men at the Wagoners' Guild house. Things that he had taken for granted could no longer be counted on. He knew he was as well prepared as he could be. His prospective pupil was only twelve years old, so the job would not be nearly so taxing as instructing one preparing for the Academy's entrance tests.

'Baron dal Ventro will see you now.'

Bryn could feel his heart skip as he stood and followed the servant through to his interview.

Dal Ventro sat at his desk with another man sitting to his right. Dal Ventro was older than Bryn expected, old to have so young a son.

'Thank you for coming, Banneret Pendollo,' dal Ventro said. 'I've been through this process a few times now, and I find the most efficient way to deal with things is to have you spar with Banneret Giaco here, and if you're up to scratch, I'll fill you in on the details.'

Bryn nodded. 'A good idea.'

'Excellent. Banneret Giaco was tutoring my son, but he's also my steward and has more pressing demands on his time these days.' Dal Ventro stood and led Bryn and Banneret Giaco through to a gallery at the back of the house. 'Are you ready to go, Banneret Pendollo?'

'I am.'

Dal Ventro took two blunt training rapiers from a wall hanger and handed one to Bryn, the other to Giaco. 'In your own time, Bannerets.'

Banneret Giaco advanced on Bryn, attacking with thrusts from his arm alone. Bryn moved back at a steady pace, parrying with the minimum amount of arm movement necessary. He made two quick thrusts to change the direction of the swordplay.

Memory and years of repeated practice were hard things to set aside, and he found himself wanting to make attacks that he knew were no longer available to him. He focussed on the things he had been working on with Bautisto; minimal movement, precision, speed. He felt his blade flex as it connected with Banneret Giaco's chest. Banneret Giaco nodded in acknowledgement of the hit. It was ungentlemanly to make a showy display in victory, and it took effort to stop himself from smiling. It was the first time he had fenced against anyone other than Bautisto since taking on this new style, and it seemed to be working. The feeling of putting a scoring hit on someone again was almost overwhelming. Right up until the moment he had felt the hit, he hadn't really believed that he would ever be able to manage it again. Every second of pain and every drop of sweat in the salon were worth it.

'I think that will be enough. Do you agree, Banneret Giaco?' dal Ventro said.

Giaco nodded.

'Thank you, Banneret Pendollo. That's an interesting style you have. I've not seen anything like it before, but it seems to be very effective.'

'I'm well versed in several styles, and am happy to instruct in any of them,' Bryn said. 'Ostian, Ruripathian, Estranzan, and of course also my own style, which is something of a work in progress, but as you say, appears effective and promising for further development.'

'I recall your name,' dal Ventro said. 'You did some duelling in the arena, did you not?'

Bryn felt his heart sink. 'Yes. I'm not duelling anymore though.'

'Well, I like what I saw here today. I'll be in touch. My man will show you out.' He gestured to the servant standing by the door.

Bryn didn't know what to think, but having dal Ventro remember his name didn't feel like a good thing. Elation to disappointment in only a moment.

〇

The second interview in Lowgarden seemed to go better. The boy's father didn't recognise Bryn's name, and having not been to the Academy himself he was far more impressed with Bryn's title than someone who had would be. Bryn felt more relaxed over the course of the interview as a result, which didn't involve any demonstration—his title was more than enough to convince the Grand Burgess of his ability.

It would be a day or two before he heard back from either of them, but he wasn't hopeful about the first interview. The second seemed more promising, and a Grand Burgess was likely to be able to pay just as well as a baron. He felt close to being able to stand on his own two feet, to finally be able to help support those who had done so much for him.

As was the case every day, he was training with Bautisto. There had been no improvement in his arms in some time, but he had enough movement, speed and strength for what Bautisto required of him. Each day they pushed a little harder and Bautisto introduced a new element for Bryn to practice and perfect. He was attempting to do exactly that when there was a commotion by the door.

Bryn lowered his sword and turned his attention away from the practice dummy to the door. A portly, ruddy-faced man with a bald head and a thick white moustache had entered, followed by two men who were obviously subservient to him.

Bryn groaned as he remembered the face. Ricoveri dal Corsi, the old banneret who scheduled all of the duels in the Amphitheatre. The last time Bryn had seen him was before his duel against Amero. As displeased as he was at seeing the old man again, Bryn was curious. What was he doing at Bautisto's salon? Bautisto hadn't mentioned any promising pupils, but that would not be unlike him. He only hoped that whoever the swordsman was, he had a better experience of the Amphitheatre than Bryn did.

'Pendollo? That you?' dal Corsi said.

Bryn furrowed his brow. 'Yes…'

'Excellent. I was told you're back in training, and looking tasty enough to boot. I've a proposal for you.'

'How did you know I'm back training?' Bryn said.

'Pal of mine from the Academy, Serrol dal Ventro, said he had you in to interview for tutoring his son. Remembered who you are. Said you fenced like nothing he's ever seen, and that you weren't half bad.'

Bautisto emerged from the back room. 'Banneret dal Corsi. What brings you back to my salon?'

'Was just telling Pendollo here,' dal Corsi said, 'that I've an opportunity for him.'

'And what might that be?' Bautisto said, blatantly hostile to dal Corsi's presence in his salon.

'Well, I'd like to chat with Pendollo alone if that's all right,' dal Corsi said, as though affronted by Bautisto's chilly reception.

'I don't think there's anything you could say that's of interest to me,' Bryn said.

'How about a rematch with dal Moreno?'

CHAPTER FORTY-SIX

A REMATCH WITH AMERO was the last thing that Bryn expected. He wandered around the city for hours after leaving the salon, trying to order his thoughts and separate them from his emotions, but he wasn't having much luck.

Dal Corsi was an arrogant old prick, and a bully if the way he treated his two underlings was anything to go by. Quite how any self-respecting banneret would put up with that treatment was beyond Bryn, but he supposed the reward of a match in the Amphitheatre was enough to make most overlook his behaviour. Naturally he had expected Bryn to jump at the chance to fight in the Amphitheatre again. Dal Corsi was so full of his own self-importance that he was flabbergasted when Bryn didn't sign an appearance contract there and then.

Bryn needed to make sense of it all before deciding. Why was he being offered this chance? There was no way the offer was made without Amero's contrivance, but what was in it for the bastard? Could it be that he now felt so secure in his position that he was extending the hand of charity to Bryn? A gesture motivated out of guilt after the way he behaved? That felt like such a ridiculous notion Bryn laughed aloud as he walked down the street, attracting several curious glances.

The reason why was one thing, but his own feelings about the match were just as important. He knew what to expect from Amero now. He knew the dirty tricks he would try, and how he would deal with them. Now, as then, he felt he could beat Amero. Even after all that had happened, he knew he had it in him to win. Just as Amero's new style had surprised and devastated all of his opponents, Bryn's tight, punchy style of swordsmanship was something that Amero would never have seen before. He knew it was effective and with a couple of months dedicated to its perfection, he was convinced he would be as good as he ever was; perhaps better. It would be as much of a surprise to Amero as his flashy new technique had been to Bryn when he first revealed it.

The memory of all that had happened angered Bryn every time it popped into his head. The thought of having the chance to settle the score was impossible to ignore. Tutoring jobs would always be available, and they could wait until after any rematch. It was only a few more weeks, and then he could let the whole episode rest with satisfactory resolution and not have to give it another thought for the rest of his life. He would have to ensure that Amero wasn't able to get to him in any way this time, either into his head or by causing physical injury.

The idea of standing over a defeated Amero on the Amphitheatre floor set Bryn's heart racing. The chance to wipe the smile off the smug bastard's face was too much to resist. Bryn realised that the decision was already made. He had no idea how he would break the news to everyone at home.

'Otto. What brings you to Ostenheim?' Amero said. To the best of his knowledge, Otto, the family steward, had not left Moreno in decades.

'Your father, my Lord. I'm so terribly sorry. He's dead,' Otto said.

Renald dead? 'Has the date for my investiture been set?' Amero said.

Otto frowned. 'Don't you want to know what happened, my Lord?'

'Would it change the fact that he's dead?'

'Well, I, well, no, my Lord.'

'My investiture. When will it take place?' Amero said.

'We haven't gotten to that yet. We thought you should be notified immediately—'

'You best attend to it then,' Amero said, 'and stop prattling around here like an old woman.'

Amero returned to his couch and looked out the window, out at the ships in the inner harbour. He wondered what changes being count would bring to his life. He saw no reason for any. The draw of the arena was too strong to turn his back on. If anything, the power being the most famed duellist in the city brought him felt as though it eclipsed that of being an elector count.

Bryn waited until dinner was over and he was helping his mother wash the dishes before he brought up his news. He hadn't mentioned it during the meal as he didn't want to be outnumbered at the table.

'I bumped into someone interesting today,' Bryn said.

'Really?' she said, not looking up from the dish she was cleaning. 'About a job?'

'Yes,' Bryn said. 'After a fashion.'

She stopped what she was doing and looked up at him. 'After a fashion?' Her voice was the same as it had been when he was a child, and caught out on a lie.

'The scheduler from the Amphitheatre called by the salon.'

'Aren't you supposed to be looking for a job?'

'I am, that's how he found out I was training again. One of the interviews I took, the employer knows the scheduler.'

'So you're going to take a duel then?'

'I don't know. I'm thinking about it.'

'Well, then you're an even bigger fool than I took you for. Did you not learn your lesson last time? Months of hard work only to look a laughing stock in front of the entire city.'

Bryn swallowed hard. 'They want to give me a rematch against Amero.'

She looked at him with complete astonishment. 'You're going to make exactly the same mistake? Again? Going back to the arena at all is daft enough, but this? Did you bang your head in the north as well?'

'I can beat him. Wipe the smile of his face. Put things to right.'

'No you can't. Even I know he's gone unbeaten for months, and I hate duelling. You need to get your head straight. I can't believe you'd even consider this. You come home exhausted every night, and barely utter a single word to that girl. How do you think that makes her feel? She thinks you don't want her around anymore, that you regret bringing her back with you. She saved your life and I'd say you're an idiot for not seeing the way she looks at you, but you've proved that already tonight.'

Bryn dipped his head.

'Keep carrying on as you are and you risk losing the only good thing that's happened to you in a very long time.'

'The money would help too,' Bryn said, not feeling at all confident now.

'I hope it's enough to pay rent. Because that's what you'll have to do. Take this duel and I don't want you around here anymore.'

He felt a flush of anger. 'I have to beat him. I can't let him get away with what he did.'

'Get out.'

Bryn stayed at an inn not far from his mother's apartment that night. He might as well have spent the night pacing the streets for all the sleep that he got. The more he thought about it, the more his anger at Amero burned.

Dal Corsi's offer had crystallised Bryn's opinion of Amero and his desire to get his own back—he couldn't let it nag away at him for the rest of his life. He could see the other things in his life, but they seemed peripheral. Amero was in the centre of his focus—until he was dealt with Bryn knew he could not give proper attention to the other things. It would all be over with in only a few weeks, a couple of months at the most, then he would be able to devote more time to the people he cared about and have the money to do it properly. Everything would be different. Better.

'You realise why the offer was made, don't you?' Bautisto said, as they put their training blades away for the day.

Bryn looked over at him. 'What do you mean?'

'The duel. Why they offered it to you.'

'I've never thought it a smart idea to question good fortune. It's not like I see all that much of it,' Bryn said.

'Perhaps you should start. Amero has been unbeaten since he first fought in the Amphitheatre. He raced to one hundred and twenty-five points so quickly, fighting twice in one day on some occasions, he had the city in a frenzy. It was impatient of him, and foolish. Once he got there, what then? What could he do to top that and keep the crowds interested? Before you got back to the city, people were beginning to say that his new style could not be bested, that his thrust is perfect and cannot be defended against.'

Bryn laughed. The thrust for which there was no defence was the elixir that had driven swordsmen throughout the ages mad. It was a myth, something unattainable, something that did not exist except in the minds of those who believed it was possible. There was no way Amero had happened upon it.

'My point is,' Bautisto said, 'people are bored with him now. He has nothing left to keep them interested.'

Bryn raised an eyebrow.

'They see the same thing every week. Three touches, duel over. The last time I went to the Amphitheatre, it was half empty by the time Amero scored his first touch. Lower ranked swordsmen are drawing bigger crowds, because people don't know what the result will be. Filling the Amphitheatre and the money that means for everyone involved is only part of it. No one will bet on his duels now, and that's where the real money lies. If he didn't have the right of top billing as First Blade of Ostia, they'd have thrown him to the gutter weeks ago. They can't get rid of him, and they can't make enough money out of him. He's not at all popular with the promoters, and it's only a matter of time before he gets completely side-lined, and he knows it. This offer is proof of the fact.'

'My heart bleeds for him,' Bryn said.

'That's exactly what he wants. If they get you back on the sand with him, Amero is going to kill you. I'm sure of it. It will solidify his reputation as an arena killer, and that will drive the people back into their frenzy. You'll be his second and most tragic kill; his former friend but now bitter enemy. That will have the crowds back in their thousands, and they'll bet on whether Amero wins by touches or by kill. He'll make the arena no better than the Black Carpet.'

'You say it like it's a certainty,' Bryn said. 'That he'll kill me.'

'He's gotten very good, Bryn. Far better than he was. The new style he developed, it's perfect for him. I don't like him any more than you do, but I have to give him credit for that.'

'I can't leave what happened unanswered. I can beat him. I

know I can. You've seen how much I've improved. I'm as good as I ever was. Better even. And our new style? It'll take him by surprise.'

Bautisto shook his head. 'You've far exceeded my expectations and hopes, Bryn. I've never seen such hard work from a pupil, and I agree you're probably better now than you ever were. The new technique is a very good match for you, but I'm not convinced it's enough.'

Bryn shook his head and started to open his mouth, but Bautisto cut him off.

'I despise Amero for what he did, but he has grown into a truly magnificent swordsman and the risk now is too great. If all you had to worry about was losing, I would say go for it, take the money and maybe you'd win, maybe not. That's not the case this time. Amero doesn't want to just win. He has to prove to the promoters that he can fill arenas, and as I see it there's only one way for him to do that. To kill again. The risk is too great. It's not worth it.'

'I thought you of all people would stand by me on this. Show a little more belief in me.'

'I do believe in you, Bryn. Surely all the hours I've spent with you over the past weeks have demonstrated that. It is your choice, and if you decide to fight, I will stand with you, but I wouldn't be doing right by you if I didn't speak up.'

'Have you been speaking to my mother?'

Bautisto laughed, and shook his head.

'We'll just have to work harder then,' Bryn said.

CHAPTER FORTY-SEVEN

AUTISTO WAS ALONE in the salon, but had a paying client later in the morning, and Bryn would be returning for his second session of the day after that, so he took the opportunity to tidy up. Business was steadily improving, and as a consequence he had to put more effort into keeping the salon clean. It might be a dump, but he couldn't abide dirt. He was sweeping dust into a pan when he noticed that a man had come into the salon, so quietly that Bautisto did not hear him. He was of medium height, wiry, and had a rapier strapped to his waist. His black hair, pulled back into a tight ponytail, was showing the first signs of grey.

'Can I help you?' Bautisto said. He set the pan on the ground, and stood straight. It was a little embarrassing for a banneret to be happened upon doing the cleaning, particularly by another banneret, but needs must.

'Perhaps,' the man said. 'I'm looking for Banneret of the Blue Bryn Pendollo. To whom do I speak?'

Bautisto relaxed. 'Banneret of the Starry Field Baltasar Bautisto. I'm afraid Banneret Pendollo is not here at present. Might I pass on a message?'

'Ah, the Estranzan maestro. Pleased to make your

acquaintance.' He nodded in salute. 'I'm Banneret of the Blue Willard Dornish. No need for a message, I'll call again in a day or two.'

He nodded again before leaving, a gesture Bautisto mirrored and then returned to his dustpan and brush.

⊘

Bryn's mother rarely spoke without meaning what she said, and it was no different with her ordering him out of the apartment. Bautisto's classes were now well enough subscribed to allow him to rent an apartment elsewhere in the city, leaving the cot in the back room of the salon free for Bryn's use. With virtually no money it was the most luxurious accommodation he could hope for.

He was punishing himself with such a gruelling workload that he was glad of only having to go a few paces before he could collapse into his bed each evening.

There was no vitriolic build up to worry about this time, but Bryn was under no illusion that this was out of any consideration on Amero's part. It was because Bryn made it an express condition of his taking part in the duel. The duel would be prepared for in secret, and only be announced the morning before. At the first sign of leak, or any hate campaign against him, he would withdraw.

The thought of having to go through another ordeal like the last one was the only thing that made the prospect of a rematch unpalatable, no matter how attractive the terms. He insisted on this, making it clear to Amero's flunkies that this was a deal breaker.

The fat walrus dal Corsi had thought keeping it a secret to be a great idea, confident that surprising the city with a big event at the last minute would stir their passions to a crescendo. He reckoned that tickets would be sold out by lunchtime, and the gambling would be furious, as Amero faced the last man to put a touch on him once again.

Even after only so short a time away from home, he missed his mother and sister. Above all, he missed Ayla. There was something about her presence that made him feel at peace, a sense of happiness and contentment that left him feeling hollow without her. As he lay alone on his cot in the cold, damp back room each night, he thought of their journey back from her ruined town. Of the nights they had spent in that draughty little shack while he prayed for his shoulders to heal. Despite it all, the memories filled him with happiness.

Alone in the darkness of his thoughts, he dwelled on what Bautisto had said. Was Amero really that good now? Could Bryn beat him? Was he as big a fool as his mother said? The match was only a few days away, so there was no backing out now. Not that he wanted to. He would win, or he would die. Either outcome felt better than letting Amero away with it.

The night before the duel, Bryn lay in his small cot, staring at the damp patches on the roof. He wasn't sleepy and felt incredibly alone. He had tried to keep Bautisto engaged in conversation—a difficult thing to do at the best of times—but even that had failed to delay his departure, leaving Bryn alone with his thoughts in the ramshackle old fencing salon.

It was not late—he had gone to bed early in preparation for the duel—so he got out of his cot, dressed, and headed for his mother's apartment. If anything, his nerves grew as he walked through the quiet evening streets. He had no idea what his reception would be like. The last words he had exchanged with his mother were harsh. He couldn't even remember what his last words with Ayla had been. He brought her to the city to repay her for her kindness to him, for saving his life. He hadn't been able to do anything for her at all. If it hadn't been for his family, like as not she'd have been living on the streets by now. In one more day, everything would change. He would win, and he would give them everything they deserved, and more.

Bryn knocked on the door and waited, listening for the sounds on the other side. His sister opened the door and raised her eyebrows when she saw Bryn standing there.

'Well,' Gilia said. 'Can't say I expected to see you. Come to your senses? Better late than never, I suppose.'

'Can I come in?' Bryn said.

She stepped back from the door to let him pass.

'I wanted to come over to ask you all to come to the Amphitheatre tomorrow,' Bryn said.

His mother looked up from the table where she was sitting. 'I'm not sure if that's a good idea.'

'I'd like you all to be there,' he said. 'After tomorrow, everything will be better. I promise.'

'Better like the last time?' Gilia said, joining their mother at the table.

Bryn looked around. 'Where's Ayla? Still at work?'

'Ayla's gone,' his mother said.

'What? Where?'

'She's gone back north. She was able to contact some cousins in Ruripathia. She decided she should be with her family. You'd know all this if you'd been around the past couple of weeks.'

'Where do they live?'

'She never said. Just said that she'd let us know when she was settled.'

'When did she leave?'

'This morning,' Gilia said.

'How?'

'She took a post carriage. We tried to stop her. The roads are still dangerous.'

'I know,' Bryn said. 'There's still fighting up around the border. What was she thinking?'

'She was thinking she had no reason to stay. If you'd been around, shown any sign that you wanted her to stay, she would have.'

Bryn felt dizzy. He had thought he had time, that he could make amends later when he had fixed everything. What a fool he had been.

'I have to go and bring her back,' he said.

Bryn didn't hesitate before turning and rushing out of the apartment to start after Ayla. He had gotten to the corner before he realised he was going nowhere fast. Without money, there was no way he would catch up with her until long after she had reached wherever she was going.

The post carriage, along with most land traffic, took the one main road north. It would stay on it until she branched off for her specific destination, so it wouldn't be difficult to follow her for the first few days of the journey. That was meaningless though, unless he could move faster than she was. The post carriage was not the fastest way north, but it was the cheapest. It meant that Bryn would be able to go faster by almost any method other than walking. Without any money, walking was all that was available to him.

He turned on his heel and backtracked to his mother's apartment. He knocked on the door. His mother opened it, a leather purse in her hand.

'Bring her back safe,' she said. She handed him the purse.

He nodded in thanks and took it, breaking into a run as he headed for the north gate and the stables outside the city walls.

When he arrived, he stood outside the stables and weighed the options of hiring a horse or taking an express carriage. If she had taken the post, which stopped each night at one of the many coaching inns along the road, Bryn reckoned he had a good chance of catching up to her. She had only left that morning, so was possibly still within the range of a day's hard ride. That would exhaust the horse, so if she had gone any farther an express would be a better idea. If he were to have any hope of being back in time for the duel, he needed to move as fast as possible. He decided to hire a horse.

He cast his eye over several of the animals, checking them for one that looked well rested and injury free. Settling on a dappled grey, he paid the tired looking stable hand. He bought a water-skin, a bag of apples and a near stale loaf of bread from the stall of an opportunistic vendor by the stable while the stable hand saddled the horse.

Bryn jumped onto the horse as soon as it was led outside, and spurred it on to a gallop. He tried to adopt as comfortable a position as he could, knowing that he would be in that saddle for many hours to come.

After several hours on the road, Bryn's entire body ached. His backside and thighs burned from chafing and he determined that once this journey was over, he wouldn't go near another horse for at least a year. He reckoned it could well take the same length of time before he was able to sit down again. There was a growing bright line on the horizon and he knew it wouldn't be long before the sun rose.

Since learning that Ayla was gone, he hadn't thought of anything other than getting her back. The duel seemed insignificant by comparison, but as his thoughts returned to it, he realised his hope of getting back to the city in time was forlorn. Even if he did manage it, he would be exhausted by the ride. It was almost dawn and he had been riding hard all night. He reined the horse back to a halt. Unless he turned around now, there was no way he would be back in the city in time for the duel.

The horse circled and snorted. Its blood was up and it was agitated by Bryn's hesitation. He looked back in the direction of Ostenheim, and realised he didn't care about the duel. He thought of Amero's smug face, and for the first time felt nothing. He thought of Ayla's lazy smile when they woke that morning under the tree. He felt a flash of despair. He spurred the horse on.

CHAPTER FORTY-EIGHT

WHILE BRYN HAD been gaining good ground all night, with dawn now a couple of hours behind him, Ayla would most likely be on the move again. His hope was to catch up with her when she stopped that coming night, if not before.

His own pace was necessarily slowed. He had to give his horse longer breaks, stopping completely rather than mixing the halts with periods of walking alongside it. There might be the opportunity to trade it for a fresh mount at the next inn but he couldn't count on it. Each second he stopped felt like an age and he was anxious to get going again. It was as though he could feel Ayla getting farther away. Reason dictated that by resting the horse he was going to be able to make better time, but it was difficult to convince himself of that fact.

As he stood next to the horse, Bryn worried that the rest he was affording the animal was still not enough. As eager as he was to catch Ayla, he couldn't afford to have it drop dead underneath him. He didn't know this horse well enough to be sure of how hard he could push it.

He still thought of her departure as sudden, but after what his mother said, he knew that it was only sudden to him. He wondered if he'd ever learn. He'd let Amero get back inside his head, but it wasn't just Amero. Bryn had spent his entire life dreaming of being a swordsman and a duellist. It was too deeply ingrained in him to easily let go of. He had convinced himself he could have it all; the people he cared about and the dream he so desperately wanted to realise. His mother was right that he was a fool. Even with Bautisto putting the facts right in front of him, he refused to see the whole thing for what it was. There were things in life that were more important than settling a score, and they were too valuable to sacrifice for something as hollow as revenge. There was nothing as important, not even a dream. His horse was staring at him. Even he knew it was time to move on.

It was dusk when a coaching inn came into view farther down the road. He smiled as he wondered how Amero had reacted to his absence, the appointed hour for their duel now long past. His thoughts didn't dwell long on Amero, however. Bryn couldn't think of anything he wanted more than a hot meal and a warm bed, but if Ayla wasn't there he would have to make do with the meal—probably cold—before riding on.

The inn was quieter than Bryn would have expected. He slowed as he approached it and watched carefully. The war was a long way to the north, so Bryn didn't think it likely marauding soldiers had raided this far south. That didn't mean that there wasn't something wrong, though. The roads were dangerous at the best of times, and banditry was always worse during times of war. Once you were a few miles from a city or town and beyond the protection of their watchmen, the roads were dangerous places, war or peace.

There was something about the scene that bothered him, but he could not put his finger on what it was. He dismounted before he reached the inn and secured his horse to a tree. Bryn drew his sword and started forward. The inn's windows glowed with the light from inside, and he could hear movement in the stable to the inn's side. He peered in to see the shapes of several horses in the darkness. He continued forward, stopping at the first window. It was made up of dozens of lozenge-shaped pieces of glass held in place by lead cames. It was an old window, and the pane had flexed outward, distorting the view of the interior.

There were several people moving around inside, and Bryn saw nothing to support his concerns. He watched a moment longer, but everything going on within was as he would expect of an ordinary coaching inn. He sheathed his sword and went inside.

'Evening there, traveller. Pardon me, Banneret,' the innkeeper said, as soon as Bryn closed the door behind him.

Bryn self-consciously pulled his cloak back over the hilt of his rapier, and nodded to the innkeeper before surveying the taproom. Four other men, all minding their own business. Nothing threatening.

'Can I get you anything, Banneret?' the innkeeper said.

'Water,' Bryn said. 'And some food. Whatever's hot. Please.'

'There's still some stew in the pot,' the innkeeper said. 'Cider's good too, if you fancy something more interesting than water.'

Bryn shook his head. 'Is there a stable boy? My horse could do with some feed and water.'

'Erco!' the innkeeper shouted.

A boy of no more than sixteen appeared from the back room. 'Take care of the Banneret's horse.'

'Just a light feed,' Bryn said. 'I might be riding on tonight.' He flipped the boy a penny, which was dextrously caught as the boy headed for the door.

Bryn sat by the bar to wait for the food. 'When did the last post carriage stop here?'

'Few hours ago. Didn't stop long though. Continued on to make the next inn before dark. Next one north should stop tomorrow afternoon. If you're looking to take it?'

'No,' Bryn said. 'I'm looking for someone that was on it. Do you have any fresh horses I could trade you for?'

The innkeeper shook his head. 'Not at the moment. Sorry.' He flicked his eyes toward someone behind Bryn. 'I'll get your stew,' he said.

Bryn turned to look at the other occupants of the taproom. They were all sitting alone, keeping to themselves. They were a rough looking bunch, not necessarily what he would have expected, but a life on the road can have that effect on a man. He remembered his own appearance the last time he had called at a rural inn, so Bryn didn't think too much of it.

The innkeeper returned from the kitchen with a bowl of stew in his hand. He placed it down on the bar counter in front of Bryn and smiled. His teeth were in bad condition, the kind of teeth a man accustomed to violence had.

Bryn looked down at the bowl as the innkeeper withdrew his hand. His knuckles were bruised, with traces of dried blood on them. Not something Bryn would have expected, unless he was using his fists to tenderise meat.

The innkeeper watched him, as though waiting for Bryn to start eating. He caught Bryn's strange look. 'Best eat up before it gets cold.'

'What happened to your hand?' Bryn said, nodding to the bloodied knuckles.

'Ah. These.' The innkeeper smiled and raised his hand up. 'Shoulda washed 'em better I suppose.'

'Customer didn't pay up?'

'Something like that.' The innkeeper's eyes flicked to some-one behind Bryn again.

He was communicating with one of the men. Something

was up. 'When did you buy the place?' Bryn said, his suspicions all but confirmed.

'Whatcha mean?' the innkeeper said.

'Well, when I passed this way a couple of months ago, there was a different owner.' Bryn heard a chair move behind him. The innkeeper kept staring at Bryn, but said nothing. Bryn stood and drew his sword as soon as he heard a second chair move.

'I don't know what you lads are up to, but it's none of my business, and I don't want any trouble.' It was his second lie in as many minutes, but there were five of them, six including the stable boy and he needed to put them off guard. If they had taken over the inn, it was with the intention of robbing whatever travellers passed through. There was no way a post carriage had gotten through untouched.

All of the men stood and slowly moved around Bryn, who backed toward the door.

"Fraid you've found it, Banneret. Bad luck for you. Good luck for us. If you've anything worth having.'

'Last chance, lads. Tell me what you did with the post carriage, and I'll let you go.'

The innkeeper and his friends all roared with laughter.

Bryn only needed one alive to tell him what they had done to the carriage. The thought that they might have hurt Ayla filled him with rage. He lunged at the closest.

The men had all drawn weapons of some description; swords, hand axes and clubs. Bryn had spent so much of his life training to fight skilled swordsmen that it came as a surprise to fight one that wasn't. The first man didn't react to Bryn's lunge at all, and still didn't seem to have registered his injury even after Bryn had pulled his sword free. Bryn had already moved on to his closest colleague by the time he started his collapse to the floor.

Bryn cut down the next in the same movement. The third charged at Bryn with his small axe raised in the air. He roared with anger, but Bryn dodged his clumsy attack and stabbed him through the back when his momentum carried him past.

The fourth was more wary—smarter perhaps, or now fore-warned. He made two feints with his short sword and bounced on the balls of his feet as though to give the impression he possessed some skill. Bryn thrust and stabbed him through the eye. He was turning to face the innkeeper before the bandit collapsed to the ground.

That left only the innkeeper in the taproom and their young accomplice outside, who would be galloping away as fast as he could by now if he had any sense. That meant Bryn needed the phoney innkeeper alive. Seeing his friends cut down with so little effort seemed to have robbed him of any desire to fight. He backed away from Bryn, his mouth opening and closing, but no sound came out. A cudgel hung limply from his fingers, and his eyes flicked from left to right as though he was looking for an escape route.

'The post carriage that stopped here today. There was a woman travelling on it.'

The innkeeper shook his head. 'We didn't touch her. Honest.'

'Where is she then?' Bryn took a step toward him and aimed the point of his rapier at the innkeeper's throat.

'Upstairs. Upstairs. Locked in a room. She's fine. See for yourself. We didn't lay a finger on her. You arrived before we could—' The innkeeper snapped his mouth shut, clearly fearful that he had said too much.

'Before you could do what?' Bryn said. He felt a flush of anger. He took a deep breath and restrained himself. 'Show me where she is.'

'And you'll let me live?'

Bryn shrugged. 'Depends on how she is.'

The innkeeper nodded emphatically and beckoned for Bryn to follow him as he made for the staircase.

Bryn followed him at a distance, aware of the possibility that there might be more brigands hiding upstairs. He kept a lookout over his shoulder for the stable boy, although the threat posed by an unarmed boy was not a concern if his grown friends were anything to go by. Bryn suspected he was long gone anyway.

The innkeeper stopped outside a door on the upper landing and fumbled in his pocket for a key. His hands were shaking as he put the key in the lock, but Bryn was under no illusions; he might be frightened, but he would stick a knife in Bryn's back the first chance he got.

He smiled congenially as he opened the door, trying to ingratiate himself with Bryn.

'Stay away! I'll cut you if you come anywhere near me!' a woman snarled. Ayla.

Bryn couldn't help but smile, but his relief was far greater than his amusement. He realised how frightened she must be, and didn't want to prolong her ordeal. He gave the barkeeper a hard kick in the backside and sent him sprawling into the room. Bryn followed him.

'Bryn?' Ayla said.

'I'm sorry,' Bryn said. It was all he could think of, and was something that was overdue.

'What are you doing here?' she said.

'I came to get you. To bring you home.'

'I don't have a home anymore,' she said. 'It was burned to the ground.'

'Yes you do. I'm sorry that I didn't make that clearer to you. There were so many things from before I left the city, before I met you, that felt... unfinished. I thought I had to deal with them. Now I realise they aren't worth it. I want you to come back with me.'

'Bryn!'

The ardour of her response came as a surprise, and it took Bryn an instant to realise it was a warning. He turned in time to see the fake innkeeper lunge at him with a small knife. Bryn stepped back and out of the way. His reflexes were too well conditioned to be tested by a bandit. His thrust was an automatic response, and the fake innkeeper was dead before Bryn gave the attack any thought.

He pulled his sword free and looked to Ayla, concerned by her reaction of having seen him kill a man. She seemed unmoved. 'Come back with me,' he said. 'Please.'

The hard look on her face faltered. 'Things will be different?'

'They will,' Bryn said. 'I promise. I know what's important now. I can't lose you.'

CHAPTER FORTY-NINE

ESPITE THE STORM of abuse Bryn was sure awaited him back in the city, he felt better than he had in months as he and Ayla rode back to Ostenheim. All of the things that had been gnawing away at him were forgotten, or seemed so small as to barely be worthy of notice. His only regret was the guilt he felt knowing that Bautisto had been left to deal with the mess when they realised that Bryn wasn't showing up for the duel.

For the first time, Bryn felt completely free of the addictive grip the desire to settle the score with Amero had placed on him. When he thought of it now, he couldn't understand how he had ever been willing to sacrifice a single thing for it.

Amero was driven by his own demons; a desire to step out from the shadow of his family name, ambition, greed, arrogance. There were many that Bryn could think of, vices all, and in the end they would consume him entirely. Bryn even felt a small measure of pity for his former friend, but the farther he could put himself from it all, the happier he would be. With Ayla beside him, Bryn knew he had all he could ever want, or need.

There was no hostile mob waiting for him when he got back to

Ostenheim, the worst-case scenario he had envisioned. He left his horse back at the stables, and sold the second one he had taken from the inn for Ayla—the brigands had no more use for it, and he considered it a modest payment for the public service he had done. That brought a handful of coins, which were gratefully received.

From there, they walked back to his mother's house. As they went, Bryn tried to eavesdrop on every conversation, both curious to hear if they were about his non-appearance and terrified that they would be. All he heard was gossip and idle chat; no mention of his name. It was as though they had never even heard of the intended duel. He expected that his mother or Gilia would be able to fill him in on how the city reacted.

When they arrived back at the door, his mother embraced Ayla without saying a word. Even Gilia gave Bryn a grudging nod of approval.

At the first opportunity, Bryn took his mother aside.

'What was the reaction?' he said. He'd wanted to ask from the moment they got back, but knew he had to tread carefully. There was still much work to be done to repair the damage he had caused.

'The duel?'

Bryn nodded.

'I knew you wouldn't be back in time, so I went to see Maestro Bautisto after you left and told him what had happened,' she said.

Bryn grimaced, not sure if he wanted to hear any more. At least Bautisto had been forewarned.

'I think he was relieved, if anything,' his mother said. 'He sent a note to Amero's people, said there was a gang of youths chanting abuse outside the salon. He said he was withdrawing you from the duel and was going to sue for breach of contract. He assured me that it would work, but didn't explain why. It seemed to do the trick though, I didn't hear anything said about it after that.'

Bryn sighed with relief and then smiled. He had worried that him not showing up would have made it all but impossible to find work in Ostenheim—there was only so much abuse a reputation could take before it was irreparable. He had resolved that he would leave the city if needs be. His brother-in-law's business in Tanosa had seemed like his best bet, but perhaps that wouldn't be necessary. He would have to get the full details of how it all played out from Bautisto.

'Maestro Bautisto sent this around this morning,' his mother said. She handed him a fat leather purse. 'The note that came with it said it was in full and final settlement of any dispute arising out of the contract. Bautisto said in it that Amero's people were worried that any fuss would harm Amero's standing, so they require us to never talk about any of it again. Bautisto agreed on our behalf, and said that he'd explain it all to you when he sees you again.'

Bryn raised his eyebrows. Amero must have been very worried about his standing with the arena promoters if he was that eager to hush things up. It seemed like too much success might not be such a good thing after all. Either way, Bryn found that he really didn't care. He opened the purse—it was stuffed to capacity with gold crowns. At a glance, it looked enough to live on for two years if he was careful with it. If *they* were careful with it.

Bryn continued to help Bautisto out in the salon while he looked for tutoring jobs. He felt it was the least he could do, after all Bautisto had done for him.

He was cleaning and oiling the training swords when dal Corsi blustered into the salon with his usual sense of entitlement, his little retinue of lickspittles scurrying after him. Bautisto was out giving a private lesson, so Bryn was the only one there. He groaned when he saw dal Corsi walk through the door.

'Do you have an appointment?' Bryn said.

'Do I have an appointment?' dal Corsi said, incredulously. 'Do you hear that? Do I have an appointment?' he said to his two aides. He turned back to Bryn. 'You're the one who had an appointment, lad. And you fucking missed it!'

It was the only time Bryn had ever heard anything other than arrogance in dal Corsi's voice.

'Didn't feel like being used by you again,' Bryn said. 'You'll have to find some other poor fool to make Amero look good.'

'Oh, I will. You can count on that. You're the bloody fool though. I'll make sure you never get work in this city again. You can count yourself lucky that Amero's having such trouble with opponents at the moment. If he wasn't so concerned at upsetting the other promoters, you'd be getting pilloried right now. Don't think for a minute that anyone fell for your breach of contract stunt. Absolute bullshit, and we all know it. If it were up to me I'd see you called a coward from here to Highgarden, and not fit to wear the Blue. Don't think you can walk away from it all with no consequence though, you little shit. There won't be a door open to you in this city. Mark my word.'

'Maybe I am a fool,' Bryn said, with a smile. 'I didn't think a fat old boor like you had the influence.' Bryn looked at the broom and dustpan lying on the floor ready for his next chore. 'There's always shit to be shovelled, Banneret dal Corsi. It just won't be your shit that I shovel. I think I'll get by.'

Dal Corsi bristled with indignation, but there was nothing he could do. He was too old to draw his sword, and he had already levelled every threat he could at Bryn. He had nothing left, so he stormed out.

Bryn watched the door for a moment after dal Corsi left. He didn't know what he was supposed to feel, but his general sentiment these days was contentment, and that was unchanged. As soon as he resumed his sweeping, he heard the door open again.

'Finally thought of a smart retort? Why don't you just...' He looked up at the door. 'Master Dornish.'

'Expecting someone else, Bryn?'

'Yes, well, no.' He laughed. 'What brings you here?'

'Death and the opportunities it brings,' Dornish said, with his usual sardonic humour. 'But more of that in a moment. I hear tell you've been working on a new technique.'

'I have,' Bryn said. 'I'm surprised word of it has reached far beyond these four walls though.'

'Well, all sorts of morsels of information come my way these days, and I like to keep abreast of what my former students are up to.' He unbuttoned his cloak, letting it drop to the floor, and tapped the hilt of his rapier. 'Any chance of a demonstration?'

Bryn shrugged his shoulders. 'Why not?' He pulled his rapier from where it hung in its scabbard. He took his guard, and Dornish stepped forward to meet him.

Dornish attacked with slow, probing thrusts; nothing that challenged Bryn.

'I know I was injured,' Bryn said, 'but give me some credit.'

Dornish nodded and Bryn launched into a blistering combination of attacks; tight, punchy and aggressive. It was ugly, but brutally effective. Above all, it was fast. He drove Dornish back across the salon floor, revelling in the way each strike flowed into the next, sword and body moving in perfect harmony. It was what he loved more than anything—almost anything—and losing it would have been something he would never have been able to come to terms with.

Dornish nodded and raised his eyebrows. 'Quite a change from the last time we did this,' Dornish said, wiping the sheen of sweat from his brow. 'Not sure I've ever seen anything quite like it.'

'Not surprised,' Bryn said. 'It's entirely a creation of Bautisto's Salon of Arms. I don't have as good a range of motion in my shoulders anymore; they healed tight, so it's tailored to allow for that. I'm trying to convince him to write an instruction manual for the style.'

'It's certainly effective,' Dornish said.

Bryn raised an eyebrow.

'More than effective,' Dornish acknowledged. 'I can imagine it will be very popular with Bannerets of a certain age who aren't quite ready to hang up their swords, among others.' He cleared his throat self referentially and attacked again.

He came at Bryn faster now, age obviously not having slowed or impeded him as much as he might have implied. Bryn was well able to deal with it. Indeed, better able than he was the last time they had fenced for his final Collegium examination at the Academy. There was no consideration for pride or style in what he did, only efficiency.

His attack spent, Dornish lowered his sword to indicate the bout was over, and saluted.

'I'm impressed, he said, 'and it confirms a decision I had all but made.'

Bryn furrowed his brow and gave Dornish a quizzical look.

'Death and opportunities,' Dornish said again. 'Major dal Damaso passed away a short time ago.'

'I'm sorry to hear that,' Bryn said. He hadn't been keeping up on Academy news with all the preparation for the rematch. 'I always liked him.'

'As did I. But that brings me to the topic of opportunity. I've been appointed as Master of the Academy.'

'Congratulations,' Bryn said, genuinely pleased for his former tutor.

'The appointment of a new master always brings changes; people move on, some take it as time to retire. I want some fresh blood in the masters' ranks, and was hoping you'd consider coming to teach.'

There were some formalities to be complied with to become an instructor at the Academy; paperwork to be completed mainly. With it all done, he left the Bannerets' Hall, excited by the challenge that lay ahead.

Dornish had seen to it that Bryn was paid his first term's salary in advance, which covered the cost of his impending wedding, which he had to admit made him more nervous than any duel he had ever fought.

He stepped out into the street and almost stumbled into Joranna dal Verrara. It took a moment for them both to realise who the other was, followed by an uncomfortable silence while they both tried to decide what to do.

For Bryn, the discomfort was only fleeting. She represented a life that he no longer wanted, and a time he was happy to forget. Once it had passed, he felt nothing, except perhaps for pity. Joranna looked well, but she always did. It was a requirement for someone trying to find herself a wealthy husband, something it looked as though she had yet to achieve. He smiled at her, and as she was beginning to open her mouth to say something, he walked away.

EPILOGUE

HUNDREDS OF EYES, expectant, nervous, afraid, were locked on him as he walked to the front of the hall. Their owners had all fallen silent the moment he entered, and the thumping of the heels of his boots on the polished wooden floor were the only sounds to be heard. Hundreds of young men, deathly silent, all waiting to see what he would do next. Once at the front of the hall, he stopped and surveyed the gathered throng. It would be an uphill battle to earn the respect of his students after all that had been said about him, but in his experience that was true of everything in life. It was just one more obstacle to face, but with Ayla by his side, he would not be facing this one alone.

'I am Banneret of the Blue Bryn Pendollo. I will be your chief instructor for the year. Take up your swords, and we shall begin.'

ABOUT THE AUTHOR

Duncan is a writer of fantasy fiction novels and short stories that are set in a world influenced by Renaissance Europe. He has a Master's Degree in History, and is particularly interested in the Medieval and Renaissance periods.

His debut novel, The Tattered Banner (Society of the Sword 1) was featured on Buzzfeed's 12 Greatest Fantasy Books of 2013.

He doesn't live anywhere particularly exotic, and when not writing he enjoys cycling, skiing and windsurfing.

You can keep up to date with Duncan at his website, duncanmhamilton.com.